Percy Bysshe Shelley, Richard Herne Shepherd

The Prose Works of Percy Bysshe Shelley - From the Original

Editions

Vol. I

Percy Bysshe Shelley, Richard Herne Shepherd

The Prose Works of Percy Bysshe Shelley - From the Original Editions
Vol. I

ISBN/EAN: 9783337078560

Printed in Europe, USA, Canada, Australia, Japan

Cover: Foto ©Andreas Hilbeck / pixelio.de

More available books at **www.hansebooks.com**

THE PROSE WORKS

OF

PERCY BYSSHE SHELLEY

FROM THE ORIGINAL EDITIONS

EDITED, PREFACED, AND ANNOTATED

BY

RICHARD HERNE SHEPHERD

IN TWO VOLUMES

VOL. I.

London

CHATTO AND WINDUS, PICCADILLY

1888

Ballantyne Press
BALLANTYNE, HANSON AND CO.
EDINBURGH AND LONDON

EDITOR'S PREFACE.

THESE two volumes contain a complete collection of Shelley's Prose Writings ; the two
youthful prose romances of *Zastrozzi* and *St. Irvyne;*
the Dublin and Marlow pamphlets ; the long-lost
and lately-found *Refutation of Deism;* the Letter to
Lord Ellenborough ; the curious review of Hogg's
romance of Alexy Haimatoff, recently unearthed by
Professor Dowden; a number of minor papers originally published by Medwin ; and the entire collection of " Essays and Letters from Abroad," first issued
by Mrs. Shelley in 1840, and which throw so much
light on Shelley's character and genius.   The Biblio-
graphy appended to the second volume will, it is
hoped, be of real service to all lovers and students
of Shelley.

Shelley is another instance of the fact that a great
master of verse is always a good writer of prose.
Whatever may be thought of the crudity of his
juvenile romances—and the greatest Shelleyan enthu-
siasts, Browning, Swinburne, and Rossetti, have suc-

cessively laughed at them—they contain at least vivid descriptions of natural appearances; while his political pamphlets, as a recent writer has pointed out, are weighty and sententious to a wonderful degree, considering the age at which they were written. That he was a delightful letter-writer, full of grace and easy fluency, the letters to Peacock and to Leigh Hunt abundantly prove; while of his critical powers, especially in regard to sculpture and painting, both these and the posthumous papers published by Medwin give us no mean idea, though we may not be prepared to go quite so far as Mr. Matthew Arnold does when he says that he doubts whether Shelley's "delightful Essays and Letters, which deserve to be far more read than they are now, will not resist the wear and tear of time better, and finally come to stand higher, than his poetry."

RICHARD HERNE SHEPHERD.

KINGSTON VALE,
Lent, 1888.

CONTENTS.

PAGE

ZASTROZZI,

A ROMANCE.

BY

P. B. S.

—— That their God
May prove their foe, and with repenting hand
Abolish his own works.—This would surpass
Common revenge.

PARADISE LOST.

LONDON,

PRINTED FOR G. WILKIE AND J. ROBINSON :

57, PATERNOSTER ROW.

1810.

I.   A

ZASTROZZI.

A ROMANCE.

CHAPTER I.

TORN from the society of all he held dear on earth, the victim of secret enemies, and exiled from happiness, was the wretched Verezzi !

All was quiet ; a pitchy darkness involved the face of things, when, urged by fiercest revenge, Zastrozzi placed himself at the door of the inn where, undisturbed, Verezzi slept.

Loudly he called the landlord. The landlord, to whom the bare name of Zastrozzi was terrible, trembling obeyed the summons.

" Thou knowest Verezzi the Italian ? He lodges here."

" He does," answered the landlord.

" Him, then, have I devoted to destruction," exclaimed Zastrozzi. " Let Ugo and Bernardo follow you to his apartment ; I will be with you to prevent mischief."

Cautiously they ascended—successfully they executed their revengeful purpose, and bore the sleeping Verezzi to the place, where a chariot waited to convey the vindictive Zastrozzi's prey to the place of its destination.

Ugo and Bernardo lifted the still sleeping Verezzi into the chariot. Rapidly they travelled onwards for several hours. Verezzi was still wrapped in deep sleep, from which all the movements he had undergone had been insufficient to rouse him.

Zastrozzi and Ugo were masked, as was Bernardo, who acted as postilion.

It was still dark, when they stopped at a small inn, on a remote and desolate heath; and waiting but to change horses, again advanced. At last day appeared—still the slumbers of Verezzi remained unbroken.

Ugo fearfully questioned Zastrozzi as to the cause of his extraordinary sleep. Zastrozzi, who, however, was well acquainted with it, gloomily answered, "I know not."

Swiftly they travelled during the whole of the day, over which Nature seemed to have drawn her most gloomy curtain. They stopped occasionally at inns, to change horses and obtain refreshments.

Night came on—they forsook the beaten track, and, entering an immense forest, made their way slowly through the rugged underwood.

At last they stopped—they lifted their victim from the chariot, and bore him to a cavern, which yawned in a dell close by.

Not long did the hapless victim of unmerited persecution enjoy an oblivion which deprived him of a knowledge of his horrible situation. He awoke—and overcome by excess of terror, started violently from the ruffians' arms.

They had now entered the cavern; Verezzi supported himself against a fragment of rock which jutted out.

"Resistance is useless," exclaimed Zastrozzi. "Following us in submissive silence can alone procure the slightest mitigation of your punishment."

Verezzi followed as fast as his frame, weakened by unnatural sleep, and enfeebled by recent illness, would permit; yet, scarcely believing that he was awake, and not thoroughly convinced of the reality of the scene before him, he viewed everything with that kind of inexplicable horror which a terrible dream is wont to excite.

After winding down the rugged descent for some time, they arrived at an iron door, which at first sight appeared to be part of the rock itself. Everything had till now been obscured by total darkness; and Verezzi, for the first time, saw the masked faces of his persecutors, which a torch brought by Bernardo rendered visible.

The massy door flew open.

The torches from without rendered the darkness which reigned within still more horrible; and Verezzi beheld the interior of this cavern as a place whence he was never again about to emerge—as his grave. Again he struggled with his persecutors, but his enfeebled frame was insufficient to support a conflict with the strong-nerved Ugo, and, subdued, he sank fainting into his arms.

His triumphant persecutor bore him into the damp cell, and chained him to the wall. An iron chain encircled his waist; his limbs, which not even a little straw kept from the rock, were fixed by immense staples to the flinty floor; and but one of his hands was left at liberty, to take the scanty pittance of bread and water which was daily allowed him.

Everything was denied him but thought, which, by comparing the present with the past, was his greatest torment.

Ugo entered the cell every morning and evening, to bring coarse bread and a pitcher of water, seldom, yet sometimes, accompanied by Zastrozzi.

In vain did he implore mercy, pity, and even death: useless were all his inquiries concerning the cause of his barbarous imprisonment—a stern silence was maintained by his relentless gaoler.

Languishing in painful captivity, Verezzi passed days

and nights seemingly countless, in the same monotonous uniformity of horror and despair. He scarcely
now shuddered when the slimy lizard crossed his naked
and motionless limbs. The large earth-worms, which
turned themselves in his long and matted hair, almost
ceased to excite sensations of horror.

Days and nights were undistinguishable from each
other; and the period which he had passed there,
though in reality but a few weeks, was lengthened by
his perturbed imagination into many years. Sometimes
he scarcely supposed that his torments were earthly,
but that Ugo, whose countenance bespoke him a
demon, was the fury who blasted his reviving hopes.
His mysterious removal from the inn near Munich
also confused his ideas, and he never could bring his
thoughts to any conclusion on the subject which occupied them.

One evening, overcome by long watching, he sank
to sleep, for almost the first time since his confinement,
when he was aroused by a loud crash, which seemed
to burst over the cavern. Attentively he listened—he
even hoped, though hope was almost dead within his
breast. Again he listened—again the same noise
was repeated : it was but a violent thunderstorm which
shook the elements above.

Convinced of the folly of hope, he addressed a
prayer to his Creator—to Him who hears a suppliant
from the bowels of the earth. His thoughts were
elevated above terrestrial enjoyments—his sufferings
sank into nothing on the comparison.

Whilst his thoughts were thus employed, a more
violent crash shook the cavern. A scintillating flame
darted from the ceiling to the floor. Almost at the
same instant the roof fell in.

A large fragment of the rock was laid athwart the
cavern ; one end being grooved into the solid wall, the
other having almost forced open the massy iron door.

Verezzi was chained to a piece of rock which remained immovable. The violence of the storm was past, but the hail descended rapidly, each stone of which wounded his naked limbs. Every flash of lightning, although now distant, dazzled his eyes, unaccustomed as they had been to the least ray of light.

The storm at last ceased, the pealing thunders died away in indistinct murmurs, and the lightning was too faint to be visible. Day appeared—no one had yet been to the cavern. Verezzi concluded that they either intended him to perish with hunger, or that some misfortune, by which themselves had suffered, had occurred. In the most solemn manner, therefore, he now prepared himself for death, which he was fully convinced within himself was rapidly approaching.

His pitcher of water was broken by the falling fragments, and a small crust of bread was all that now remained of his scanty allowance of provisions.

A burning fever raged through his veins; and, delirious with despairing illness, he cast from him the crust which alone could now retard the rapid advances of death.

Oh! what ravages did the united efforts of disease and suffering make on the manly and handsome figure of Verezzi! His bones had almost started through his skin; his eyes were sunken and hollow; and his hair, matted with the damps, hung in strings upon his faded cheek. The day passed as had the morning—death was every instant before his eyes—a lingering death by famine—he felt its approaches; night came, but with it brought no change. He was aroused by a noise against the iron door: it was the time when Ugo usually brought fresh provisions. The noise lessened; at last it totally ceased—with it ceased all hope of life in Verezzi's bosom. A cold tremor pervaded his limbs—his eyes but faintly presented to his imagination the ruined cavern—he sank, as far as the chains which

strong proofs of his imprisonment, which the deep marks of the chains had left till now, was impossible.

Had not those marks remained, he would have conceived the horrible events which had led him thither to have been but the dreams of his perturbed imagination. He, however, thought it better to yield, since, as Ugo and Bernardo attended him in the short walks he was able to take, an escape was impossible, and its attempt would but make his situation more unpleasant.

He often expressed a wish to write to Julia, but the old woman said she had orders neither to permit him to write nor receive letters—on pretence of not agitating his mind—and, to avoid the consequences of despair, knives were denied him.

As Verezzi recovered, and his mind obtained that firm tone which it was wont to possess, he perceived that it was but a device of his enemies that detained him at the cottage, and his whole thoughts were now bent upon the means for effecting his escape.

It was late one evening, when, tempted by the peculiar beauty of the weather, Verezzi wandered beyond the usual limits, attended by Ugo and Bernardo, who narrowly watched his every movement. Immersed in thought, he wandered onwards, till he came to a woody eminence, whose beauty tempted him to rest a little, in a seat carved in the side of an ancient oak. Forgetful of his unhappy and dependent situation, he sat there some time, until Ugo told him that it was time to return.

In their absence Zastrozzi had arrived at the cottage. He had impatiently inquired for Verezzi.

"It is the baron's custom to walk every evening," said Bianca ; "I soon expect him to return."

Verezzi at last arrived.

Not knowing Zastrozzi as he entered, he started back, overcome by the likeness he bore to one of the men he had seen in the cavern.

He was now convinced that all the sufferings he had undergone in that horrible abode of misery were not imaginary, and that he was at this instant in the power of his bitterest enemy.

Zastrozzi's eyes were fixed on him with an expression too manifest to be misunderstood ; and, with an air in which he struggled to disguise the natural malevolence of his heart, he said, that he hoped Verezzi's health had not suffered from the evening air.

Enraged beyond measure at this hypocrisy, from a man whom he now no longer doubted to be the cause of all his misfortunes, he could not forbear inquiring for what purpose he had conveyed him hither, and told him instantly to release him.

Zastrozzi's cheeks turned pale with passion, his lips quivered, his eyes darted revengeful glances, as thus he spoke :—

"Retire to your chamber, young fool, which is the fittest place for you to reflect on, and repent of, the insolence shown to one so much your superior."

"I fear nothing,". interrupted Verezzi, "from your vain threats and empty denunciations of vengeance. Justice—Heaven ! is on my side, and I must eventually triumph."

What can be a greater proof of the superiority of virtue, than that the terrible, the dauntless Zastrozzi trembled ? for he did tremble ; and, conquered by the emotions of the moment, paced the circumscribed apartment with unequal steps. For an instant he shrunk within himself; he thought of his past life, and his awakened conscience reflected images of horror. But again revenge drowned the voice of virtue—again passion obscured the light of reason, and his steeled soul persisted in its scheme.

Whilst he still thought, Ugo entered. Zastrozzi, smothering his stinging conscience, told Ugo to follow him to the heath. Ugo obeyed.

CHAPTER III.

GO and Zastrozzi proceeded along the heath, on the skirts of which stood the cottage. Verezzi leaned against the casement, when a low voice, which floated in indistinct murmurs on the silence of the evening, reached his ear. He listened attentively. He looked into the darkness, and saw the towering form of Zastrozzi, and Ugo, whose awkward, ruffian-like gait could never be mistaken. He could not hear their discourse, except a few detached words which reached his ears. They seemed to be denunciations of anger: a low tone afterwards succeeded, and it appeared as if a dispute, which had arisen between them, was settled: their voices at last died away in distance.

Bernardo now left the room. Bianca entered; but Verezzi plainly heard Bernardo lingering at the door.

The old woman continued sitting in silence at a remote corner of the chamber. It was Verezzi's hour for supper: he desired Bianca to bring it. She obeyed, and brought some dried raisins in a plate. He was surprised to see a knife was likewise brought; an indulgence he imputed to the inadvertency of the old woman. A thought started across his mind—it was now time to escape.

He seized the knife—he looked expressively at the old woman—she trembled. He advanced from the casement to the door: he called for Bernardo—Bernardo entered, and Verezzi, lifting his arm high, aimed a knife at the villain's heart. Bernardo started aside, and the knife was fixed firmly in the door-case. Verezzi attempted by one effort to extricate it. The effort was vain. Bianca, as fast as her tottering limbs could carry her, hastened through the opposite door, calling loudly for Zastrozzi.

Verezzi attempted to rush through the open door, but Bernardo opposed himself to it. A long and violent contest ensued, and Bernardo's superior strength was on the point of overcoming Verezzi, when the latter, by a dexterous blow, precipitated him down the steep and narrow staircase.

Not waiting to see the event of his victory, he rushed through the opposite door, and meeting with no opposition, ran swiftly across the heath.

The moon, in tranquil majesty, hung high in air, and showed the immense extent of the plain before him. He continued rapidly advancing, and the cottage was soon out of sight. He thought that he heard Zastrozzi's voice in every gale. Turning round, he thought Zastrozzi's eye glanced over his shoulder. But even had Bianca taken the right road, and found Zastrozzi, Verezzi's speed would have mocked pursuit.

He ran several miles, still the dreary extent of the heath was before him : no cottage yet appeared, where he might take shelter. He cast himself for an instant on the bank of a rivulet, which stole slowly across the heath. The moonbeam played upon its surface—he started at his own reflected image—he thought that voices were wafted on the western gale, and, nerved anew, pursued his course across the plain.

The moon had gained the zenith before Verezzi rested again. Two pine-trees, of extraordinary size, stood on a small eminence: he climbed one, and found a convenient seat in its immense branches.

Fatigued, he sank to sleep.

Two hours he lay hushed in oblivion, when he was awakened by a noise. It is but the hooting of the night-raven, thought he.

Day had not yet appeared, but faint streaks in the east presaged the coming morn. Verezzi heard the clattering of hoofs. What was his horror to see that Zastrozzi, Bernardo, and Ugo, were the horsemen!

Overcome by terror, he clung to the rugged branch. His persecutors advanced to the spot—they stopped under the tree wherein he was.

"Eternal curses," exclaimed Zastrozzi, "upon Verezzi ! I swear never to rest until I find him, and then I will accomplish the purpose of my soul.   But come, Ugo, Bernardo, let us proceed."

" Signor," said Ugo, " let us the rather stop here to refresh ourselves and our horses.   You, perhaps, will not make this pine your couch, but I will get up, for I think I spy an excellent bed above there."

" No, no," answered Zastrozzi ; "did not I resolve never to rest until I had found Verezzi ?   Mount, villain, or die."

Ugo sullenly obeyed.   They galloped off and were quickly out of sight.

Verezzi returned thanks to Heaven for his escape ; for he thought that Ugo's eye, as the villain pointed to the branch where he reposed, met his.

It was now morning.   Verezzi surveyed the heath, and thought he saw buildings at a distance.   Could he gain a town or city, he might defy Zastrozzi's power.

He descended the pine-tree, and advanced as quickly as he could towards the distant buildings.   He proceeded across the heath for half an hour, and perceived that, at last, he had arrived at its termination.

The country assumed a new aspect, and the number of cottages and villas showed him that he was in the neighbourhood of some city.   A large road which he now entered confirmed his opinion.   He saw two peasants, and asked them where the road led,—" To Passau," was the answer.

It was yet very early in the morning, when he walked through the principal street of Passau.   He felt very faint with his recent and unusual exertions ; and, overcome by languor, sank on some lofty stone steps, which led to a magnificent mansion, and, resting his head on his arm, soon fell asleep.

He had been there nearly an hour, when he was awakened by an old woman. She had a basket on her arm, in which were flowers, which it was her custom to bring to Passau every market-day. Hardly knowing where he was, he answered the old woman's inquiries in a vague and unsatisfactory manner. By degrees, however, they became better acquainted ; and, as Verezzi had no money, nor any means of procuring it, he accepted of an offer which Claudine (for that was the old woman's name) made him, to work for her, and share her cottage, which, together with a little garden, was all she could call her own. Claudine quickly disposed of her flowers, and, accompanied by Verezzi, soon arrived at a little cottage near Passau. It was situated on a pleasant and cultivated spot ; at the foot of a small eminence, on which it was situated, flowed the majestic Danube, and on the opposite side was a forest belonging to the Baron of Schwepper, whose vassal Claudine was.

Her little cottage was kept extremely neat ; and, by the charity of the Baron, wanted none of those little comforts which old age requires.

Verezzi thought that, in so retired a spot, he might at least pass his time tranquilly, and elude Zastrozzi.

"What induced you," said he to Claudine, as in the evening they sat before the cottage door, "what induced you to make that offer this morning to me ? "

"Ah !" said the old woman, "it was but last week that I lost my dear son, who was everything to me ; he died by a fever which he caught by his too great exertions in obtaining a livelihood for me ; and I came to the market yesterday, for the first time since my son's death, hoping to find some peasant who would fill his place, when chance threw you in my way.

"I had hoped that he would have outlived me, as I

am quickly hastening to the grave, to which I look forward as to the coming of a friend, who would relieve me from those cares which, alas ! but increase with my years."

Verezzi's heart was touched with compassion for the forlorn situation of Claudine. He tenderly told her that he would not forsake her; but if any opportunity occurred for ameliorating her situation, she should no longer continue in poverty.

CHAPTER IV.

BUT let us return to Zastrozzi. He had walked with Ugo on the heath, and had returned late. He was surprised to see no light in the cottage. He advanced to the door, he rapped violently ; no one answered. "Very strange !" exclaimed Zastrozzi, as he burst open the door with his foot. He entered the cottage—no one was there. He searched it, and at last saw Bernardo lying, seemingly lifeless, at the foot of the staircase. Zastrozzi advanced to him, and lifted him from the ground ; he had been but in a trance, and immediately recovered.

As soon as his astonishment was dissipated, he told Zastrozzi what had happened.

"What !" exclaimed Zastrozzi, interrupting him, "Verezzi escaped ! Hell and furies ! Villain, you deserve instant death ; but thy life is at present necessary to me. Arise, go instantly to Rosenheim, and bring three of my horses from the inn there—make haste !—begone !"

Bernardo trembling arose, and obeying Zastrozzi's commands, crossed the heath quickly towards Rosenheim, a village about half a league distant on the north.

Whilst he was gone, Zastrozzi, agitated by contending passions, knew scarcely what to do. With hurried strides he paced the cottage. He sometimes spoke lowly to himself. The feelings of his soul flashed from his eyes—his frown was terrible.

"Would I had his heart reeking on my dagger, signor!" said Ugo. "Kill him when you catch him, which you soon will, I am sure."

"Ugo," said Zastrozzi, "you are my friend; you advise me well. But no! he must not die. Ah! by what horrible fetters am I chained—fool that I was—Ugo! he shall die—die by the most hellish torments. I give myself up to fate;—I will taste revenge, for revenge is sweeter than life; and even were I to die with him, and, as the punishment of my crime, be instantly plunged into eternal torments, I should taste superior joy in recollecting the sweet moment of his destruction. Oh! would that destruction could be eternal!"

The clattering of hoofs was heard, and Zastrozzi was now interrupted by the arrival of Bernardo—they instantly mounted, and the high-spirited steeds bore them swiftly across the heath.

Rapidly, for some time, were Zastrozzi and his companions borne across the plain. They took the same road as Verezzi had. They passed the pines where he reposed. They hurried on.

The fainting horses were scarce able to bear their guilty burthens. No one had spoken since they had left the clustered pines.

Bernardo's horse, overcome by excessive fatigue, sank on the ground; that of Zastrozzi scarce appeared in better condition. They stopped.

"What!" exclaimed Zastrozzi, "must we give up the search? Ah! I am afraid we must; our horses can proceed no further—curse on the horses! But let us proceed on foot; Verezzi shall not escape me; nothing shall now retard the completion of my just revenge."

I. B

As he thus spoke, Zastrozzi's eye gleamed with impatient revenge; and with rapid steps he advanced towards the south of the heath.

Daylight at length appeared; still were the villains' efforts to find Verezzi insufficient. Hunger, thirst, and fatigue conspired to make them relinquish the pursuit. They lay at intervals upon the stony soil.

"This is but an uncomfortable couch, signor," muttered Ugo.

Zastrozzi, whose whole thoughts were centred in revenge, heeded him not, but, nerved anew by impatient vengeance, he started from the bosom of the earth, and muttering curses upon the innocent object of his hatred, proceeded onwards. The day passed as had the morning and preceding night. Their hunger was scantily allayed by the wild berries which grew amid the heathy shrubs; and their thirst but increased by the brackish pools of water which alone they met with. They perceived a wood at some distance. "That is a likely place for Verezzi to have retired to, for the day is hot, and he must want repose as well as ourselves," said Bernardo. "True," replied Zastrozzi, as he advanced towards it. They quickly arrived at its borders: it was not a wood, but an immense forest, which stretched southward as far as Schaffhausen. They advanced into it.

The tall trees rising above their heads warded off the meridian sun; the mossy banks beneath invited repose; but Zastrozzi, little recking a scene so fair, hastily scrutinized every recess which might afford an asylum to Verezzi.

Useless were all his researches—fruitless his endeavours: still, however, though, faint with hunger and weary with exertion, he nearly sank upon the turf, his mind was superior to corporeal toil; for *that*, nerved by revenge, was indefatigable.

Ugo and Bernardo, overcome by the extreme fatigue

which they had undergone, and strong as the assassins were, fell fainting on the earth.

The sun began to decline; at last it sank beneath the western mountain, and the forest-tops were tinged by its departing ray. The shades of night rapidly thickened.

Zastrozzi sat awhile upon the decayed trunk of a scathed oak.

The sky was serene; the blue ether was spangled with countless myriads of stars: the tops of the lofty forest-trees waved mournfully in the evening wind; and the moonbeam penetrating at intervals, as they moved, through the matted branches, threw dubious shades upon the dark underwood beneath.

Ugo and Bernardo, conquered by irresistible torpor, sank to rest upon the dewy turf.

A scene so fair—a scene so congenial to those who can reflect upon their past lives with pleasure, and anticipate the future with the enthusiasm of innocence, ill accorded with the ferocious soul of Zastrozzi, which at one time agitated by revenge, at another by agonising remorse, or contending passions, could derive no pleasure from the past—anticipate no happiness in futurity.

Zastrozzi sat for some time immersed in heart-rending contemplations; but though conscience for awhile reflected his past life in images of horror, again was his heart steeled by fiercest vengeance; and, aroused by images of insatiate revenge, he hastily arose, and, waking Ugo and Bernardo, pursued his course.

The night was calm and serene—not a cloud obscured the azure brilliancy of the spangled concave above—not a wind ruffled the tranquillity of the atmosphere below.

Zastrozzi, Ugo, and Bernardo advanced into the forest. They had tasted no food, save the wild berries of the wood, for some time, and were anxious to arrive at some cottage, where they might procure refreshments.

For some time the deep silence which reigned was uninterrupted.

"What is that?" exclaimed Zastrozzi, as he beheld a large and magnificent building, whose battlements rose above the lofty trees. It was built in the Gothic style of architecture, and appeared to be inhabited.

The building reared its pointed casements loftily to the sky; their treillaged ornaments were silvered by the clear moonlight, to which the dark shades of the arches beneath formed a striking contrast. A large portico jutted out: they advanced towards it, and Zastrozzi attempted to open the door.

An open window on one side of the casement arrested Zastrozzi's attention. "Let us enter that," said he. They entered. It was a large saloon, with many windows. Everything within was arranged with princely magnificence. Four ancient and immense sofas in the apartment invited repose.

Near one of the windows stood a table, with an escrutoire on it; a paper lay on the ground near it.

Zastrozzi, as he passed, heedlessly took up the paper. He advanced nearer to the window, thinking his senses had deceived him when he read, "La Contessa di Laurentini"; but they had not done so, for La Contessa di Laurentini still continued on the paper. He hastily opened it; and the letter, though of no importance, convinced him that this must have been the place to which Matilda said that she had removed.

Ugo and Bernardo lay sleeping on the sofas. Zastrozzi, leaving them as they were, opened an opposite door—it led into a vaulted hall—a large flight of stairs rose from the opposite side—he ascended them. He advanced along a lengthened corridor—a female in white robes stood at the other end—a lamp burnt near her on the balustrade. She was in a reclining attitude, and had not observed his approach. Zastrozzi recognized her for Matilda. He approached her, and beholding Zastrozzi before her, she started back with surprise. For awhile she gazed on him in silence, and at last exclaimed, "Zastrozzi! ah! are we revenged on Julia? am I happy? Answer me quickly. Well by your silence do I perceive that our plans have been put into execution. Excellent Zastrozzi! accept my most fervent thanks, my eternal gratitude."

"Matilda!" returned Zastrozzi, "would I could say that we were happy! but, alas! it is but misery and disappointment that cause this my so unexpected visit. I know nothing of the Marchesa de Strobazzo—less of Verezzi. I fear that I must wait till age has unstrung my now so fervent energies; and when time has damped your passion, perhaps you may gain Verezzi's love. Julia is returned to Italy—is even now in Naples; and, secure in the immensity of her possessions, laughs at our trifling vengeance. But it shall not be always thus," continued Zastrozzi, his eyes sparkling with inexpressible brilliancy; "I will accomplish my purpose; and, Matilda, thine shall likewise be effected. But, come, I have not tasted food for these two days."

"Oh! supper is prepared below," said Matilda. Seated at the supper-table, the conversation, enlivened by wine, took an animated turn. After some subjects, irrelevant to this history, being discussed, Matilda said, "Ha! but I forgot to tell you, that I have done some good. I have secured that diabolical Paulo, Julia's servant, who was of great service to her, and, by penetrating our schemes, might have even discomfited our grand design. I have lodged him in the lowest cavern of those dungeons which are under this building—will you go and see him?" Zastrozzi answered in the affirmative, and seizing a lamp which burnt in a recess of the apartment, followed Matilda.

The rays of the lamp but partially dissipated the darkness as they advanced through the antiquated

passages. They arrived at a door : Matilda opened
it, and they quickly crossed a grass-grown courtyard. ·

The grass which grew on the lofty battlements waved
mournfully in the rising blast, as Matilda and Zastrozzi
entered a dark and narrow casement. Cautiously they
descended the slippery and precipitous steps. The
lamp, obscured by the vapours, burnt dimly as they
advanced. They arrived at the foot of the staircase.
"Zastrozzi!" exclaimed Matilda. Zastrozzi turned
quickly, and, perceiving a door, obeyed Matilda's directions.

On some straw, chained to the wall, lay Paulo.

"O pity! stranger, pity!" exclaimed the miserable
Paulo.

No answer, save a smile of most expressive scorn,
was given by Zastrozzi. They again ascended the narrow
staircase; and, passing the courtyard, arrived at the
supper-room.

"But," said Zastrozzi, again taking his seat, "what
use is that fellow Paulo in the dungeon ? Why do you
keep him there ?"

"Oh!" answered Matilda, "I know not ; but if you
wish——"

·· She paused, but her eye expressively filled up the
sentence.

Zastrozzi poured out an overflowing goblet of wine.
He summoned Ugo and Bernardo—"Take that," said
Matilda, presenting them a key. One of the villains
took it, and in a few moments returned with the hapless
Paulo.

"Paulo!" exclaimed Zastrozzi, loudly, "I have prevailed on La Contessa to restore your freedom : here,"
added he, "take this ; I pledge to your future happiness."

Paulo bowed low—he drank the poisoned potion to
the dregs, and, overcome by sudden and irresistible
faintness, fell at Zastrozzi's feet. Sudden convulsions
shook his frame, his lips trembled, his eyes rolled hor-

ribly, and, uttering an agonised and lengthened groan, he expired.

"Ugo ! Bernardo ! take that body and bury it immediately," cried Zastrozzi. "There, Matilda, by such means must Julia die : you see, that the poisons which I possess are quick in their effect."

A pause ensued, during which the eyes of Zastrozzi and Matilda spoke volumes to each guilty soul.

The silence was interrupted by Matilda. Not shocked at the dreadful outrage which had been committed, she told Zastrozzi to come out into the forest, for that she had something for his private ear.

"Matilda," said Zastrozzi, as they advanced along the forest, "I must not stay here, and waste moments in inactivity, which might be more usefully employed. I must quit you to-morrow—I must destroy Julia."

"Zastrozzi," returned Matilda, "I am so far from wishing you to spend your time here in ignoble listlessness, that I will myself join your search. You shall to Italy—to Naples—watch Julia's every movement, attend her every step, and, in the guise of a friend, destroy her ; but beware, whilst you assume the softness of the dove, to forget not the cunning of the serpent. On you I depend for destroying her ; my own exertions shall find Verezzi ; I myself will gain his love —Julia must die, and expiate the crime of daring to rival me, with her hated blood."

Whilst thus they conversed, whilst they planned these horrid schemes of destruction, the night wore away.

The moonbeam darting her oblique rays from under volumes of lowering vapour, threatened an approaching storm. The lurid sky was tinged with a yellowish lustre—the iorest-tops rustled in the rising tempest— big drops fell—a flash of lightning, and, instantly after, a peal of bursting thunder, struck with sudden terror the bosom of Matilda. She, however, immediately overcame it, and, regarding the battling element with indifference, continued her discourse with Zastrozzi.

They wore out the night in many visionary plans for the future, and now and then a gleam of remorse assailed Matilda's heart. Heedless of the storm, they had remained in the forest late. Flushed with wickedness, they at last sought their respective couches, but sleep forsook their pillow.

In all the luxuriance of extravagant fancy, Matilda portrayed the symmetrical form, the expressive countenance, of Verezzi; whilst Zastrozzi, who played a double part, anticipated, with ferocious exultation, the torments which he she loved was eventually fated to endure, and changed his plan, for a sublimer mode of vengeance was opened to his view.

Matilda passed a night of restlessness and agitation; her mind was harassed by contending passions, and her whole soul wound up to deeds of horror and wickedness. Zastrozzi's countenance, as she met him in the breakfast-parlour, wore a settled expression of determined revenge—" I almost shudder," exclaimed Matilda, " at the sea of wickedness on which I am about to embark! But still, Verezzi—ah! for him would I even lose my hopes of eternal happiness. In the sweet idea of calling him mine, no scrupulous delicacy, no mistaken superstitious fear, shall prevent me from deserving him by daring acts—No! I am resolved," continued Matilda, as, recollecting his graceful form, her soul was assailed by tenfold love.

"And I am likewise resolved," said Zastrozzi; " I am resolved on revenge—my revenge shall be gratified. Julia shall die, and Verezzi——"

Zastrozzi paused; his eye gleamed with a peculiar expression, and Matilda thought he meant more than he had said—she raised her eyes—they encountered his.

The guilt-bronzed cheek of Zastrozzi was tinged with a momentary blush, but it quickly passed away, and his countenance recovered its wonted firm and determined expression.

"Zastrozzi !" exclaimed Matilda. "Should you be false—should you seek to deceive me—— But no ; it is impossible. Pardon, my friend—I meant not what I said—my thoughts are crazed——"

"'Tis well," said Zastrozzi, haughtily.

"But you forgive my momentary, unmeaning doubt?" said Matilda, and fixed her unmeaning eyes on his countenance.

"It is not for us to dwell on vain, unmeaning expressions, which the soul dictates not," returned Zastrozzi ; "and I sue for pardon from you, for having, by ambiguous expressions, caused the least agitation ; but, believe me, Matilda, we will not forsake each other ; your cause is mine ; distrust between us is foolish. But, farewell for the present ; I must order Bernardo to go to Passau to purchase horses."

The day passed on ; each waited with impatience for the arrival of Bernardo. "Farewell, Matilda," exclaimed Zastrozzi, as he mounted the horses which Bernardo brought ; and, taking the route of Italy, galloped off.

CHAPTER V.

HER whole soul wrapped up in one idea, the guilty Matilda threw herself into a chariot which waited at the door, and ordered the equipage to proceed towards Passau.

Left to indulge reflection in solitude, her mind recurred to the object nearest her heart—to Verezzi.

Her bosom was scorched by an ardent and unquenchable fire ; and while she thought of him, she even shuddered at the intenseness of her own sensations.

"He shall love me—he shall be mine—mine for ever," mentally ejaculated Matilda.

The streets of Passau echoed to La Contessa di Laurentini's equipage, before, roused from her reverie, she found herself at the place of her destination ; and she was seated in her hotel in that city, before she had well arranged her unsettled ideas. She summoned Ferdinand, a trusty servant, to whom she confided everything. " Ferdinand," said she, " you have many claims on my gratitude. I have never had cause to reproach you with infidelity in executing my purposes —add another debt to that which I already owe you ; find Il Conte Verezzi within three days, and you are my best friend." Ferdinand bowed, and prepared to execute her commands. Two days passed, during which Matilda failed not to make every personal inquiry, even in the suburbs of Passau.

Alternately depressed by fear, and revived by hope, for three days was Matilda's mind in a state of disturbance and fluctuation. The evening of the third day, of the day on which Ferdinand was to return, arrived. Matilda's mind, wound up to the extreme of impatience, was the scene of conflicting passions. She paced the room rapidly.

A servant entered, and announced supper.

" Is Ferdinand returned ?" hastily inquired Matilda.

The domestic answered in the negative. She sighed deeply, and struck her forehead.

Footsteps were heard in the ante-chamber without.

"There is Ferdinand !" exclaimed Matilda, exultingly, as he entered. "Well, well ! have you found Verezzi? Ah ! speak quickly ! Ease me of this horrible suspense."

"Signora !" said Ferdinand, " it grieves me much to be obliged to declare that all my endeavours have been inefficient to find Il Conte Verezzi——"

" Oh, madness ! madness !" exclaimed Matilda, " is

it for this that I have plunged into the dark abyss of crime?—is it for this that I have despised the delicacy of my sex, and, braving consequences, have offered my love to one who despises me—who shuns me, as does the barbarous Verezzi? But if he is in Passau—if he is in the environs of the city, I will find him."

Thus saying, despising the remonstrances of her domestics, casting off all sense of decorum, she rushed into the streets of Passau. A gloomy silence reigned through the streets of the city; it was past midnight, and every inhabitant seemed to be sunk in sleep—sleep which Matilda was almost a stranger to. Her white robes floated on the night air—her shadowy and dishevelled hair flew over her form, which, as she passed the bridge, seemed to strike the boatmen below with the idea of some supernatural and ethereal form.

She hastily crossed the bridge. She entered the fields on the right—the Danube, whose placid stream was scarcely agitated by the wind, reflected her symmetrical form, as, scarcely knowing what direction she pursued, Matilda hastened along its banks. Sudden horror, resistless despair, seized her brain, maddened as it was by hopeless love.

"What have I to do in this world, my fairest prospect blighted, my fondest hope rendered futile?" exclaimed the frantic Matilda, as, wound up to the highest pitch of desperation, she attempted to plunge herself into the river.

But life fled; for Matilda, caught by a stranger's arm, was prevented from the desperate act.

Overcome by horror, she fainted.

Some time did she lie in a state of torpid insensibility, till the stranger, filling his cup with water, and sprinkling her pallid countenance with it, recalled to life the miserable Matilda.

What was her surprise, what was her mingled emotion of rapture and doubt, when the moonbeam

disclosed to her view the countenance of Verezzi, as in
anxious solicitude he bent over her elegantly-propor-
tioned form !

' "By what chance," exclaimed the surprised Verezzi,
"do I see here La Contessa di Laurentini? Did not I
leave you at your Italian castella? I had hoped you
would have ceased to persecute me, when I told you that
I was irrevocably another's."

"Oh, Verezzi!" exclaimed Matilda, casting herself
at his feet, "I adore you to madness—I love you to
distraction. If you have one spark of compassion, let
me not sue in vain—reject not one who feels it impossible to overcome the fatal, resistless passion which
consumes her."

"Rise, Signora," returned Verezzi—"rise ; this discourse is improper—it is not suiting the dignity of
your rank, or the delicacy of your sex : but suffer me
to conduct you to yon cottage, where, perhaps, you may
deign to refresh yourself, or pass the night."

The moonbeams played upon the tranquil waters of
the Danube, as Verezzi silently conducted the beautiful
Matilda to the humble dwelling where he resided.

Claudine waited at the door, and had begun to fear
that some mischance had befallen Verezzi, as, when he
arrived at the cottage-door, it was long past his usual
hour of return.

It was his custom, during those hours when the
twilight of evening cools the air, to wander through
the adjacent rich scenery, though he seldom prolonged
his walks till midnight.

He supported the fainting form of Matilda as he
advanced towards Claudine. The old woman's eyes
had lately failed her, from extreme age ; and it was
not until Verezzi called to her that she saw him, accompanied by La Contessa di Laurentini.

"Claudine," said Verezzi, "I have another claim upon
your kindness ; this lady, who has wandered beyond

her knowledge, will honour our cottage so far as to pass the night here. If you would prepare the pallet which I usually occupy for her, I will repose this evening on the turf, and will now get supper ready. Signora," continued he, addressing Matilda, "some wine would, I think, refresh your spirits; permit me to fill you a glass of wine."

Matilda silently accepted his offer—their eyes met—those of Matilda were sparkling and full of meaning.

"Verezzi!" exclaimed Matilda, "I arrived but four days since at Passau—I have eagerly inquired for you —oh! how eagerly! Will you accompany me to-morrow to Passau?"

"Yes," said Verezzi, hesitatingly.

Claudine soon joined them. Matilda exulted in the success of her schemes, and Claudine being present, the conversation took a general turn. The lateness of the hour, at last, warned them to separate.

Verezzi, left to solitude and his own reflections, threw himself on the turf, which extended to the Danube below. Ideas of the most gloomy nature took possession of his soul; and, in the event of the evening, he saw the foundation of the most bitter misfortunes.

He could not love Matilda; and though he never had seen her but in the most amiable light, he found it impossible to feel any sentiment towards her, save cold esteem. .. Never had he beheld those dark shades in her character, which, if developed, could excite nothing but horror and detestation; he regarded her as a woman of strong passions, who, having resisted them to the utmost of her power, was at last borne away in the current—whose brilliant virtues one fault had obscured—as such he pitied her: but still he could not help observing a comparison between her and Julia, whose feminine delicacy shrunk from the slightest suspicion, even, of indecorum. Her fragile form, her mild, heavenly countenance, was contrasted with all the partiality of love, to the scintillating eye, the commanding countenance, the bold expressive gaze, of Matilda.

He must accompany her on the morrow to Passau. During their walk, he determined to observe a strict silence ; or, at all events, not to hazard one equivocal expression, which might be construed into what it was not meant for.

The night passed away—morning came, and the tops of the far-seen mountains were gilded by the rising sun.

Exulting in the success of her schemes, and scarcely able to disguise the vivid feelings of her heart, the wily Matilda, as early as she descended to the narrow parlour, where Claudine had prepared a simple breakfast, affected a gloom she was far from feeling.

An unequivocal expression of innocent and mild tenderness marked her manner towards Verezzi : her eyes were cast on the ground, and her every movement spoke meekness and sensibility.

At last, breakfast being finished, the time arrived when Matilda, accompanied by Verezzi, pursued the course of the river, to retrace her footsteps to Passau. A gloomy silence for some time prevailed—at last Matilda spoke :

"Unkind Verezzi ! is it thus that you will ever slight me ? is it for this that I have laid aside the delicacy of my sex, and owned to you a passion which was but too violent to be concealed ? Ah ! at least pity me ! I love you : oh ! I adore you to madness !"

She paused—the peculiar expression which beamed in her dark eye, told the tumultuous wishes of her bosom.

"Distress not yourself and me, Signora," said Verezzi, "by these unavailing protestations. Is it for you—is it for Matilda," continued he, his countenance assuming a smile of bitterest scorn, "to talk of love to the lover of Julia ?"

Rapid tears coursed down Matilda's cheek. She sighed—the sigh seemed to rend her inmost bosom.

So unexpected a reply conquered Verezzi. He had been prepared for reproaches, but his feelings could not withstand Matilda's tears.

"Ah! forgive me, Signora," exclaimed Verezzi, "if my brain, crazed by disappointments, dictated words which my heart intended not."

"Oh," replied Matilda, "it is I who am wrong: led on by the violence of my passion, I have uttered words, the bare recollection of which fills me with horror. Oh! forgive, forgive an unhappy woman, whose only fault is loving you too well."

As thus she spoke, they entered the crowded streets of Passau, and, proceeding rapidly onwards, soon arrived at La Contessa di Laurentini's hotel.

CHAPTER VI.

HE character of Matilda has been already so far revealed, as to render it unnecessary to expatiate upon it farther. Suffice it to say, that her syren illusions and well-timed blandishments, obtained so great a power over the imagination of Verezzi, that his resolution to return to Claudine's cottage before sunset became every instant fainter and fainter.

"And will you thus leave me?" exclaimed Matilda, in accents of the bitterest anguish, as Verezzi prepared to depart. "Will you thus leave unnoticed, her who, for your sake alone, casting aside the pride of high birth, has wandered, unknown, through foreign climes? Oh! if I have (led away by love for you) outstepped the bounds of modesty, let me not, oh! let me not be injured by others with impunity. Stay, I entreat thee, Verezzi, if yet one spark of compassion lingers in your breast—stay, and defend me from those who vainly seek one who is irrevocably thine."

With words such as these did the wily Matilda work upon the generous passions of Verezzi. Emotions of pity, of compassion, for one whose only fault he supposed to be love for him, conquered Verezzi's softened soul.

"Oh! Matilda," said he, "though I cannot love thee—though my soul is irrevocably another's—yet, believe me, I esteem, I admire thee; and it grieves me that a heart, fraught with so many and so brilliant virtues, has fixed itself on one who is incapable of appreciating its value."

The time passed away, and each returning sun beheld Verezzi still at Passau—still under Matilda's roof. That softness, that melting tenderness, which she knew so well how to assume, began to convince Verezzi of the injustice of the involuntary hatred which had filled his soul towards her. Her conversation was fraught with sense and elegant ideas. She played to him in the cool of the evening; and often, after sunset, they rambled together into the rich scenery and luxuriant meadows which are washed by the Danube.

Claudine was not forgotten: indeed, Matilda first recollected her, and, by placing her in an independent situation, added a new claim to the gratitude of Verezzi.

In this manner three weeks passed away. Every day did Matilda practise new arts, employ new blandishments, to detain under her roof the fascinated Verezzi.

The most select parties in Passau, flitted in varied movements to exquisite harmony, when Matilda perceived Verezzi's spirits to be ruffled by recollection.

When he seemed to prefer solitude, a moonlight walk by the Danube was proposed by Matilda; or, with skilful fingers, she drew from her harp sounds of the most heart-touching, most enchanting melody. Her behaviour towards him was soft, tender, and quiet, and might rather have characterised the mild, serene love of a friend or sister, than the ardent, unquenchable fire which burnt, though concealed, within Matilda's bosom.

It was one calm evening that Matilda and Verezzi sat in a back saloon, which overlooked the gliding Danube. Verezzi was listening, with all the enthusiasm of silent rapture, to a favourite soft air which Matilda sang, when a loud rap at the hall-door startled them. A domestic entered, and told Matilda that a stranger, on particular business, waited to speak with her.

"Oh!" exclaimed Matilda, "I cannot attend to him now; bid him wait."

The stranger was impatient, and would not be denied.

"Desire him to come in, then," said Matilda.

The domestic hastened to obey her commands.

Verezzi had arisen to leave the room. "No," cried Matilda, "sit still; I shall soon dismiss the fellow; besides, I have no secrets from you." Verezzi took his seat.

The wide folding-doors which led into the passage were open.

Verezzi observed Matilda, as she gazed fixedly through them, to grow pale.

He could not see the cause, as he was seated on a sofa at the other end of the saloon.

Suddenly she started from her seat; her whole frame seemed convulsed by agitation, as she rushed through the door.

Verezzi heard an agitated voice exclaim, "Go! go! —to-morrow morning!"

Matilda returned. She seated herself again at the harp, which she had quitted, and essayed to compose herself; but it was in vain, she was too much agitated.

Her voice, as she again attempted to sing, refused to perform its office; and her humid hands, as they swept the strings of the harp, violently trembled.

"Matilda," said Verezzi, in a sympathising tone,

"what has agitated you? Make me a repository of your sorrows; I would, if possible, alleviate them."

"Oh, no," said Matilda, affecting unconcern, "nothing—nothing has happened. . I was even myself unconscious that I appeared agitated."

Verezzi affected to believe her, and assumed a composure which he felt not. The conversation changed, and Matilda assumed her wonted mien. The lateness of the hour at last warned them to separate.

The more Verezzi thought upon the evening's occurrence, the more did a conviction in his mind, inexplicable even to himself, strengthen, that Matilda's agitation originated in something of consequence. He knew her mind to be superior to common circumstance, and fortuitous casualty, which might have ruffled an inferior soul. Besides, the words which he had heard her utter —"Go! go!—to-morrow morning!"—and though he resolved to disguise his real sentiments, and seem to let the subject drop, he determined narrowly to scrutinise Matilda's conduct, and particularly to know what took place on the following morning. An indefinable presentiment that something horrible was about to occur, filled Verezzi's mind. A long chain of retrospection ensued—he could not forget the happy hours he had passed with Julia ; her interesting softness, her ethereal form, pressed on his aching sense.

Still did he feel his soul irresistibly softened towards Matilda—her love for him flattered his vanity; and though he could not feel reciprocal affection towards her, yet her kindness in rescuing him from his former degraded situation, her altered manner towards him, and her unremitting endeavours to please, to humour him in everything, called for his warmest, his sincerest gratitude.

The morning came—Verezzi arose from a sleepless couch, and descending into the breakfast-parlour, there found Matilda.

He endeavoured to appear the same as usual, but in vain; for an expression of reserve and scrutiny was apparent on his features.

Matilda perceived it, and shrunk abashed from his keen gaze.

The meal passed away in silence.

"Excuse me for an hour or two," at last stammered out Matilda—"my steward has accounts to settle;" and she left the apartment.

Verezzi had now no doubt but that the stranger, who had caused Matilda's agitation the day before, was now returned to finish his business.

He moved towards the door to follow her—he stopped.

"What right have I to pry into the secrets of another?" thought Verezzi; "besides, the business which this stranger has with Matilda cannot possibly concern me."

Still was he compelled, by an irresistible fascination, as it were, to unravel what appeared to him so mysterious an affair. He endeavoured to believe it to be as she affirmed; he endeavoured to compose himself; he took a book, but his eyes wandered insensibly.

Thrice he hesitated—thrice he shut the door of the apartment; till at last, a curiosity, unaccountable even to himself, propelled him to seek Matilda.

Mechanically he moved along the passage. He met one of the domestics—he inquired where Matilda was.

"In the grand saloon," was the reply.

With trembling steps he advanced towards it. The folding doors were open. He saw Matilda and the stranger standing at the remote end of the apartment.

The stranger's figure, which was towering and majestic, was rendered more peculiarly striking by the elegantly proportioned form of Matilda, who leant on a marble table near her; and her gestures, as she conversed with him, manifested the most eager impatience, the deepest interest.

At so great a distance, Verezzi could not hear their conversation; but, by the low murmurs which occasionally reached his ear, he perceived that whatever it might be, they were both equally interested in the subject.

For some time he contemplated them with mingled surprise and curiosity—he tried to arrange the confused murmurs of their voices, which floated along the immense and vaulted apartment; but no articulate sound reached his ear.

At last Matilda took the stranger's hand : she pressed it to her lips with an eager and impassioned gesture, and led him to the opposite door of the saloon.

Suddenly the stranger turned, but as quickly regained his former position, as he retreated through the door; not quickly enough, however, but, in the stranger's fire-darting eye, Verezzi recognised him who had declared eternal enmity at the cottage on the heath.

Scarcely knowing where he was, or what to believe, for a few moments Verezzi stood bewildered, and unable to arrange the confusion of ideas which floated in his brain and assailed his terror-struck imagination. He knew not what to believe—what phantom it could be that, in the shape of Zastrozzi, blasted his straining eye-balls—Could it really be Zastrozzi ? Could his most rancorous, his bitterest enemy, be thus beloved, thus confided in, by the perfidious Matilda ?

For several moments he stood doubting what he should resolve upon. At one while he determined to reproach Matilda with treachery and baseness, and overwhelm her in the mid career of wickedness; but at last concluding it to be more politic to dissemble and subdue his emotions, he went into the breakfast-parlour which he had left, and seated himself as if nothing had happened, at a drawing which he had left incomplete.

Besides, perhaps Matilda might not be guilty—perhaps she was deceived; and though some scheme of villainy and destruction to himself was preparing, she might be the dupe, and not the coadjutor, of Zastrozzi. The idea that she was innocent soothed him; for he was anxious to make up, in his own mind, for the injustice which he had been guilty of towards her: and though he could not conquer the disgusting ideas, the unaccountable detestations, which often, in spite of himself, filled his soul towards her, he was willing to overcome what he considered but as an illusion of the imagination, and to pay that just tribute of esteem to her virtues which they demanded.

Whilst these ideas, although confused and unconnected, passed in Verezzi's brain, Matilda again entered the apartment.

Her countenance exhibited the strongest marks of agitation, and full of inexpressible and confused meaning was her dark eye, as she addressed some trifling question to Verezzi, in a hurried accent, and threw herself into a chair beside him.

"Verezzi!" exclaimed Matilda, after a pause equally painful to both—"Verezzi! I am deeply grieved to be the messenger of bad news—willingly would I withhold the fatal truth from you; yet, by some other means, it may meet your unprepared ear. I have something dreadful, shocking, to relate; can you bear the recital?"

The nerveless fingers of Verezzi dropped the pencil—he seized Matilda's hand, and, in accents almost inarticulate from terror, conjured her to explain her horrid surmises.

"Oh! my friend! my sister!" exclaimed Matilda, as well-feigned tears coursed down her cheeks,—"oh! she is——"

"What! what!" interrupted Verezzi, as the idea of something having befallen his adored Julia filled his maddened brain with tenfold horror: for often had Matilda declared that since she could not become his

wife she would willingly be his friend, and had even
called Julia her sister.

"Oh!" exclaimed Matilda, hiding her face in her
hands, "Julia—Julia—whom you love, is dead."

Unable to withhold his fleeting faculties from a
sudden and chilly horror which seized them, Verezzi
sank forward, and, fainting, fell at Matilda's feet.

In vain, for some time, was every effort to recover
him. Every restorative which was administered, for
a long time, was unavailing; at last his lips unclosed—
he seemed to take his breath easier—he moved—he
slowly opened his eyes.

CHAPTER VII.

IS head reposed upon Matilda's bosom; he
started from it violently, as if stung by a
scorpion, and fell upon the floor. His eyes
rolled horribly, and seemed as if starting from their
sockets.

"Is she then dead?—is Julia dead?" in accents
scarcely articulate exclaimed Verezzi. "Ah, Matilda!
was it you then who destroyed her? was it by thy
jealous hand that she sank to an untimely grave? Ah,
Matilda! Matilda! say that she yet lives! Alas! what
have I to do in the world without Julia? an empty,
uninteresting void!"

Every word uttered by the hapless Verezzi spoke
daggers to the agitated Matilda.

Again overpowered by the acuteness of his sensations,
he sank on the floor, and, in violent convulsions, he
remained bereft of sense.

Matilda again raised him—again laid his throbbing
head upon her bosom. Again, as, recovering, the

wretched Verezzi perceived his situation—overcome by
agonising reflection, he relapsed into insensibility.

One fit rapidly followed another, and at last, in a
state of the wildest delirium, he was conveyed to bed.

Matilda found that a too eager impatience had carried her too far. She had prepared herself for violent
grief, but not for the paroxysms of madness which now
seemed really to have seized the brain of the devoted
Verezzi.

She sent for a physician—he arrived, and his
opinion of Verezzi's danger almost drove the wretched
Matilda to desperation.

Exhausted by contending passions, she threw herself
on a sofa; she thought of the deeds which she had
perpetrated to gain Verezzi's love; she considered that
should her purpose be defeated at the very instant
which her heated imagination had portrayed as the
commencement of her triumph : should all the wickedness, all the crimes, into which she had plunged herself,
be of no avail—this idea, more than remorse for her
enormities, affected her.

She sat for a time absorbed in a confusion of contending thought ; her mind was the scene of anarchy
and horror; at last, exhausted by their own violence,
a deep, a desperate calm, took possession of her
faculties. She started from the sofa, and, maddened
by the idea oɪ Verezzi's danger, sought his apartment.

On a bed lay Verezzi.

A thick film overspread his eye, and he seemed sunk
in insensibility.

Matilda approached him. She pressed her burning
lips to his. She took his hand—it was cold, and at
intervals slightly agitated by convulsions.

A deep sigh at this instant burst from his lips—a
momentary hectic flushed his cheek, as the miserable
Verezzi attempted to rise.

Matilda, though almost too much agitated to command her emotions, threw herself into a chair behind the curtain, and prepared to watch his movements.

"Julia! Julia!" exclaimed he, starting from the bed, as his flaming eye-balls were unconsciously fixed upon the agitated Matilda, "where art thou? Ah! thy fair form now moulders in the dark sepulchre! would I were laid beside thee! thou art now an ethereal spirit!" And then, in a seemingly triumphant accent, he added, "But, ere long, I will seek thy unspotted soul—ere long I will again clasp my lost Julia!" Overcome by resistless delirium, he was for an instant silent—his starting eyes seemed to follow some form, which imagination had portrayed in vacuity. He dashed his head against the wall, and sank, overpowered by insensibility, on the floor.

Accustomed as she was to scenes of horror, and firm and dauntless as was Matilda's soul, yet this was too much to behold with composure. She rushed towards him, and lifted him from the floor. In a delirium of terror, she wildly called for help. Unconscious of everything around her, she feared Verezzi had destroyed himself. She clasped him to her bosom, and called on his name, in an ecstasy of terror.

The domestics, alarmed by her exclamations, rushed in. Once again they lifted the insensible Verezzi into the bed. Every spark of life seemed now to have been extinguished; for the transport of horror which had torn his soul was almost too much to be sustained. A physician was again sent for—Matilda, maddened by desperation, in accents almost inarticulate from terror, demanded hope or despair from the physician.

He, who was a man of sense, declared his opinion, that Verezzi would speedily recover, though he knew not the event which might take place in the crisis of the disorder, which now rapidly approached.

The remonstrances of those around her were unavailing to draw Matilda from the bedside of Verezzi.

She sat there, a prey to disappointed passion, silent, and watching every turn of the hapless Verezzi's countenance, as, bereft of sense, he lay extended on the bed before her.

The animation which was wont to illumine his sparkling eye was fled, the roseate colour which had tinged his cheek had given way to an ashy paleness— he was insensible to all around him. Matilda sat there the whole day, and silently administered medicines to the unconscious Verezzi, as occasion required.

Towards night the physician again came. Matida's head thoughtfully leant upon her arm as he entered the apartment.

"Ah! what hope? what hope?" wildly she exclaimed.

The physician calmed her, and bid her not despair : then, observing her pallid countenance, he said, he believed she required his skill as much as his patient.

"Oh! heed me not," she exclaimed ; "but how is Verezzi? will he live or die?"

The physician advanced towards the emaciated Verezzi—he took his hand.

A burning fever raged through his veins.

"Oh, how is he?" exclaimed Matilda, as, anxiously watching the humane physician's countenance, she thought a shade of sorrow spread itself over his features—"but tell me my fate quickly," continued she : "I am prepared to hear the worst—prepared to hear that he is even dead already."

As she spoke this, a sort of desperate serenity overspread her features. She seized the physician's arm, and looked steadfastly on his countenance, and then, as if overcome by unwonted exertions, she sank fainting at his feet.

The physician raised her, and soon succeeded in recalling her fleeted faculties.

Overcome by its own violence, Matilda's despair be-

came softened, and the words of the physician operated
as a balm upon her soul, and bid her feel hope.

She again resumed her seat, and waited with
smothered impatience for the event of the decisive
crisis, which the physician could now no longer conceal.

She pressed his burning hand in hers, and waited,
with apparent composure, for eleven o'clock.

Slowly the hours passed—the clock of Passau tolled
each lingering quarter as they rolled away, and hastened
towards the appointed time, when the chamber-door of
Verezzi was slowly opened by Ferdinand.

"Ha! why do you disturb me now?" exclaimed
Matilda, whom the entrance of Ferdinand had roused
from a profound reverie.

"Signora!" whispered Ferdinand—"Signor Zastrozzi
waits below : he wishes to see you there."

"Ah!" said Matilda, thoughtfully, "conduct him
here."

Ferdinand departed to obey her; footsteps were heard
in the passage, and immediately afterwards Zastrozzi
stood before Matilda.

"Matilda!" exclaimed he, "why do I see you here?
What accident has happened which confines you to this
chamber?"

"Ah!" replied Matilda, in an undervoice, "look in
that bed—behold Verezzi! emaciated and insensible—
in a quarter of an hour, perhaps, all animation will be
fled—fled for ever!" continued she, as a deeper expression of despair shaded her beautiful features.

Zastrozzi advanced to the foot of the bed—Verezzi
lay, as if dead, before his eyes ; for the ashy hue of his
lips, and his sunken inexpressive eye, almost declared
that his spirit was fled.

Zastrozzi gazed upon him with an indefinable expression of insatiated vengeance—indefinable to Matilda, as
she gazed upon the expressive countenance of her coadjutor in crime.

" Matilda ! I want you : come to the lower saloon ;
I have something to speak to you of," said Zastrozzi.

" Oh ! if it concerned my soul's eternal happiness, I
could not now attend," exclaimed Matilda, energetically;
" in less than a quarter of an hour, perhaps, all I hold
dear on earth will be dead ; with him, every hope, every
wish, every tie which binds me to earth.   Oh !" exclaimed she, her voice assuming a tone of extreme
horror, " see how pale he looks !"

Zastrozzi bade Matilda farewell, and went away.

The physician yet continued watching in silence the
countenance of Verezzi: it still retained its unchanging
expression of fixed despair.

Matilda gazed upon it, and waited with the most
eager, yet subdued impatience, for the expiration of the
few minutes which yet remained—she still gazed.

The features of Verezzi's countenance were slightly
convulsed.

The clock struck eleven.

His lips unclosed—Matilda turned pale with terror ;
yet mute, and absorbed by expectation, remained rooted
to her seat.

She raised her eyes, and hope again returned, as she
beheld the countenance of the humane physician lighted
up with a beam of pleasure.

She could no longer contain herself, but, in an
ecstasy of pleasure, as excessive as her grief and horror
before had been violent, in rapid and hurried accents
questioned the physician.   The physician, with an expressive smile, pressed his finger on his lip.   She
understood the movement, and though her heart
was dilated with sudden and excessive delight, she
smothered her joy, as she had before her grief, and gazed
with rapturous emotion on the countenance of Verezzi,
as, to her expectant eyes, a blush of animation tinged his
before pallid countenance.

Matilda took his hand—the pulses yet beat with

feverish violence. She gazed upon his countenance—the film, which before had overspread his eye, disappeared ; returning expression pervaded its orbit, but it was the expression of deep, of rooted grief.

The physician made a sign to Matilda to withdraw.

She drew the curtain before her, and in anxious expectation awaited the event.

A deep, a long-drawn sigh, at last burst from Verezzi's bosom. He raised himself, his eyes seemed to follow some form which imagination had portrayed in the remote obscurity of the apartment, for the shades of night were but partially dissipated by a lamp which burnt on a table behind. He raised his almost nerveless arm, and passed it across his eyes, as if to convince himself that what he saw was not an illusion of the imagination.

He looked at the physician, who sat near to, and silent by the bedside, and patiently awaited whatever event might occur.

Verezzi slowly rose, and violently exclaimed, "Julia! Julia! my long-lost Julia, come ! " And then, more collected, he added, in a mournful tone, " Ah, no ! you are dead ; lost, lost for ever ! "

He turned round and saw the physician, but Matilda was still concealed.

" Where am I ? " inquired Verezzi, addressing the physician.

" Safe, safe," answered he, " compose yourself ; all will be well."

"Ah, but Julia ? " inquired Verezzi, with a tone so expressive of despair, as threatened returning delirium.

"Oh! compose yourself," said the humane physician ; "you have been very ill ; this is but an illusion of the imagination ; and even now, I fear that you labour under that delirium which attends a brain-fever."

Verezzi's nerveless frame again sunk upon the bed—

still his eyes were open, and fixed upon vacancy; he seemed to be endeavouring to arrange the confusion of ideas which pressed upon his brain.

Matilda undrew the curtain; but, as her eye met the physician's, his glance told her to place it in its original situation.

As she thought of the events of the day, her heart was dilated by tumultuous, yet pleasurable emotions. She conjectured that were Verezzi to recover, of which she now entertained but little doubt, she might easily erase from his heart the boyish passion which before had possessed it; might convince him of the folly of supposing that a first attachment is fated to endure for ever; and, by unremitting assiduity in pleasing him—by soft, quiet attentions, and an affected sensibility, might at last acquire the attainment of that object for which her bosom had so long and so ardently panted.

Soothed by these ideas, and willing to hear from the physician's mouth a more explicit affirmation of Verezzi's safety than his looks had given, Matilda rose, for the first time since his illness, and, unseen by Verezzi, approached the physician—" Follow me to the saloon," said Matilda.

The physician obeyed, and, by his fervent assurances of Verezzi's safety and speedy recovery, confirmed Matilda's fluctuating hopes. " But," added the physician, "though my patient will recover if his mind be unruffled, I will not answer for his re-establishment should he see you, as his disorder, being wholly on the mind, may be possibly augmented by——"

The physician paused, and left Matilda to finish the sentence; for he was a man of penetration and judgment, and conjectured that some sudden and violent emotion, of which she was the cause, occasioned his patient's illness. This conjecture became certainty, as, when he concluded, he observed Matilda's face change to an ashy paleness.

"May I not watch him—attend him?" inquired Matilda, imploringly.

"No," answered the physician; "in the weakened state in which he now is, the sight of you might cause immediate dissolution."

Matilda started, as if overcome by horror at the bare idea, and promised to obey his commands.

The morning came—Matilda arose from a sleepless couch, and with hopes yet unconfirmed, sought Verezzi's apartment.

She stood near the door listening. Her heart palpitated with tremendous violence as she listened to Verezzi's breathing—every sound from within alarmed her. At last she slowly opened the door, and, though adhering to the physician's directions in not suffering Verezzi to see her, she could not deny herself the pleasure of watching him, and busying herself in little offices about his apartment.

She could hear Verezzi question the attendant collectedly, yet as a person who was ignorant where he was, and knew not the events which had immediately preceded his present state.

At last he sank into a deep sleep. Matilda now dared to gaze on him : the hectic colour which had flushed his cheek was fled, but the ashy hue of his lips had given place to a brilliant vermilion. She gazed intently on his countenance.

A heavenly, yet faint smile diffused itself over his countenance—his hand slightly moved.

Matilda, fearing that he would awake, again concealed herself. She was mistaken, for, on looking again, he still slept.

She still gazed upon his countenance. The visions of his sleep were changed, for tears came fast from under his eyelids, and a deep sigh burst from his bosom.

Thus passed several days: Matilda still watched with

most affectionate assiduity by the bedside of the unconscious Verezzi.

The physician declared that his patient's mind was yet in too irritable a state to permit him to see Matilda, but that he was convalescent.

One evening she sat by his bedside, and gazing upon the features of the sleeping Verezzi, felt unusual softness take possession of her soul—an indefinable and tumultuous emotion shook her bosom—her whole frame thrilled with rapturous ecstasy, and seizing the hand which lay motionless beside her, she imprinted on it a thousand burning kisses.

"Ah, Julia! Julia! is it you?" exclaimed Verezzi, as he raised his enfeebled frame; but perceiving his mistake, as he cast his eyes on Matilda, sank back, and fainted.

Matilda hastened with restoratives, and soon succeeded in recalling to life Verezzi's fleeted faculties.

CHAPTER VIII.

Art thou afraid
To be the same in thine own act and valour
As thou art in desire? Wouldst thou have that
Which thou esteemest the ornament of life,
Or live a coward in thine own esteem,
Letting *I dare not* wait upon *I would?*—MACBETH.

For love is heaven, and heaven is love.
—*Lay of the Last Minstrel.*

THE soul of Verezzi was filled with irresistible disgust, as, recovering, he found himself in Matilda's arms. His whole frame trembled with chilly horror, and he could scarcely withhold himself from again fainting. He fixed his eyes upon the countenance—they met hers—an ardent fire, mingled with a touching softness, filled their orbits.

In a hurried and almost inarticulate accent, he reproached Matilda with perfidy, baseness, and even murder. The roseate colour which had tinged Matilda's cheek, gave place to an ashy hue—the animation which had sparkled in her eye, yielded to a confused expression of apprehension, as the almost delirious Verezzi uttered accusations he knew not the meaning of ; for his brain, maddened by the idea of Julia's death, was whirled round in an ecstasy of terror.

Matilda seemed to have composed every passion ; a forced serenity overspread her features, as, in a sympathising and tender tone, she entreated him to calm his emotions, and giving him a temporary medicine, left him.

She descended to the saloon.

"Ah! he yet despises me—he even hates me," ejaculated Matilda. "An irresistible antipathy—irresistible, I fear, as my love for him is ardent, has taken possession of his soul towards me. Ah! miserable, hapless being that I am! doomed to have my fondest hope, my brightest prospect, blighted."

Alive alike to the tortures of despair and the illusions of hope, Matilda, now in an agony of desperation, impatiently paced the saloon.

Her mind was inflamed by a more violent emotion of hate towards Julia, as she recollected Verezzi's fond expressions: she determined, however, that were Verezzi not to be hers, he should never be Julia's.

Whilst thus she thought, Zastrozzi entered.

The conversation was concerning Verezzi.

"How shall I gain his love, Zastrozzi ?" exclaimed Matilda. "Oh! I will renew every tender office—I will watch by him day and night, and, by unremitting attentions, I will try to soften his flinty soul. But, alas! it was but now that he started from my arms in horror, and, in accents of desperation, accused me of perfidy—of murder. Could I be perfidious to Verezzi,

my heart, which burns with so fervent a fire, declares
I could not, and murder——"

Matilda paused.

"Would thou could say thou wert guilty, or even
accessary to *that*," exclaimed Zastrozzi, his eye gleaming
with disappointed ferocity. "Would Julia of Strobazzo's heart was reeking on my dagger!"

"Fervently do I join in that wish, my best Zastrozzi,"
returned Matilda : "but, alas! what avail wishes—
what avail useless protestations of revenge, whilst Julia
yet lives?—yet lives, perhaps, again to obtain Verezzi
—to clasp him constant to her bosom—and perhaps—
oh, horror! perhaps to ——"

Stung to madness by the picture which her fancy had
portrayed, Matilda paused.

Her bosom heaved with throbbing palpitations; and,
whilst describing the success of her rival, her warring
soul shone apparent from her scintillating eyes.

Zastrozzi, meanwhile, stood collected in himself; and,
scarcely heeding the violence of Matilda, awaited the
issue of her speech.

He besought her to calm herself, nor, by those violent
emotions, unfit herself for prosecuting the attainment
of her fondest hope.

"Are you firm?" inquired Zastrozzi.

"Yes!"

"Are you resolved? Does fear, amid the other
passions, shake your soul?"

"No, no—this heart knows not to fear—this breast
knows not to shrink," exclaimed Matilda eagerly.

"Then be cool—be collected," returned Zastrozzi,
"and thy purpose is effected."

Though little was in these words which might war-
rant hope, yet Matilda's susceptible soul, as Zastrozzi
spoke, thrilled with anticipated delight.

"My maxim, therefore," said Zastrozzi, "through
life has been, wherever I am, whatever passions shake

I. D

my inmost soul, at least to *appear* collected. I generally am ; for, by suffering no common events, no fortuitous casualty to disturb me, my soul becomes steeled
to more interesting trials. I have a spirit, ardent, impetuous as thine ; but acquaintance with the world has
induced me to veil it, though it still continues to burn
within my bosom. Believe me, I am far from wishing
to persuade you from your purpose. No—any purpose
undertaken with ardour, and prosecuted with perseverance, must eventually be crowned with success.
Love is worthy of any risk—I felt it once, but revenge
has now swallowed up every other feeling of my soul—
I am alive to nothing but revenge. But even did I
desire to persuade you from the purpose on which your
heart is fixed, I should not say it was wrong to attempt
it ; for whatever procures pleasure is right, and consonant to the dignity of man, who was created for no
other purpose but to obtain happiness ; else, why were
passions given us ? why were those emotions which
agitate my breast and madden my brain implanted in
us by nature ? As for the confused hope of a future
state, why should we debar ourselves of the delights of
this, even though purchased by what the misguided
multitude calls immorality?"

Thus sophistically argued Zastrozzi. His soul,
deadened by crime, could only entertain confused
ideas of immortal happiness ; for in proportion as
human nature departs from virtue, so far are they also
from being able clearly to contemplate the wonderful
operations, the mysterious ways of Providence.

Coolly and collectedly argued Zastrozzi: he delivered
his sentiments with the air of one who was wholly
convinced of the truth of the doctrines he uttered,—a
conviction to be dissipated by shunning proof.

Whilst Zastrozzi thus spoke, Matilda remained silent,
—she paused. Zastrozzi must have strong powers of
reflection ; he must be convinced of the truth of his

own reasoning, thought Matilda, as eagerly she yet gazed on his countenance. Its unchanging expression of firmness and conviction still continued.

"Ah!" said Matilda, "Zastrozzi, thy words are a balm to my soul. I never yet knew thy real sentiments on this subject; but answer me, do you believe that the soul decays with the body, or if you do not, when this perishable form mingles with its parent earth, where goes the soul which now actuates its movements? perhaps, it wastes its fervent energies in tasteless apathy, or lingering torments."

"Matilda," returned Zastrozzi, "think not so; rather suppose that, by its own innate and energetical exertions, this soul must endure for ever, that no fortuitous occurrences, no incidental events, can affect its happiness; but by daring boldly, by striving to verge from the beaten path, whilst yet trammelled in the chains of mortality, it will gain superior advantages in a future state."

"But religion! oh, Zastrozzi!"

"I thought thy soul was daring," replied Zastrozzi; "I thought thy mind was towering; and did I then err in the different estimate I had formed of thy character? O yield not yourself, Matilda, thus to false, foolish, and vulgar prejudices—for the present, farewell."

Saying this, Zastrozzi departed.

Thus, by an artful appeal to her passions, did Zastrozzi extinguish the faint spark of religion which yet gleamed in Matilda's bosom.

In proportion as her belief of an Omnipotent power, and consequently her hopes of eternal salvation declined, her ardent and unquenchable passion for Verezzi increased, and a delirium of guilty love filled her soul.

"Shall I then call him mine for ever?" mentally inquired Matilda; "will the passion which now consumes me possess my soul to all eternity? Ah! well I know it will; and when emancipated from this

terrestrial form, my soul departs; still its fervent
energies unrepressed, will remain; and in the union
of soul to soul, it will taste celestial transports." An
ecstasy of tumultuous and confused delight rushed
through her veins; she stood for some time immersed in
thought. Agitated by the emotions of her soul, her every
limb trembled. She thought upon Zastrozzi's sentiments.
She almost shuddered as she reflected; yet was convinced by the cool and collected manner in which he
had delivered them. She thought on his advice, and
steeling her soul, repressing every emotion, she now
acquired that coolness so necessary to the attainment
of her desire.

Thinking of nothing else, alive to no idea but
Verezzi, Matilda's countenance assumed a placid
serenity—she even calmed her soul, she bid it restrain
its emotions, and the passions which so lately had
battled fiercely in her bosom were calmed.

She again went to Verezzi's apartment, but, as she
approached, vague fears lest he should have penetrated
her schemes confused her: but his mildly beaming
eyes, as she gazed upon them, convinced her that the
horrid expressions which he had before uttered were
merely the effect of temporary delirium.

"Ah, Matilda!" exclaimed Verezzi, "where have
you been?"

Matilda's soul, alive alike to despair and hope, was
filled with momentary delight as he addressed her; but
bitter hate, and disappointed love, again tortured her
bosom, as he exclaimed in accents of heart-felt agony:
"Oh! Julia, my long-lost Julia!"

"Matilda," said he, "my friend, farewell; I feel that
I am dying, but I feel pleasure,—oh! transporting
pleasure, in the idea that I shall soon meet my Julia.
Matilda," added he, in a softened accent, "farewell for
ever." Scarcely able to contain the emotions which the
idea alone of Verezzi's death excited, Matilda, though

the crisis of the disorder, she knew, had been favour-
able, shuddered—bitter hate, even more rancorous than
ever, kindled in her bosom against Julia, for to
hear Verezzi talk of her with soul-subduing tenderness,
but wound up her soul to the highest pitch of uncontrollable vengeance. Her breast heaved violently, her
dark eye, in expressive glances, told the fierce passions
of her soul; yet, sensible of the necessity of controlling
her emotions, she leaned her head upon her hand, and
when she answered Verezzi, a calmness, a melting expression of grief, overspread her features. She conjured him, in the most tender, the most soothing terms,
to compose himself; and though Julia was gone for
ever, to remember that there was yet one in the world,
one tender friend who would render the burden of life
less insupportable.

"Oh! Matilda," exclaimed Verezzi, "talk not to me of
comfort, talk not of happiness. All that constituted my
comfort, all to which I looked forward with rapturous
anticipation of happiness, is fled—fled for ever."

Ceaselessly did Matilda watch by the bedside of
Verezzi; the melting tenderness of his voice, the melancholy, interesting expression of his countenance, but
added fuel to the flame which consumed her; her soul
was engrossed by one idea; every extraneous passion
was conquered, and nerved for the execution of its
fondest purpose; a seeming tranquillity overspread her
mind, not that tranquillity which results from conscious
innocence and mild delights, but that which calms
every tumultuous emotion for a time; when, firm in a
settled purpose, the passions but pause, to break out
with more resistless violence. In the meantime, the
strength of Verezzi's constitution overcame the malignity of his disorder, returning strength again braced
his nerves, and he was able to descend to the saloon.

The violent grief of Verezzi had subsided into a deep
and settled melancholy; he could now talk of his Julia,

indeed it was his constant theme; he spoke of her virtues, her celestial form, her sensibility, and by his
ardent professions of eternal fidelity to her memory,
unconsciously almost drove Matilda to desperation.
Once he asked Matilda how she died; for on the day
when the intelligence first turned his brain, he waited
not to hear the particulars ; the bare fact drove him to
instant madness.

Matilda was startled at the question, yet ready invention supplied the place of a premeditated story.

"Oh ! my friend," said she, tenderly, "unwillingly
do I tell you that for you she died; disappointed love,
like a worm in the bud, destroyed the unhappy Julia;
fruitless were all her endeavours to find you; till at last,
concluding that you were lost to her for ever, a deep
melancholy by degrees consumed her, and gently led
to the grave.   She sank into the arms of death without
a groan."

"And there shall I soon follow her," exclaimed Verezzi, as a severer pang of anguish and regret darted
through his soul. " I caused her death, whose life was
far, far dearer to me than my own.   But now it is all
over, my hopes of happiness in this world are blasted,
blasted for ever."

As he said this, a convulsive sigh heaved his breast,
and the tears silently rolled down his cheeks ; for some
time in vain were Matilda's endeavours to calm him,
till at last, mellowed by time, and overcome by reflection, his violent and fierce sorrow was softened into
a fixed melancholy.

Unremittingly Matilda attended him, and gratified
his every wish; she, conjecturing that solitude might be
detrimental to him, often entertained parties, and endeavoured by gaiety to drive away his dejection; but if
Verezzi's spirits were elevated by company and merriment, in solitude again they sank, and a deeper melancholy, a severer regret possessed his bosom, for having

allowed himself to be momentarily interested by any
thing but the remembrance of his Julia ; for he felt a
soft, a tender and ecstatic emotion of regret, when
retrospection portrayed the blissful time long since gone
by, while, happy in the society of her whom he idolized,
he thought he could never be otherwise than then,
enjoying the sweet, the serene delights of association
with a congenial mind ; he often now amused himself
in retracing with his pencil, from memory, scenes
which, though in his Julia's society he had beheld
unnoticed, yet were now hallowed by the remembrance
of her : for he always associated the idea of Julia with
the remembrance of those scenes which she had so
often admired, and where, accompanied by her, he had
so often wandered.

Matilda, meanwhile, firm in the purpose of her soul,
unremittingly persevered ; she calmed her mind, and
though, at intervals, shook by almost superhuman
emotions, before Verezzi a fixed serenity, a well-feigned
sensibility, and a downcast tenderness, marked her
manner.   Grief, melancholy, a fixed, a quiet depression
of spirits, seemed to have calmed every fiercer feeling
when she talked with Verezzi of his lost Julia ; but,
though subdued for the present, revenge, hate, and
the fervour of disappointed love, burned her soul.

Often, when she had retired from Verezzi, when he
had talked with tenderness, as he was wont, of Julia,
and sworn everlasting fidelity to her memory, would
Matilda's soul be tortured by fiercest desperation.

One day, when conversing with him of Julia, she
ventured to hint, though remotely, at her own faithful
and ardent attachment.

"Think you," replied Verezzi, "that because my
Julia's spirit is no longer enshrined in its earthly form,
that I am the less devotedly, the less irrevocably hers?
—No! no!   I was hers, I am hers, and to all eternity
shall be hers : and when my soul, divested of mor-

tality, departs into another world, even amid the universal wreck of nature, attracted by congeniality of sentiment, it will seek the unspotted spirit of my idolized Julia. Oh, Matilda! thy attention, thy kindness, calls for my warmest gratitude—thy virtue demands my sincerest esteem ; but, devoted to the memory of my Julia, I can *love* none but her."

Matilda's whole frame trembled with unconquerable emotion, as thus determinedly he rejected her; but, calming the more violent passions, a flood of tears rushed from her eyes ; and, as she leant over the back of a sofa on which she reclined, her sobs were audible.

Verezzi's soul was softened towards her—he raised the humbled Matilda, and bid her be comforted, for he was conscious that her tenderness towards him deserved not an unkind return.

"Oh! forgive, forgive me!" exclaimed Matilda, with well-feigned humility: "I knew not what I said." She then abruptly left the saloon.

Reaching her own apartment, Matilda threw herself on the floor, in an agony of mind too great to be described. Those infuriate passions, restrained as they had been in the presence of Verezzi, now agitated her soul with inconceivable terror. Shook by sudden and irresistible emotions, she gave vent to her despair.

"Where, then, is the boasted mercy of God," exclaimed the frantic Matilda, "if he suffer his creatures to endure such agony as this? or where his wisdom, if he implant in the heart passions furious —uncontrollable—as mine, doomed to destroy their happiness?"

Outraged pride, disappointed love, and infuriate revenge, revelled through her bosom. Revenge, which called for innocent blood—the blood of the hapless Julia.

Her passions were now wound up to the highest pitch of desperation. In indescribable agony of mind, she dashed her head against the floor—she imprecated a thousand curses upon Julia, and swore eternal revenge.

At last, exhausted by their own violence, the warring passions subsided—a calm took possession of her soul—she thought again upon Zastrozzi's advice—Was she now cool? was she now collected?

She was now immersed in a chain of thought; unaccountable, even to herself, was the serenity which had succeeded.

CHAPTER X.

PERSEVERING in the prosecution of her design, the time passed away slowly to Matilda; for Verezzi's frame, becoming every day more emaciated, threatened, to her alarmed imagination, approaching dissolution — slowly to Verezzi, for he waited with impatience for the arrival of death, since nothing but misery was his in this world.

Useless would it be to enumerate the conflicts in Matilda's soul : suffice it to say that they were many, and that their violence progressively increased.

Verezzi's illness at last assumed so dangerous an appearance that Matilda, alarmed, sent for a physician.

The humane man who had attended Verezzi before was from home, but one, skilful in his profession, arrived, who declared that a warmer climate could alone restore Verezzi's health.

Matilda proposed to him to remove to a retired and picturesque spot which she possessed in the Venetian territory. Verezzi, expecting speedy dissolution, and conceiving it to be immaterial where he died, consented ; and, indeed, he was unwilling to pain one so kind as Matilda by a refusal.

The following morning was fixed for the journey.

The morning arrived, and Verezzi was lifted into the chariot, being yet extremely weak and emaciated.

Matilda, during the journey, by every care, every kind and sympathising attention, tried to drive away Verezzi's melancholy; sensible that, could the weight which pressed upon his spirits be removed, he would speedily regain health. But no! it was impossible. Though he was grateful for Matilda's attention, a still deeper shade of melancholy overspread his features; a more heart-felt inanity and languor sapped his life. He was sensible of a total distaste of former objects— objects which, perhaps, had formerly forcibly interested him. The terrific grandeur of the Alps, the dashing cataract, as it foamed beneath their feet, ceased to excite those feelings of awe which formerly they were wont to inspire. The lofty pine-groves inspired no additional melancholy, nor did the blooming valleys of Piedmont, or the odoriferous orangeries which scented the air, gladden his deadened soul.

They travelled on—they soon entered the Venetian territory, where, in a gloomy and remote spot, stood the Castella di Laurentini.

It was situated in a dark forest—lofty mountains around lifted their aspiring and craggy summits to the skies.

The mountains were clothed half up by ancient pines and plane-trees, whose immense branches stretched far; and above, bare granite rocks, on which might be seen occasionally a scathed larch, lifted their gigantic and misshapen forms.

In the centre of an amphitheatre, formed by these mountains, surrounded by wood, stood the Castella di Laurentini, whose grey turrets and time-worn battle-ments overtopped the giants of the forest.

Into this gloomy mansion was Verezzi conducted by Matilda. The only sentiment he felt was surprise at the prolongation of his existence. As he advanced, supported by Matilda and a domestic, into the castella, Matilda's soul, engrossed by one idea, confused by its own unquenchable passions, felt not that ecstatic, that calm and serene delight, only experienced by the innocent, and which is excited by a return to the place where we have spent our days of infancy.

No—she felt not this; the only pleasurable emotion which her return to this remote castella afforded was the hope that, disengaged from the tumult of, and proximity to the world, she might be the less interrupted in the prosecution of her madly-planned schemes.

Though Verezzi's melancholy seemed rather increased than diminished by the journey, yet his health was visibly improved by the progressive change of air and variation of scenery, which must, at times, momentarily alleviate the most deep-rooted grief; yet, again in a fixed spot—again left to solitude and his own torturing reflections, Verezzi's mind returned to his lost, his still adored Julia. He thought of her ever; unconsciously he spoke of her; and, by his rapturous exclamations, sometimes almost drove Matilda to desperation.

Several days thus passed away. Matilda's passion, which, mellowed by time, and diverted by the variety of objects, and the hurry of the journey, had relaxed its violence, now, like a stream pent up, burst all bounds.

But one evening, maddened by the tender protestations of eternal fidelity to Julia's memory which Verezzi uttered, her brain was almost turned.

Her tumultuous soul, agitated by contending emotions, flashed from her eyes. Unable to disguise the extreme violence of her sensations, in an ecstasy of despairing love, she rushed from the apartment where she had left Verezzi, and, unaccompanied, wandered into the forest, to calm her emotions, and concert some better plans of revenge; for, in Verezzi's presence, she scarcely dared to think.

Her infuriated soul burned with fiercest revenge: she wandered into the trackless forest, and, conscious that she was unobserved, gave vent to her feelings in wild exclamations.

"Oh, Julia! hated Julia! words are not able to express my detestation of thee. Thou hast destroyed Verezzi. Thy cursed image, revelling in his heart, has blasted my happiness for ever; but, ere I die, I will taste revenge—oh! exquisite revenge!" She paused—she thought of the passion which consumed her. "Perhaps one no less violent has induced Julia to rival me," said she. Again the idea of Verezzi's illness—perhaps his death—infuriated her soul. Pity, chased away by vengeance and disappointed passion, fled. "Did I say that I pitied thee? Detested Julia, much did my words belie the feelings of my soul. No—no—thou shalt not escape me. Pity thee!"

Again immersed in corroding thought, she heeded not the hour, till looking up, she saw the shades of night were gaining fast upon the earth. The evening was calm and serene: gently agitated by the evening zephyr, the lofty pines sighed mournfully. Far to the west appeared the evening star, which faintly glittered in the twilight. The scene was solemnly calm, but not in unison with Matilda's soul. Softest, most melancholy music, seemed to float upon the southern gale. Matilda listened—it was the nuns at a convent, chanting the requiem for the soul of a departed sister.

"Perhaps gone to heaven!" exclaimed Matilda, as, affected by the contrast, her guilty soul trembled. A chain of horrible racking thoughts pressed upon her soul; and, unable to bear the acuteness of her sensations, she hastily returned to the castella.

Thus, marked only by the varying paroxysms of the passions which consumed her, Matilda passed the time:

her brain was confused, her mind agitated by the ill
success of her schemes, and her spirits, once so light
and buoyant, were now depressed by disappointed hope.

"What shall I next concert?" was the mental inquiry
of Matilda. "Ah! I know not."

She suddenly started—she thought of Zastrozzi.

"Oh! that I should have till now forgotten Zastrozzi,"
exclaimed Matilda, as a new ray of hope darted through
her soul. "But he is now at Naples, and some time
must necessarily elapse before I can see him."

"Oh, Zastrozzi, Zastrozzi! would that you were
here!"

No sooner had she well arranged her resolutions,
which before had been confused by eagerness, than she
summoned Ferdinand, on whose fidelity she dared to
depend, and bid him speed to Naples, and bear a letter,
with which he was entrusted, to Zastrozzi.

Meanwhile Verezzi's health, as the physician had predicted, was so much improved by the warm climate and
pure air of the Castella di Laurentini, that, though yet
extremely weak and emaciated, he was able, as the
weather was fine, and the summer evenings tranquil, to
wander, accompanied by Matilda, through the surrounding scenery.

In this gloomy solitude, where, except the occasional
and infrequent visits of a father confessor, nothing occurred to disturb the uniform tenour of their life, Verezzi
was everything to Matilda—she thought of him ever:
at night, in dreams, his image was present to her enraptured imagination. She was uneasy, except in his
presence; and her soul, shook by contending paroxysms
of the passion which consumed her, was transported by
unutterable ecstasies of delirious and maddening love.

Her taste for music was exquisite; her voice of
celestial sweetness; and her skill, as she drew sounds
of soul-touching melody from the harp, enraptured the
mind to melancholy pleasure.

The affecting expression of her voice, mellowed as it was by the tenderness which at times stole over her soul, softened Verezzi's listening ear to ecstasy.

Yet, again recovering from the temporary delight which her seductive blandishments had excited, he thought of Julia. As he remembered her ethereal form, her retiring modesty, and unaffected sweetness, a more violent, a deeper pang of regret and sorrow assailed his bosom, for having suffered himself to be even momentarily interested by Matilda.

Hours, days passed lingering away. They walked in the evenings around the environs of the castella—woods, dark and gloomy, stretched far—cloud-capt mountains reared their gigantic summits high ; and, dashing amidst the jutting rocks, foaming cataracts, with sudden and impetuous course, sought the valley below.

Amid this scenery the wily Matilda usually led her victim.

One evening when the moon, rising over the gigantic outline of the mountain, silvered the far-seen cataract, Matilda and Verezzi sought the forest.

For a time neither spoke : the silence was uninterrupted, save by Matilda's sighs, which declared that violent and repressed emotions tortured the bosom within.

They silently advanced into the forest. The azure sky was spangled with stars—not a wind agitated the unruffled air—not a cloud obscured the brilliant concavity of heaven. They ascended an eminence, clothed with towering wood ; the trees around formed an amphitheatre. Beneath, by a gentle ascent, an opening showed an immense extent of forest, dimly seen by the moon, which overhung the opposite mountain. The craggy heights beyond might distinctly be seen, edged by the beams of the silver moon.

Verezzi threw himself on the turf.

" What a beautiful scene, Matilda !" he exclaimed.

" Beautiful indeed," returned Matilda. " I have admired it ever, and brought you here this evening on purpose to discover whether you thought of the works of nature as I do."

" Oh ! fervently do I admire this," exclaimed Verezzi, as, engrossed by the scene before him, he gazed enraptured.

" Suffer me to retire for a few minutes," said Matilda.

Without waiting for Verezzi's answer, she hastily entered a small tuft of trees. Verezzi gazed surprised ; and soon sounds of such ravishing melody stole upon the evening breeze, that Verezzi thought some spirit of the solitude had made audible to mortal ears ethereal music.

He still listened—it seemed to die away—and again a louder, a more rapturous swell, succeeded.

The music was in unison with the scene—it was in unison with Verezzi's soul : and the success of Matilda's artifice, in this respect, exceeded her most sanguine expectation.

He still listened—the music ceased—and Matilda's symmetrical form emerging from the wood, roused Verezzi from his vision.

He gazed on her—her loveliness and grace struck forcibly upon his senses; her sensibility, her admiration of objects which enchanted him, flattered him ; and her judicious arrangement of the music left no doubt in his mind but that, experiencing the same sensations herself, the feelings of his soul were not unknown to her.

Thus far everything went on as Matilda desired. To touch his feelings had been her constant aim : could she find anything which interested him ; anything to divert his melancholy : or could she succeed in effacing another from his mind, she had no doubt but that he would quickly and voluntarily clasp her to his bosom.

By affecting to coincide with him in everything—by

feigning to possess that congeniality of sentiment and union of idea which he thought so necessary to the existence of love, she doubted not soon to accomplish her purpose.

But sympathy and congeniality of sentiment, however necessary to that love which calms every fierce emotion, fills the soul with a melting tenderness, and, without disturbing it, continually possesses the soul, was by no means consonant to the ferocious emotions, the unconquerable and ardent passion which revelled through Matilda's every vein.

When enjoying the society of him she loved, calm delight, unruffled serenity, possessed not her soul. No —but, inattentive to every object but him, even her proximity to him agitated her with almost uncontrollable emotion.

Whilst watching his look, her pulse beat with unwonted violence, her breast palpitated, and, unconscious of it herself, an ardent and voluptuous fire darted from her eyes.

Her passion too, controlled as it was in the presence of Verezzi, agitated her soul with progressively increasing fervour. Nursed by solitude, and wound up, perhaps, beyond any pitch which another's soul might be capable of, it sometimes almost maddened her.

Still, surprised at her own forbearance, yet strongly perceiving the necessity of it, she spoke not again of her passion to Verezzi.

CHAPTER XI.

A T last the day arrived when Matilda expected Ferdinand's return. Punctual to his time, Ferdinand returned, and told Matilda that Zastrozzi had, for the present, taken up his abode at a cottage not far from thence, and that he there awaited her arrival.

Matilda was much surprised that Zastrozzi preferred a cottage to her castella ; but, dismissing that from her mind, hastily prepared to attend him.

She soon arrived at the cottage. Zastrozzi met her— he quickened his pace towards her.

" Well, Zastrozzi," exclaimed Matilda, inquiringly.

" Oh !" said Zastrozzi, " our schemes have all, as yet, been unsuccessful. Julia yet lives, and, surrounded by wealth and power, yet defies our vengeance. I was planning her destruction, when, obedient to your commands, I came here."

" Alas !" exclaimed Matilda, " I fear it must be ever thus : but, Zastrozzi, much I need your advice—your assistance. Long have I languished in hopeless love : often have I expected, and as often have my eager expectations been blighted by disappointment."

A deep sigh of impatience burst from Matilda's bosom, as, unable to utter more, she ceased.

" 'Tis but the image of that accursed Julia," replied Zastrozzi, " revelling in his breast, which prevents him from becoming instantly yours. Could you but efface that !"

" I would I could efface it," said Matilda : " the friendship which now exists between us would quickly ripen into love, and I should be for ever happy. How, Zastrozzi, can that be done ? But, before we think of happiness, we must have a care to our safety: we must destroy Julia, who yet endeavours, by every means, to know the event of Verezzi's destiny. But, surrounded by wealth and power as she is, how can that be done ? No bravo in Naples dare attempt her life : no rewards, however great, could tempt the most abandoned of men to brave instant destruction, in destroying her ; and should *we* attempt it, the most horrible tortures of the Inquisition, a disgraceful death, and that without

I.   E

the completion of our desire, would be the consequence."

"Think not so, Matilda," answered Zastrozzi; "think
not, because Julia possesses wealth, that she is less
assailable by the dagger of one eager for revenge as I
am ; or that, because she lives in splendour at Naples,
that a poisoned chalice, prepared by your hand, the
hand of a disappointed rival, could not send her writhing and convulsed to the grave. No, no ; she *can* die,
nor shall we writhe on the rack."

"Oh !" interrupted Matilda, "I care not, if, writhing
in the prisons of the Inquisition, I suffer the most excruciating torment ; I care not if, exposed to public
view, I suffer the most ignominious and disgraceful of
deaths, if, before I die—if, before this spirit seeks
another world, I gain my purposed design, I enjoy unutterable, and, as yet, inconceivable happiness."

The evening meanwhile came on, and, warned by the
lateness of the hour to separate, Matilda and Zastrozzi
parted.

Zastrozzi pursued his way to the cottage, and Matilda,
deeply musing, retraced her steps to the castella.

The wind was fresh, and rather tempestuous: light
fleeting clouds were driven rapidly across the dark-blue
sky. The moon, in silver majesty, hung high in eastern
ether, and rendered transparent as a celestial spirit the
shadowy clouds, which at intervals crossed her orbit,
and by degrees vanished like a vision in the obscurity of
distant air. On this scene gazed Matilda—a train of
confused thought took possession of her soul—her
crimes, her past life, rose in array to her terror-struck
imagination. Still burning love, unrepressed, unconquerable passion, revelled through every vein : her
senses, rendered delirious by guilty desire, were
whirled around in an inexpressible ecstasy of anticipated delight—delight, not unmixed by confused
apprehensions.

She stood thus with her arms folded, as if contemplating the spangled concavity of heaven.

It was late—later than the usual hour of return, and Verezzi had gone out to meet Matilda.

"What! deep in thought, Matilda?" exclaimed Verezzi, playfully.

Matilda's cheek, as he thus spoke, was tinged with a momentary blush; it, however, quickly passed away, and she replied, "I was enjoying the serenity of the evening, the beauty of the setting sun, and then the congenial twilight induced me to wander farther than usual."

The unsuspicious Verezzi observed nothing peculiar in the manner of Matilda; but, observing that the night air was chill, conducted her back to the castella. No art was left untried, no blandishment omitted, on the part of Matilda, to secure her victim. Everything which he liked, she affected to admire : every sentiment uttered by Verezzi was always anticipated by the observing Matilda ; but long was all in vain—long was every effort to obtain his love useless.

Often, when she touched the harp, and drew sounds of enchanting melody from its strings, whilst her almost celestial form bent over it, did Verezzi gaze enraptured, and, forgetful of everything else, yielding himself to a tumultuous oblivion of pleasure, listened entranced.

But all her art could not draw Julia from his memory ; he was much softened towards Matilda ; he felt esteem, tenderest esteem—but he yet loved not.

Thus passed the time. Often would desperation, and an idea that Verezzi would never love her, agitate Matilda with most violent agony. The beauties of nature which surrounded the castella had no longer power to interest ; borne away on swelling thought, often in the solitude of her own apartment, her spirit was wafted on the wings of anticipating fancy. Sometimes imagination portrayed the most horrible images

for futurity ; Verezzi's hate, perhaps his total dereliction
of her, his union with Julia, pressed upon her brain,
and almost drove her to distraction, for Verezzi alone
filled every thought ; nourished by restless reveries, the
most horrible anticipations blasted the blooming
Matilda. Sometimes, however, a gleam of sense shot
across her soul, deceived by visions of unreal bliss, she
acquired new courage, and fresh anticipations of delight,
from a beam which soon withdrew its ray ; for, usually
sunk in gloom, her dejected eyes were fixed on the
ground ; though sometimes an ardent expression,
kindled by the anticipation of gratified desire, flashed
from their fiery orbits.

Often, whilst thus agitated by contending emotions,
her soul was shook, and, unconscious of its intentions,
knew not the most preferable plan to pursue: would she
seek Zastrozzi : on him, unconscious why, she relied ˙
much—his words were those of calm reflection and
experience ; and his sophistry, whilst it convinced her
that a superior being exists not, who can control our
actions, brought peace to her mind—peace to be succeeded by horrible and resistless conviction of the falsehood of her coadjutor's arguments ; still, however,
they calmed her ; and, by addressing her reason and
passions at the same time, deprived her of the power of
being benefited by either.

The health of Verezzi, meanwhile, slowly mended :
his mind, however, shook by so violent a trial as it had
undergone, recovered not its vigour, but, mellowed by
time, his grief, violent and irresistible as it had been at
first, now became a fixed melancholy, which spread
itself over his features, was apparent in every action,
and, by resistance, inflamed Matilda's passion to tenfold fury.

The touching tenderness of Verezzi's voice, the
dejected softened expression of his eye, touched her
soul with tumultuous yet milder emotions. In his pre-

sence she felt calmed ; and those passions which, in solitude, were almost too fierce for endurance, when with him were softened into a tender though confused delight.

It was one evening, when no previous appointment existed between Matilda and Zastrozzi, that, overcome by disappointed passion, Matilda sought the forest.

The sky was unusually obscured, the sun had sunk beneath the western mountain, and its departing ray tinged the heavy clouds with a red glare. The rising blast sighed through the towering pines, which rose loftily above Matilda's head : the distant thunder, hoarse as the murmurs of the grove, in indistinct echoes mingled with the hollow breeze ; the scintillating lightning flashed incessantly across her path, as Matilda, heeding not the storm, advanced along the trackless forest.

The crashing thunder now rattled madly above, the lightnings flashed a larger curve, and at intervals, through the surrounding gloom, showed a scathed larch, which, blasted by frequent storms, reared its bare head on a height above.

Matilda sat upon a fragment of jutting granite, and contemplated the storm which raged around her. The portentous calm, which at intervals occurred amid the reverberating thunder, portentous of a more violent tempest, resembled the serenity which spread itself over Matilda's mind—a serenity only to be succeeded by a fiercer paroxysm of passion.

CHAPTER XII.

TILL sat Matilda upon the rock—she still contemplated the tempest which raged around her.

The battling elements paused : an uninterrupted

silence, deep, dreadful as the silence of the tomb, succeeded. Matilda heard a noise—footsteps were distinguishable, and, looking up, a flash of vivid lightning
disclosed to her view the towering form of Zastrozzi.

His gigantic figure was again involved in pitchy
darkness, as the momentary lightning receded. A peal
of crashing thunder again madly rattled over the zenith,
and a scintillating flash announced Zastrozzi's approach,
as he stood before Matilda.

Matilda, surprised at his approach, started as he
addressed her, and felt an indescribable awe, when she
reflected on the wonderful casualty which, in this terrific and tempestuous hour, had led them to the same
spot.

"Doubtless his feelings are violent and irresistible as
mine: perhaps *these* led him to meet me here."

She shuddered as she reflected: but smothering the
sensations of alarm which she had suffered herself to be
surprised by, she asked him what had led him to the
forest.

"The same which led you here, Matilda," returned
Zastrozzi: "the same influence which actuates us both,
has doubtless inspired that congeniality which, in this
frightful storm, led us to the same spot."

"Oh!" exclaimed Matilda, "how shall I touch the
obdurate Verezzi's soul? He still despises me—he
declares himself to be devoted to the memory of his
Julia; and that although she be dead, he is not the
less devotedly hers. What can be done?"

Matilda paused; and, much agitated, awaited Zastrozzi's reply.

Zastrozzi, meanwhile, stood collected in himself, and
firm as the rocky mountain which lifts its summit to
heaven.

"Matilda," said he, "to-morrow evening will pave
the way for that happiness which your soul has so long
panted for; if, indeed, the event which will then occur

does not completely conquer Verezzi. But the violence of the tempest increases—let us seek shelter."

"Oh! heed not the tempest," said Matilda, whose expectations were raised to the extreme of impatience by Zastrozzi's dark hints; "heed not the tempest, but proceed, if you wish not to see me expiring at your feet."

"You fear not the tumultuous elements—nor do I," replied Zastrozzi. "I assert again, that if to-morrow evening you lead Verezzi to this spot—if, in the event which will here occur, you display that presence of mind which I believe you to possess, Verezzi is yours."

"Ah! what do you say, Zastrozzi, that Verezzi will be mine?" inquired Matilda, as the anticipation of inconceivable happiness dilated her soul with sudden and excessive delight.

"I say again, Matilda," returned Zastrozzi, "that if you dare to brave the dagger's point—if you but make Verezzi owe his life to you ——"

Zastrozzi paused, and Matilda acknowledged her insight of his plan, which her enraptured fancy represented as the basis of her happiness.

"Could he, after she had, at the risk of her own life, saved his, unfeelingly reject her? Would those noble sentiments, which the greatest misfortunes were unable to extinguish, suffer that? No."

Full of these ideas, her brain confused by the ecstatic anticipation of happiness which pressed upon it, Matilda retraced her footsteps towards the castella.

The violence of the storm which so lately had raged was passed—the thunder, in low and indistinct echoes, now sounded through the chain of rocky mountains, which stretched far to the north—the azure, and almost cloudless ether, was studded with countless stars, as Matilda entered the castella, and, as the hour was late, sought her own apartment.

Sleep fled not, as usual, from her pillow; but, overcome by excessive drowsiness, she soon sank to rest.

Confused dreams floated in her imagination, in which she sometimes supposed that she had gained Verezzi; at others, that, snatched from her ardent embrace, he was carried by an invisible power over rocky mountains, or immense and untravelled heaths, and that, in vainly attempting to follow him, she had lost herself in the trackless desert.

Awakened from disturbed and unconnected dreams, she arose.

The most tumultuous emotions of rapturous exultation filled her soul as she gazed upon her victim, who was sitting at a window which overlooked the waving forest.

Matilda seated herself by him, and most enchanting, most pensive music, drawn by her fingers from a harp, thrilled his soul with an ecstasy of melancholy; tears rolled rapidly down his cheeks; deep drawn, though gentle sighs heaved his bosom: his innocent eyes were mildly fixed upon Matilda, and beamed with compassion for one whose only wish was gratification of her own inordinate desires, and destruction to his opening prospects of happiness.

She, with a ferocious pleasure, contemplated her victim; yet, curbing the passions of her soul, a meekness, a well-feigned sensibility, characterised her downcast eye.

She waited, with the smothered impatience of expectation, for the evening : then had Zastrozzi affirmed that she would lay a firm foundation for her happiness.

Unappalled, she resolved to brave the dagger's point : she resolved to bleed ; and though her life-blood were to issue at the wound, to dare the event.

The evening at last arrived ; the atmosphere was obscured by vapour, and the air more chill than usual; yet, yielding to the solicitations of Matilda, Verezzi accompanied her to the forest.

Matilda's bosom thrilled with inconceivable happiness, as she advanced towards the spot; her limbs, trembling with ecstasy, almost refused to support her. Unwonted sensations—sensations she had never felt before, agitated her bosom; yet, steeling her soul, and persuading herself that celestial transports would be the reward of firmness, she fearlessly advanced.

The towering pine-trees waved in the squally wind— the shades of twilight gained fast on the dusky forest —the wind died away, and a deep, a gloomy silence reigned.

They now had arrived at the spot which Zastrozzi had asserted would be the scene of an event which might lay the foundation of Matilda's happiness.

She was agitated by such violent emotions that her every limb trembled, and Verezzi tenderly asked the reason of her alarm.

"Oh, nothing, nothing!" returned Matilda; but, stung by more certain anticipation of ecstasy by his tender inquiry, her whole frame trembled with tenfold agitation, and her bosom was filled with more unconquerable transport.

On the right, the thick umbrage of the forest trees rendered undistinguishable any one who might lurk *there;* on the left, a frightful precipice yawned, at whose base a deafening cataract dashed with tumultuous violence; around, misshapen and enormous masses of rock; and beyond, a gigantic and blackened mountain, reared its craggy summit to the skies.

They advanced towards the precipice. Matilda stood upon the dizzy height—her senses almost failed her, and she caught the branch of an enormous pine which impended over the abyss.

"How frightful a depth!" exclaimed Matilda.

"Frightful indeed," said Verezzi, as thoughtfully he contemplated the terrific depth beneath.

They stood for some time gazing on the scene in silence.

Footsteps were heard—Matilda's bosom thrilled with mixed sensations of delight and apprehension, as, summoning all her fortitude, she turned round. A man advanced towards them.

"What is your business?" exclaimed Verezzi.

"Revenge!" returned the villain, as, raising a dagger high, he essayed to plunge it in Verezzi's bosom, but Matilda lifted her arm, and the dagger piercing it, touched not Verezzi. Starting forward, he fell to the earth, and the ruffian instantly dashed into the thick forest.

Matilda's snowy arm was tinged with purple gore: the wound was painful, but an expression of triumph flashed from her eyes, and excessive pleasure dilated her bosom: the blood streamed fast from her arm, and tinged the rock whereon they stood with a purple stain.

Verezzi started from the ground, and seeing the blood which streamed down Matilda's garments, in accents of terror demanded where she was wounded.

"Oh! think not upon that," she exclaimed, "but tell me—ah! tell me," said she, in a voice of well-feigned alarm, "are you wounded mortally? Oh! what sensations of terror shook me, when I thought that the dagger's point, after having pierced my arm, had drunk your life-blood."

"Oh!" answered Verezzi, "I am not wounded; but let us haste to the castella."

He then tore part of his vest, and with it bound Matilda's arm. Slowly they proceeded towards the castella.

"What villain, Verezzi," said Matilda, "envious of my happiness, attempted his life, for whom I would ten thousand times sacrifice my own? Oh! Verezzi, how I thank God, who averted the fatal dagger from thy heart!"

Verezzi answered not; but his heart, his feelings, were irresistibly touched by Matilda's behaviour. Such noble contempt of danger, so ardent a passion, as to risk her life to preserve his, filled his breast with a tenderness towards her; and he felt that he could now deny her nothing, not even the sacrifice of the poor remains of his happiness, should she demand it.

Matilda's breast meanwhile swelled with sensations of unutterable delight: her soul, borne on the pinions of anticipated happiness, flashed in triumphant glances from her fiery eyes. She could scarcely forbear clasping Verezzi in her arms, and claiming him as her own; but prudence, and a fear of in what manner a premature declaration of love might be received, prevented her.

They arrived at the castella, and a surgeon from the neighbouring convent was sent for by Verezzi.

The surgeon soon arrived, examined Matilda's arm, and declared that no unpleasant consequences could ensue. Retired to her own apartment, those transports, which before had been allayed by Verezzi's presence, now unrestrained by reason, involved Matilda's senses in an ecstasy of pleasure.

She threw herself on the bed, and, in all the exaggerated colours of imagination, portrayed the transports which Zastrozzi's artifice had opened to her view.

Visions of unreal bliss floated during the whole night in her disordered fancy; her senses where whirled around in alternate ecstasies of happiness and despair, as almost palpable dreams pressed upon her disturbed brain.

At one time she imagined that Verezzi, consenting to their union, presented her his hand: that at her touch the flesh crumbled from it, and, a shrieking spectre, he fled from her view: again, silvery clouds floated across her sight, and unconnected, disturbed visions occupied her imagination till the morning.

Verezzi's manner, as he met Matilda the following

morning, was unusually soft and tender; and in a voice of solicitude, he inquired concerning her health.

The roseate flush of animation which tinged her cheek, the triumphant glance of animation which danced in her scintillating eye, seemed to render the inquiry unnecessary.

A dewy moisture filled her eyes, as she gazed with an expression of tumultuous, yet repressed rapture upon the hapless Verezzi.

Still did she purpose, in order to make her triumph more certain, to protract the hour of victory; and, leaving her victim, wandered into the forest to seek Zastrozzi. When she arrived at the cottage, she learnt that he had walked forth.—She soon met him.

"Oh! Zastrozzi—my best Zastrozzi!" exclaimed Matilda, " what a source of delight have you opened to me! Verezzi is mine—oh! transporting thought! will be mine for ever. That distant manner which he usually affected towards me, is changed to a sweet, an ecstatic expression of tenderness. Oh! Zastrozzi, receive my best, my most fervent thanks."

"Julia need not die then," muttered Zastrozzi; "when once you possess Verezzi, her destruction is of little consequence."

The most horrible scheme of revenge at this instant glanced across Zastrozzi's mind.

"Oh! Julia must die," said Matilda, "or I shall never be safe; such an influence does her image possess over Verezzi's mind, that I am convinced, were he to know that she lived, an estrangement from me would be the consequence. Oh! quickly let me hear that she is dead. I can never enjoy uninterrupted happiness until her dissolution."

"What you have just pronounced is Julia's death-warrant," said Zastrozzi, as he disappeared among the thick trees.

Matilda returned to the castella.

Verezzi, at her return, expressed a tender apprehension, lest, thus wounded, she should have hurt herself by walking; but Matilda quieted his fears, and engaged him in interesting conversation, which seemed not to have for its object the seduction of his affection; though the ideas conveyed by her expressions were so artfully connected with it, and addressed themselves so forcibly to Verezzi's feelings, that he was convinced he ought to love Matilda, though he felt *that* within himself which, in spite of reason—in spite of reflection—told him that it was impossible.

CHAPTER XIII.

The enticing smile, the modest-seeming eye,
Beneath whose beauteous beams, belying heaven,
Lurk searchless cunning, cruelty, and death.
                                                                THOMSON.

TILL did Matilda's blandishments—her unremitting attention—inspire Verezzi with a softened tenderness towards her. He regarded her as one who, at the risk of her own life, had saved his; who loved him with an ardent affection, and whose affection was likely to be lasting : and though he could not regard her with that enthusiastic tenderness with which he even yet adored the memory of his Julia, yet he might esteem her—faithfully esteem her—and felt not that horror at uniting himself with her as formerly. But a conversation which he had with Julia recurred to his mind : he remembered well, that when they had talked of their speedy marriage, she had expressed an idea, that a union in this life might endure to all eternity; and that the chosen of his heart on earth, might, by congenialty of sentiment, be united in heaven.

The idea was hallowed by the remembrance of his Julia; but chasing it, as an unreal vision, from his mind, again his high sentiments of gratitude prevailed.

Lost in these ideas, involved in a train of thought, and unconscious where his footsteps led him, he quitted the castella. His reverie was interrupted by low murmurs, which seemed to float on the silence of the forest; it was scarcely audible, yet Verezzi felt an undefinable wish to know what it was. He advanced towards it—it was Matilda's voice.

Verezzi approached nearer, and from within heard her voice in complaints. He eagerly listened. Her sobs rendered the words which in passionate exclamations burst from Matilda's lips, almost inaudible. He still listened—a pause in the tempest of grief which shook Matilda's soul seemed to have taken place.

" Oh! Verezzi—cruel, unfeeling Verezzi!" exclaimed Matilda, as a fierce paroxysm of passion seized her brain—"will you thus suffer one who adores you to linger in hopeless love, and witness the excruciating agony of one who idolizes you, as I do, to madness?"

As she spoke thus, a long-drawn sigh closed the sentence.

Verezzi's mind was agitated by various emotions as he stood; but rushing in at last, [he] raised Matilda in his arms, and tenderly attempted to comfort her.

She started as he entered—she heeded not his words; but, seemingly overcome by shame, cast herself at his feet, and hid her face in his robe.

He tenderly raised her, and his expressions convinced her that the reward of all her anxiety was now about to be reaped.

The most triumphant anticipation of transports to come filled her bosom; yet, knowing it to be necessary to dissemble—knowing that a shameless claim on his affections would but disgust Verezzi, she said:

"Oh! Verezzi, forgive me: supposing myself to be

alone—supposing no one overheard the avowal of the secret of my soul, with which, believe me, I never more intended to have importuned you, what shameless sentiments—shameless even in solitude—have I not given vent to. I can no longer conceal, that the passion with which I adore you is unconquerable, irresistible; but, I conjure you, think not upon what you have this moment heard to my disadvantage; nor despise a weak unhappy creature, who feels it impossible to overcome the fatal passion which consumes her.

"Never more will I give vent, even in solitude, to my love—never more shall the importunities of the hapless Matilda reach your ears. To conquer a passion fervent, tender as mine is impossible."

As she thus spoke, Matilda, seemingly overcome by shame, sank upon the turf.

A sentiment stronger than gratitude, more ardent than esteem, and more tender than admiration, softened Verezzi's heart as he raised Matilda. Her symmetrical form shone with tenfold loveliness to his heated fancy; inspired with sudden fondness, he cast himself at her feet.

A Lethean torpor crept upon his senses; and, as he lay prostrate before Matilda, a total forgetfulness of every former event of his life swam in his dizzy brain. In passionate exclamations he avowed unbounded love.

"Oh Matilda! dearest, angelic Matilda!" exclaimed Verezzi, "I am even now unconscious what blinded me—what kept me from acknowledging my adoration of thee!—adoration never to be changed by circumstances—never effaced by time."

The fire of voluptuous, of maddening love scorched his veins, as he caught the transported Matilda in his arms, and, in accents almost inarticulate with passion, swore eternal fidelity.

"And accept my oath of everlasting allegiance to

thee, adored Verezzi," exclaimed Matilda; "accept my vows of eternal, indissoluble love."

Verezzi's whole frame was agitated by unwonted and ardent emotions. He called Matilda his wife—in the delirium of sudden fondness, he clasped her to his bosom—"and though love like ours," exclaimed the infatuated Verezzi, "wants not the vain ties of human laws, yet, that our love may want not any sanction which could possibly be given to it, let immediate orders be given for the celebration of our union."

Matilda exultingly consented ; never had she experienced sensations of delight like these : the feelings of her soul flushed in exulting glances from her fiery eyes. Fierce, transporting triumph filled her soul as she gazed on her victim, whose mildly-beaming eyes were now characterised by a voluptuous expression. Her heart beat high with transport: and as they entered the castella, the swelling emotions of her bosom were too tumultuous for utterance.

Wild with passion, she clasped Verezzi to her beating breast; and, overcome by an ecstasy of delirious passion, her senses were whirled round in confused and inexpressible delight. A new and fierce passion raged likewise in Verezzi's breast ; he returned her embrace with ardour, and clasped her in fierce transports.

But the adoration with which he now regarded Matilda, was a different sentiment from that chaste and mild emotion which had characterised his love for Julia : that passion, which he had fondly supposed would end but with his existence, was effaced by the arts of another.

Now was Matilda's purpose attained—the next day would behold her his bride—the next day would behold her fondest purpose accomplished.

With the most eager impatience, the fiercest anticipation of transport, did she wait for its arrival.

Slowly passed the day, and slowly did the clock toil each lingering hour as it rolled away.

The following morning at last arrived: Matilda arose from a sleepless couch—fierce, transporting triumph flashed from her eyes as she embraced her victim. He returned it—he called her his dear and ever-beloved spouse; and, in all the transports of maddening love, declared his impatience for the arrival of the monk who was to unite them. Every blandishment—every thing which might dispel reflection, was this day put in practice by Matilda.

The monk at last arrived : the fatal ceremony—fatal to the peace of Verezzi—was performed.

A magnificent feast had been previously arranged : every luxurious viand, every expensive wine, which might contribute to heighten Matilda's triumph, was present in profusion.

Matilda's joy, her soul-felt triumph, was too great for utterance—too great for concealment. The exultation of her inmost soul flashed in expressive glances from her scintillating eyes, expressive of joy intense—unutterable.

Animated with excessive delight, she started from the table, and seizing Verezzi's hand, in a transport of inconceivable bliss, dragged him in wild sport and varied movements to the sound of swelling and soul touching melody.

"Come, my Matilda," at last exclaimed Verezzi, "come, I am weary of transport—sick with excess of unutterable pleasure: let us retire, and retrace in dreams the pleasures of the day."

Little did Verezzi think that this day was the basis of his future misery ; little did he think that, amid the roses of successful and licensed voluptuousness, regret, horror, and despair would arise, to blast the prospects which, Julia being forgot, appeared so fair, so ecstatic.

The morning came. Inconceivable emotions—inconceivable to those who have never felt them—dilated Matilda's soul with an ecstasy of inexpressible bliss ; every barrier to her passion was thrown down—every

I.   F opposition conquered; still was her bosom the scene of fierce and contending passions.

Though in possession of every thing which her fancy had portrayed with such excessive delight, she was far from feeling that innocent and calm pleasure which soothes the soul, and, calming each violent emotion, fills it with a serene happiness. No—*her* brain was whirled around in transports; fierce, confused transports of visionary and unreal bliss : though her every pulse, her every nerve, panted with the delight of gratified and expectant desire ; still was she not happy : she enjoyed not that tranquillity which is necessary to the existence of happiness.

In this temper of mind, for a short period she left Verezzi, as she had appointed a meeting with her coadjutor in wickedness.

She soon met him.

"I need not ask," exclaimed Zastrozzi, "for well do I see, in those triumphant glances, that Verezzi is thine ; that the plan which we concerted when last we met, has put you in possession of that which your soul panted for."

"Oh ! Zastrozzi !" said Matilda,—"kind, excellent Zastrozzi ; what words can express the gratitude which I feel towards you—what words can express the bliss, exquisite, celestial, which I owe to your advice ? yet still, amid the roses of successful love—amid the ecstasies of transporting voluptuousness—fear, blighting chilly fear, damps my hopes of happiness. Julia, the hated, accursed Julia's image, is the phantom which scares my otherwise certain confidence of eternal delight : could she but be hurled to destruction—could some other artifice of my friend sweep her from the number of the living——"

"'Tis enough, Matilda," interrupted Zastrozzi ; "'tis enough : in six days hence meet me here ; meanwhile, let not any corroding anticipations destroy your present happiness ; fear not ; but, on the arrival of your faithful Zastrozzi, expect the earnest of the happiness which you wish to enjoy for ever."

Thus saying, Zastrozzi departed, and Matilda retraced her steps to her castella.

Amid the delight, the ecstasy, for which her soul had so long panted—amid the embraces of him whom she had fondly supposed alone to constitute all terrestrial happiness, racking, corroding thoughts possessed Matilda's bosom.

Deeply musing on schemes of future delight—delight established by the gratification of most diabolical revenge, her eyes fixed upon the ground, heedless what path she pursued, Matilda advanced along the forest.

A voice aroused her from her reverie—it was Verezzi's—the well-known, the tenderly-adored tone, struck upon her senses forcibly; she started, and hastening towards him, soon allayed those fears which her absence had excited in the fond heart of her spouse, and on which account he had anxiously quitted the castella to search for her.

Joy, rapturous, ecstatic happiness, untainted by fear, unpolluted by reflection, reigned for six days in Matilda's bosom.

Five days passed away, the sixth arrived, and, when the evening came, Matilda, with eager and impatient steps, sought the forest.

The evening was gloomy, dense vapours overspread the air; the wind, low and hollow, sighed mournfully in the gigantic pine-trees, and whispered in low hissings among the withered shrubs which grew on the rocky prominences.

Matilda waited impatiently for the arrival of Zastrozzi. At last his towering form emerged from an interstice in the rocks.

He advanced towards her.

"Success! Victory! my Matilda," exclaimed Zastrozzi, in an accent of exultation—" Julia is——"

" You need add no more," interrupted Matilda: "kind, excellent Zastrozzi, I thank thee ; but yet do say how you destroyed her—tell me by what racking, horrible torments you launched her soul into eternity. Did she perish by the dagger's point ? or did the torments of poison send her, writhing in agony, to the tomb ? "

" Yes," replied Zastrozzi ; " she fell at my feet, overpowered by resistless convulsions. Who more ready than myself to restore the Marchesa's fleeted senses— who more ready than myself to account for her fainting, by observing, that the heat of the assembly had momentarily overpowered her ? But Julia's senses were fled for ever ; and it was not until the swiftest gondola in Venice had borne me far towards your castella, that *il consiglio di dieci* searched for, without discovering the offender.

"Here I must remain ; for, were I discovered, the fatal consequences to us both are obvious. Farewell for the present," added he ; " meanwhile, happiness attend you ; but go not to Venice."

" Where have you been so late, my love ? " tenderly inquired Verezzi as she returned. " I fear lest the night air, particularly that of so damp an evening as this, might affect your health."

" No, no, my dearest Verezzi, it has not," hesitatingly answered Matilda.

" You seem pensive, you seem melancholy, my Matilda," said Verezzi ; " lay open your heart to me. I am afraid something, of which I am ignorant, presses upon your bosom. Is it the solitude of this remote castella which represses the natural gaiety of your soul ? Shall we go to Venice ? "

" Oh ! no, no ! " hastily and eagerly interrupted Matilda : " not to Venice—we must not go to Venice."
. Verezzi was slightly surprised, but imputing her manner to indisposition, it passed off.

Unmarked by events of importance, a month passed away. Matilda's passion, unallayed by satiety, unconquered by time, still raged with its former fierceness—still was every earthly delight centred in Verezzi; and in the air-drawn visions of her imagination, she portrayed to herself that this happiness would last for ever.

It was one evening that Verezzi and Matilda sat, happy in the society of each other, that a servant entering, presented the latter with a sealed paper.

The contents were: "Matilda Contessa di Laurentini is summoned to appear before the Holy Inquisition—to appear before its tribunal, immediately on the receipt of this summons."

Matilda's cheek, as she read it, was blanched with terror. The summons—the fatal, irresistible summons, struck her with chilly awe. She attempted to thrust it into her bosom; but, unable to conceal her terror, she assayed to rush from the apartment—but it was in vain : her trembling limbs refused to support her, and she sank fainting on the floor.

Verezzi raised her—he restored her fleeting senses; he cast himself at her feet, and in the tenderest, most pathetic accents, demanded the reason of her alarm. "And if," said he, "it is any thing of which I have unconsciously been guilty—if it is any thing in my conduct which has offended you, oh! how soon, how truly would I repent. Dearest Matilda, I adore you to madness : tell me then quickly—confide in one who loves you as I do."

"Rise, Verezzi," exclaimed Matilda, in a tone expressive of serene horror : "and since the truth can no longer be concealed, peruse that letter."

She presented him the fatal summons. He eagerly snatched it; breathless with impatience, he opened it. But what words can express the consternation of the affrighted Verezzi, as the summons, mysterious and inexplicable to him, pressed upon his straining eyeball?

For an instant he stood fixed in mute and agonizing thought. At last, in the forced serenity of despair, he demanded what was to be done.

Matilda answered not : for her soul, borne on the pinions of anticipation, at that instant portrayed to itself ignominious and agonizing dissolution.

"What is to be done?" again, in a deeper tone of despair, demanded Verezzi.

"We must instantly to Venice," returned Matilda, collecting her scattered faculties; " we must to Venice; there, I believe, we may be safe. But in some remote corner of the city we must for the present fix our habitation ; we must condescend to curtail our establishment ; and above all, we must avoid particularity. But will my Verezzi descend from the rank of life in which his birth has placed him, and with the outcast Matilda's fortunes quit grandeur ? "

"Matilda ! dearest Matilda ! " exclaimed Verezzi, "talk not thus ; you know I am ever yours ; you know I love you, and with you, could conceive a cottage elysium."

Matilda's eyes flashed with momentary triumph as Verezzi spoke thus, amid the alarming danger which impended her : under the displeasure of the inquisition, whose motives for prosecution are inscrutable, whose decrees are without appeal, her soul, in the possession of all it held dear on earth, secure of Verezzi's affection, thrilled with pleasurable emotions, yet not unmixed with alarm.

She now prepared to depart. Taking, therefore, out of all her domestics, but the faithful Ferdinand, Matilda, accompanied by Verezzi, although the evening was far advanced, threw herself into a chariot, and leaving every one at the castella unacquainted with her intentions, took the road through the forest which led to Venice.

The convent bell, almost inaudible from distance,

tolled ten as the carriage slowly ascended a steep which rose before it.

"But how do you suppose, my Matilda," said Verezzi, "that it will be possible for us to evade the scrutiny of the inquisition?"

"Oh!" returned Matilda, "we must not appear in our true characters—we must disguise them."

"But," inquired Verezzi, "what crime do you suppose the inquisition to allege against you?"

"Heresy, I suppose," said Matilda. "You know an enemy has nothing to do but lay an accusation of heresy against any unfortunate and innocent individual, and the victim expires in horrible tortures, or lingers the wretched remnant of his life in dark and solitary cells."

A convulsive sigh heaved Verezzi's bosom.

"And is that then to be my Matilda's destiny?" he exclaimed in horror. "No—Heaven will never permit such excellence to suffer."

Meanwhile they had arrived at the Brenta. The Brenta's stream glided silently beneath the midnight breeze towards the Adriatic.

Towering poplars, which loftily raised their spiral forms on its bank, cast a gloomier shade upon the placid wave.

Matilda and Verezzi entered a gondola, and the grey tints of approaching morn had streaked the eastern ether, before they entered the Grand Canal at Venice; and passing the Rialto, proceeded onwards to a small, though not inelegant mansion, in the eastern suburbs.

Everything here, though not grand, was commodious; and as they entered it, Verezzi expressed his approbation of living here retired.

Seemingly secure from the scrutiny of the inquisition, Matilda and Verezzi passed some days of uninterrupted happiness.

At last, one evening, Verezzi, tired even with mono-

tony of ecstasy, proposed to Matilda to take the gondola, and go to a festival which was to be celebrated at
St. Mark's Place.

CHAPTER XIV.

HE evening was serene. Fleecy clouds floated
on the horizon—the moon's full orb, in cloudless
majesty, hung high in air, and was reflected in
silver brilliancy by every wave of the Adriatic, as,
gently agitated by the evening breeze, they dashed
against innumerable gondolas which crowded the
Laguna.

Exquisite harmony, borne on the pinions of the
tranquil air, floated in varying murmurs; it sometimes
died away, and then again swelling louder, in melo-
dious undulations, softened to pleasure every listening
ear.

Every eye which gazed on the fairy scene beamed
with pleasure; unrepressed gaiety filled every heart but
Julia's, as, with a vacant stare, unmoved by feelings of
pleasure, unagitated by the gaiety which filled every
other soul, she contemplated the varied scene. A magnificent gondola carried the Marchesa di Strobazzo;
and the innumerable flambeaux which blazed around
her rivalled the meridian sun.

It was the pensive, melancholy Julia, who, immersed
in thought, sat unconscious of every external object,
whom the fierce glance of Matilda measured with a
haughty expression of surprise and revenge. The dark
fire which flashed from her eye, more than told the
feelings of her soul, as she fixed it on her rival; and
had it possessed the power of the basilisk's, Julia would
have expired on the spot.

It was the ethereal form of the now forgotten Julia
which first caught Verezzi's eye. For an instant he

gazed with surprise upon her symmetrical figure, and was about to point her out to Matilda, when, in the downcast countenance of the enchanting female, he recognised his long-lost Julia.

To paint the feelings of Verezzi—as Julia raised her head from the attitude in which it was fixed, and disclosed to his view that countenance which he had formerly gazed on in ecstasy, the index of that soul to which he had sworn everlasting fidelity—is impossible.

The Lethean torpor, as it were, which before had benumbed him ; the charm, which had united him to Matilda, was dissolved.

All the air-built visions of delight, which had but a moment before floated in gay variety in his enraptured imagination, faded away, and, in place of these, regret, horror, and despairing repentance, reared their heads amid the roses of momentary voluptuousness.

He still gazed entranced, but Julia's gondola, indistinct from distance, mocked his straining eyeball.

For a time neither spoke : the gondola rapidly passed onwards, but, immersed in thought, Matilda and Verezzi heeded not its rapidity.

They had arrived at St. Mark's Place, and the gondolier's voice, as he announced it, was the first interruption of the silence.

They started.—Verezzi now, for the first time, aroused from his reverie of horror, saw that the scene before him was real ; and that the oaths of fidelity which he had so often and so fervently sworn to Julia were broken.

The extreme of horror seized his brain—a frigorific torpidity of despair chilled every sense, and his eyes, fixedly, gazed on vacancy.

" Oh ! return—instantly return ! " impatiently replied Matilda to the question of the gondolier.

The gondolier, surprised, obeyed her, and they returned.

The spacious canal was crowded with gondolas ; merriment and splendour reigned around ; enchanting harmony stole over the scene ; but, listless of the music, heeding not the splendour, Matilda sat lost in a maze of thought.

Fiercest vengeance revelled through her bosom, and, in her own mind, she resolved a horrible purpose.

Meanwhile, the hour was late, the moon had gained the zenith, and poured her beams vertically on the un-ruffled Adriatic, when the gondola stopped before Matilda's mansion.

A sumptuous supper had been prepared for their return. Silently Matilda entered—silently Verezzi followed.

Without speaking, Matilda seated herself at the supper-table ; Verezzi, with an air of listlessness, threw himself into a chair beside her.

For a time neither spoke.

"You are not well to-night," at last stammered out Verezzi : "what has disturbed you ? "

"Disturbed me !" repeated Matilda : "why do you suppose that any thing has disturbed me ? "

A more violent paroxysm of horror seemed now to seize Verezzi's brain. He pressed his hand to his burning forehead—the agony of his mind was too great to be concealed—Julia's form, as he had last seen her, floated in his fancy, and, overpowered by the resistlessly horrible ideas which pressed upon them, his senses failed him : he faintly uttered Julia's name—he sank forward, and his throbbing temples reclined on the table.

"Arise! awake! prostrate, perjured Verezzi, awake!" exclaimed the infuriate Matilda, in a tone of gloomy horror.

Verezzi started up, and gazed with surprise upon the countenance of Matilda, which, convulsed by passion, flashed desperation and revenge.

" 'Tis plain," said Matilda, gloomily, " 'tis plain, he loves me not."

A confusion of contending emotions battled in Verezzi's bosom : his marriage vow—his faith plighted to Matilda—convulsed his soul with indescribable agony.

Still did she possess a great empire over his soul— still was her frown terrible—and still did the hapless Verezzi tremble at the tones of her voice, as, in a frenzy of desperate passion, she bade him quit her for ever : " And," added she, " go, disclose the retreat of the outcast Matilda to her enemies ; deliver me to the inquisition, that a union with her you detest may fetter you no longer."

Exhausted by breathless agitation, Matilda ceased : the passions of her soul flashed from her eyes ; ten thousand conflicting emotions battled in Verezzi's bosom : he knew scarce what to do ; but, yielding to the impulse of the moment, he cast himself at Matilda's feet, and groaned deeply.

At last the words, " I am ever yours, I ever shall be yours," escaped his lips.

For a time Matilda stood immovable. At last she looked on Verezzi ; she gazed downwards upon his majestic and youthful figure, she looked upon his soul-illumined countenance, and tenfold love assailed her softened soul. She raised him—in an oblivious delirium of sudden fondness she clasped him to her bosom, and, in wild and hurried expressions, asserted her right to his love.

Her breast palpitated with fiercest emotions ; she pressed her burning lips to his ; most fervent, most voluptuous sensations of ecstasy revelled through her bosom.

Verezzi caught the infection ; in an instant of oblivion, every oath of fidelity which he had sworn to another, like a baseless cloud, dissolved away ; a Lethean torpor crept over his senses; he forgot Julia, or remembered her only as an uncertain vision, which floated before his fancy more as an ideal being of another world, whom he might hereafter adore there, than as an enchanting and congenial female, to whom his oaths of eternal fidelity had been given.

Overcome by unutterable transports of returning bliss, she started from his embrace—she seized his hand— her face was overspread with a heightened colour as she pressed it to her lips.

"And are you then mine—mine for ever?" rapturously exclaimed Matilda.

"Oh! I am thine—thine to all eternity," returned the infatuated Verezzi: "no earthly power shall sever us; joined by congeniality of soul, united by a bond to which God himself bore witness."

He again clasped her to his bosom—again, as an earnest of fidelity, imprinted a fervent kiss on her glowing cheek; and, overcome by the violent and resistless emotions of the moment, swore, that nor heaven nor hell should cancel the union which he here solemnly and unequivocally renewed.

Verezzi filled an overflowing goblet.

"Do you love me?" inquired Matilda.

"May the lightning of heaven consume me, if I adore thee not to distraction! may I be plunged in endless torments, if my love for thee, celestial Matilda, endures not for ever!"

Matilda's eyes flashed fiercest triumph; the exultingly delightful feelings of her soul were too much for utterance—she spoke not, but gazed fixedly on Verezzi's countenance.

CHAPTER XV.

" That no compunctious visitings of nature
Shake my fell purpose, nor keep peace between
The effect and it. Come to my woman's breasts,
And take my milk for gall, ye murdering ministers,
Wherever, in your sightless substances,
Ye wait on nature's mischief."—MACBETH.

EREZZI raised the goblet which he had just filled, and exclaimed, in an impassioned tone—
" My adored Matilda! this is to thy happiness—this is to thy every wish; and if I cherish a single thought which centres not in thee, may the most horrible tortures which ever poisoned the peace of man, drive me instantly to distraction. God of heaven! witness thou my oath, and write it in letters never to be erased! Ministering spirits, who watch over the happiness of mortals, attend! for here I swear eternal fidelity, indissoluble, unalterable affection to Matilda!"

He said—he raised his eyes towards heaven — he gazed upon Matilda. Their eyes met—hers gleamed with a triumphant expression of unbounded love.

Verezzi raised the goblet to his lips—when, lo! on a sudden, he dashed it to the ground— his whole frame was shook by horrible convulsions—his glaring eyes, starting from their sockets, rolled wildly around : seized with sudden madness, he drew a dagger from his girdle, and with fellest intent raised it high——

What phantom blasted Verezzi's eyeball! what made the impassioned lover dash a goblet to the ground, which he was about to drain as a pledge of eternal love to the choice of his soul! and why did he, infuriate, who had, but an instant before, imagined Matilda's arms an earthly paradise, attempt to rush unprepared into the presence of his Creator!—It was the mildly-beaming eyes of the lovely but forgotten Julia, which spoke reproaches to the soul of Verezzi—it was her celestial countenance, shaded by dishevelled ring-lets, which spoke daggers to the false one ; for, when he had raised the goblet to his lips—when, sublimed by the maddening fire of voluptuousness to the height of enthusiastic passion, he swore indissoluble fidelity to another—Julia stood before him !

Madness—fiercest madness—revelled through his brain. He raised the poniard high, but Julia rushed forwards, and, in accents of distinction, in a voice of alarmed tenderness, besought him to spare himself—to spare her—for all might yet be well.

"Oh ! never, never !" exclaimed Verezzi, frantically ; " no peace but in the grave for me.——I am—I am—married to Matilda."

Saying this, he fell backwards upon a sofa, in strong convulsions, yet his hand still grasped the fatal poniard.

Matilda, meanwhile, fixedly contemplated the scene. Fiercest passions raged through her breast—vengeance, disappointed love—disappointed in the instant too when she had supposed happiness to be hers for ever, ren-dered her bosom the scene of wildest anarchy.

Yet she spoke not—she moved not—but, collected in herself, stood waiting the issue of that event, which had so unexpectedly dissolved her visions of air-built ecstasy.

Serened to firmness from despair, Julia administered everything which could restore Verezzi with the most unremitting attention. At last he recovered. He slowly raised himself, and starting from the sofa where he lay, his eyes rolling wildly, and his whole frame convulsed by fiercest agitation, he raised the dagger which he still retained, and, with a bitter smile of exultation, plunged it into his bosom ! His soul fled without a groan, and his body fell to the floor, bathed in purple blood.

Maddened by this death-blow to all anticipation of

happiness, Matilda's faculties, as she stood, whirled in wild confusion : she scarce knew where she was.

At last, a portentous, a frightful calm, spread itself over her soul. Revenge, direst revenge, swallowed up every other feeling. Her eyes scintillated with a fiend-like expression. She advanced to the lifeless corse of Verezzi—she plucked the dagger from his bosom—it was stained with his life's blood, which trickled fast from the point to the floor. She raised it on high, and impiously called upon the God of nature to doom her to endless torments, should Julia survive her vengeance.

She advanced towards her victim, who lay bereft of sense on the floor : she shook her rudely, and grasping a handful of her dishevelled hair, raised her from the earth.

" Knowest thou me ? " exclaimed Matilda, in frantic passion—" knowest thou the injured Laurentini ? Behold this dagger, reeking with my husband's blood —behold that pale corse, in whose now cold breast thy accursed image revelling, impelled to commit the deed which deprives me of happiness for ever."

Julia's senses, roused by Matilda's violence, returned. She cast her eyes upwards, with a timid expression of apprehension, and beheld the infuriate Matilda convulsed by fiercest passion, and a blood-stained dagger raised aloft, threatening instant death.

"Die ! detested wretch," exclaimed Matilda, in a paroxysm of rage, as she violently attempted to bathe the stiletto in the life-blood of her rival ; but Julia starting aside, the weapon slightly wounded her neck, and the ensanguined stream stained her alabaster bosom.

She fell on the floor, but suddenly starting up, attempted to escape her bloodthirsty persecutor.

Nerved anew by this futile attempt to escape her vengeance, the ferocious Matilda seized Julia's floating hair, and holding her back with fiend-like strength,

stabbed her in a thousand places; and, with exulting
pleasure, again and again buried the dagger to the
hilt in her body, even after all remains of life were
annihilated.

At last the passions of Matilda, exhausted by their
own violence, sank into a deadly calm; she threw the
dagger violently from her, and contemplated the terrific
scene before her with a sullen gaze.

Before her, in the arms of death, lay him on whom
her hopes of happiness seemed to have formed so firm
a basis.

Before her lay her rival, pierced with innumerable
wounds, whose head reclined on Verezzi's bosom, and
whose angelic features, even in death, a smile of affection pervaded.

There she herself stood, an isolated guilty being.
A fiercer paroxysm of passion now seized her: in an
agony of horror, too great to be described, she tore her
hair in handfuls—she blasphemed the power who had
given her being, and imprecated eternal torments upon
the mother who had borne her.

"And is it for this," added the ferocious Matilda—
"is it for horror, for torments such as these, that He,
whom monks call all-merciful, has created me?"

She seized the dagger which lay on the floor.

"Ah, friendly dagger," she exclaimed, in a voice of
fiend-like horror, "would that thy blow produced annihilation! with what pleasure then would I clasp thee to
my heart!"

She raised it high—she gazed on it—the yet warm
blood of the innocent Julia trickled from its point.

The guilty Matilda shrunk at death—she let fall the
upraised dagger—her soul had caught a glimpse of the
misery which awaits the wicked hereafter, and, spite of
her contempt of religion—spite of her, till now, too
firm dependence on the doctrines of atheism, she trembled at futurity; and a voice from within, which

whispers, "thou shalt never die!" spoke daggers to Matilda's soul.

Whilst thus she stood entranced in a delirium of despair, the night wore away, and the domestic who attended her, surprised at the unusual hour to which they had prolonged the banquet, came to announce the lateness of the hour; but opening the door, and perceiving Matilda's garments stained with blood, she started back with affright, without knowing the full extent of horror which the chamber contained, and alarmed the other domestics with an account that Matilda had been stabbed.

In a crowd they all came to the door, but started back in terror when they saw Verezzi and Julia stretched lifeless on the floor.

Summoning fortitude from despair, Matilda loudly called for them to return : but fear and horror overbalanced her commands, and, wild with affright, they all rushed from the chamber, except Ferdinand, who advanced to Matilda, and demanded an explanation.

Matilda gave it, in few and hurried words.

Ferdinand again quitted the apartment, and told the credulous domestics, that an unknown female had surprised Verezzi and Matilda ; that she had stabbed Verezzi, and then committed suicide.

The crowd of servants, as in mute terror they listened to Ferdinand's account, entertained not a doubt of the truth. Again and again they demanded an explanation of the mysterious affair, and employed their wits in conjecturing what might be the cause of it ; but the more they conjectured, the more were they puzzled ; till at last, a clever fellow named Pietro, who, hating Ferdinand on account of the superior confidence with which his lady treated him, and supposing more to be concealed in this affair than met the ear, gave information to the police, and, before morning, Matilda's

dwelling was surrounded by a party of officials belonging to il Consiglio di dieci.

Loud shouts rent the air as the officials attempted
the entrance. Matilda still was in the apartment where,
during the night, so bloody a tragedy had been acted :
still in speechless horror was she extended on the sofa,
when a loud rap at the door aroused the horror-tranced
wretch. She started from the sofa in wildest perturbation, and listened attentively. Again was the noise
repeated, and the officials rushed in.

They searched every apartment ; at last they entered
that in which Matilda, motionless with despair,
remained.

Even the stern officials, hardy, unfeeling as they
were, started back with momentary horror as they
beheld the fair countenance of the murdered Julia ; fair
even in death, and her body disfigured with numberless
ghastly wounds.

"This cannot be suicide," muttered one, who by his
superior manner, seemed to be their chief, as he raised
the fragile form of Julia from the ground, and the blood,
scarcely yet cold, trickled from her vestments.

"Put your orders in execution," added he.

Two officials advanced towards Matilda, who, standing apart with seeming tranquillity, awaited their
approach.

"What wish you with me ? " exclaimed Matilda
haughtily.

The officials answered not ; but their chief, drawing a
paper from his vest, which contained an order for the
arrest of Matilda La Contessa di Laurentini, presented
it to her.

She turned pale ; but, without resistance, obeyed the
mandate, and followed the officials in silence to the
canal, where a gondola waited, and in a short time she
was in the gloomy prisons of il Consiglio di dieci.

A little straw was the bed of the haughty Laurentini ;

a pitcher of water and bread was her sustenance;
gloom, horror, and despair pervaded her soul; all the
pleasures which she had but yesterday tasted; all the
ecstatic blisses which her enthusiastic soul had painted
for futurity, like the unreal vision of a dream, faded
away; and, confined in a damp and narrow cell,
Matilda saw that all her hopes of future delight would
end in speedy and ignominious dissolution.

Slow passed the time—slow did the clock at St.
Mark's toll the revolving hours as languidly they passed
away.

Night came on, and the hour of midnight struck
upon Matilda's soul as her death knell.

A noise was heard in the passage which led to the
prison.

Matilda raised her head from the wall against which
it was reclined, and eagerly listened, as if in expectation of an event which would seal her future fate. She
still gazed, when the chains of the entrance were un-
locked. The door, as it opened, grated harshly on its
hinges, and two officials entered.

"Follow me," was the laconic injunction which
greeted her terror-struck ear.

Trembling, Matilda arose: her limbs, stiffened by
confinement, almost refused to support her; but collecting fortitude from desperation, she followed the relentless officials in silence.

One of them bore a lamp, whose rays, darting in
uncertain columns, showed, by strong contrasts of light
and shade, the extreme massiness of the passages.

The Gothic frieze above was worked with art; and
the corbels, in various and grotesque forms, jutted from
the tops of clustered pilasters.

They stopped at a door. Voices were heard from
within: their hollow tones filled Matilda's soul with
unconquerable tremors. But she summoned all her
resolution—she resolved to be collected during the

trial ; and even, if sentenced to death, to meet her fate with fortitude, that the populace, as they gazed, might not exclaim—"The poor Laurentini dared not to die."

These thoughts were passing in her mind during the delay which was occasioned by the officials conversing with another whom they met there.

At last they ceased—an uninterrupted silence reigned : the immense folding doors were thrown open, and disclosed to Matilda's view a vast and lofty apartment. In the centre was a table, which a lamp, suspended from the centre, overhung, and where two stern-looking men, habited in black vestments, were seated.

Scattered papers covered the table, with which the two men in black seemed busily employed.

Two officials conducted Matilda to the table where they sat, and, retiring, left her there.

CHAPTER XVI.

"Fear, for their scourge, mean villains have ;
Thou art the torturer of the brave."

MARMION.

ONE of the inquisitors raised his eyes ; he put back the papers which he was examining, and in a solemn tone asked her name.

"My name is Matilda ; my title La Contessa di Laurentini," haughtily she answered ; "nor do I know the motive for that inquiry, except it were to exult over my miseries, which you are, I suppose, no stranger to."

"Waste not your time," exclaimed the inquisitor, sternly, "in making idle conjectures upon our conduct ; but do you know for what you are summoned here ? "

"No," replied Matilda.

"Swear that you know not for what crime you are here imprisoned," said the inquisitor.

Matilda took the oath required. As she spoke, a dewy sweat burst from her brow, and her limbs were convulsed by the extreme of horror, yet the expression of her countenance was changed not.

" What crime have you committed which might subject you to the notice of this tribunal ? " demanded he, in a determined tone of voice.

Matilda gave no answer, save a smile of exulting scorn. She fixed her regards upon the inquisitor : her dark eyes flashed fiercely, but she spoke not.

" Answer me," exclaimed he, "what to confess might save both of us needless trouble."

Matilda answered not, but gazed in silence upon the inquisitor's countenance.

He stamped thrice—four officials rushed in, and stood at some distance from Matilda.

" I am unwilling," said the inquisitor, " to treat a female of high birth with indignity ; but, if you confess not instantly, my duty will not permit me to withhold the question."

A deeper expression of contempt shaded Matilda's beautiful countenance : she frowned, but answered not.

"You will persist in this foolish obstinacy ? " exclaimed the inquisitor. " Officials, do your duty."

Instantly the four, who till now had stood in the background, rushed forwards : they seized Matilda, and bore her into the obscurity of the apartment.

Her dishevelled ringlets floated in negligent luxuriance over her alabaster bosom : her eyes, the contemptuous glance of which had now given way to a confused expression of alarm, were almost closed ; and her symmetrical form, as borne away by the four officials, looked interestingly lovely.

The other inquisitor, who, till now, busied by the papers which lay before him, had heeded not Matilda's examination, raised his eyes, and, beholding the form of a female, with a commanding tone of voice, called to the officials to stop.

Submissively they obeyed his order. Matilda, released from the fell hands of these relentless ministers of justice, advanced to the table.

Her extreme beauty softened the inquisitor who had spoken last. He little thought that, under a form so celestial, so interesting, lurked a heart depraved, vicious as a demon's.

He therefore mildly addressed her; and telling her that, on some future day, her examination would be renewed, committed her to the care of the officials, with orders to conduct her to an apartment better suited to her rank.

The chamber to which she followed the officials was spacious and well furnished, but large iron bars secured the windows, which were high, and impossible to be forced.

Left again to solitude, again to her own gloomy thoughts—her retrospection but horror and despair— her hopes of futurity none—her fears many and horrible—Matilda's situation is better conceived than described.

Floating in wild confusion, the ideas which presented themselves to her imagination were too horrible for endurance.

Deprived, as she was, of all earthly happiness, fierce as had been her passion for Verezzi, the disappointment of which sublimed her brain to the most infuriate delirium of resistless horror, the wretched Matilda still shrunk at death—she shrunk at the punishment of those crimes, in whose perpetration no remorse had touched her soul, for which, even now, she repented not, but as they had deprived her of terrestrial enjoyments.

She thought upon the future state—she thought upon

the arguments of Zastrozzi against the existence of a
Deity : her inmost soul now acknowledged their falsehood, and she shuddered as she reflected that her condition was irretrievable.

Resistless horror revelled through her bosom : in an
intensity of racking thought she rapidly paced the
apartment ; at last, overpowered, she sank upon a sofa.

At last the tumultuous passions, exhausted by their
own violence, subsided : the storm, which so lately had
agitated Matilda's soul, ceased : a serene calm succeeded, and sleep quickly overcame her faculties.

Confused visions flitted in Matilda's imagination
whilst under the influence of sleep; at last they
assumed a settled shape.

Strangely brilliant and silvery clouds seemed to flit
before her sight : celestial music, enchanting as the
harmony of the spheres, serened Matilda's soul, and,
for an instant, her situation forgotten, she lay entranced.

On a sudden the music ceased ; the azure concavity
of heaven seemed to open at the zenith, and a being,
whose countenance beamed with unutterable beneficence, descended.

It seemed to be clothed in a transparent robe of
flowing silver: its eye scintillated with superhuman
brilliancy, whilst her dream, imitating reality almost to
exactness, caused the entranced Matilda to suppose
that it addressed her in these words:—

"Poor sinning Matilda! repent, it is not yet too
late.—God's mercy is unbounded. Repent ! and thou
mayest yet be saved."

These words yet tingled in Matilda's ears; yet were
her eyes lifted to heaven, as if following the visionary
phantom who had addressed her in her dream, when,
much confused, she arose from the sofa.

A dream, so like reality, made a strong impression
upon Matilda's soul.

The ferocious passions, which so lately had battled fiercely in her bosom, were calmed : she lifted her eyes to heaven : they beamed with an expression of sincerest penitence; for sincerest penitence at this moment, agonised whilst it calmed Matilda's soul.

"God of mercy! God of heaven!" exclaimed Matilda ; "my sins are many and horrible, but I repent."

Matilda knew not how to pray ; but God, who from the height of heaven penetrates the inmost thoughts of terrestrial hearts, heard the outcast sinner, as in tears of true and agonising repentance, she knelt before him.

She despaired no longer. She confided in the beneficence of her Creator ; and, in the hour of adversity, when the firmest heart must tremble at his power, no longer a hardened sinner, demanded mercy. And mercy, by the All-benevolent of heaven, is never refused to those who humbly, yet trusting in his goodness, ask it.

Matilda's soul was filled with a celestial tranquillity. She remained upon her knees in mute and fervent thought : she prayed ; and, with trembling, asked forgiveness of her Creator.

No longer did that agony of despair torture her bosom. True, she was ill at ease : remorse for her crimes deeply affected her ; and though her hopes of salvation were great, her belief in God and a future state firm, the heavy sighs which burst from her bosom, showed that the arrows of repentance had penetrated deeply.

Several days passed away, during which the conflicting passions of Matilda's soul, conquered by penitence, were mellowed into a fixed and quiet depression.

CHAPTER XVII.

Si fractus illabatur orbis,
Impavidum ferient ruinæ.
HORACE.

T last the day arrived, when, exposed to a public trial, Matilda was conducted to the tribunal of il Consiglio di Dieci.

The inquisitors were not, as before, at a table in the middle of the apartment; but a sort of throne was raised at one end, on which a stern-looking man, whom she had never seen before, sat: a great number of Venetians were assembled, and lined all sides of the apartment.

Many, in black vestments, were arranged behind the superior's throne; among whom Matilda recognised those who had before examined her.

Conducted by two officials, with a faltering step, a pallid cheek, and downcast eye, Matilda advanced to that part of the chamber where sat the superior.

The dishevelled ringlets of her hair floated unconfined over her shoulders : her symmetrical and elegant form was enveloped in a thin white robe.

The expression of her sparkling eyes was downcast and humble; yet, seemingly unmoved by the scene before her, she remained in silence at the tribunal.

The curiosity and pity of every one, as they gazed on the loveliness of the beautiful culprit, was strongly excited.

"Who is she? who is she?" ran in inquiring whispers round the apartment. No one could tell.

Again deep silence reigned—not a whisper interrupted the appalling calm.

At last the superior, in a sternly solemn voice, said—

"Matilda Contessa di Laurentini, you are here arraigned on the murder of La Marchesa di Strobazzo:

canst thou deny it? canst thou prove to the contrary?
My ears are open to conviction. Does no one speak
for the accused?"

He ceased: uninterrupted silence reigned. Again
he was about—again, with a look of detestation and
horror, he had fixed his penetrating eye upon the
trembling Matilda, and had unclosed his mouth to utter
the fatal sentence, when his attention was arrested by a
man who rushed from the crowd, and exclaimed, in a
hurried tone—

" La Contessa di Laurentini is innocent."

" Who are you, who dare assert that?" exclaimed
the superior, with an air of doubt.

" I am," answered he, " Ferdinand Zeilnitz, a German, the servant of La Contessa di Laurentini, and I
dare assert that she is innocent."

" Your proof," exclaimed the superior, with a severe
frown.

" It was late," answered Ferdinand, " when I entered
the apartment, and then I beheld two bleeding bodies,
and La Contessa di Laurentini, who lay bereft of sense
on the sofa."

" Stop!" exclaimed the superior.

Ferdinand obeyed.

The superior whispered to one in black vestments,
and soon four officials entered, bearing on their
shoulders an open coffin.

The superior pointed to the ground: the officials
deposited their burden, and produced, to the terror-
struck eyes of the gazing multitude, Julia, the lovely
Julia, covered with innumerable and ghastly gashes.

All present uttered a cry of terror—all started,
shocked and amazed, from the horrible sight; yet
some, recovering themselves, gazed at the celestial loveliness of the poor victim to revenge, which, unsubdued
by death, still shone from her placid features.

A deep-drawn sigh heaved Matilda's bosom; tears,

spite of all her firmness, rushed into her eyes; and she had nearly fainted with dizzy horror; but, overcoming it, and collecting all her fortitude, she advanced towards the corse of her rival, and, in the numerous wounds which covered it, saw the fiat of her future destiny.

She still gazed on it—a deep silence reigned—not one of the spectators, so interested were they, uttered a single word—not a whisper was heard through the spacious apartment.

"Stand off! guilt-stained, relentless woman," at last exclaimed the superior fiercely: "is it not enough that you have persecuted, through life, the wretched female who lies before you—murdered by you? Cease, therefore, to gaze on her with looks as if your vengeance was yet insatiated. But retire, wretch: officials, take her into your custody; meanwhile, bring the other prisoner."

Two officials rushed forward, and led Matilda to some distance from the tribunal: four others entered, leading a man of towering height and majestic figure. The heavy chains with which his legs were bound rattled as he advanced.

Matilda raised her eyes—Zastrozzi stood before her. She rushed forwards—the officials stood unmoved.

"Oh Zastrozzi!" she exclaimed—"dreadful, wicked has been the tenor of our lives; base, ignominious, will be its termination: unless we repent, fierce, horrible, may be the eternal torments which will rack us, ere four-and-twenty hours are elapsed. Repent then, Zastrozzi; repent! and as you have been my companion in apostasy from virtue, follow me likewise in dereliction of stubborn and determined wickedness."

This was pronounced in a low and faltering voice.

"Matilda," replied Zastrozzi, whilst a smile of contemptuous atheism played over his features—"Matilda, fear not: fate wills us to die: and I intend to meet death, to encounter annihilation, with tranquillity. Am I not convinced of the non-existence of a Deity? am I not convinced that death will but render this soul more free, more unfettered ? Why need I then shudder at death ? why need any one, whose mind has risen above the shackles of prejudice, the errors of a false and injurious superstition."

Here the superior interposed, and declared he could allow private conversation no longer.

Quitting Matilda, therefore, Zastrozzi, unappalled by the awful scene before him, unshaken by the near approach of agonising death, which he now fully believed he was about to suffer, advanced towards the superior's throne.

Every one gazed on the lofty stature of Zastrozzi, and admired his dignified mien and dauntless composure, even more than they had the beauty of Matilda.

Every one gazed in silence, and expected that some extraordinary charge would be brought against him.

The name of Zastrozzi, pronounced by the superior, had already broken the silence, when the culprit, gazing disdainfully on his judge, told him to be silent, for he would spare him much needless trouble.

"I am a murderer," exclaimed Zastrozzi; "I deny it not : I buried my dagger in the heart of him who injured me ; but the motives which led me to be an assassin were at once excellent and meritorious : for I swore, at a loved mother's death-bed, to avenge her betrayer's falsehood.

"Think you that whilst I perpetrated the deed I feared the punishment ? or whilst I revenged a parent's cause, that the futile torments which I am doomed to suffer here, had any weight in my determination ? No —no. If the vile deceiver, who brought my spotless mother to a tomb of misery, fell beneath the dagger of one who swore to revenge her—if I sent him to another world, who destroyed the peace of one I loved more than myself in this, am I to be blamed ?"

Zastrozzi ceased, and with an expression of scornful triumph, folded his arms.

"Go on!" exclaimed the superior.

"Go on! go on!" echoed from every part of the immense apartment.

He looked around him. His manner awed the tumultuous multitude; and, in uninterrupted silence, the spectators gazed upon the unappalled Zastrozzi, who, towering as a demi-god, stood in the midst.

"Am I then called upon," said he, "to disclose things which bring painful remembrances to my mind? Ah, how painful! But no matter; you shall know the name of him who fell beneath this arm: you shall know him, whose memory, even now, I detest more than I can express. I care not who knows my actions, convinced as I am, and convinced to all eternity as I shall be, of their rectitude. Know then, that Olivia Zastrozzi was my mother; a woman in whom every virtue, every amiable and excellent quality, I firmly believe to have been centred.

"The father of him, who, by my arts committed suicide but six days ago in La Contessa di Laurentini's mansion, took advantage of a moment of weakness, and disgraced her who bore me. He swore, with the most sacred oaths, to marry her—but he was false.

"My mother soon brought me into the world. The seducer married another; and, when the destitute Olivia begged a pittance to keep her from starving, her proud betrayer spurned her from his door, and tauntingly bade her exercise her profession. 'The crime I committed with thee, perjured one!' exclaimed my mother, as she left his door, 'shall be my last!'—and, by heavens! she acted nobly. A victim to falsehood, she sank early to the tomb; and, ere her thirtieth year, she died—her spotless soul fled to eternal happiness. Never shall I forget—though but fourteen when she died—never shall I forget her last commands. 'My

son,' said she, 'my Pietrino, revenge my wrongs—
revenge them on the perjured Verezzi—revenge them on
his progeny for ever !'

"And, by heaven ! I think I have revenged them.
Ere I was twenty-four, the false villain, though surrounded by seemingly impenetrable grandeur ; though
forgetful of the offence to punish which this arm was
nerved, sank beneath my dagger. But I destroyed his
body alone," added Zastrozzi, with a terrible look of
insatiated vengeance: "time has taught me better: his
son's *soul* is hell-doomed to all eternity : he destroyed
himself ; but my machinations, though unseen, effected
his destruction.

"Matilda di Laurentini ! Hah ! why do you shudder ? When, with repeated stabs, you destroyed her
who now lies lifeless before you in her coffin, did you
not reflect upon what must be your fate ? You have
enjoyed him whom you adored—you have even been
married to him—and, for the space of more than a
month, have tasted unutterable joys ; and yet you are
unwilling to pay the price of your happiness—by heavens, I am not !" added he, bursting into a wild laugh.
"Ah, poor fool, Matilda, did you think it was from
friendship I instructed you to gain Verezzi ? No, no—
it was revenge which induced me to enter into your
schemes with zeal ; which induced me to lead her
whose lifeless form lies yonder, to your house, fore-
seeing the effect it would have upon the strong passions
of your husband.

"And now," added Zastrozzi, "I have been candid
with you. Judge, pass your sentence—but I know my
doom ; and, instead of horror, experience some degree
of satisfaction at the arrival of death, since all I have
to do on earth is completed."

Zastrozzi ceased ; and, unappalled, fixed his expressive gaze upon the superior.

Surprised at Zastrozzi's firmness, and shocked at the

crimes of which he had made so unequivocal an avowal, the superior turned away in horror.

Still Zastrozzi stood unmoved, and fearlessly awaited the fiat of his destiny.

The superior whispered to one in black vestments. Four officials rushed in, and placed Zastrozzi on the rack.

Even whilst writhing under the agony of almost insupportable torture his nerves were stretched, Zastrozzi's firmness failed him not; but, upon his soul-illumined countenance, played a smile of most disdainful scorn—and, with a wild, convulsive laugh of exulting revenge, he died.

THE END.

ST. IRVYNE;

OR,

THE ROSICRUCIAN:

A ROMANCE.

_____

BY

A GENTLEMAN

OF THE UNIVERSITY OF OXFORD.

_____

LONDON:
PRINTED FOR J. J. STOCKDALE,
41, PALL MALL.
1811.

I.   H

ST. IRVYNE;

OR,

THE ROSICRUCIAN.

CHAPTER I.

RED thunder-clouds, borne on the wings of the midnight whirlwind, floated, at fits, athwart the crimson-coloured orbit of the moon : the rising fierceness of the blast sighed through the stunted shrubs, which, bending before its violence, inclined towards the rocks whereon they grew : over the blackened expanse of heaven, at intervals, was spread the blue lightning's flash ; it played upon the granite heights, and, with momentary brilliancy, disclosed the terrific scenery of the Alps, whose gigantic and misshapen summits, reddened by the transitory moonbeam, were crossed by black fleeting fragments of the tempest-cloud. The rain, in big drops, began to descend, and the thunder-peals, with louder and more deafening crash, to shake the zenith, till the long-protracted war echoing from cavern to cavern, died, in indistinct murmurs, amidst the far-extended chain of mountains. In this scene, then, at this horrible and tempestuous hour, without one existent earthly being whom he might claim as friend, without one resource to which he might fly as an asylum from the horrors of neglect and poverty, stood Wolfstein ;—he gazed upon the con-

flicting elements ; his youthful figure reclined against a
jutting granite rock ; he cursed his wayward destiny, and
implored the Almighty of Heaven to permit the thunder-
bolt, with crash terrific and exterminating, to descend
upon his head, that a being useless to himself and to
society might no longer, by his existence, mock Him
who ne'er made aught in vain. "And what so horrible
crimes have I committed," exclaimed Wolfstein, driven
to impiety by desperation ; "what crimes which merit
punishment like this?   What, what is death?   Ah,
dissolution ! thy pang is blunted by the hard hand of
long-protracted suffering — suffering unspeakable, indescribable !"   As thus he spoke, a more terrific
paroxysm of excessive despair revelled through every
vein ; his brain swam around in wild confusion, and,
rendered delirious by excess of misery, he started from
his flinty seat, and swiftly hastened towards the precipice, which yawned widely beneath his feet.   "For
what then should I longer drag on the galling chain of
existence?" cried Wolfstein ; and   his impious expression was borne onwards by the hot and sulphurous
thunder-blast.

The midnight meteors danced above the gulf upon
which Wolfstein wistfully gazed.   Palpable, impenetrable darkness seemed to hang upon it ; impenetrable
even by the flaming thunderbolt. " Into this then shall
I plunge myself?" soliloquized the wretched outcast,
"and by one rash act endanger, perhaps, eternal happiness ;—deliver myself up, perhaps, to the anticipation
and experience of never-ending torments?   Art thou
the God then, the Creator of the universe, whom cant·
ing monks call the God of mercy and forgiveness, and
sufferest thou thy creatures to become the victims of
tortures such as fate has inflicted on me?   Oh, God !
take my soul ; why should I longer live?" Thus having
spoken, he sank on the rocky bosom of the mountains.
Yet, unheeding the exclamations of the maddened

Wolfstein, fiercer raged the tempest. The battling elements, in wild confusion, seemed to threaten nature's dissolution ; the ferocious thunderbolt, with impetuous violence, danced upon the mountains, and, collecting more terrific strength, severed gigantic rocks from their else eternal basements ; the masses, with sound more frightful than the bursting thunder-peal, dashed towards the valley below. Horror and desolation marked their track. The mountain-rills, swoln by the waters of the sky, dashed with direr impetuosity from the Alpine summits ; their foaming waters were hidden in the darkness of midnight, or only became visible when the momentary scintillations of the lightning rested on their whitened waves. Fiercer still than nature's wildest uproar were the feelings of Wolfstein's bosom ; his frame, at last, conquered by the conflicting passions of his soul, no longer was adequate to sustain the un-equal contest, but sank to the earth. His brain swam wildly, and he lay entranced in total insensibility.

What torches are those that dispel the distant dark-ness of midnight, and gleam, like meteors, athwart the blackness of the tempest ? They throw a wavering light over the thickness of the storm : they wind along the mountains : they pass the hollow valleys. Hark ! the howling of the blast has ceased,—the thunder-bolts have dispersed, but yet reigns darkness. Distant sounds of song are borne on the breeze ; the sounds approach. A low bier holds the remains of one whose soul is floating in the regions of eternity : a black pall covers him. Monks support the lifeless clay : others precede, bearing torches, and chanting a requiem for the salvation of the departed one. They hasten towards the convent of the valley, there to deposit the lifeless limbs of one who has explored the frightful path of eternity before them. And now they had arrived where lay Wolfstein : "Alas !" said one of the monks, "there reclines a wretched traveller. He is dead ;

murdered, doubtlessly, by the fell bandits who infest these wild recesses."

They raised from the earth his form : yet his bosom throbbed with the tide of life : returning animation once more illumed his eye : he started on his feet, and wildly inquired why they had awakened him from that slumber which he had hoped to have been eternal. Unconnected were his expressions, strange and impetuous the fire darting from his restless eyeballs. At length, the monks succeeded in calming the desperate tumultuousness of his bosom, calming at least in some degree ; for he accepted their proffered tenders of a lodging, and essayed to lull to sleep, for awhile, the horrible idea of dereliction which pressed upon his loaded brain.

While thus they stood, loud shouts rent the air, and, before Wolfstein and the monks could well collect their scattered faculties, they found that a troop of Alpine bandits had surrounded them. Trembling, from apprehension, the monks fled every way. None, however, could escape. "What! old grey-beards," cried one of the robbers, " do you suppose that we will permit you to evade us : you who feed upon the strength of the country, in idleness and luxury, and have compelled many of our noble fellows, who otherwise would have been ornaments to their country in peace, thunderbolts to their enemies in war, to seek precarious subsistence as Alpine bandits? If you wish for mercy, therefore, deliver unhesitatingly your joint riches." The robbers then despoiled the monks of whatever they might adventitiously have taken with them, and, turning to Wolfstein, the apparent chieftain told him to yield his money likewise. Unappalled, Wolfstein advanced towards them. The chief held a torch ; its red beams disclosed the expression of stern severity and unyielding loftiness which sate upon the brow of Wolfstein. "Bandit," he answered fearlessly, " I have none,—no money

—no hope—no friends ; nor do I care for existence!
Now judge if such a man be a fit victim for fear ! No!
I never trembled ! "

A ray of pleasure gleamed in the countenance of the
bandit as Wolfstein spoke. Grief, in inerasible traces,
sate deeply implanted on the front of the outcast. At
last, the chief, advancing to Wolfstein, who stood at
some little distance, said, " My companions think that
so noble a fellow as you appear to be, would be no unworthy member of our society ; and, by Heaven, I am
of their opinion. Are you willing to become one of us ? "

Wolfstein's dark gaze was fixed upon the ground : his
contracted eyebrow evinced deep thought : he started
from his reverie, and, without hesitation, consented to
their proposal.

Long was it past the hour of midnight when the
banditti troop, with their newly-acquired associate,
advanced along the pathless Alps. The red glare of
the torches which each held, tinged the rocks and pine-
trees, through woods of which they occasionally passed,
and alone dissipated the darkness of night. Now
had they arrived at the summit of a wild and rocky
precipice, but the base indeed of another which mingled
its far-seen and gigantic outline with the clouds of
heaven. A door, which before had appeared part of
the solid rock, flew open at the chieftain's touch, and
the whole party advanced into the spacious cavern.
Over the walls of the lengthened passages putrefaction
had spread a bluish clamminess ; damps hung around,
and, at intervals, almost extinguished the torches, whose
glare was scarcely sufficient to dissipate the impenetrable
obscurity. After many devious windings they advanced
into the body of the cavern : it was spacious and lofty.
A blazing wood fire threw its dubious rays upon the
misshapen and ill-carved walls. Lamps suspended from
the roof, dispersed the subterranean gloom, not so completely however, but that ill-defined shades lurked in

the arched distances, whose hollow recesses led to
different apartments.

The gang had sate down in the midst of the cavern
to supper, which a female, whose former loveliness had '
left scarce any traces on her cheek, had prepared. The
most exquisite and expensive wines apologised for the
rusticity of the rest of the entertainment, and induced
freedom of conversation, and wild, boisterous merriment,
which reigned until the bandits, overcome by the
fumes of the wine which they had drunk, sank to sleep.
Wolfstein, left again to solitude and silence, reclining
on his mat in a corner of the cavern, retraced, in mental,
sorrowing review, the past events of his life: ah!
that eventful existence whose fate had dragged the
heir of a wealthy potentate in Germany from the lap of
luxury and indulgence, to become a vile associate of
viler bandits, in the wild and trackless deserts of the
Alps. Around their dwellings, lofty inaccessible acclivities reared their barren summits ; they echoed to no
sound save the wild hoot of the night-raven, or the impatient yelling of the vulture, which hovered on the
blast in quest of scanty sustenance. These were the
scenes without : noisy revelry and tumultuous riot
reigned within. The mirth of the bandits appeared to
arise independently of themselves ; their hearts were
void and dreary. Wolfstein's limbs pillowed on the
flinty bosom of the earth : those limbs which had been
wont to recline on the softest, the most luxurious sofas.
Driven from his native country by an event which imposed upon him an insuperable barrier to ever again
returning thither, possessing no friends, not having one
single resource from which he might obtain support,
where could the wretch, the exile, seek for an asylum
but with those whose fortunes, expectations, and characters were desperate, and marked as darkly, by fate,
as his own?

Time fled, and each succeeding day inured Wolfstein

more and more to the idea of depriving his fellow-creatures of their possessions. In a short space of time the high-souled and noble Wolfstein, though still high-souled and noble, became an experienced bandit. His magnanimity and courage, even whilst surrounded by the most threatening dangers, and the unappalled expression of countenance with which he defied the dart of death, endeared him to the robbers ; whilst with him they all asserted that they felt, as it were, instinctively impelled to deeds of horror and danger, which, otherwise, must have remained unattempted even by the boldest. His was every daring expedition, his the scheme which demanded depth of judgment and promptness of execution. Often, whilst at midnight the band lurked perhaps beneath the overhanging rocks, which were gloomily impended above them, in the midst, perhaps, of one of those horrible tempests whereby the air, in those Alpine regions, is so frequently convulsed, would the countenance of the bandits betray some slight shade of alarm and awe ; but that of Wolfstein was fixed, unchanged, by any variation of scenery or action. One day it was when the chief communicated to the banditti notice which he had received by means of spies, that an Italian Count of immense wealth was journeying from Paris to his native country, and, at a late hour the following evening, would pass the Alps near this place ; "They have but few attendants," added he, " and those few will not come this way ; the postilion is in our interest, and the horses are to be overcome with fatigue when they approach the destined spot : you understand."

The evening came. " I," said Wolfstein, "will roam into the country, but will return before the arrival of our wealthy victim." Thus saying, he left the cavern, and wandered out amidst the mountains.

It was autumn. The mountain-tops, the scattered oaks which occasionally waved their lightning-blasted heads on the summits of the far-seen piles of rock, were gilded by the setting glory of the sun ; the trees, yellowed by the waning year, reflected a glowing teint from their thick foliage ; and the dark pine-groves which were stretched half-way up the mountain sides, added a more deepened gloom to the shades of evening, which already began to gather rapidly above the scenery.

It was at this dark and silent hour, that Wolfstein, unheeding the surrounding objects,—objects which might have touched with awe, or heightened to devotion, any other breast,—wandered alone—pensively he wandered—dark images for futurity possessed his soul : he shuddered when he reflected upon what had passed ; nor was his present situation calculated to satisfy a mind eagerly panting for liberty and independence. Conscience too, awakened conscience, upbraided him for the life which he had selected, and, with silent whisperings, stung his soul to madness. Oppressed by thoughts such as these, Wolfstein yet proceeded, forgetful that he was to return before the arrival of their destined victim—forgetful indeed was he of every external existence ; and, absorbed in himself, with arms folded, and eyes fixed upon the earth, he yet advanced. At last he sank on a mossy bank, and, guided by the impulse of the moment, inscribed on a tablet the following lines ; for the inaccuracy of which, the perturbation of him who wrote them, may account ; he thought of past times while he marked the paper with—

'Twas dead of the night, when I sat in my dwelling ;
One glimmering lamp was expiring and low ;
Around, the dark tide of the tempest was swelling,
Along the wild mountains night-ravens were yelling,—
They bodingly presaged destruction and woe.

'Twas then that I started !—the wild storm was howling,
Nought was seen, save the lightning, which danced in the sky ;
Above me, the crash of the thunder was rolling,
And low, chilling murmurs, the blast wafted by.

My heart sank within me : unheeded the war
  Of the battling clouds, on the mountain-tops, broke ;
Unheeded the thunder-peal crash'd in mine ear—
This heart, hard as iron, is stranger to fear ;
  But conscience in low, noiseless whispering spoke.

'Twas then that her form on the whirlwind upholding,
  The ghost of the murder'd Victoria strode ;
In her right hand a shadowy shroud she was holding,
  She swiftly advanced to my lonesome abode.
I wildly then call'd on the tempest to bear me——

Overcome by the wild retrospection of ideal horror, which these swiftly-written lines excited in his soul, Wolfstein tore the paper, on which he had written them, to pieces, and scattered them about him. He arose from his recumbent posture, and again advanced through the forest. Not far had he proceeded, ere a mingled murmur broke upon the silence of night—it was the sound of human voices. An event so unusual in these solitudes, excited Wolfstein's momentary surprise ; he started, and looking around him, essayed to discover whence those sounds proceeded. What was the astonishment of Wolfstein, when he found that a detached party, who had been sent in pursuit of the Count, had actually overtaken him, and, at this instant, were dragging from the carriage the almost lifeless form of a female, whose light symmetrical figure, as it leant on the muscular frame of the robber who supported it, afforded a most striking contrast. They had, before his arrival, plundered the Count of all his riches, and, enraged at the spirited defence which he had made, had inhumanly murdered him, and cast his lifeless body adown the yawning precipice. Transfixed by a jutting point of granite rock, it remained there to be devoured by the ravens. Wolfstein joined the banditti ; and, although he could not recall the deed, lamented the wanton cruelty which had been practised upon the Count. As for the female, whose grace and loveliness

made so strong an impression upon him, he demanded
that every soothing attention should be paid to her, and
his desire was enforced by the commands of the chief,
whose dark eye wandered wildly over the beauties of
the lovely Megalena de Metastasio, as if he had secretly
destined them for himself.

At last they arrived at the cavern ; every resource
which the cavern of a gang of lawless and desperate
villains might afford, was brought forward to restore
the fainted Megalena to life : she soon recovered—she
slowly opened her eyes, and started with surprise to
behold herself surrounded by a rough set of despera-
does, and the gloomy walls of the cavern, upon which
darkness hung, awfully visible. Near her sate a female,
whose darkened expression of countenance seemed perfectly to correspond with the horror prevalent throughout the cavern ; her face, though bearing the marks of
an undeniable expression of familiarity with wretchedness, had some slight remains of beauty.

It was long past midnight when each of the robbers
withdrew to repose. But his mind was too much
occupied by the events of the evening to allow the unhappy Wolfstein to find quiet ;—at an early hour he
rose from his sleepless couch, to inhale the morning
breeze. The sun had but just risen ; the scene was
beautiful ; everything was still, and seemed to favour
that reflection, which even propinquity to his abandoned associates imposed no indefinably insuperable
bar to. In spite of his attempts to think upon other
subjects, the image of the fair Megalena floated in his
mind. Her loveliness had made too deep an impression
on it to be easily removed ; and the hapless Wolfstein,
ever the victim of impulsive feeling, found himself
bound to her by ties, more lasting than he had now conceived the transitory tyranny of woe could have imposed.
For never had Wolfstein beheld so singularly beautiful a
form ;—her figure cast in the mould of most exact

symmetry; her blue and love-beaming eyes, from which occasionally emanated a wild expression, seemingly almost superhuman ; and the auburn hair which hung in unconfined tresses down her damask cheek—formed a resistless *tout ensemble.*

Heedless of every external object, Wolfstein long wandered. The protracted sound of the bandits' horn struck at last upon his ear, and aroused him from his reverie. On his return to the cavern, the robbers were assembled at their meal ; the chief regarded him with marked and jealous surprise as he entered, but made no remark. They then discussed their uninteresting and monotonous topics, and the meal being ended, each villain departed on his different business.

Megalena, finding herself alone with Agnes (the only woman, save herself, who was in the cavern, and who served as an attendant on the robbers), essayed, by the most humble entreaties and supplications, to excite pity in her breast : she conjured her to explain the cause for which she was thus imprisoned, and wildly inquired for her father. The guilt-bronzed brow of Agnes was contracted by a sullen and malicious frown: it was the only reply which the inhuman female deigned to return. After a pause, however, she said, "Thou thinkest thyself my superior, proud girl ; but time may render us equals. Submit to that, and you may live on the same terms as I do."

There appeared to lurk a meaning in these words, which Megalena found herself incompetent to develop ; she answered not, therefore, and suffered Agnes to depart unquestioned. The wretched Megalena, a prey to despair and terror, endeavoured to revolve in her mind the events which had brought her to this spot, but an unconnected stream of ideas pressed upon her brain. The sole light in her cell was that of a dismal lamp which, by its uncertain flickering, only dissipated the almost palpable obscurity, in a sufficient degree more assuredly to point out the circumambient horrors. She gazed wistfully around, to see if there were any outlet; none there was, save the door whereby Agnes had entered, which was strongly barred on the outside. In despair she threw herself on the wretched pallet. "For what cause, then, am I thus entombed alive?" soliloquized the hapless Megalena; "would it not be preferable at once to annihilate the spark of life which burns but faintly within my bosom? O my father! where art thou? Thy tombless corpse, perhaps, is torn into a thousand pieces by the fury of the mountain cataract. —Little didst thou presage misfortunes such as these! —little didst thou suppose that our last journey would have caused thy immature dissolution—my infamy and misery, not to end but with my hapless existence! Here there is none to comfort me, none to participate my miseries!" Thus speaking, overcome by a paroxysm of emotion, she sank on the bed, and bedewed her fair face with tears.

Whilst, oppressed by painful retrospection, the outcast orphan was yet kneeling, Agnes entered, and, not even noticing her distress, bade her prepare to come to the banquet where the troop of bandits was assembled. In silence, along the vaulted and gloomy passages, she followed her conductress, from whose stern and forbidding gaze her nature shrunk back enhorrored, till they reached that apartment of the cavern where the revelry waited but for her arrival to commence. On her entering, Cavigni, the chief, led her to a seat on his right hand, and paid her every attention which his froward nature could stoop to exercise towards a female; she received his civilities with apparent complacency; but her eye was frequently fascinated, as it were, towards the youthful Wolfstein, who had caught her attention the evening before. His countenance, spite of the shade of woe with which the hard hand of suffering had marked it, was engaging and beautiful ; not that beauty which may be freely acknowledged, but inwardly confessed by every beholder with sensations penetrating and resistless ; his figure majestic and lofty, and the fire which flashed from his expressive eye, indefinably to herself, penetrated the inmost soul of the isolated Megalena. Wolfstein regarded Cavigni with indignation and envy ; and, though almost ignorant himself of the dreadful purpose of his soul, resolved in his own mind an horrible deed. Cavigni was enraptured with the beauty of Megalena, and secretly vowed that no pains should be spared to gain to himself the possession of an object so lovely. The anticipated delight of gratified voluptuousness revelled in every vein as he gazed upon her ; his eye flashed with a triumphant expression of lawless love, yet he determined to defer the hour of his happiness till he might enjoy more free, unrestrained delight, with his adored fair one. She gazed on the chief, however, with an ill-concealed aversion ; his dark expression of countenance, the haughty severity, and contemptuous frown, which habitually sate on his brow, invited not, but rather repelled a reciprocality of affection, which the haughty chief, after his own attachment, entertained not the most distant doubt of. He was, notwithstanding, conscious of her coldness, but attributing it to virgin modesty, or to the novel situation into which she had suddenly been thrown, paid her every attention ; nor did he omit to promise her every little comfort which might induce her to regard him with esteem. Still, though veiled beneath the most artful dissimulation, did the fair Megalena pant ardently for liberty—for, oh! liberty is sweet, sweeter even than all the other pleasures of life, to full satiety, without it.

Cavigni essayed, by every art, to gain her over to his desires ; but Megalena, regarding him with aversion, answered with an haughtiness which she was unable to conceal, and which his proud spirit might ill brook.

Cavigni could not disguise the vexation which he felt, when, increased by resistance, Megalena's dislike towards him remained no longer a secret: "Megalena," said he, at last, "fair girl, thou shalt be mine—we will be wedded to-morrow, if you think the bands of love not sufficiently forcible to unite us."

"No bands shall ever unite me to you!" exclaimed Megalena. "Even though the grave were to yawn beneath my feet, I would willingly precipitate myself into its gulf, if the alternative of that, or an union with you, were proposed to me."

Rage swelled Cavigni's bosom almost to bursting— the conflicting passions of his soul were too tumultuous for utterance;—in an hurried tone, he commanded Agnes to show Megalena to her cell: she obeyed, and they both quitted the apartment.

Wolfstein's soul, sublimed by the most infuriate paroxysms of contending emotions, battled wildly. His countenance retained, however, but one expression,—it was of dark and deliberate revenge. His stern eye was fixed upon Cavigni;—he decided at this instant to perpetrate the deed he had resolved on. Leaving his seat, he intimated his intention of quitting the cavern for an instant.

Cavigni had just filled his goblet. Wolfstein, as he passed, dexterously threw a little white powder into the wine of the chief.

When Wolfstein returned, Cavigni had not yet quaffed the deadly draught: rising, therefore, he exclaimed aloud, "Fill your goblets, all." Every one obeyed, and sat in expectation of the toast which he was about to propose.

"Let us drink," he exclaimed, "to the health of the chieftain's bride—let us drink to their mutual happiness." A smile of pleasure irradiated the countenance of the chief:—that he whom he had supposed to be a dangerous rival, should thus publicly forego any claim to the affections of Megalena, was indeed pleasure.

"Health and mutual happiness to the chieftain and his bride!" re-echoed from every part of the table.

Cavigni raised the goblet to his lips : he was about to quaff the tide of death, when Ginotti, one of the robbers, who sat next to him, upreared his arm, and dashed the cup of destruction to the earth. A silence, as if in expectation of some terrible event, reigned throughout the cavern.

Wolfstein turned his eyes towards the chief ;—the dark and mysterious gaze of Ginotti arrested his wandering eyeball ; its expression was too marked to be misunderstood :—he trembled in his inmost soul, but his countenance yet retained its unchangeable expression. Ginotti spoke not, nor willed he to assign any reason for his extraordinary conduct ; the circumstance was shortly forgotten, and the revelry went on undisturbed by any other event.

Ginotti was one of the boldest of the robbers ; he was the distinguished favourite of the chief, and, although mysterious and reserved, his society was courted with more eagerness, than such qualities might, abstractedly considered, appear to deserve. None knew his history—*that* he concealed within the deepest recesses of his own bosom ; nor could the most suppliant entreaties, or threats of the most horrible punishments, have wrested from him one particular concerning it. Never had he once thrown off the mysterious mask, beneath which his character was veiled, since he had become an associate of the band. In vain the chief required him to assign some reason for his late extravagant conduct ; he said it was mere accident, but with an air, which more than convinced every one that something lurked behind which yet remained unknown. Such, however, was their respect for Ginotti, that the occurrence passed almost without a comment.

I.   I

Long now had the hour of midnight gone by, and
the bandits had retired to repose. Wolfstein retired
too to his couch, but sleep closed not his eyelids; his
bosom was a scene of the wildest anarchy; the conflicting passions revelled dreadfully in his burning
brain : — love, maddening, excessive, unaccountable
idolatry, as it were, which possessed him for Megalena,
urged him on to the commission of deeds which conscience represented as beyond measure wicked, and
which Ginotti's glance convinced him were by no means
unsuspected. Still so unbounded was his love for
Megalena (madness rather than love), that it overbalanced every other consideration, and his unappalled
soul resolved to persevere in its determination even to
destruction !

Cavigni's commands respecting Megalena had been
obeyed :—the door of her cell was fastened, and the
ferocious chief resolved to let her lie there till the
suffering and confinement might subdue her to his will.
Megalena endeavoured, by every means, to soften the
obdurate heart of her attendant ; at length, her mildness of manner induced Agnes to regard her with pity ;
and before she quitted her cell, they were so far recon-
ciled to each other that they entered into a comparison
of their mutual situations ; and Agnes was about to
relate to Megalena the circumstances which had brought
her to the cavern, when the fierce Cavigni entered, and,
commanding Agnes to withdraw, said, " Well, proud
girl, are you now in a better humour to return the
favour with which your superior regards you ?"

" No !" heroically answered Megalena.

" Then," rejoined the chief, " if within four-and-
twenty hours you hold yourself not in readiness to
return my love, force shall wrest the jewel from its
casket." Thus having said, he abruptly quitted the
cell.

So far had Wolfstein's proposed toast, at the banquet,

gained on the unsuspecting ferociousness of Cavigni,
that he accepted the former's artful tender of service, in
the way of persuasion with Megalena, supposing, by
Wolfstein's manner, that they had been cursorily acquainted before. Wolfstein, therefore, entered the apartment of Megalena.

At the sight of him Megalena arose from her recumbent posture, and hastened joyfully to meet him ; for
she remembered that Wolfstein had rescued her from
the insults of the banditti, on the eventful evening
which had subjected her to their control.

" Lovely, adored girl," he exclaimed, "short is my
time : pardon, therefore, the abruptness of my address.
The chief has sent me to persuade you to become
united to him ; but I love you, I adore you to madness.
I am not what I seem. Answer me !—time is short."

An indefinable sensation, unfelt before, swelled
through the passion-quivering frame of Megalena.
" Yes, yes," she cried, " I will—I love you——" At
this instant the voice of Cavigni was heard in the passage. Wolfstein started from his knees, and pressing
the fair hand presented to his lips with exulting ardour,
departed hastily to give an account of his mission to
the anxious Cavigni, who restrained himself in the
passage without, and, slightly mistrusting Wolfstein,
was about to advance to the door of the cell to listen
to their conversation, when Wolfstein quitted Megalena.

Megalena, again in solitude, began to reflect upon
the scenes which had been lately acted. She thought
upon the words of Wolfstein, unconscious wherefore
they were a balm to her mind : she reclined upon her
wretched pallet. It was now night : her thoughts took
a different turn ; the melancholy wind sighing along
the crevices of the cavern, and the dismal sound of
rain, which pattered fast, inspired mournful reflection.
She thought of her father,—her beloved father ;—a
solitary wanderer on the face of the earth ; or, most

probably, thought she, his soul rests in death. Horrible idea ! If the latter, she envied his fate; if the former, she even supposed it preferable to her present abode.   She again thought of Wolfstein ; she pondered on his last words :—an escape from the cavern : oh, delightful idea !   Again her thoughts recurred to her father : tears bedewed her cheeks ; she took a pencil, and, actuated by the feelings of the moment, inscribed on the wall of her prison these lines :—

> Ghosts of the dead ! have I not heard your yelling
>   Rise on the night-rolling breath of the blast,*
> When o'er the dark ether the tempest is swelling,
>   And on eddying whirlwind the thunder-peal past ?
>
> For oft have I stood on the dark height of Jura,
>   Which frowns on the valley that opens beneath ;
> Oft have I braved the chill night-tempest's fury,
>   Whilst around me, I thought, echo'd murmurs of death.
>
> And now, whilst the winds of the mountain are howling,
>   O father ! thy voice seems to strike on mine ear ;
> In air whilst the tide of the night-storm is rolling,
>   It breaks on the pause of the elements' jar.
>
> On the wing of the whirlwind which roars o'er the mountain
>   Perhaps rides the ghost of my sire who is dead ;
> On the mist of the tempest which hangs o'er the fountain,
>   Whilst a wreath of dark vapour encircles his head.

Here she paused, and, ashamed of the exuberance of her imagination, obliterated from the wall the characters which she had traced : the wind still howled dreadfully ; in fearful anticipation of the morrow, she threw herself on the bed, and, in sleep, forgot the misfortunes which impended over her.

Meantime, the soul of Wolfstein was disturbed by ten thousand conflicting passions ; revenge and disappointed love agonized his soul to madness ; and he resolved to quench the rude feelings of his bosom in the blood of his rival.   But, again he thought of Ginotti ;

* Taken almost word for word from the poem of Lachin y Gair in Byron's *Hours of Idleness.* Newark, 1807, p. 130.—ED.

he thought of the mysterious intervention which his dark glances proved not to be accidental. To him it was an inexplicable mystery; which the more he reflected upon, the less able was he to unravel. He had mixed the poison, unseen, as he thought, by any one; certainly unseen by Ginotti, whose back was unconcernedly turned at the time. He planned, therefore, a second attempt, unawed by what had happened before, for the destruction of Cavigni, which he resolved to put into execution this night.

Before he had become an associate with the band of robbers, the conscience of Wolfstein was clear; clear, at least, from the commission of any wilful and deliberate crime; for, alas! an event almost too dreadful for narration, had compelled him to quit his native country, in indigence and disgrace. His courage was equal to his wickedness; his mind was unalienable from its purpose; and whatever his will might determine, his boldness would fearlessly execute, even though hell and destruction were to yawn beneath his feet, and essay to turn his unappalled soul from the accomplishment of his design. Such was the guilty Wolfstein; a disgraceful fugitive from his country, a vile associate of a band of robbers, and a murderer, at least in intent, if not in deed. He shrunk not at the commission of crimes; he was now the hardened villain; eternal damnation, tortures inconceivable on earth, awaited him. " Foolish, degrading idea ! " he exclaimed, as it momentarily glanced through his mind; " am I worthy of the celestial Megalena, if I shrink at the price which it is necessary I should pay for her possession ? " This idea banished every other feeling from his heart; and, smothering the stings of conscience, a decided resolve of murder took possession of him—the determining, within himself, to destroy the very man who had given him an asylum, when driven to madness by the horrors of neglect and poverty. He stood in the night-storm on the mountains ; he cursed the intervention of Ginotti, and secretly swore that nor heaven nor hell again should dash the goblet of destruction from the mouth of the detested Cavigni.   The soul of Wolfstein too, insatiable in its desires, and panting for liberty, ill could brook the confinement of idea, which the cavern of the bandits must necessarily induce.   He longed again to try his fortune ; he longed to re-enter that world which he had never tried but once, and that indeed for a short time ; sufficiently long, however, to blast his blooming hopes, and to graft on the stock, which otherwise might have produced virtue, the fatal seeds of vice.

CHAPTER II.

The fiends of fate are heard to rave,
And the death-angel flaps his broad wing o'er the wave.

IT was midnight ; and all the robbers were assembled in the banquet-hall, amongst whom, bearing in his bosom a weight of premeditated crime, was Wolfstein ; he sat by the chief.   They discoursed on indifferent subjects ; the sparkling goblet went round ; loud laughter succeeded.   The ruffians were rejoicing over some plunder which they had taken from a traveller, whom they had robbed of immense wealth ; they had left his body a prey to the vultures of the mountains. The table groaned. with the pressure of the feast. Hilarity reigned around : reiterated were the shouts of merriment and joy ; if such could exist in a cavern of robbers.

It was long past midnight : another hour, and Megalena must be Cavigni's.   This idea rendered Wolfstein callous to every sting of conscience ; and he eagerly awaited an opportunity when he might, unperceived, infuse poison into the goblet of one who confided in him.   Ginotti sat opposite to Wolfstein : his arms were folded, and his gaze rested fixedly upon the fearless countenance of the murderer. Wolfstein shuddered when he beheld the brow of the mysterious Ginotti contracted, his marked features wrapped in inexplicable mystery.

All were now heated by wine, save the wily villain who destined murder; and the awe-inspiring Ginotti, whose reservedness and mystery, not even the hilarity of the present hour could dispel.

Conversation appearing to flag, Cavigni exclaimed, "Steindolph, you know some old German stories ; cannot you tell one, to deceive the lagging hours?"

Steindolph was famed for his knowledge of metrical spectre tales, and the gang were frequently wont to hang delighted on the ghostly wonders which he related.

"Excuse, then, the mode of my telling it," said Steindolph, "and I will with pleasure. I learnt it whilst in Germany ; my old grandmother taught it me, and I can repeat it as a ballad."—"Do, do," re-echoed from every part of the cavern.—Steindolph thus began :

BALLAD.

I.

The death-bell beats !
The mountain repeats
The echoing sound of the knell ;
And the dark monk now
Wraps the cowl round his brow,
As he sits in his lonely cell.

II.

And the cold hand of death
Chills his shuddering breath,
As he lists to the fearful lay
Which the ghosts of the sky,
As they sweep wildly by,
Sing to departed day.
And they sing of the hour
When the stern fates had power
To resolve Rosa's form to its clay.

III.

But that hour is past ;
And that hour was the last
Of peace to the dark monk's brain.
   Bitter tears, from his eyes, gush'd silent and fast :
And he strove to suppress them in vain.

IV.

Then his fair cross of gold he dash'd on the floor,
When the death-knell struck on his ear,
   Delight is in store
   For her evermore ;
But for me is fate, horror, and fear.

V.

   Then his eyes wildly roll'd,
   When the death-bell toll'd,
And he raged in terrific woe.
   And he stamp'd on the ground,
   But when ceased the sound
Tears again began to flow.

VI.

   And the ice of despair
   Chill'd the wide throb of care,
And he sat in mute agony still ;
   Till the night-stars shone through the cloudless air.
And the pale moonbeam slept on the hill.

VII.

   Then he knelt in his cell :—
   And the horrors of hell
Were delights to his agonized pain.
   And he pray'd to God to dissolve the spell,
Which else must for ever remain.

VIII.

And in fervent prayer he knelt on the ground,
   Till the abbey bell struck One :
His feverish blood ran chill at the sound :
A voice hollow and horrible murmur'd around,
   " The term of thy penance is done ! "

IX.

Grew dark the night ;
The moonbeam bright
Wax'd faint on the mountain high ;
And, from the black hill,
Went a voice cold and still, —
" Monk ! thou art free to die."

X.

Then he rose on his feet,
And his heart loud did beat,
And his limbs they were palsied with dread ;
Whilst the grave's clammy dew
O'er his pale forehead grew ;
And he shudder'd to sleep with the dead.

XI.

And the wild midnight storm
Raved around his tall form,
As he sought the chapel's gloom :
And the sunk grass did sigh
To the wind, bleak and high,
As he searched for the new-made tomb.

XII.

And forms, dark and high,
Seem'd around him to fly,
And mingle their yells with the blast
And on the dark wall
Half-seen shadows did fall,
As enhorror'd he onward pass'd.

XIII.

And the storm-fiend's wild rave
O'er the new-made grave,
And dread shadows, linger around.
The Monk call'd on God his soul to save,
And, in horror, sank on the ground.

XIV.

Then despair nerved his arm
To dispel the charm,
And he burst Rosa's coffin asunder.

And the fierce storm did swell
More terrific and'fell,
And louder peal'd the thunder.

XV.

And laugh'd, in joy, the fiendish throng,
Mix'd with ghosts of the mouldering dead;
And their grisly wings, as they floated along,
Whistled in murmurs dread.

XVI.

And her skeleton form the dead Nun rear'd,
Which dripp'd with the chill dew of hell.
In her half-eaten eyeballs two pale flames appear'd,
And triumphant their gleam on the dark Monk glared,
As he stood within the cell.

XVII.

And her lank hand lay on his shuddering brain ;
But each power was nerved by fear.—
" I never, henceforth, may breathe again ;
Death now ends mine anguish'd pain.—
The grave yawns,—we meet there."

XVIII.

And her skeleton lungs did utter the sound,
So deadly, so lone, and so fell,
That in long vibrations shudder'd the ground ;
And as the stern notes floated around,
A deep groan was answer'd from hell.

As Steindolph concluded, an universal shout of ap-
plause echoed through the cavern. Every one had
been so attentive to the recitation of the robber, that no
opportunity of perpetrating his resolve had appeared to
Wolfstein. Now all again was revelry and riot, and
the wily designer eagerly watched for the instant when
universal confusion might favour his attempt to drop,
unobserved, the powder into the goblet of the chief.
With a gaze of insidious and malignant revenge was
the eye of Wolfstein fixed upon the chieftain's countenance. Cavigni perceived it not ; for he was heated

with wine, or the unusual expression of his associate's face must have awakened suspicion, or excited remark. Yet was Ginotti's gaze fixed upon Wolfstein, who, like a sanguinary and remorseless ruffian, sat expectantly waiting the instant of death. The goblet passed round : —at the moment when Wolfstein mingled the poison with Cavigni's wine, the eyes of Ginotti, which before had regarded him with the most dazzling scrutiny, were intentionally turned away. He then arose from the table, and, complaining of sudden indisposition, retired. Cavigni raised the goblet to his lips—

" Now, my brave fellows," he exclaimed, " the hour is late ; but before we retire, I here drink success and health to every one of you."

Wolfstein involuntarily shuddered.—Cavigni quaffed the liquor to the dregs!—the cup fell from his trembling hand. The chill dew of death sat upon his forehead : in terrific convulsions he fell headlong; and, inarticulately uttering, " I am poisoned," sank seemingly lifeless on the earth. Sixty robbers at once rushed forward to raise him ; and, reclining in their arms, with an horrible and harrowing shriek, the spark of life fled from his body for ever. A robber, skilled in surgery, opened a vein ; but no blood followed the touch of the lancet.—Wolfstein advanced to the body, unappalled by the crime which he had committed ; and tore aside the vest from its bosom ; that bosom was discoloured by large spots of livid purple, which, by their premature appearance, declared the poison which had been used to destroy him, to be excessively powerful.

Every one regretted the death of the brave Cavigni ; every one was surprised at the mode of his death ; and, by his abruptly quitting the apartment, the suspicion fell upon Ginotti, who was consequently sent for by Ardolph, a robber whom they had chosen chieftain, Wolfstein having declined the proffered distinction.

Ginotti arrived. His stern countenance was changed

not by the execrations showered on him by everyone.
He yet remained unmoved, and apparently careless
what sentiments others might entertain of him ; he
deigned not even to deny the charge. This coolness
seemed to have convinced everyone, the new chief in
particular, of his innocence.

" Let every one," said Ardolph, "be searched ; and
if his pockets contain poison which could have effected
this, let him die." This method was universally
applauded. As soon as the acclamations were stilled,
Wolfstein advanced forwards and spoke thus :

"Any longer to conceal that it was I who perpetrated the deed, were useless. Megalena's loveliness
inflamed me :—I envied one who was about to possess
it.—I have murdered him ! "

Here he was interrupted by the shouts of the bandits ;
and he was about to be delivered to death, when
Ginotti advanced. His superior and towering figure
inspired awe even in the hearts of the bandits. They
were silent.

"Suffer Wolfstein," he exclaimed, "to depart un-
hurt. *I* will answer for his never publishing our
retreat : *I* will promise that never more shall you
behold him."

Every one submitted to Ginotti : for who could
resist the superior Ginotti ? From the gaze of Ginotti
Wolfstein's soul shrank, enhorrored, in confessed
inferiority : he who had shrunk not at death, had
shrunk not to avow himself guilty of murder, and had
prepared to meet its reward, started from Ginotti's
eye-beam as from the emanation of some superior and
preter-human being.

"Quit the cavern ! " said Ginotti.—"May I not
remain here until the morrow ? " inquired Wolfstein.—
" If to-morrow's rising sun finds you in this cavern,"
returned Ginotti, "I must deliver you up to the
vengeance of those whom you have injured."

Wolfstein retired to his solitary cell, to retrace, in his mind, the occurrences of this eventful night. What was he now ? an isolated wicked wanderer ; not a being on earth whom he could call a friend, and carrying with him that never-dying tormentor—conscience. In half-waking dreams passed the night ; the ghost of him whom he had so inhumanly destroyed, seemed to cry for justice at the throne of God ; bleeding, pale, and ghastly, it pressed on his agonized brain ; and confused, inexplicable visions flitted in his imagination, until the freshness of the morning breeze warned him to depart. He collected together all those valuables which had fallen to his share as plunder, during his stay in the cavern: they amounted to a large sum. He rushed from the cavern ; he hesitated ;—he knew not whither to fly. He walked fast, and essayed, by exercise, to smother the feelings of his soul ; but the attempt was fruitless. Not far had he proceeded, ere, stretched on the earth apparently lifeless, he beheld a female form. He advanced towards it—it was Megalena !

A tumult of exulting and inconceivable transport rushed through his veins as he beheld her—her for whom he had plunged into the abyss of crime. She slept, and, apparently overcome by the fatigues which she had sustained, her slumber was profound. Her head reclined upon the jutting root of a tree ; the tint of health and loveliness sat upon her cheek.

When the fair Megalena awakened, and found herself in the arms of Wolfstein, she started : yet, turning her eyes, she beheld it was no enemy, and the expression of terror gave way to pleasure. In the general confusion had Megalena escaped from the abode of the bandits. The destinies of Wolfstein and Megalena were assimilated by similarity of situations ; and, before they quitted the spot, so far had this reciprocal feeling prevailed, that they swore mutual affection. Megalena then related her escape from the cavern, and showed Wolfstein jewels, to an immense amount, which she had secreted.

"At all events, then," said Wolfstein, "we may defy poverty ; for I have about me jewels to the value of ten thousand zechins."

"We will go to Genoa," said Megalena.

"We will, my fair one.   There, entirely devoted to each other, we will defy the darts of misery."

Megalena returned no answer, save a look of else inexpressible love.

It was now the middle of the day ; neither Wolfstein nor Megalena had tasted food since the preceding night ; and faint from fatigue, Megalena scarce could move onwards.   "Courage, my love," said Wolfstein ; "yet a little way, and we shall arrive at a cottage, a sort of inn, where we may wait until the morrow, and hire mules to carry us to Placenza, whence we can easily proceed to the goal of our destination."

Megalena collected her strength : in a short time they arrived at the cottage, and passed the remainder of the day in plans respecting the future.   Wearied with unusual exertions, Megalena early retired to an inconvenient bed, which, however, was the best the cottage could afford ; and Wolfstein, lying along the bench by the fireplace, resigned himself to meditation ; for his mind was too much disturbed to let him sleep.

Although Wolfstein had every reason to rejoice at the success which had crowned his schemes ; although the very event had occurred which his soul had so much and so eagerly panted for ; yet, even now, in possession of all he held valuable on earth, was he ill at ease. Remorse for his crimes tortured him : yet, steeling his conscience, he essayed to smother the fire which burned in his bosom ; to change the tenour of his thoughts— in vain ! he could not.   Restless passed the night, and the middle of the day beheld Wolfstein and Megalena far from the habitation of the bandits.

They intended, if possible, to reach Breno that night, and thence, on the following day, to journey towards Genoa. They had descended the southern acclivity of the Alps. It was now hastening towards spring, and the whole country began to gleam with the renewed loveliness of nature. Odoriferous orange-groves scented the air. Myrtles bloomed on the sides of the gentle eminences which they occasionally ascended. The face of nature was smiling and gay; so was Megalena's heart : with exulting and speechless transport it bounded within her bosom. She gazed on him who possessed her soul ; although she felt no inclination in her bosom to retrace the events, by means of which an obscure bandit, undefinable to herself, had gained the eternal love of the former haughty Megalena de Metastasio.

They soon arrived at Breno. Wolfstein dismissed the muleteer, and conducted Megalena into the interior of the inn, ordering at the same time a supper. Again were repeated protestations of eternal affection, avowals of indissoluble love ; but it is sufficient to conceive what cannot be so well described.

It was near midnight ; Wolfstein and Megalena sat at supper, and conversed with that unrestrainedness and gaiety which mutual confidence inspired, when the door was opened, and the innkeeper announced the arrival of a man who wished to speak with Wolfstein.

" Tell him," exclaimed Wolfstein, rather surprised, and wishing to guard against the possibility of danger, " that I will not see him."

The landlord left the room, and in a short time returned. A man accompanied him : he was of gigantic stature, and masked. " He would take no denial, signor," said the landlord, in exculpation, as he left the room.

The stranger advanced to the table at which Wolfstein and Megalena sat : he threw aside his mask, and disclosed the features of—Ginotti ! Wolfstein's frame became convulsed with involuntary horror : he started. Megalena was surprised.

Ginotti, at length, broke the terrible silence.

"Wolfstein," he said, "I saved you from, otherwise, inevitable death ; by *my* means alone have you gained Megalena:—what do I then deserve in return?" Wolfstein looked on the countenance : it was stern and severe, yet divested of the terrible expression which had before caused his frame to shudder with excess of alarm.

"My eternal gratitude," returned Wolfstein, hesitatingly.

"Will you promise, that when, destitute and a wanderer, I demand your protection, when I beseech you to listen to the tale which I shall relate, you *will* listen to me ; that, when I am dead, you will bury me, and suffer my soul to rest in the endless slumber of annihilation ? Then will you repay me for the benefits which I have conferred upon you."

"I will," replied Wolfstein ; "I will perform all that you require."

"Swear it !" exclaimed Ginotti.

"I swear."

Ginotti then abruptly quitted the apartment; the sound of his footsteps was heard descending the stairs ; and, when they were no longer audible, a weight seemed to have been taken from the breast of Wolfstein.

"How did that man save your life ?" inquired Megalena.

"He was one of our band," replied Wolfstein, evasively;" and, on a plundering excursion, his pistol-ball entered the heart of the man, whose sabre, lifted aloft, would else have severed my head from my body."

"Dear Wolfstein, who are you ?—whence came you ? —for you were not always an Alpine bandit ?"

"That is true, my adored one ; but fate presents an

insuperable barrier to my ever relating the events which occurred previously to my connexion with the banditti. Dearest Megalena, if you love me, never question me concerning my *past* life, but rest satisfied with the conviction, that my future existence shall be devoted to you, and to you alone." Megalena felt surprise ; but, although eagerly desiring to unravel the mystery in which Wolfstein shrouded himself, desisted from inquiry.

Ginotti's mysterious visit had made too serious an impression on the mind of Wolfstein to be lightly erased. In vain he essayed to appear easy and unembarrassed, while he conversed with Megalena. He attempted to drown thought in wine—but in vain :— Ginotti's strange injunction pressed, like a load of ice, upon his breast. At last, the hour being late, they both retired to their respective rooms.

Early on the following morning, Wolfstein arose, to arrange the necessary preparations for their journey to Genoa ; whither he had sent a servant whom he hired at Breno, to prepare accommodations for their arrival· Needless were it minutely to describe each trivial event which occurred during their journey to Genoa.

On the morning of the fourth day, they found themselves within a short distance of the city. They determined on the plan they should adopt, and, in a short space of time, arriving at Genoa, took up their residence in a mansion on the outermost extremity of the city.

CHAPTER III.

Whence, and what art thou, execrable shape,
That darest, though grim and terrible, advance
Thy miscreated front athwart my way?—
PARADISE LOST.

IME passed ; and, settled in their new habitation, Megalena and Wolfstein appeared to defy the arrows of vengeful destiny.

Wolfstein resolved to allow some time to elapse before he spoke of the subject nearest to his heart, of herself, to Megalena. One evening, however, overcome by the passion which, by mutual indulgence, had become resistless, he cast himself at her feet, and, avowing most unbounded love, demanded the promised return. A slight spark of virtue yet burned in the bosom of the wretched girl ; she essayed to fly from temptation ; but Wolfstein, seizing her hand, said, "And is my adored Megalena a victim then to prejudice ? Does she believe, that the Being who created us gave us passions which never were to be satiated ? Does she suppose that Nature created us to become the tormentors of each other ? "

"Ah ! Wolfstein," Megalena said tenderly, "rise !— You know too well the chain which unites me to you is indissoluble ; you know that I must be thine ; where, therefore, is there an appeal ? "

"To thine own heart, Megalena ; for, if my image implanted there is not sufficiently eloquent to confirm your hesitating soul, I would wish not for a casket that contains a jewel unworthy of my possession."

Megalena involuntarily started at the strength of his expression ; she felt how completely she was his, and turned her eyes upon his countenance, to read in it the meaning of his words.—His eyes gleamed with excessive and confiding love.

"Yes," exclaimed Megalena, "yes, prejudice avaunt !

once more reason takes her seat, and convinces me that
to be Wolfstein's is not criminal. O Wolfstein ! if for
a moment Megalena has yielded to the imbecility of
nature, believe that she yet knows how to recover herself, to reappear in her proper character. Ere I knew
you, a void in my heart, and a tasteless carelessness of
those objects which now interest me, confessed your
unseen empire ; my heart longed for something which
now it has attained. I scruple not, Wolfstein, to aver
that it is you :—Be mine, then, and let our affection
end not but with our existence ! "

"Never, never shall it end !" enthusiastically exclaimed Wolfstein. " Never !—What can break the
bond joined by congeniality of sentiment, cemented by
an union of soul which must endure till the intellectual
particles which compose it become annihilated ? Oh !
never shall it end ; for when, convulsed by nature's
latest ruin, sinks the fabric of this perishable globe ;
when the earth is dissolved away, and the face of
heaven is rolled from before our eyes like a scroll ;
then will we seek each other, and, in eternal, indi-
visible, although immaterial union, shall we exist to all
eternity."

Yet the love with which Wolfstein regarded Megalena, notwithstanding the strength of his expressions,
though fervent and excessive, at first, was not of that
nature which was likely to remain throughout existence ;
it was like the blaze of the meteor at midnight, which
glares amid the darkness for awhile, and then expires ;
yet did he love her now ; at least if heated admiration
of her person and accomplishments, independently of
mind, be love.

    *   *   *   *   *

Blessed in mutual affection, if so it may be called,
the time passed swift to Wolfstein and Megalena. No
incident worthy of narration occurred to disturb the
uninterrupted tenour of their existence. Tired, at last,

even with delight, which had become monotonous from
long continuance, they began to frequent the public
places. It was one evening, nearly a month subsequent
to their first residence at Genoa, that they went to a
party at the Duca di Thice. It was there that he beheld
the gaze of one of the crowd fixed upon him. Indefinable
to himself were the emotions which shook him ; in
vain he turned to every part of the saloon to avoid the
scrutiny of the stranger's gaze ; he was not able to
give formation, in his own mind, to the ideas which
struck him ; they were acknowledged, however, in his
heart, by sensations awful, and not to be described.
He knew that he had before seen the features of the
stranger ; but he had forgotten Ginotti ; for it was
Ginotti — from whose scrutinizing glance Wolfstein
turned appalled ;—it was Ginotti, of whose strangely
and fearfully gleaming eyeball Wolfstein endeavoured
to evade the fascination in vain. His eyes, resistlessly
attracted to the sphere of chill horror that played
around Ginotti's glance, in vain were fixed on vacuity ;
in vain attempted to notice other objects. Complaining
to Megalena of sudden and violent indisposition, Wolfstein with her retired, and they quickly reached the
steps of their mansion. Arrived there, Megalena tenderly inquired the cause of Wolfstein's illness, but his
vague answers and unconnected exclamations, soon led
her to suppose it was not corporeal. She entreated him
to acquaint her with the reason of his indisposition ;
Wolfstein, however, wishing to conceal from Megalena
the true cause of his emotions, evasively told her that
he had felt excessively faint from the heat of the assembly ; she well knew, by his manner, that he had not
told her truth, but affected to be satisfied, resolving,
at some future period, to develop the mystery with
which he evidently was environed. Retired to rest,
Wolfstein's mind, torn by contending paroxysms of
passion, admitted not of sleep ; he ruminated on the

mysterious reappearance of Ginotti ; and the more he reflected, the more did the result of his reflections lead him astray. The strange gaze of Ginotti, and the consciousness that he was completely in the power of so indefinable a being ; the consciousness that, wheresoever he might go, Ginotti would still follow him, pressed upon Wolfstein's heart. Ignorant of what connexion they could have with this mysterious observer of his actions, his crimes recurred in hideous and disgustful array to the bewildered mind of Wolfstein ; he reflected, that, although now exulting in youthful health and vigour, the time would come, the dreadful day of retribution, when endless damnation would yawn beneath his feet, and he would shrink from eternal punishment before the tribunal of that God whom he had insulted. To evade death, unconscious why, became an idea on which he dwelt with earnestness ; he thought on it for a time, and being mournfully convinced of its impossibility, strove to change the tenour of his reflections.

While these thoughts dwelt in his mind, sleep crept imperceptibly over his senses ; yet, in his visions, was Ginotti present. He dreamed that he stood on the brink of a frightful precipice, at whose base, with deafening and terrific roar, the waves of the ocean dashed ; that, above his head, the blue glare of the lightning dispelled the obscurity of midnight, and the loud crashing of the thunder was rolled franticly from rock to rock ; that, along the cliff on which he stood, a figure, more frightful than the imagination of man is capable of portraying, advanced towards him, and was about to precipitate him headlong from the summit of the rock whereon he stood, when Ginotti advanced, and rescued him from the grasp of the monster ; that no sooner had he done this, than the figure dashed Ginotti from the precipice—his last groans were borne on the blast which swept the bosom of the ocean.

Confused visions then obliterated the impressions of
the former, and he rose in the morning restless and
unrefreshed.

A weight which his utmost efforts could not remove,
pressed upon the bosom of Wolfstein; his mind, superior and towering as it was, found all its energies inefficient to conquer it. As a last resource, therefore,
this wretched victim of vice and folly sought the
gaming-table; a scene which alone could raise the
spirits of one who required something important, even
in his pastimes, to interest him. He staked large
sums; and, although he concealed his haunts from
Megalena, she soon discovered them. For a time, fortune
smiled; till one evening he entered his mansion,
desperate from ill luck, and, accusing his own hapless
destiny, could no longer conceal the truth from Megalena. She reproved him mildly, and her tenderness
had such an effect on Wolfstein that he burst into
tears, and promised her that never again would he yield
to the vicious influence of folly.

The rapid days rolled on, and each one brought the
conviction to Wolfstein more strongly, that Megalena
was not the celestial model of perfection which his
warm imagination had portrayed; he began to find in
her, not the exhaustless mine of interesting converse
which he had once supposed. Possession, which, when
unassisted by real, intellectual love, clogs man, increases
the ardent, uncontrollable passions of woman even to
madness. Megalena yet adored Wolfstein with most
fervent love :—although yet greatly attached to Megalena, although he would have been uneasy were she
another's, Wolfstein no longer regarded her with that
idolatrous affection which had filled his bosom towards
her. Feelings of this nature naturally drove Wolfstein
occasionally from home to seek for employment—and
what employment, save gaming, could Genoa afford to
Wolfstein? In what other occupation was it possible

that he could engage? It was done: he broke his promise to Megalena, and became even a more devoted votary to gambling than before.

How powerful are the attractions of delusive vice! Wolfstein soon staked large sums—larger even than ever. With what anxiety did he watch the dice! How were his eyeballs strained with mingled anticipation of wealth and poverty! Now fortune smiled; yet he concealed even his good luck from Megalena. At length the tide changed again: he lost immense sums; and desperate from a series of ill success, cursed his hapless destiny, and with wildest emotions rushed into the street. Again he solemnly swore to Megalena, that never more would he risk their mutual happiness by his folly.

Still, hurried away by the impulse of a burning desire of interesting his deadened feelings, did Wolfstein, false to his promise, seek the gaming-table; he had staked an enormous amount; and the fatal throw was at this instant about to decide the fate of the unhappy Wolfstein.

A pause, as if some dreadful event were about to occur, ensued; each gazed upon the countenance of Wolfstein, which, desperate from danger, retained, however, an expressive firmness.

A stranger stood before Wolfstein on the opposite side of the table. He appeared to have no interest in what was going forward, but, with unmoved gaze, fixed his eyes upon his countenance.

Wolfstein felt an instinctive shuddering thrill through his frame, when, oh horrible confirmation of his wildest apprehensions! it was—Ginotti!—the terrible, the mysterious Ginotti, whose dire scrutiny, resting upon Wolfstein, chilled his soul with excessive affright.

A sensation of extreme and conflicting emotions shook the inmost recesses of Wolfstein's heart; for an instant his brain swam around in wildest commotion, yet he steeled his resolution, even to the horrors of

hell and destruction; he gazed on the mysterious
scrutineer who stood before him, and, regardless of
the sum he had staked, and which before had engaged
his whole attention, and excited his liveliest interest,
dashed the box convulsively upon the table, and followed Ginotti, who was about to quit the apartment,
resolving to clear up a fatality which hung around him,
and appeared to blast his prospects; for of the misfortunes which had succeeded his association with the
bandits, he had not the slightest doubt in his own
mind, that Ginotti was the cause.

With reflections a scene of the wildest anarchy,
Wolfstein resolved to unravel the mystery in which he
saw Ginotti was shrouded; and resolved, therefore, to
devote that night towards finding out his abode.
With feelings such as these, he rushed into the street,
and followed the gigantic form of Ginotti, who stalked
onwards majestically, as if conscious of safety, and
wholly ignorant of the eager scrutiny with which
Wolfstein watched his every movement.

It was midnight—yet they continued to advance; a
feeling of desperation urged Wolfstein onwards; he
resolved to follow Ginotti, even to the extremity of the
universe.   They passed through many bye and narrow
streets; the darkness was complete; but the rays of the
lamps, as they fell upon the lofty form of Ginotti,
guided the footsteps of Wolfstein.

They had reached the end of the Strada Nuova; the
lengthened sound of Ginotti's footsteps was all that
struck upon Wolfstein's ear.   On a sudden, Ginotti's
figure disappeared from Wolfstein's gaze; in vain he
looked around him, in vain he searched every recess,
wherein he might have secreted himself—Ginotti was
gone!

To describe the surprise mingled with awe, which
possessed Wolfstein's bosom, is impossible.   In vain he
searched every part.   He proceeded to the bridge; a

party of fishermen were waiting there; he inquired of them, had they seen a man of superior stature pass? they appeared surprised at his question, and unanimously answered in the negative. While varying emotions tumultuously contended within his bosom, Wolfstein, ever the victim of extraordinary events, paused awhile, revolving the mystery both of Ginotti's appearance and disappearance. That business of an important nature led him to Genoa, he doubted not; his indifference at the gaming-table, his particular regard of Wolfstein, left, in the mind of the latter, no doubt, but that he took a terrible and mysterious interest in whatever related to him.

All now was silent. The inhabitants of Genoa lay wrapped in sleep, and, save the occasional conversation of the fishermen who had just returned, no sound broke on the uninterrupted stillness, and thick clouds obscured the star-beams of heaven.

Again Wolfstein searched that part of the city which lay near Strada Nuova; but no one had seen Ginotti; although all wondered at the wild expressions and disordered mien of Wolfstein. The bell tolled the hour of three ere Wolfstein relinquished his pursuit; finding, however, further inquiry fruitless, he engaged a chair to take him to his habitation, where he doubted not that Megalena anxiously awaited his return.

Proceeding along the streets, the obscurity of the night was not so great but that he observed the figure of one of the chairmen to be above that of common men, and that he had drawn his hat forwards to conceal his countenance. His appearance, however, excited no remark; for Wolfstein was too much absorbed in the idea which related individually to himself, to notice what, perhaps, at another time, might have excited wonder. The wind sighed moaningly along the stilly colonnades, and the grey light of morning began to appear above the eastern eminences.

They entered the street which soon led to the abode of Wolfstein, who fixed his eyes upon the chairman. His gigantic proportions struck him with involuntary awe : such is the unaccountable connexion of idea in the mind of man. He shuddered. Such a man, thought he, is Ginotti : such a man is he who watches my every action, whose power I feel within myself is resistless, and not to be evaded. He sighed deeply when he reflected on the terrible connexion, dreadful although mysterious, which subsisted between himself and Ginotti. His soul sank within him at the idea of his own littleness, when a fellow-mortal might be able to gain so strong, though sightless, an empire over him. He felt that he was no longer independent. Whilst these thoughts agitated his mind, the chair had stopped at his habitation. He turned round to discharge the chairman's fare, when, casting his eyes on his countenance, which hitherto had remained concealed—oh, horrible and chilling conviction! he recognized in his dark features those of the terrific Ginotti. As if hell had yawned at the feet of the hapless Wolfstein, as if some spectre of the night had blasted his straining eyeball, so did he stand transfixed. His soul shrank with mingled awe and abhorrence from a being who, even to himself, was confessedly superior to the proud and haughty Wolfstein. Ere well he could calm his faculties, agitated by so unexpected an interview, Ginotti said,

"Wolfstein! long have I known you ; long have I marked you as the only man who now exists, worthy, and appreciating the value of what I have in store for you. Inscrutable are my intentions ; seek not, therefore, to develop them : time will do it in a far more complete manner. You shall not now know the motive for my, to you, unaccountable actions : strive not, therefore, to unravel them : You may frequently see me : never attempt to speak or follow ; for, if you do——"
Here the eyes of Ginotti flashed with coruscations of

inexpressible fire, and his every feature became animated by the tortures which he was about to describe; but he suddenly checked himself, and only added: "Attend to these my directions, but try, if possible, to forget me. I am not what I seem. The time may come, *will* most probably arrive, when I shall appear in my real character to you. You, Wolfstein, have I singled out from the whole world to make the depositary——" He ceased, and abruptly quitted the spot.

CHAPTER IV.

—Nature shrinks back
Enhorror'd from the lurid gaze of vengeance,
E'en in the deepest caverns, and the voice
Of all her works lies hush'd.

OLYMPIA.

N Wolfstein's return to his habitation, he found Megalena in anxious expectation of his arrival. She feared that some misfortune had befallen him. Wolfstein related to her the events of the preceding night; they appeared to her mysterious and inexplicable : nor could she offer any consolation to the wretched Wolfstein.

The occurrences of the preceding evening left a load upon his breast, which all the gaieties of Genoa were insufficient to dispel : eagerly he longed for the visit of Ginotti. Slow dragged the hours : each day did he expect it, and each succeeding day brought but disappointment to his expectations.

Megalena too, the beautiful, the adored Megalena, was no longer what formerly she was, the innocent girl hanging on his support, and depending wholly upon him for defence and protection ; no longer, with mild and love-beaming eyes, she regarded the haughty Wolfstein as a superior being, whose look or slightest

word was sufficient to decide her on any disputed
point. No; dissipated pleasures had changed the
former mild and innocent Megalena. Far, far different was she than when she threw herself into his
arms on their escape from the cavern, and, with a
blush, smiled upon the first declaration of Wolfstein's
affection.

Now, immersed in a succession of gay pleasures,
Megalena was no longer the gentle interesting she,
whose soul of sensibility would tremble if a worm
beneath her feet expired; whose heart would sink
within her at the tale of others' woe. She had become a
fashionable belle, and forgot, in her new character, the
fascinations of her old one. Still, however, was she
ardently, solely, and resistlessly attached to Wolfstein :
his image was implanted in her soul, never to be effaced
by casualty, never erased by time. No coolness apparently took place between them; but, although unperceived and unacknowledged by each, an indifference
evidently did exist between them. Among the various
families whom their residence in Genoa had rendered
familiar to Wolfstein and Megalena, none were more
so than that of il Conte della Anzasca; it consisted of
himself, la Contessa, and a daughter of exquisite loveliness, named Olympia.

This girl, mistress of every fascinating accomplishment, uniting in herself to great brilliancy and playfulness of wit, a person alluring beyond description,
was in her eighteenth year. From habitual indulgence,
her passions, naturally violent and excessive, had become irresistible; and when once she had fixed a
determination in her mind, that determination must
either be effected, or she must cease to exist. Such,
then, was the beautiful Olympia, and as such she conceived a violent and unconquerable passion for Wolfstein. His towering and majestic form, his expressive
and regular features, beaming with somewhat of soft-

ness ; yet pregnant with a look as if woe had beat to
the earth a mind whose native and unconfined energies
aspired to heaven—all, all told her, that, without him,
she must either cease to be, or drag on a life of endless
and irremediable woe. Nourished by restless imagination, her passion soon attained a most unbridled
height : instead of conquering a feeling which honour,
generosity, virtue, all forbade ever to be gratified, she
gloried within herself at having found one on whom
she might with justice fix her burning attachment ;
for although the object of them had never before been
present to her mind, the desires for that object, although
unseen, had taken root long, long ago. A false system
of education, and a wrong expansion of ideas, as they
became formed, had been put in practice with respect
to her youthful mind ; and indulgence strengthened the
passions which it behoved restraint to keep within
proper bounds, and which have unfolded themselves as
coadjutors of virtue, and not as promoters of vicious
and illicit love. Fiercer, nevertheless, in proportion as
greater obstacles appeared in the prosecution of her
resolve, flamed the passion of the devoted Olympia.
Her brain was whirled round in the fiercest convulsions
of expectant happiness ; the anticipation of gratified
voluptuousness swelled her bosom even to bursting, yet
did she rein-in the boiling emotions of her soul, and
resolved to be sufficiently cool, more certainly to accomplish her purpose.

It was one night when Wolfstein's mansion was the
scene of gaiety, that this idea first suggested itself to
the mind of Olympia, and unfolded itself to her, as it
really was, love for Wolfstein. In vain the suggestions
of generosity, the voice of conscience, which told her
how doubly wicked would be the attempt of alienating
from her the lover of her friend Megalena, in audible,
though noiseless, accents spoke ; in vain the native
modesty of her sex represented in its real and hideous

colours what she was about to do : still Olympia was resolved.

That night, in the solitude of her own chamber, in the palazzo of her father, she retraced in her mind the various events which had led to her present uncontrollable passion, which had employed her whole thoughts, and rendered her, as it were, dead to every other outward existence. The wild transports of maddening desire raved terrific within her breast : she endeavoured to smother the ideas which presented themselves; but the more she strove to erase them from her mind, the more vividly were they represented in her heated and enthusiastic imagination. "And will he not return my love ? " she exclaimed : " will he not ?—ah ! a bravo's dagger shall pierce his heart, and thus will I reward him for his contempt of Olympia della Anzasca. But no ! it is impossible. I will cast myself at his feet ; I will avow to him the passion which consumes me,—will swear to be ever, ever his ! Can he then cast me from him ? Can he despise a woman whose only fault is love, nay, idolatry, adoration for him ? "

She paused.—The tumultuous passions of her soul were now too fierce for utterance—too fierce for concealment or restraint. The hour was late ; the moon poured its mildly-lustrous beams upon the lengthened colonnades of Genoa, when Olympia, overcome by emotions such as these, quitted her father's palazzo, and hastened, with rapid and unequal footsteps, towards the mansion of Wolfstein. The streets were by no means crowded ; but those who yet lingered in them gazed with slight surprise on the figure of Olympia, which, light and symmetrical as a celestial sylphid, passed swiftly onwards.

She soon arrived at the habitation of Wolfstein, and sent the domestic to announce that one wished to speak with him, whose business was pressing and secret.

She was conducted into an apartment, and there awaited the arrival of Wolfstein. A confused expression of awe played upon his features as he entered ; but it suddenly gave place to that of surprise. He started upon perceiving Olympia, and said,

"To what, Lady Olympia, do I owe the unforeseen pleasure of your visit ? What so mysterious business have you with me?" continued he playfully. " But come, we had just sat down to supper; Megalena is within."—— "Oh ! if you wish to see me expire in horrible torments at your feet, inhuman Wolfstein, call for Megalena ! and then will your purpose be accomplished."—" Dearest Lady Olympia, compose yourself, I beseech you," said Wolfstein : "what, what agitates you ?"—" Oh ! pardon, pardon me," she exclaimed, with maniac wildness, "pardon a wretched female who knows not what she does ! Oh ! resistlessly am I impelled to this avowal : resistlessly am I impelled to declare to you, that I love you! adore you to distraction !—Will you return my affection ? But ah ! I rave ! Megalena, the beloved Megalena, claims you as her own ; and the wretched Olympia must moan the blighted prospects which were about to open fair before her eyes."

" For Heaven's sake, dear lady, compose yourself; recollect who you are; recollect the loftiness of birth and loveliness of form which are so eminently yours. This, this is far beneath Olympia."

" Oh ! " she exclaimed, franticly casting herself at his feet, and bursting into a passion of tears, " what are birth, fame, fortune, and all the advantages which are casually given to me ! I swear to thee, Wolfstein, that I would sacrifice not only these, but even all my hopes of future salvation, even the forgiveness of my Creator, were it required from me. O Wolfstein, kind, pitying Wolfstein, look down with an eye of indulgence on a female whose only crime is resistless, unquenchable adoration of you."

She panted for breath, her pulses beat with violence, her eyes swam, and overcome by the conflicting passions of her soul, the frame of Olympia fell, sickening with faintness, on the ground. Wolfstein raised her, and tenderly essayed to recall the senses of the hapless girl. Recovering, and perceiving her situation, Olympia started, seemingly, horrified, from the arms of Wolfstein. The energies of her high mind instantly resumed their functions, and she exclaimed, "Then, base and ungrateful Wolfstein, you refuse to unite your fate with mine? My love is ardent and excessive, but the revenge which may follow the despiser of it is far more impetuous; reflect well then ere you drive Olympia della Anzasca to despair."—"No reflection, in the present instance, is needed, lady," replied Wolfstein, coolly, yet determinedly. "What man of honour needs a moment's rumination to discover what nature has so inerasibly implanted in his bosom—the sense of right and wrong? I am connected with a female whom I love, who confides in me; in what manner should I merit her confidence, if I join myself to another? nor can the loveliness, the exquisite, the unequalled loveliness of the beautiful Olympia della Anzasca compensate me for breaking an oath sworn to another."

He paused.—Olympia spake not, but appeared to be awaiting the dreadful fiat of her destiny.

"Olympia," Wolfstein continued, "pardon me! Were I not irrevocably Megalena's, I must be thine: I esteem you, I admire you, but my love is another's."

The passion which before had choked Olympia's utterance, appeared to give way to the impetuousness of her emotions.

"Then," she said, as a solemnity of despair toned her voice to firmness, "then you are irrevocably another's?"

"I am compelled to be explicit; I am compelled to say, I am another's for ever!" fervently returned Wolfstein.

Again fainting from the excess of painful feeling which vibrated through her frame, Olympia fell at Wolfstein's feet: again he raised her, and, in anxious solicitude, watched her varying countenance. At the critical instant when Olympia had just recovered from the faintness which had oppressed her, the door burst open, and disclosed to the view of the passion-grieving Olympia, the detested form of Megalena. A silence, resembling that when a solemn pause in the midnight-tempest announces that the elements only hesitate to collect more terrific force for the ensuing explosion, took place, while Megalena surveyed Olympia and Wolfstein. Still she spoke not; yet the silence, even more terrible than the commotion which followed, continued to prevail. Olympia dashed by Megalena, and faintly articulating "Vengeance!" rushed into the street, and bent her rapid flight to the Palazzo di Anzasca.

"Wolfstein," said Megalena, her voice quivering with excessive emotion, "Wolfstein, how have I deserved this? How have I deserved a dereliction so barbarous and unprovoked? But no!" she added in a firmer tone, "no, I will leave you! I will show that I can bear the tortures of disappointed love, better than you can evade the scrutiny of one who did adore thee."

In vain Wolfstein put in practice every soothing art to tranquillize the agitation of Megalena. Her frame trembled with violent shuddering; yet her soul, as it were, superior to the form which enshrined it, loftily towered, and retained its firmness amidst the frightful chaos which battled within.

"Now," said she to Wolfstein, "I will leave you."

"O God! Megalena, dearest, adored Megalena!" exclaimed Wolfstein, passionately, "stop—I love you, must ever love you: deign, at least, to hear me."

"What good would accrue from that?" gloomily inquired Megalena.

I.   L

Wolfstein rushed towards her ; he threw himself at
her feet and exclaimed, " If ever, for one instant, my
soul was alienated from thee—if ever it swerved from
the affection which I have sworn to thee—may the red
right hand of God instantaneously dash me beneath the
lowest abyss of hell ! O Megalena ! is it as a victim
of groundless jealousy that I have immolated myself at
the altar of thy perfections ? Have I only raised myself
to this summit of happiness to feel more deeply the fall
of which thou art the cause ? O Megalena ! if yet one
spark of thy former love lingers in thy breast, oh !
believe one who swears that he must be thine even till
the particles which compose the soul devoted to thee,
become annihilated."—He paused.

Megalena heard his wildly enthusiastic expressions
in sullen silence. She looked upon him with a stern
and severe gaze :—he yet lay at her feet, and, hiding his
face upon the earth, groaned deeply. "What proof,"
exclaimed Megalena, impatiently, "what proof will
Wolfstein, the deceiver, bring to satisfy me that his love
is still mine ? "

" Seek for proof in my heart," returned Wolfstein,
" that heart which yet is bleeding from the thorns which
thou, cruel girl, hast implanted in it : seek it in my
every action, and then will the convinced Megalena
know that Wolfstein is hers irrevocably—body and soul,
for ever ! "

" Yet, I believe thee not ! " said Megalena : " for the
haughty Olympia della Anzasca would scarcely recline in
the arms of a man who was not entirely devoted to her."

Yet were the charms of Megalena unfaded ; yet their
empire over Wolfstein excessive and complete.

"Still I believe thee not," continued she, as a smile
of expectant malice sat upon her cheek. " I require
some proof which will assuredly convince me that I
am yet beloved : give me proof, and Megalena will
again be Wolfstein's."—" Oh ! " said Wolfstein, mourn-

fully, "what farther proof can I give, but my oath, that
never in soul or body have I broken the allegiance that
I formerly swore to thee ? "

"The death of Olympia!" gloomily returned
Megalena.

"What mean you ?" said Wolfstein, starting.

"I mean," continued Megalena, collectedly, as if
what she was about to utter had been the result of
serious cogitation : "I mean that, if ever you wish
again to possess my affections, ere to-morrow morning,
Olympia must expire !"

"Murder the innocent Olympia ?"

"Yes !"

A pause ensued, during which the mind of Wolfstein,
torn by ten thousand warring emotions, knew not on
what to resolve. He gazed upon Megalena : her
symmetrical form shone with tenfold loveliness to his
enraptured imagination : again he resolved to behold
those eyes beam with affection for him, which were now
gloomily fixed upon the ground. "Will nothing else
convince Megalena that Wolfstein is eternally hers ? "

"Nothing."

"'Tis done, then," exclaimed Wolfstein, "'tis done.
Yet," he muttered, "I may suffer for this premeditated act tortures now inconceivable ; I may writhe,
convulsed, in immaterial agony, for ever and for ever—
ah ! I cannot. No !" he continued, "Megalena, I am
again yours ; I will immolate the victim which thou
requirest as a sacrifice to our love. Give me a dagger,
which may sweep off from the face of the earth one
who is hateful to thee ! Adored creature, give me the
dagger, and I will restore it to thee dripping with
Olympia's hated blood ; it shall have first been buried
in her heart."

"Then, then again art thou mine own ! again art
thou the idolized Wolfstein, whom I was wont to love !"
said Megalena, enfolding him in her embrace. Per-

ceiving her returning softness, Wolfstein essayed to
induce her to spare him the frightful proof of the ardour
of his attachment ; but she started from his arms as he
spoke, and exclaimed :

"Ah ! base deceiver, do you hesitate ?"

"Oh, no ! I do not hesitate, dearest Megalena ;—
give me a dagger, and I go."

Here, follow me then," returned Megalena. He
followed her to the supper-room.

" It is useless to go yet, it has but yet struck one ;
the inhabitants of il Palazzo della Anzasca will, about
two, be nearly all retired to rest ; till then, let us converse on what we were about to do." So far did
Megalena's seductive blandishment, her artful selection
of converse, win upon Wolfstein, that, when the
destined hour approached, his sanguinary soul thirsted
for the blood of the comparatively innocent Olympia.

"Well !" he cried, swallowing down an overflowing
goblet of wine, "now the time is come ; now suffer
me to go, and tear the soul of Olympia from her hated
body." His fury amounted almost to delirium, as,
masked, and having a dagger, which Megalena had
given him, concealed beneath his garments, he proceeded rapidly along the streets towards the Palazzo
della Anzasca. So eager was he to shed the life-blood
of Olympia, that he flew, rather than ran, along the
silent streets of Genoa. The colonnades of the lofty
Palazzo della Anzasca resounded to his rapid footsteps;
he stopped at its lofty portal :—it was open; unperceived
he entered, and, hiding himself behind a column, according to the directions of Megalena, waited there.
Soon advancing through the hall, he saw the sylph-like
figure of the lovely Olympia ; with silent tread he
followed it, experiencing not the slightest sentiment of
remorse within his bosom for the deed which he was
about to perpetrate. He followed her to her apartment,
and secreting himself until Olympia might have sunk

into sleep, with sanguinary and remorseless patience, when her loud breathing convinced him that her slumber was profound, he arose from his place of concealment, and advanced to the bed, wherein Olympia lay. Her light tresses, disengaged from the band which had confined them, floated around a countenance, superhumanly beautiful, and whose expression, even in slumber, appeared to be tinted by Wolfstein's refusal; convulsive sighs heaved her fair bosom, and tears, starting from under her eyelids, fell profusely down her damask cheek. Wolfstein gazed upon her in silence. "Cruel, inhuman Megalena!" he mentally soliloquized, "could nothing but immolation of this innocence appease thee?" Again he stifled the stings of rebelling conscience; again the unquenchable ardour of his love for Megalena stimulated him to the wildest pitch of fury: he raised high the dagger, and, drawing aside the covering which veiled her alabaster bosom, paused an instant, to decide in what place it were most instantaneously destructive to strike. Again a mournful smile irradiated her lovely features; it played with a sweet softness on her countenance: it seemed as though she smiled in defiance of the arrows of destiny, but that her soul, nevertheless, lingered with the wretch who sought her life. Maddened by the sight of so much beauteous innocence, even the desperate Wolfstein, forgetful of the danger which he must thereby incur, hurled the dagger from him. The sound awakened Olympia: she started up in surprise; but her alarm was changed into ecstasy, when she beheld the idolized possessor of her soul standing before her.

"I was dreaming of you," said Olympia, scarcely knowing whether this were not a dream; but, impulsively following the first emotions of her soul. "I dreamed that you were about to murder me. It is not so, Wolfstein, no! you would not murder one who adores you?"

"Murder Olympia! O God! no!—I take Heaven to witness, that I never *now* could do it!"

"Nor could you ever, I hope, dear Wolfstein; but drive away thoughts like these, and remember that Olympia lives but for thee; and the moment which takes from her your affections seals the death-like fiat of her destiny." These asseverations, strengthened by the most solemn and deadly vows that he would return to Megalena the destroyer of Olympia, flashed across Wolfstein's mind. Perpetrate the deed, now, he could not; his soul became a scene of most terrific agony. "Wilt thou be mine?" exclaimed the enraptured Olympia, as a ray of hope arose in her mind. "Never! never can I," groaned the agitated Wolfstein; "I am irrevocably, indissolubly another's." Maddened by this death-blow to all expectations of happiness, which the deluded Olympia had so fondly anticipated, she leaped wildly from the bed. A light and flowing night-dress alone veiled her form, her alabaster bosom was shaded by the light ringlets of her hair which rested unconfined upon it. She threw herself at the feet of Wolfstein. On a sudden, as if struck by some thought, she started convulsively from the earth: for an instant she paused.

The rays of a lamp, which stood in a recess of the apartment, fell full upon the dagger of Wolfstein. Eagerly Olympia sprung towards it; and, ere Wolfstein was aware of her dreadful intent, plunged it into her bosom. Weltering in purple gore, she fell; no groan, no sigh escaped her lips. A smile, which the pangs of dissolution could not dispel, played on her convulsed countenance; it irradiated her features with celestially awful, although terrific expression. "Ineffectually have I endeavoured to conquer the ardent feelings of my soul; now I overcome them," were her last words. She uttered them in a tone of firmness, and, falling back, expired in torments, which her fine, her expressive features declared that she gloried in.

All was silent in the chamber of death : the stillness was frightful. The agonies which Wolfstein endured were past description: for a time he neither moved nor spoke. The pale glare of the lamp fell upon the features of Olympia, from which the tinge of life had fled for ever. Suddenly, and in despite of himself, were the affections of Wolfstein turned from Megalena: he could not but now regard her as a fiend, who had been the cause of Olympia's destruction ; who had urged him to a deed from which his nature now shrunk as from annihilation. A wild paroxysm of awful alarm seized upon him : he knelt by the side of Olympia's corpse ; he kissed it, bathed it with his tears, and imprecated a thousand curses on himself. Her features, although convulsed by the agonies of violent disolution, retained an unchanging image of loveliness, which never might fade away. Her beautiful bosom, in which her hand yet held the fatal dagger, was discoloured with blood, and those affection-beaming orbs were now closed in the never-ending slumber of the grave. Unable longer to endure a sight of so much horror, Wolfstein started up, and forgetful of everything save the frightful deed which he had witnessed, rushed from the Palazzo della Anzasca, and mechanically retraced his way towards his own habitation.

· Not once that night had Megalena closed her eyes. Her infuriate passions had wound her soul up to a deadly calmness of expectation. She had not, during the whole of the night, retired to rest, but sat, with sanguinary patience, cursing the lagging hours that they passed so slowly, and waiting to hear tidings of death. Morning had begun to streak the eastern sky with gray, when Wolfstein hurried into the supper-room, where Megalena still sat, wildly exclaming, " The deed is done ! " Megalena entreated him to be calm, and more collectedly, to communicate the events which had occurred during the night.

" In the first place," he said in an accent of feigned
horror, " the officers of justice are alarmed ! "

Deadly affright chilled the soul of Megalena : she
turned pale, and, gasping for breath, inquired eagerly
respecting the success of his attempt.

" O God ! " exclaimed Wolfstein, " that has succeeded but too well ! the hapless Olympia welters in
her life-blood ! "

"Joy ! joy ! " franticly exclaimed Megalena, her eagerness for revenge overcoming, for the moment, every
other feeling.

"But, Megalena," continued Wolfstein, " she fell not
by my hand : no, she smiled on me in her sleep, and
when she awoke, finding me deaf to her solicitations,
snatched my dagger, and buried it in her bosom."

" Did you *wish* to prevent the deed ? " inquired
Megalena.

"Oh, good God of Heaven ! thou knowest my
heart : I would sacrifice every remaining earthly good
were Olympia again alive ! "

Megalena spoke not, but a smile of exquisitely gratified malice illumined her features with terrific flame.

" We must instantly quit Genoa," said Wolfstein :
"the name on the mask which I left in the Palazzo
della Anzasca, will remove all doubt that I was the
murderer of Olympia. Yet indeed I care not much
for death ; if you will it so, Megalena, we will even,
as it is, remain in Genoa."

"Oh ! no, no ! " eagerly cried Megalena : "Wolfstein,
I love you beyond expression, and Genoa is destruction :
let us seek, therefore, some retired spot, where we may
for awhile at least secrete ourselves. But, Wolfstein,
are you persuaded that I love you ? need there more
proof be required than that I wished the death of
another for thee ? it was on *that* account alone that I
desired the destruction of Olympia, that thou mightest
be more completely and irresistibly mine."

Wolfstein answered not : the feelings of his soul were far different ; the expression of his countenance plainly evinced them : and Megalena regretted that her effervescent passions should have led her to so rash an avowal of her contempt of virtue. They then separated to arrange their affairs, prior to their departure, which, on account of the pressing necessity of the case, must take place immediately. They took with them but two domestics, and collecting all their stock of money, they were soon far from pursuit and Genoa.

CHAPTER VII.

Yes! 'tis the influence of that sightless fiend,
Who guides my every footstep, that I feel:
An iron grasp arrests each fluttering sense,
And a fell voice howls in mine anguish'd ear,
" Wretch, thou mayest rest no more."

OLYMPIA.

HOW sweet are the scenes endeared to us by ideas which we have cherished in the society of one we have loved! How melancholy to wander amongst them again after an absence, perhaps of years; years, which have changed the tenour of our existence,—have changed even the friend, the dear friend, for whose sake alone the landscape lives in the memory, for whose sake tears flow at the each varying feature of the scenery, which catches the eye of one who has never seen them since he saw them with the being who was dear to him !

Dark, autumnal, and gloomy was the hour ; the winds whistled hollow, and over the expanse of heaven was spread an unvarying sombreness of vapour : nothing was heard save the melancholy shriekings of the night-bird, which, soaring on the evening blast, broke the stillness of the scene, interrupting the meditations of frenzied enthusiasm; mingled with the sighing of the wind, which swept in languid and varying cadence amidst the leafless boughs.

Ah! of whom shall the poor outcast wanderer demand protection? Far, far, has she wandered. The vice and unkindness of the world hath torn her tender heart. In whose bosom shall she repose the secret of her sufferings? Who will listen with pity to the narrative of her woe, and heal the wounds which the selfish unkindness of man hath made, and then sent her with them, unbound, on the wide and pitiless world? Lives there one whose confidence the sufferer might seek?

Cold and dreary was the night: November's blast had chilled the air. Is the blast so pitiless as ingratitude and selfishness? Ah, no! thought the wanderer; it is unkind indeed, but not *so* unkind as that. Poor Eloise de St. Irvyne! many, many are in thy situation; but few have a heart so full of sensibility and excellence for the demoniac malice of man to deform, and then glut itself with hellish pleasure in the conviction of having ravaged the most lovely of the works of their Creator. She gazed upon the sky: the moon had just risen; its full orb was occasionally shaded by a passing cloud : it rose from behind the turrets of le Château de St. Irvyne. The poor girl raised her eyes towards it, streaming with tears : she scarce could recognize the once-loved building. She thanked God for permitting her again to behold it; and hastened on with steps tottering from fatigue, yet nerved with the sanguineness of anticipation.

Yes, St. Irvyne was the same as when she had left it five years ago. The same ivy mantled the western tower ; the same jasmine, which bloomed so luxuriantly when she left it, was still there, though leafless from the season. Thus was it with poor Eloise : she had left St. Irvyne, blooming, and caressed by every one ; she returned to it, pale, downcast, and friendless. The jasmine encircled the twisted pillars which supported the portal. Alas! whose assistance had prevented Eloise from sinking to the earth?—no one's. She knocked at the door—it was opened, and an instant's space beheld her in the arms of a beloved sister. Needless were it to describe the mutual pleasure, needless to describe the delight, of recognition ; suffice it to say, that Eloise once more enjoyed the society of her dearest friend ; and, in the happiness of her society, forgot the horrors which had preceded her return to St. Irvyne.

Now were it well to leave Eloise at St. Irvyne, and retrace the events which, since five years, had so darkly tinged the fate of the unsuspecting female, who trusted to the promises of man. It was a beautiful morning in May, and the loveliness of the season had spread a deeper shade of gloom over the features of Eloise, for she knew that not long would her mother live. They journeyed on towards Geneva, whither the physicians had ordered Madame de St. Irvyne to repair, as the last resort of a hope that she might, thereby, escape a rapid decline. On account of the illness of her mother, they proceeded slowly ; and ere long they had entered the region of the Alps, the shades of evening, which rapidly began to increase, announced approaching night. They had expected, before this time, to have reached a town ; but, either owing to a miscalculation of their route, or the remissness of the postilion, they had not yet done so. The majestic moon which hung above their heads, tinged with silver the fleecy clouds which skirted the far-seen horizon ; and, borne on the soft wing of the evening zephyr, shadowy lines of vapour, at intervals, crossed her orbit ; then vanishing into the dark blue expansiveness of ether, their fantastic forms, like the phantoms of midnight, became invisible. Now might we almost suppose, that the sightless spirits of the departed good, enthroned on the genial breeze of night, watched over

those whom they had loved on earth, and poured into
the bosom, to the dictates of which, in this world, they
had listened with idolatrous attention, that tranquillity
and confidence in the goodness of the Creator, which is
necessary for us to experience ere we go to the next.
Such tranquillity felt Madame de St. Irvyne: she tried
to stifle the ideas which arose within her mind; but the
more she strove to repress them, in the more vivid
characters were they imprinted on the imagination.

Now had they gained the summit of the mountain,
when, suddenly, a crash announced that the carriage
had given way.

"What is to be done?" inquired Eloise. The
postilion appeared to take no notice of her question.
"What is to be done?" again she inquired.

"Why, I scarcely know," answered the postilion;
"but 'tis impossible to proceed."

"Is there no house nearer than―――― "

"Oh yes," replied he; "here is a house quite near,
but a little out of the way; and, perhaps, Ma'am'selle
will not――――"

"Oh, lead on, lead on to it," quickly rejoined Eloise.

They followed the postilion, and soon arrived at
the house. It was large and plain; and although there
were lights in some of the windows, it bore an indefinable appearance of desolation.

In a large hall sat three or four men, whose marked
countenances almost announced their profession to be
bandits. *One* of superior and commanding figure,
whispering to the rest, and himself advancing with the
utmost and most unexpected politeness, accosted the
travellers. For the ideas with which the countenance
of this man inspired Eloise she in vain endeavoured to
account. It appeared to her that she had seen him
before; that the deep tone of his voice was known to
her; and that eye, scintillating with a coruscation of
mingled sternness and surprise, found some counterpart

in herself. Of gigantic stature, yet formed in the mould of exactest symmetry, was the figure of the stranger who sate before Eloise. His countenance of excessive beauty even, but dark, emanated with an expression of superhuman loveliness; not that grace which may freely be admired, but acknowledged in the inmost soul by sensations mysterious, and before unexperienced. He tenderly inquired, whether the night air had injured the ladies, and pressed them to partake of a repast which the other three men had prepared; he appeared to unbend a severity, which evidently was habitual, and by extreme brilliancy and playfulness of wit, joined to talents for conversation possessed by few, made Madame de St. Irvyne forget that she was dying; and her daughter, as in rapturous attention she listened to each accent of the stranger, remembered no more that she was about to lose her mother.

In the stranger's society, they almost forgot the lapse of time : a pause in the conversation at last occurred.

" Can Ma'am'selle sing ? " inquired the stranger.

" I can," replied Eloise ; " and with pleasure."

Song.

How swiftly through heaven's wide expanse
　　Bright day's resplendent colours fade !
How sweetly does the moonbeam's glance
　　With silver tint St. Irvyne's glade !

No cloud along the spangled air,
　　Is borne upon the evening breeze ;
How solemn is the scene ! how fair
　　The moonbeams rest upon the trees !

Yon dark gray turret glimmers white,
　　Upon it sits the mournful owl ;
Along the stillness of the night,
　　Her melancholy shriekings roll.

But not alone on Irvyne's tower,
　　The silver moonbeam pours her ray ;
It gleams upon the ivied bower,
　　It dances in the cascade's spray.

"Ah ! why do darkening shades conceal
  The hour, when man must cease to be ?*
Why may not human minds unveil
  The dim mists of futurity?

"The keenness of the world hath torn
  The heart which opens to its blast;
Despised, neglected, and forlorn,
  Sinks the wretch in death at last."

She ceased ;—the thrilling accents of her interestingly sweet voice died away in the vacancy of stillness ;
—yet listened the charmed auditors; their imaginations
prolonged the tender strain ; the uncouth attendants of
the stranger were chained in silence, and the enthusiastic gaze of their host was fixed upon the timid
countenance of Eloise with wild and mysterious expression.   It seemed to say to Eloise, "We meet again ;"—
and, as the idea struck her imagination, convulsed by
a feeling of indescribable and excessive awe, she started.

At last, the hour being late, they all retired.   Eloise
sought the couch prepared for her ; her mind, perturbed by emotions, the cause of which she in vain
essayed to develop, could bring its intellectual energies
to act on no one particular point ; her imagination was
fertile, and, under its fantastic guidance, she felt her
judgment and reason irresistibly fettered.   The image
of the fascinating, yet awful stranger, dwelt on her
mind.   She sank on her knees to return thanks to her
Creator for his mercies ; yet even then, faithless to the
task on which it was employed, her mind returned to
the stranger.   She felt no particular affection or esteem
for him ;—no, she rather feared him ; and, when she
endeavoured to connect the chain of ideas which
pressed upon her mind, tears started into her eyes, and
she looked around the apartment with the timid terror
of a person who converses at midnight on a subject at
once awful and interesting : but poor Eloise was no
philosopher ; and to explain sensations like these, were

* These two lines are taken *verbatim* from Byron's *Hours of Idleness.*—ED.

even beyond the power of the wisest of them. She felt alarmed, herself, at the violence of the feelings which shook her bosom, and attempted to compose herself to sleep. Yet even in her dream was the stranger present. She thought that she met him on a flowery plain ; that the feelings of her bosom, whether she would or not, impelled her towards him ; that, before she had been enfolded in his arms, a torrent of scintillating flame, accompanied by a terrific crash of thunder, made the earth yawn beneath her feet ;—the gay vision vanished from her fancy, and, in place of the flowery plain, a rugged and desolate heath extended far before her ; its monotonous solitude unbroken, save by the low and barren rocks which rose occasionally from its surface. From dreams such as these, dreams which left on her mind painful presentiments of her future life, Eloise arose, restless and unrefreshed from slumber.

Why gleams that dark eyeball upon the countenance of Eloise, as she tenderly inquired for the health of her mother ? Why did a hidden expression of exulting joy light up that demoniac gaze, when Madame de St. Irvyne said to her daughter, "I feel rather faint to-day, my child ;—would we were at Geneva !" It beams with hell and destruction !—Let me look again : that, when I see another eye which gleams so fiendishly, I may know that it is a villain's.—Thus might have thought the sightless minister of the beneficence of God, as it hovered round the spotless Eloise. But, hush ! what was that scream which was heard by the ear of listening enthusiasm ? It was the shriek of the fair Eloise's better genius ; it screamed to see the foe of the innocent girl so near—it is fled fast to Geneva. "There, Eloise, will we meet again," methought it whispered ; whilst a low hollow tone, hoarse from the dank vapours of the grave, seemed lowly to howl in the ear of rapt Fancy, "We meet again likewise."

Their courteous host conducted Madame de St. Irvyne and Eloise to their chaise, which was now repaired, and ready for the journey; the stranger bowed respectfully as they went away. The expression of his dark eye, as he beheld them for the last time, was even stronger than ever ; it seemed not to affect her mother; but the mystic feelings which it excited in the bosom of Eloise were beyond description powerful. The paleness of Madame de St. Irvyne's cheek, on which the only teint was an occasional and hectic flush, announced that the illness which consumed her, rapidly increased, and would soon lead her gently to the gates of death. She talked calmly of her approaching dissolution, and only regretted, that to no one protector could she entrust the care of her orphaned daughters. Marianne, her eldest daughter, had, by her mother's particular desire, remained at the château ; and though much wishing to accompany her mother, she urged it no longer, when she knew Madame de St. Irvyne to be resolved against it. Now had the illness which had attacked her assumed so serious and so decided an appearance, that she could no longer doubt the event ; could no longer doubt that she was quickly about to enter a better world.

"My daughter," said she, "there is a banker at Geneva, a worthy man, to whom I shall bequeath the guardianship of my child; on that head are all my doubts quieted. But, Eloise, my child, you are yet young ; you know not the world ; but bear in mind these words of your dying mother, so long as you remember herself :—When you see a man enveloped in deceit and mystery; when you see him dark, reserved, and suspicious, carefully avoid him. Should such a man seek your friendship or affection, should he seek, by any means, to confer an obligation upon you, or make you confer one on him, spurn him from you as you would a serpent ; as one who aimed to lure your unsuspecting innocence to the paths of destruction."

The affecting solemnity of her voice, as thus she spoke, touched Eloise deeply; she wept. "I must remember my mother for ever," was her almost inarticulate reply; deep sobs burst from her agitated bosom; and the varying crowds of imagery which followed each other in her mind, were too complicated to be defined. Still, though deeply grieved at the approaching death of her mother, was the mysterious stranger uppermost in her thoughts; his image excited ideas painful and unpleasant. She wished to turn the tide of them; but the more she attempted it, with the more painful recurrence of almost *mechanical* force, did his recollection press upon her disturbed intellect.

Eloise de St. Irvyne was a girl, whose temper and disposition was most excellent; she was, indeed, too, possessed of uncommon sensibility; yet was her mind moulded in an inferior degree of perfection. She was susceptible of prejudice, to a great degree; and resigned herself, careless of the consequences which might follow, to the feelings of the moment. Every accomplishment, it is true, she enjoyed in the highest excellence; and the very convent at which she was educated, which afforded the adventitious advantages so highly esteemed by the world, prevented her mind from obtaining that degree of expansiveness and excellence which, otherwise, might have rendered Eloise nearer approaching to perfection; the very routine of a convent education gave a false and pernicious bias to the ideas, as, luxuriant in youth, they unfolded themselves; and those sentiments which, had they been allowed to take the turn which nature intended, would have become coadjutors of virtue, and strengtheners of that mind, which now they had rendered *comparatively* imbecile. Such was Eloise, and as such she required unexampled care to prevent those feelings which agitate every mind of sensibility, to get the better of the judgment which had, by an erroneous

I. M

system of education, become relaxed. Her mother was
about to die—who now would care for Eloise ?

They entered Geneva at the close of a fine, yet sultry
day. The illness of Madame de St. Irvyne had increased so as now to threaten instant danger : she was
conveyed to bed. A deadly paleness sat on her cheek :
it was flushed, however, as she spoke, with momentary
hectics ; and, as she conversed with her daughter, a fire,
which almost partook of ethereality, shone in her sunken
eye. It was evening ; the yellow beams of the sun, as
his orb shed the parting glory on the verge of the
horizon, penetrated the bed-curtains ; and by their
effulgence contrasted the deadliness of her countenance.
The poor Eloise sat, watching, with eyes dimmed by
tears, each variation in the countenance of her mother.
Silent, from an ecstasy of grief, she gazed fixedly upon
her, and felt every earthly hope die within her, when
the conviction of a fast-approaching dissolution pressed
upon her disturbed brain. Madame de St. Irvyne, at
length exhausted, fell into a quiet slumber ; Eloise
feared to disturb her, but, motionless with grief, sate
behind the curtain.· Now had sunk the orb of day, and
the shades of twilight began to scatter duskiness
through the chamber of death. All was silent ; and,
save by the catchings of breath in her mother's slumber,
the stillness was uninterrupted. Yet even in this awful,
this terrific crisis of her existence, the mind of Eloise
seemed compelled to exert its intellectual energies but on
one subject ;—in vain she essayed to pray ;—in vain she
attempted to avert the horror of her meditations, by contemplating the pallid features of her dying mother; her
thoughts were not within her own control, and she
trembled as she reflected on the appalling and mysterious influence which the image of a man, whom she
had seen but once, and whom she neither loved nor
cared for, had gained over her mind. With the indefinable terror of one who dreads to behold some phan-

tom, Eloise fearfully cast her eyes around the gloomy apartment; occasionally she shrank from the ideal form which an unconnected imagination had conjured up, and could scarcely but suppose that the *stranger's* gaze, as last he had looked upon her, met her own with an horrible and mixed scintillation of mysterious cunning and interest. She felt no prepossession in his favour ; she rather detested him, and gladly would never have again beheld him. Yet, were the circumstances which introduced him to their notice alluded to, she would turn pale, and blush, by turns ; and Jeanette, their maid, was fully persuaded in her own mind, and prided herself on her penetration in the discovery, that Ma'am'selle was violently in love with the hospitable Alpine hunter.

Madame de St. Irvyne had now awakened; she beckoned her daughter to approach. Eloise obeyed ; and, kneeling, kissed the chill hand of her mother, in a transport of sorrow, and bathed it with her tears.

"Eloise," said her mother, her voice trembling from excessive weakness, "Eloise, my child, farewell—farewell for ever. I feel I am about to die ; but, before I die, willingly would I say much to my dearest daughter. You are now left on the hard-hearted, pitiless world ; and perhaps, oh! perhaps, about to become an immolated victim of its treachery. Oh !——" Here, overcome by extreme pain, she fell backwards ; a transient gleam of animation lighted up her expressive countenance ; she smiled, and—expired. All was still ; and over the gloomy chamber reigned silence and horror. The yellow moonbeam, with sepulchral effulgence, gleamed on the countenance of her who had expired, and lighted her features, sweet even in death, with a dire and horrible contrast to the dimness which prevailed around ! Ah ! such was the contrast of the peace enjoyed by the spirit of the departed one, with the misery which awaited the wretched Eloise. Poor Eloise! she had now lost almost her only friend !

In excessive and silent grief, knelt the mourning girl; she spoke not, she wept not ; her sorrow was too violent for tears, but, oh ! her heart was torn by pangs of unspeakable acuteness. But even amid the alarm which so melancholy an event must have excited, the idea of the *stranger in the Alps* sublimed the soul of Eloise to the highest degree of horror, and despair the most infuriate. For the ideas which crowded into her mind at this crisis, so eventful, so terrific, she endeavoured to account ; but, alas ! her attempt was fruitless ! Still knelt she ; still did she press to her burning lips the lifeless hand of departed excellence, when the morning's ray announced to her that longer continuing there might excite suspicion of intellectual derangement. She arose, therefore, and, quitting the apartment, announced the melancholy event which had taken place. She gave orders for the funeral ; it was to be solemnized as soon as decency would permit, as the poor friendless Eloise wished speedily to quit Geneva. She wrote to announce the fatal event to her sister. Slowly dragged the time. Eloise followed to its latest bed the corpse of her mother, and was returning from the convent, when a stranger put into her hand a note, and quickly disappeared :—

"Will Eloise de St. Irvyne meet her friend at —— Abbey, to-morrow night, at ten o'clock ? "

CHAPTER VIII.

—— Why then unbidden gush'd the tear?
 *   *   *   *   *
Then would cold shudderings seize his brain,
  As gasping he labour'd for breath ;
The strange gaze of his meteor eye,
Which, frenzied, and rolling dreadfully,
  Glared with hideous gleam,
Would chill like the spectre gaze of Death,
  As, conjured by feverish dream,
He seems o'er the sick man's couch to stand,
And shakes the fell lance in his skeleton hand.
WANDERING JEW.*

ES ;—they fled from Genoa ; they had eluded pursuit and justice, but could not escape the torments of an outraged and avenging conscience, which, with stings the most acute, pursued them whithersoever they might go. Fortune even seemed to favour them : for fortune will, sometimes, in this world, appear to side with the wicked. Wolfstein had received notice that an uncle, possessed of immense wealth, had died in Bohemia, and bequeathed to him the whole of his estate. Thither, then, with Megalena, went Wolfstein. Their journey produced no event of consequence; suffice it to say, that they arrived at the spot where Wolfstein's possessions were situated.

Dark and desolate were the scenes which surrounded the no less desolate castle. Gloomy heaths, in unvarying sadness of immensity, stretched far and wide. A scathed pine or oak, blasted by the thunderbolts of heaven, alone broke the monotonous sameness of the imagery. Needless were it to describe the castle, built like all those of the Bohemian barons, in mingled Gothic and barbarian architecture. Over the dark expanse the dim moon beaming, and faintly, with its sepulchral

* See vol. iii., p. 91.

radiance, dispersing the thickness of the vapours whicʰ
lowered around (for her waning horn, which hung low
above the horizon, added but tenfold horror to the
terrific desolation of the scene); the night-raven pouring
on the dull ear of evening her frightful screams, and
breaking on the otherwise uninterrupted stillness,—were
the melancholy greetings to their new habitation.

They alighted at the antique entrance, and passing
through a vast and comfortless hall, were conducted
into a saloon not much less so. The coolness of the
evening, for it was late in the autumn, made the wood
fire, which had been lighted, disperse a degree of comfort; and Wolfstein, having arranged his domestic
concerns, continued talking with Megalena until midnight.

"But you have never yet correctly explained to me,"
said Megalena, "the mystery which encircled that
strange man whom we met at the inn at Breno. I think
I have seen him once since, or I should not now have
thought of the circumstance."

"Indeed, Megalena, I know of no mystery. I suppose the man was mad, or wished to make us think so;
for my part, I have never thought of him since; nor
intend to think of him."

"Do you not?" exclaimed a voice, which enchained
motionless to his seat the horror-struck Wolfstein—
when turning round, and starting in agonized frenzy
from his chair, Ginotti himself—*Ginotti*—from whose
terrific gaze never had he turned unappalled, stood in
cool and fearless contempt before him!

"Do you not?" continued the mysterious stranger.
"Never again intendest thou to think of me?—me!
who have watched each expanding idea, conscious to
what I was about to apply them, conscious of the great
purpose for which each was formed. Ah! Wolfstein,
by my agency shalt thou——" He paused, assuming
a smile expressive of exultation and superiority.

"Oh! do with me what thou wilt, strange, inexplicable being!—Do with me what thou wilt!" exclaimed Wolfstein, as an ecstasy of frenzied terror
overpowered his astonished senses. Megalena still sat
unmoved : she was surprised, it is true ; but most was
she surprised, that an event like this should have power
so to shake Wolfstein ; for even then he stood gazing
in enhorrored silence on the majestic figure of Ginotti.

"Fool, then, that thou art, to deny me!" continued
Ginotti, in a tone less solemn, but more severe. "Wilt
thou promise me that, when I come to demand what
thou covenantedst with me at Breno, I meet no fears, no
scruples, but that, then, thou wilt perform what there
thou didst swear, and that *this* oath shall be in-
violable ? "

" It shall," replied Wolfstein.

" Swear it."

"As I keep my vows with you, may God reward me
hereafter ! "

" 'Tis done, then," returned Ginotti. " Ere long shall
I claim the performance of this covenant—now farewell." Speaking thus, Ginotti dashed away ; and,
mounting a horse which stood at the gate, sped swiftly
across the heath His form lessened in the clear moonlight ; and when it was no longer visible to the straining eyeballs of Wolfstein, he felt, as it were, a spell
which had enthralled him, to be dissolved.

Reckless of Megalena's earnest entreaties, he threw
himself into a chair, in deep and gloomy melancholy ;
he answered them not, but, immersed in a train of
corroding ideas, remained silent. Even when retired
to repose, and he could, occasionally, sink into a transitory slumber, would he again start from it, as he thought
that Ginotti's majestic form leaned over him, and that
the glance which, last, his fearful eye had thrown,
chilled his breast with indescribable agony. Slowly
lagged the time to Wolfstein : Ginotti, though now

gone, and far away perhaps, dwelt in his disturbed
mind; his image was there imprinted in characters
terrific and indelible. Oft would he wander along the
desolate heath; on every blast of wind which sighed
over the scattered remnants of what was once a forest,
Ginotti's, the terrific Ginotti's voice seemed to float;
and in every dusky recess, favoured by the descending
shades of gloomy night, his form appeared to lurk,
and, with frightful glare, his eye to penetrate the con-
science-stricken Wolfstein as he walked. A falling
leaf, or a hare starting from her heathy seat, caused
him to shrink with affright; yet, though dreading loneli-
ness, he was irresistibly compelled to seek for solitude.
Megalena's charms had now no longer power to speak
comfort to his soul: ephemeral are the friendships of
the wicked, and involuntary disgust follows the attachment founded on the visionary fabric of passion or
interest. It sinks in the merited abyss of ennui, or is
followed by apathy and carelessness, which amply its
origin deserved.

The once ardent and excessive passion of Wolfstein
for Megalena, was now changed into disgust and almost
detestation; he sought to conceal it from her, but it
was evident, in spite of his resolution. He regarded
her as a woman capable of the most shocking enormities; since, without any adequate temptation to vice,
she had become sufficiently depraved to consider an
inconsequent crime the wilful and premeditated destruction of a fellow-creature; still, whether it were from
the indolence which he had contracted, or an indefinably
sympathetic connexion of soul, which forbade them to
part during their mortal existence, was Wolfstein
irremediably linked to his mistress, who was as depraved as himself, though originally of a better disposition. He likewise had, at first, resisted the allurements
of vice; but, overpowered by its incitements, had resigned himself, indeed reluctantly, to its influence. But

Megalena had courted its advances, and endeavoured
to conquer neither the suggestions of crime, nor the
dictates of a nature prone to the attacks of *appetite*—
let me not call it passion.

Fast advanced winter ; cheerless and solitary were
the days. Wolfstein, occasionally, followed the chase ;
but even *that* was wearisome : and the bleeding image
of the murdered Olympia, or the still more dreaded
idea of the terrific Ginotti, haunted him in the midst
of its tumultuous pleasures, and embittered every moment of his existence. The pale corpse too of Cavigni,
blackened by poison, reigned in his chaotic imagination
and stung his soul with tenfold remorse, when he reflected
that he had murdered one who never had injured
him, for the sake of a being whose depraved society
every succeeding day rendered more monotonous and
insipid.

It was one evening when, according to his custom,
Wolfstein wandered late : it was in the beginning of
December, and the weather was peculiarly mild for the
season and latitude. Over the cerulean expanse of ether
the dim moon, shrouded in the fleeting fragments of
vapour, which, borne on the pinions of the northern
blast, crossed her pale orb ; at intervals, the dismal
hooting of the owl, which, searching for prey, flitted
her white wings over the dusky heath ; the silver beams
which slept on the outline of the far-seen forests, and the
melancholy stillness, uninterrupted save by these con-
comitants of gloom, conduced to sombre reflection.
Wolfstein reclined upon the heath ; he retraced, in
mental review, the past events of his life, and shuddered
at the darkness of his future destiny. He strove to
repent of his crimes ; but, though conscious of the connexion which existed between the ideas, as often as
repentance presented itself to his mind, Ginotti rushed
upon his troubled imagination, and a dark veil seemed
to separate him for ever from contrition, notwithstanding

he was constantly subjected to the tortures inflicted by
it. At last, wearied with the corroding recollections,
the acme of which progressively increased, he bent his
steps again towards his habitation.

As he was entering the portal, a grasp of iron arrested
his arm, and, turning round, he recognized the tall
figure of Ginotti, which, enveloped in a mantle, had
leaned against a jutting buttress. Amazement, for a
time, chained the faculties of Wolfstein in motionless
surprise : at last he recollected himself, and, in a voice
trembling from agitation, inquired, did he now demand
the performance of the promise ?

"I come," he said, "I come to demand it, Wolfstein !
Art thou willing to perform what thou hast promised ?
—but come——."

A degree of solemnity, mixed with concealed fierceness, toned his voice as he spoke; yet was he fixed in the
attitude in which first he had addressed Wolfstein.
The pale ray of the moon fell upon his dark features,
and his coruscating eye fixed on his trembling victim's
countenance, flashed with almost intolerable brilliancy.
A chill horror darted through Wolfstein's sickening
frame; his brain swam around wildly, and most appalling
presentiments of what was about to happen, pressed
upon his agonized intellect. "Yes, yes, I have promised, and I will perform the covenant I have entered
into," said Wolfstein; "I swear to you that I will!"
and as he spoke, a kind of mechanical and inspired feeling steeled his soul to fortitude; it seemed to arise
independently of himself; nor could he, though he
eagerly desired to do so, control in the least his *own*
resolves. Such an impulse as this had first induced
him to promise at all. Ah ! how often in Ginotti's
absence had he resisted it ! but when the mysterious
disposer of the events of his existence was before him, a
consciousness of the inutility of his refusal compelled
him to submit to the mandates of a being, whom his

heart sickening to acknowledge, it unwillingly confessed as a superior.

"Come," continued Ginotti; "the hour is late, I must dispatch."

Unresisting, yet speaking not, Wolfstein conducted Ginotti to an apartment.

"Bring wine, and light a fire," said he to his servant, who quickly obeyed him. Wolfstein swallowed an overflowing goblet, hoping thereby to acquire courage; for he found that, with every moment of Ginotti's stay, the visionary and awful terrors of his mind augmented.

"Do you not drink?"

"No," replied Ginotti, sullenly.

A pause ensued; during which the eyes of Ginotti, glaring with demoniacal scintillations, spoke tenfold terrors to the soul of Wolfstein. He knitted his brows, and bit his lips, in vain attempting to appear unembarrassed. "Wolfstein!" at last said Ginotti, breaking the fearful silence; "Wolfstein!"

The colour fled from the cheek of his victim, as thus Ginotti spoke: he moved his posture, and awaited, in anxious and horrible solicitude, the declaration which was, as he supposed, to ensue. "My name, my family, and the circumstances which have attended my career through existence, it neither boots you to know, nor me to declare."

"Does it not?" said Wolfstein, scarcely knowing what to say; yet convinced, from the pause, that something was expected.

"No! nor canst thou, nor any other existent being, even attempt to dive into the mysteries which envelope me. Let it be sufficient for you to know, that every event in your life has not only been known to me, but has occurred under my particular machinations."

Wolfstein started. The terror which had blanched his cheek now gave way to an expression of fierceness

and surprise ; he was about to speak, but Ginotti,
noticing not his motion, thus continued :

"Every opening idea which has marked, in so
decided and so eccentric an outline, the fiat of your
future destiny, has not been unknown to or unnoticed
by me. I rejoiced to see in you, whilst young, the progress of that genius which in mature time would entitle
you to the reward which I destine for you, and for you
alone. Even when far, far away, when the ocean perhaps has roared between us, have I known your
thoughts, Wolfstein ; yet have I known them neither
by conjecture nor inspiration. Never would your mind
have attained that degree of expansion or excellence,
had not I watched over its every movement, and taught
the sentiment, as it unfolded itself, to despise contented
vulgarity. For this, and for an event far more important than any your existence yet has been subjected
to, have I watched over you : say, Wolfstein, have I
watched in vain ? "

Each feeling of resentment vanished from Wolfstein's
bosom, as the mysterious intruder spoke : his voice at
last died, in a clear and melancholy cadence, away ;
and his expressive eye, divested of its fierceness and
mystery, rested on Wolfstein's countenance with a mild
benignity.

"No, no ; thou hast not watched in vain, mysterious
disposer of my existence. Speak ! I burn with curiosity
and solicitude to learn for what thou hast thus super-
intended me : " and, as thus he spoke, a feeling of
resistless anxiety to know what would be the conclusion
of the night's adventure, took place of horror. Inquiringly he gazed on the countenance of Ginotti, the
features of whom were brightened with unwonted animation. "Wolfstein," said Ginotti, "often hast thou
sworn that I should rest in the grave in peace :—now
listen."

CHAPTER IX.

If Satan had never fallen,
Hell had been made for thee.
                    THE REVENGE.

H! poor, unsuspecting innocence! and is that fair flower about to perish in the blasts of dereliction and unkindness? Demon indeed must be he who could gaze on those mildly-beaming eyes, on that perfect form, the emblem of sensibility, and yet plunge the spotless mind of which it was an index, into a sea of repentance and unavailing sorrow. I should scarce suppose even a demon would act so, were there not many with hearts more depraved even than those of fiends, who first have torn some unsophisticated soul from the pinnacle of excellence, on which it sat smiling, and then triumphed in their hellish victory when it writhed in agonized remorse, and strove to hide its unavailing regret in the dust from which the fabric of her virtues had arisen. *"Ah! I fear me, the unsuspecting girl will go;"* she knows not the malice and the wiles of perjured man—and she is gone!

It was late in the evening, and Eloise had returned from her mother's funeral, sad and melancholy; yet, even amidst the oppression of grief, surprise, and astonishment, pleasure and thankfulness, that any one should notice her, possessed her mind as she read over and over the characters traced on the note which she still held in her hand. The hour was late, the moon was down, yet countless stars bedecked the almost boundless hemisphere. The mild beams of Hesper slept on the glassy surface of the lake, as, scarcely agitated by the zephyr of evening, its waves rolled in slow succession; the solemn umbrage of the pine-trees, mingled with the poplar, threw their undefined shadows on the water; and the nightingale, sitting solitary in the hawthorn, poured on the listening stillness of evening, her grateful lay of melancholy. Hark! her full strains swell on the silence of night; and now they die away, with lengthened and solemn cadence, insensibly into the breeze, which lingers, with protracted sweep, along the valley. Ah! with what enthusiastic ecstasy of melancholy does he whose friend, whose dear friend, is far, far away, listen to such strains as these! perhaps he has heard them with that friend,—with one he loves: never again may they meet his ear. Alas! 'tis melancholy; I even now see him sitting on the rock which looks over the lake, in frenzied listlessness; and counting in mournful review, the days which are past since they fled so quickly with one who was dear to him.

It was to the ruined abbey which stood on the southern side of the lake that, so swiftly, Eloise is hastening. A presentiment of awe filled her mind; she gazed, in inquiring terror, around her, and scarce could persuade herself that shapeless forms lurked not in the gloomy recesses of the scenery.

She gained the abbey; in melancholy fallen grandeur its vast ruins reared their pointed casements to the sky. Masses of disjointed stone were scattered around; and, save by the whirrings of the bats, the stillness which reigned, was uninterrupted. Here then was Eloise to meet the strange one who professed himself to be her friend. Alas! poor Eloise believed him. It yet wanted an hour to the time of appointment; the expiration of that hour Eloise awaited. The abbey brought to her recollection a similar ruin which stood near St. Irvyne; it brought with it the remembrance of a song which Marianne had composed soon after her brother's death. She sang, though in a low voice :—

SONG.

How stern are the woes of the desolate mourner,
  As he bends in still grief o'er the hallowed bier,

As enanguish'd he turns from the laugh of the scorner,
  And drops, to perfection's remembrance, a tear ;
When floods of despair down his pale cheek are streaming,
When no blissful hope on his bosom is beaming,
Or, if lull'd for awhile, soon he starts from his dreaming,
  And finds torn the soft ties to affection so dear.

Ah! when shall day dawn on the night of the grave,
  Or summer succeed to the winter of death?
Rest awhile, hapless victim, and Heaven will save
  The spirit, that faded away with the breath.
Eternity points in its amaranth bower,
Where no clouds of fate o'er the sweet prospect lower,
Unspeakable pleasure, of goodness the dower,
  When woe fades away like the mist of the heath.

She ceased : the melancholy cadence of her angelic voice died in faint reverberations of echo away, and once again reigned stillness.

Now fast approached the hour; and, ere ten had struck, a stranger of towering and gigantic proportions walked along the ruined refectory : without stopping to notice other objects, he advanced swiftly to Eloise, who sat on a misshapen piece of ruin, and throwing aside the mantle which enveloped his figure, discovered to her astonished sight the stranger of the Alps, who of late had been incessantly present to her mind. Amazement, for a time, chained each faculty in stupefaction; she would have started from her seat, but the stranger, with gentle violence grasping her hand, compelled her to remain where she was.

" Eloise," said the stranger, in a voice of the most fascinating tenderness—" Eloise ! "

The softness of his accents changed, in an instant, what was passing in the bosom of Eloise. She felt no surprise that he knew her name : she experienced no dread at this mysterious meeting with a person, at the bare mention of whose name she was wont to tremble : no, the ideas which filled her mind were indefinable,

She gazed upon his countenance for a moment, then, hiding her face in her hands, sobbed loudly.

"What afflicts you, Eloise?" said the stranger: "how cruel, that such a breast as thine should be tortured by pain!"

"Ah!" cried Eloise, forgetting that she spoke to a stranger; "how can one avoid sorrow, when there, perhaps, is scarce a being in the world whom I can call my friend; when there is no one on whom I lay claim for protection?"

"Say not, Eloise," cried the stranger, reproachfully, yet benignly; "say not that you can claim none as a friend—you may claim me. Ah! that I had ten thousand existences, that each might be devoted to the service of one whom I love more than myself! Make me then the repository of your every sorrow and secret. I love you, indeed I do, Eloise, and why will you doubt me?"

"I do not doubt you, stranger," replied the unsuspecting girl; "why should I doubt you? for you could have no interest in saying so, if you did not.—I thank you for loving one who is quite, quite friendless; and, if you will allow me to be your friend, I will love you too. I never loved any one, before, but my poor mother and Marianne. Will you then, if you are a friend to me, come and live with me and Marianne, at St. Irvyne's?"

"St. Irvyne's!" exclaimed the stranger, almost convulsively, as he interrupted her; then, as fearing to betray his emotions, he paused, yet quitted not the grasp of Eloise's hand, which trembled within his with feelings which her mind distrusted not.

"Yes, sweet Eloise, I love you indeed," at last he said, affectionately. "And I thank you much for believing me; but I cannot live with you at St. Irvyne's. Farewell, for to-night, however; for my poor Eloise has need of sleep." He then was quitting the abbey, when Eloise stopped him to inquire his name.

" Frederic de Nempere."

"Ah! then I shall recollect Frederic de Nempere, as the name of a friend, even if I never again behold him."

" Indeed I am not faithless ; soon shall I see you again. Farewell, beloved Eloise." Thus saying, with rapid step he quitted the ruin.

Though he was now gone, the sound of his tender farewell yet seemed to linger on the ear of Eloise ; but with each moment of his absence, became lessened the conviction of his friendship, and heightened the suspicions which, though unaccountable to herself, possessed her bosom. She could not conceive what motive could have led her to own her love for one whom she feared, and felt a secret terror, from the conviction of the resistless empire which he possessed within her : yet though she shrank from the bare idea of ever becoming his, did she ardently, though scarcely would she own it to herself, desire again to see him.

Eloise now returned to Geneva : she resigned herself to sleep, but even in her dreams was the image of Nempere present to her imagination. Ah ! poor deluded Eloise, didst thou think a *man* would merit thy love through disinterestedness? didst thou think that one who supposed himself superior, yet inferior in reality, to you, in the scale of existent beings, would desire thy society from *love ?* yet superior as the fool here supposes himself to be to the creature whom he injures, superior as he boasts himself, he may howl with the fiends of darkness, in never-ending misery, whilst thou shalt receive, at the throne of the God whom thou hast loved, the rewards of that unsuspecting excellence, which he who boasts his superiority, shall *suffer* for trampling upon. Reflect on *this*, ye libertines, and, in the full career of the lasciviousness which has unfitted your souls for enjoying the *slightest* real happiness here or hereafter, tremble ! Tremble ! I say ; for the day of retribution will arrive. But the poor Eloise need not

I. N

tremble ; the victims of your detested cunning need not
fear that day: no !—then will the cause of the broken-
hearted be avenged by Him to whom their wrongs
cry for redress.

Within a few miles of Geneva, Nempere possessed a
country-house : thither did he persuade Eloise to go
with him ; " For," said he, " though I cannot come to
St. Irvyne's, yet my friend will live with me."

" Yes, indeed I will," replied Eloise ; for, whatever
she might feel when he was absent, in his presence she
felt insensibly softened, and a sentiment nearly approaching to love would, at intervals, take possession of
her soul.   Yet was it by no means an easy task to lure
Eloise from the paths of virtue ; it is true she knew but
little, nor was the expansion of her mind such as might
justify the exultations of a fiend at a triumph over her
virtue ; yet was it that very timid, simple innocence
which prevented Eloise from understanding to what the
deep-laid sophistry of her false friend tended ; and, not
understanding it, she could not be influenced by its
arguments. Besides, the principles and morals of Eloise
were such as could not *easily* be shaken by the allurements which temptation might throw out to her unsophisticated innocence.

" Why," said Nempere, " are we taught to believe
that the union of two who love each other is wicked,
unless authorized by certain rites and ceremonials,
which certainly cannot change the tenour of sentiments
which it is destined that these two people should entertain of each other ? "

" It is, I suppose," answered Eloise, calmly, " because
God has willed it so ; besides," continued she, blushing
at she knew not what, " it would ——

" And is then the superior and towering soul of
Eloise subjected to sentiments and prejudices so stale
and vulgar as these ? " interrupted Nempere indig-
nantly.   " Say, Eloise, do not you think it an insult to

two souls, united to each other in the irrefragable cove-
nants of love and congeniality, to promise, in the sight
of a Being whom they know not, that fidelity which is
certain otherwise ?"

"But I do know that Being!" cried Eloise, with
warmth ; "and when I cease to know him, may I die !
I pray to him every morning, and, when I kneel at
night, I thank him for the mercy which he has shown
to a poor friendless girl like me ! He is the protector
of the friendless, and I love and adore him !"

"Unkind Eloise ! how canst thou call thyself friendless ? Surely, the adoration of two beings unfettered
by restraint, must be most acceptable !—But, come,
Eloise, this conversation is nothing to the purpose: I
see we both think alike, although the *terms* in which
we express our sentiments are different. Will you sing
to me, dear Eloise ?" Willingly did Eloise fetch her
harp ; she wished not to scrutinize what was passing
in her mind, but, after a short prelude, thus began :—

SONG.

I.

Ah ! faint are her limbs, and her footstep is weary,
  Yet far must the desolate wanderer roam ;
Though the tempest is stern, and the mountain is dreary,
  She must quit at deep midnight her pitiless home.
I see her swift foot dash the dew from the whortle,
As she rapidly hastes to the green grove of myrtle ;
And I hear, as she wraps round her figure the kirtle,
  "Stay thy boat on the lake,—dearest Henry, I come."

II.

High swell'd in her bosom the throb of affection
  As lightly her form bounded over the lea,
And arose in her mind every dear recollection ;
  "I come, dearest Henry, and wait but for thee."
How sad, when dear hope every sorrow is soothing,
When sympathy's swell the soft bosom is moving,
And the mind the mild joys of affection is proving,
  Is the stern voice of fate that bids happiness flee !

III.

Oh! dark lower'd the clouds on that horrible eve,
And the moon dimly gleam'd through the tempested air ;
Oh! how could fond visions such softness deceive ?
Oh! how could false hope rend a bosom so fair ?
Thy love's pallid corse the wild surges are laving,
O'er his form the fierce swell of the tempest is raving ;
But, fear not, parting spirit ; thy goodness is saving,
In eternity's bowers, a seat for thee there.

"How soft is that strain!" cried Nempere, as she concluded.

"Ah!" said Eloise, sighing deeply: "'tis a melancholy song; my poor brother wrote it, I remember, about ten days before he died. 'Tis a gloomy tale concerning him; he ill deserved the fate he met. Some future time I will tell it you ; but now, 'tis very late.—Good-night."

Time passed, and Nempere, finding that he must proceed more warily, attempted no more to impose upon the understanding of Eloise by such palpably baseless arguments ; yet, so great and so unaccountable an influence had he gained on her unsuspecting soul, that ere long, on the altar of vice, pride, and malice, was immolated the innocence of the spotless Eloise. Ah, ye proud! in the severe consciousness of unblemished reputation, in the fallacious opinion of the world, why turned ye away, as if fearful of contamination, when yon poor frail one drew near ? See the tears which steal adown her cheek!—*She* has repented, *ye* have not!

And thinkest thou, libertine, from a principle of depravity—thinkest thou that thou hast raised thyself to the level of Eloise, by trying to sink her to thine own ?—No!—Hopest thou that thy curse has passed away unheeded or unseen ? The God whom thou hast insulted has marked thee!—In the everlasting tablets of heaven, is thine offence written!—but poor Eloise's crime is obliterated by the mercy of Him, who knows the innocence of her heart.

* * * * * *

Yes—thy sophistry hath prevailed, Nempere!—'tis but blackening the memoir of thine offences! Hark! what shriek broke upon the enthusiastic silence of twilight? 'Twas the fancied scream of one who loved Eloise long ago, but now is—dead. It warns thee— alas! 'tis unavailing!!—'Tis fled, but not for ever.

It is evening; the moon, which rode in cloudless and unsullied majesty, in the leaden-coloured east, hath hidden her pale beams in a dusky cloud, as if blushing to contemplate a scene of so much wickedness.

'Tis done; and amidst the vows of a transitory delirium of pleasure, regret, horror, and misery, arise! they shake their Gorgon locks at Eloise! appalled she shudders with affright, and shrinks from the contemplation of the consequences of her imprudence. Beware, Eloise!—a precipice, a frightful precipice yawns at thy feet! advance yet a step further, and thou perishest! No, give not up thy religion—it is that alone which can support thee under the miseries, with which imprudence has so darkly marked the progress of thine existence!

CHAPTER X.

The elements respect their Maker's seal !
   Still like the scathed pine-tree's height,
   Braving the tempests of the night,
Have I 'scaped the bickering flame.
Like the scathed pine, which a monument stands
Of faded grandeur, which the brands
   Of the tempest-shaken air
Have riven on the desolate heath ;
Yet it stands majestic even in death,
   And rears its wild form there.

WANDERING JEW.

YET, in an attitude of attention, Wolfstein was fixed, and, gazing upon Ginotti's countenance, awaited his narrative.

"Wolfstein," said Ginotti, "the circumstances which I am about to communicate to you are, many of them, you may think, trivial ; but I must be minute, and, however the recital may excite your astonishment, suffer me to proceed without interruption."

Wolfstein bowed affirmatively—Ginotti thus proceeded :—

"From my earliest youth, before it was quenched by complete satiation, *curiosity*, and a desire of unveiling the latent mysteries of nature, was the passion by which all the other emotions of my mind were intellectually organized. This desire first led me to cultivate, and with success, the various branches of learning which led to the gates of wisdom. I then applied myself to the cultivation of philosophy, and the éclât with which I pursued it, exceeded my most sanguine expectations. *Love* I cared not for ; and wondered why men perversely sought to ally themselves with weakness. Natural philosophy at last became the peculiar science to which I directed my eager inquiries ; thence was I led into a train of labyrinthic meditations. I thought of *death*—I shuddered when I reflected, and shrank in horror from the idea, *selfish and self-interested* as I was, of entering a new existence to which I was a stranger. I must either dive into the recesses of futurity, or I must not, I cannot die. 'Will not this nature—will not the *matter* of which it is composed—exist to all eternity? Ah! I know it will; and, by the exertions of the energies with which nature has gifted me, well I know it shall.' This was my opinion at that time: I then believed that there existed no God. Ah! at what an exorbitant price have I bought the conviction that there is one !!! Believing that priestcraft and superstition were all the religion which *man* ever practised, it could not be supposed that I thought there existed supernatural beings of any kind. I believed *nature* to be self-sufficient and excelling; I supposed not, therefore, that there could be anything beyond nature.

"I was now about seventeen: I had dived into the depths of metaphysical calculations. With sophistical arguments had I convinced myself of the non-existence of a First Cause, and, by every combined modification of the essences of matter, had I apparently proved that no existences could possibly be, unseen by human vision. I had lived, hitherto, completely for myself; I cared not for others; and, had the hand of fate swept from the list of the living every one of my youthful associates, I should have remained immoved and fearless. I had not a friend in the world ;—I cared for nothing but *self*. . Being fond of calculating the effects of poison, I essayed one, which I had composed, upon a youth who had offended me; he lingered a month, and then expired in agonies the most terrific. It was returning from his funeral, which all the students of the college where I received my education (Salamanca) had attended, that a train of the strangest thought pressed upon my mind. I feared, more than ever, now, to die; and, although I had no right to form hopes or expecta-

tions for longer life than is allotted to the rest of
mortals, yet did I think it were possible to protract
existence. And why, reasoned I with myself, relapsing
into melancholy, why am I to suppose that these
muscles or fibres are made of stuff more durable than
those of other men? I have no right to suppose otherwise than that, at the end of the time allotted by
nature, for the existence of the atoms which compose my
being, I must, like all other men, perish, perhaps ever-
lastingly. Here, in the bitterness of my heart, I cursed
that nature and chance which I believed in ; and, in a
paroxysmal frenzy of contending passions, cast myself,
in desperation, at the foot of a lofty ash-tree, which
reared its fantastic form over a torrent which dashed
below.

"It was midnight; far had I wandered from Salamanca; the passions which agitated my brain, almost
to delirium, had added strength to my nerves, and
swiftness to my feet; but, after many hours' incessant
walking, I began to feel fatigued. No moon was up,
nor did one star illume the hemisphere. The sky was
veiled by a thick covering of clouds; and, to my
heated imagination, the winds, which in stern cadence
swept along the night-scene, whistled tidings of death
and annihilation. I gazed on the torrent, foaming
beneath my feet; it could scarcely be distinguished
through the thickness of the gloom, save at intervals,
when the white-crested waves dashed at the base of the
bank on which I stood. 'Twas then that I contemplated self-destruction ; I had almost plunged into the
tide of death, had rushed upon the unknown regions of
eternity, when the soft sound of a bell from a neighbouring convent, was wafted in the stillness of the night.
It struck a chord in unison with my soul ; it vibrated
on the secret springs of rapture. I thought no more
of suicide, but, reseating myself at the root of the ash-
tree, burst into a flood of tears ;—never had I wept

before; the sensation was new to me; it was inexplicably pleasing. I reflected by what rules of science I could account for it : *there* philosophy failed me. I acknowledged its inefficacy; and, almost at *that* instant, allowed the existence of a superior and beneficent *Spirit*, in whose image is made the soul of man ; but quickly chasing these ideas, and, overcome by excessive and unwonted fatigue of mind and body, I laid my head upon a jutting projection of the tree, and, forgetful of every thing around me, sank into a profound and quiet slumber. Quiet, did I say? No—It was not quiet. I dreamed that I stood on the brink of a most terrific precipice, far, far above the clouds, amid whose dark forms which lowered beneath, was seen the dashing of a stupendous cataract : its roarings were borne to mine ear by the blast of night. Above me rose, fearfully embattled and rugged, fragments of enormous rocks, tinged by the dimly gleaming moon ; their loftiness, the grandeur of their misshapen proportions, and their bulk, staggering the imagination ; and scarcely could the mind itself scale the vast loftiness of their aërial summits. I saw the dark clouds pass by, borne by the impetuosity of the blast, yet felt no wind myself. Methought darkly gleaming forms rode on their almost palpable prominences.

" Whilst thus I stood, gazing on the expansive gulf which yawned before me, methought a silver sound stole on the quietude of night. The moon became as bright as polished silver, and each star sparkled with scintillations of inexpressible whiteness. Pleasing images stole imperceptibly upon my senses, when a ravishingly sweet strain of dulcet melody seemed to float around. Now it was wafted nearer, and now it died away in tones to melancholy dear. Whilst I thus stood enraptured, louder swelled the strain of seraphic harmony ; it vibrated on my inmost soul, and a mysterious softness lulled each impetuous passion to repose. I

gazed in eager anticipation of curiosity on the scene
before me; for a mist of silver radiance rendered every
object but myself imperceptible; yet was it brilliant as
the noon-day sun.   Suddenly, whilst yet the full strain
swelled along the empyrean sky, the mist in one place
seemed to dispart, and through it, to roll clouds of
deepest crimson.   Above them, and seemingly reclining
on the viewless air, was a form of most exact and
superior symmetry.   Rays of brilliancy, surpassing expression, fell from his burning eye, and the emanations
from his countenance tinted the transparent clouds below with silver light.   The phantasm advanced towards
me; it seemed then, to my imagination, that his figure ·
was borne on the sweet strain of music which filled
the circumambient air.   In a voice which was fascination itself, the being addressed me, saying, 'Wilt
thou come with me? wilt thou be mine?'   I felt a
decided wish never to be his.   'No, no,' I unhesitatingly cried, with a feeling which no language can
either explain or describe.   No sooner had I uttered
these words, than methought a sensation of deadly
horror chilled my sickening frame; an earthquake
rocked the precipice beneath my feet; the beautiful
being vanished; clouds, as of chaos, rolled around,
and from their dark masses flashed incessant meteors.
I heard a deafening noise on every side; it appeared
like the dissolution of nature; the blood-red moon,
whirled from her sphere, sank beneath the horizon.
My neck was grasped firmly, and, turning round in an
agony of horror, I beheld a form more hideous than
the imagination of man is capable of portraying, whose
proportions, gigantic and deformed, were seemingly
blackened by the inerasible traces of the thunderbolts
of God; yet in its hideous and detestable countenance,
though seemingly far different, I thought I could recognize that of the lovely vision: 'Wretch!' it exclaimed,
in a voice of exulting thunder; 'saidst thou that thou

wouldst not be mine? Ah! thou art mine beyond
redemption; and I triumph in the conviction, that no
power can ever make thee otherwise. Say, art thou
willing to be mine?' Saying this, he dragged me to
the brink of the precipice : the contemplation of approaching death frenzied my brain to the highest pitch
of horror. 'Yes, yes, I am thine,' I exclaimed. No
sooner had I pronounced these words than the visionary
scene vanished, and I awoke. But even when awake,
the contemplation of what I had suffered, whilst under
the influence of sleep, pressed upon my disordered
fancy; my intellect, wild with unconquerable emotions,
could fix on no one particular point to exert its energies; they were strained beyond their power of
exerting.

"Ever, from that day, did a deep-corroding melancholy usurp the throne of my soul. At last, during
the course of my philosophical inquiries, I ascertained
the method by which *man* might exist for ever, and it
was connected with my dream. It would unfold a
tale of too much horror to trace, in review, the circumstances as then they occurred ; suffice it to say, that I
became acquainted that a *superior* being really exists :
and ah! how dear a price have I paid for the knowledge! To one man alone, Wolfstein, may I communicate this secret of immortal life : then must I forego
my claim to it,—and oh! with what pleasure shall I
forego it! To you I bequeath the secret; but first
you must swear that if . . . . you wish God
may . . . ."

" I swear," cried Wolfstein, in a transport of delight;
burning ecstasy revelled through his veins ; pleasurable
coruscations were emitted from his eyes. "I swear,"
continued he; "and if ever . . . . . may
God . . . ."

"Needless were it for me," continued Ginotti, "to
expatiate further upon the *means* which I have used

to become master over your every action; that will be sufficiently explained when you have followed my directions. Take," continued Ginotti, "——— and ——— and ———; mix them according to the directions which this book will communicate to you. Seek, at midnight, the ruined abbey near the castle of St. Irvyne, in France; and there—I need say no more —there you will meet with me."

CHAPTER XI.

THE varying occurrences of time and change, which bring anticipation of better days, brought none to the hapless Eloise. Nempere now having gained the point which his villainy had projected, felt little or no attachment left for the unhappy victim of his baseness; he treated her indeed most cruelly, and his unkindness added greatly to the severity of her afflictions. One day, when, weighed down by the extreme asperity of her woes, Eloise sat leaning her head on her hand, and mentally retracing, in sickening and mournful review, the concatenated occurrences which had led her to become what she was, she sought to change the bent of her ideas, but in vain. The feelings of her soul were but exacerbated by the attempt to quell them. Her dear brother's death, that brother so tenderly beloved, added a sting to her sensations. Was there any one on earth to whom she was now attracted by a wish of pouring in the friend's bosom ideas and feelings indefinable to any one else? Ah, no! that friend existed not; never, never more would she know such a friend. Never did she really love any one; and now had she sacrificed her conviction oi right and wrong to a man who neither knew how to appreciate her excellence, nor was adequate to excite other sensation than of terror and dread.

Thus were her thoughts engaged, when Nempere entered the apartment, accompanied by a gentleman, whom he unceremoniously announced as the Chevalier Mountfort, an Englishman of rank, and his friend. He was a man of handsome countenance and engaging manners. He conversed with Eloise with an ill-disguised conviction of his own superiority, and seemed indeed to assert, as it were, a right of conversing with her ; nor did Nempere appear to dispute his apparent assumption. The conversation turned upon music ; Mountfort asked Eloise her opinion ; "Oh !" said Eloise, enthusiastically, "I think it sublimes the soul to heaven ; I think it is, of all earthly pleasures, the most excessive. Who, when listening to harmoniously-arranged sounds of music, exists there, but must forget his woes, and lose the memory of every earthly existence in the ecstatic emotions which it excites ? Do you not think so, Chevalier ?" said she ; for the liveliness of his manner enchanted Eloise, whose temper, naturally elastic and sprightly, had been damped as yet by misery and seclusion. Mountfort smiled at the energetic avowal of her feelings ; for, whilst she yet spoke, her expressive countenance became irradiated by the emanation of sentiment.

"Yes," said Mountfort, "it is indeed powerfully efficient to excite the interests of the soul ; but does it not, by the very act of resuscitating the feelings, by working upon the, perhaps, long dead chords of secret and enthusiastic rapture, awaken the powers of grief as well as pleasure ?"

"Ah ! it may do both," said Eloise, sighing.

He approached her at that instant. Nempere arose, as if intentionally, and left the room. Mountfort pressed her hand to his heart with earnestness : he kissed it, and then resigning it, said, "No, no, spotless un

tainted Eloise; untainted even by surrounding depravity : not for worlds would I injure you. Oh! I
can conceal it no longer—will conceal it no longer—
Nempere is a villain."

"Is he?" said Eloise, apparently resigned, *now*, to
the severest shocks of fortune : "then, then indeed I
know not with whom to seek an asylum.　Methinks all
are villains."

"Listen then, injured innocence, and reflect in whom
thou hast confided.　Ten dáys ago, in the gaming-
house at Geneva, Nempere was present.　He engaged
in play with me, and I won of him considerable sums.
He told me that he could not pay me now, but that
he had a beautiful girl, whom he would give to me, if I
would release him from the obligation.　'Est elle une
fille de joie?' I inquired.　'Oui, et de vertu prati-
cable.'　This quieted my conscience.　In a moment of
licentiousness, I acceded to his proposal ; and, as
money is almost valueless to me, I tore the bond for
three thousand zechins : but did I think that an angel
was to be sacrificed to the degraded avarice of the being
to whom her fate was committed?　By heavens, I will
this moment seek him—upbraid him with his inhuman
depravity,—and——" "Oh! stop, stop," cried Eloise,
"do not seek him ; all, all is well—I will leave him.
Oh! how I thank you, stranger, for this unmerited pity
to a wretch who is, alas! too conscious that she deserves it not."—"Ah! you deserve every thing," interrupted the impassioned Mountfort; "you deserve
paradise.　But leave this perjured ,villain ; and do not
say, unkind fair-one, that you have no friend : indeed,
you have a most warm, disinterested friend in me."—
"Ah! but," said Eloise, hesitatingly, "what will
the——"

"World say," she was about to have added; but the
conviction of having so lately and so flagrantly violated
every regard to its opinion—she only sighed.　"Well,"

continued Mountfort, as if not perceiving her hesitation; "you will accompany me to a cottage ornée, which I possess at some little distance hence? Believe that your situation shall be treated with the deference which it requires; and, however I may have yielded to habitual licentiousness, I have too much honour to disturb the sorrows of one who is a victim to that of another." Licentious and free as had been the career of Mountfort's life, it was by no means the result of a nature naturally prone to vice; it had been owing to the unchecked sallies of an imagination not sufficiently refined. At the desolate situation of Eloise, however, every good propensity in his nature urged him to take compassion on her. His heart, originally susceptible of the finest feelings, was touched, and he really and sincerely—yes, a libertine, but not one from principle, sincerely meant what he said.

"Thanks, generous stranger," said Eloise, with energy; "indeed I *do* thank you." For not yet had acquaintance with the world sufficiently bidden Eloise distrust the motives of its disciples. "I accept your offer, and only hope that my compliance may not induce you to regard me otherwise than I am."

"Never, never can I regard you as other than a suffering angel," replied the impassioned Mountfort. Eloise blushed at what the energetic force of Mountfort's manner assured her was not intended as a compliment.

"But may I ask my generous benefactor, *how, where,* and *when* am I to be released?"

"Leave that to me," returned Mountfort: "be ready to-morrow night at ten o'clock. A chaise will wait beneath."

Nempere soon entered; their conversation was uninterrupted, and the evening passed away uninteresting and slow.

Swiftly fled the intervening hours, and fast advanced

the moment when Eloise was about to try, again, the
compassion of the world.   Night came, and Eloise
entered the chaise ; Mountfort leaped in after her.
For awhile her agitation was excessive.   Mountfort at
last succeeded in calming her ; " Why, my dearest
Ma'am'selle," said he, " why will you thus needlessly
agitate yourself ?   I *swear* to hold your honour far
dearer than my own life ; and my companion ——"
   " What companion ?" Eloise interrupted him, inquiringly.

   " Why," replied he, " a friend of mine, who lives at
my cottage ; he is an Irishman, and so *very* moral, and
so averse to every species of *gaieté de cœur*, that you
need be under no apprehensions.   In short, he is a
love-sick swain, without ever having found what he
calls a *congenial* female.   He wanders about, writes
poetry, and, in short, is much *too sentimental* to occasion
you any alarm on that account.   And, I assure you,'
added he, assuming a more serious tone, " although I
may not be quite so far gone in romance, yet I have
feelings of honour and humanity which teach me to
respect your sorrows as my own."

   " Indeed, indeed I believe you, generous stranger ;
nor do I think that you *could* have a friend whose
principles are dishonourable."

   Whilst yet she spoke, the chaise stopped, and
Mountfort springing from it, handed Eloise into his
habitation.   It was neatly fitted up in the English
taste.

   " Fitzeustace," said Mountfort to his friend, " allow
me to introduce you to Madame Eloise de ——"
Eloise blushed, as did Fitzeustace.

   " Come," said Fitzeustace, to conquer *mauvaise honte,*
" supper is ready, and the lady doubtlessly ıatigued."

   Fitzeustace was finely formed, yet there was a languor
which pervaded even his whole figure : his eyes were
dark and expressive, and as, occasionally, they met

those of Eloise, gleamed with excessive brilliancy, awakened doubtlessly by curiosity and interest. He said but little during supper, and left to his more vivacious friend the whole of Eloise's conversation, who, animated at having escaped a persecutor, and one she hated, displayed extreme command of social powers. Yes, once again was Eloise vivacious : the sweet spirit of social intercourse was not dead within,—that spirit which illumes even slavery, which makes its horrors less terrific, and is not annihilated in the dungeon itself.

At last arrived the hour of retiring.—Morning came.

The cottage was situated in a beautiful valley. The odorous perfume of roses and jasmine wafted on the zephyr's wing, the flowery steep which rose before it, and the umbrageous loveliness of the surrounding country, rendered it a spot the most fitted for joyous seclusion. Eloise wandered out with Mountfort and his friend to view it ; and so accommodating was her spirit, that, ere long, Fitzeustace became known to her as familiarly as if they had been acquainted all their lives.

Time fled on, and each day seemed only to succeed the other purposely to vary the pleasures of this delightful retreat. Eloise sung in the summer evenings, and Fitzeustace, whose taste for music was most exquisite, accompanied her on his oboe.

By degrees the society of Fitzeustace, to which before she had preferred Mountfort's, began to be more interesting. He insensibly acquired a power over the heart of Eloise, which she herself was not aware of. She involuntarily almost sought his society ; and when, which frequently happened, Mountfort was absent at Geneva, her sensations were indescribably ecstatic in the society of his friend. She sat in mute, in silent rapture, listening to the notes of his oboe, as they floated on

I.   O the stillness of evening : she feared not for the future, but, as it were, in a dream of rapturous delight, supposed that she must ever be as now—happy ; not reflecting that, were he who caused that happiness absent, it would exist no longer.

Fitzeustace madly, passionately doted on Eloise ; in all the energy of incontaminated nature, he sought but the happiness of the object of his whole affections. He sought not to investigate the causes of his woe ; sufficient was it for him to have found one who could *understand*, could *sympathize in*, the feelings and sensations which every child of nature, whom the world's refinements and luxury have not vitiated, must feel,— that affection, that contempt of selfish gratification, which every one, whose soul towers at all above the multitude, must acknowledge. He destined Eloise, in his secret soul, for his own. He resolved to die—he wished to live with her; and would have purchased one instant's happiness for her with ages of hopeless torments to be inflicted on himself. He loved her with passionate and excessive tenderness: were he absent from her but a moment, he would sigh with love's impatience for her return ; yet he feared to avow his flame, lest this, perhaps, baseless dream of rapturous and enthusiastic happiness might fade ;—then, indeed, Fitzeustace felt that he must die.

Yet was Fitzeustace mistaken : Eloise loved him with all the tenderness of innocence ; she confided in him unreservedly ; and, though unconscious of the nature of the love she felt for him, returned each enthusiastically energetic prepossession of his towering mind with ardour excessive and unrestrained. Yet did Fitzeustace suppose that she loved him not. Ah ! why did he think so ?

Late one evening, Mountfort had gone to Geneva, and Fitzeustace wandered with Eloise towards that spot which Eloise selected as their constant evening ramble

on account of its superior beauty. The tall ash and
oak, in mingled umbrage, sighed far above their heads;
beneath them were walks, artificially cut, yet imitating
nature. They wandered on, till they came to a pavilion
which Mountfort had caused to be erected. It was
situated on a piece of land entirely surrounded by water,
yet peninsulated by a rustic bridge which joined it to
the walk.

Hither, urged mechanically, for their thoughts were
otherwise employed, wandered Eloise and Fitzeustace.
Before them hung the moon in cloudless majesty ; her
orb was reflected by every movement of the crystalline
water, which, agitated by the gentle zephyr, rolled tranquilly. Heedless yet of the beauties of nature, the
loveliness of the scene, they entered the pavilion.

Eloise convulsively pressed her hand on her forehead.

" What is the matter, my dearest Eloise ? " inquired
Fitzeustace, whom awakened tenderness had thrown off
his guard.

" Oh ! nothing, nothing ; but a momentary faintness.
It will soon go off ; let us sit down."

They entered the pavilion.

" 'Tis nothing but drowsiness," said Eloise, affecting
gaiety; " 'twill soon go off. I sate up late last night ;
that I believe was the occasion."

" Recline on this sofa, then," said Fitzeustace, reaching another pillow to make the couch easier; " and I
will play some of those Irish tunes which you admire
so much."

Eloise reclined on the sofa, and Fitzeustace, seated
on the floor, began to play ; the melancholy plaintive-
ness of his music touched Eloise ; she sighed, and
concealed her tears in her handkerchief. At length she
sunk into a profound sleep : still Fitzeustace continued
playing, noticing not that she slumbered. He now per-

ceived that she spoke, but in so low a tone, that he knew she slept.

He approached. She lay wrapped in sleep ; a sweet and celestial smile played upon her countenance, and irradiated her features with a tenfold expression of etheriality. Suddenly the visions of her slumbers appeared to have changed ; the smile yet remained, but its expression was melancholy; tears stole gently from under her eyelids :—she sighed.

Ah ! with what eagerness of ecstasy did Fitzeustace lean over her form ! He dared not speak, he dared not move ; but pressing a ringlet of hair which had escaped its band, to his lips, waited silently.

"Yes, yes ; I think—it may——" at last she muttered ; but so confusedly, as scarcely to be distinguishable.

Fitzeustace remained rooted in rapturous attention, listening.

"I thought, I thought he looked as if he could love me," scarcely articulated the sleeping Eloise. "Perhaps, though he may not love me, he may allow me to love him.—Fitzeustace ! "

On a sudden, again were changed the visions of her slumbers ; terrified she started from sleep, and cried, "Fitzeustace ! "

CHAPTER XII.

For love is heaven, and heaven is love.
                    LAY OF THE LAST MINSTREL.

NEEDLESS were it to expatiate on their transports ; they loved each other, and that is enough for those who have felt like Eloise and Fitzeustace.

One night, rather later indeed than it was Mountfort's custom to return from Geneva, Eloise and Fitz-eustace sat awaiting his arrival. At last it was too late any longer even to expect him; and Eloise was about to bid Fitzeustace good-night, when a knock at the door aroused them. Instantly, with a hurried and disordered step, his clothes stained with blood, his countenance convulsed and pallid as death, in rushed Mountfort.

An involuntary exclamation of surprise burst from the terrified Eloise.

"What—what is the matter?"

"Oh, nothing, nothing!" answered Mountfort, in a tone of hurried, yet desperate agony. The wildness of his looks contradicted his assertions. Fitzeustace, who had been inquiring whether he was wounded, on finding that he was not, flew to Eloise.

"Oh! go, go!" she exclaimed. "Something, I am convinced, is wrong. Tell me, dear Mountfort, what it is—in pity tell me."

"Nempere is dead!" replied Mountfort, in a voice of deliberate desperation; then, pausing for an instant, he added in an under tone: "And the officers of justice are in pursuit of me. Adieu, Eloise!—Adieu, Fitz-eustace! You know I must part with you—you know how unwillingly. My address is at—London.—Adieu! —once again adieu!"

Saying this, as by a convulsive effort of despairing energy, he darted from the apartment, and, mounting a horse which stood at the gate, swiftly sped away. Fitz-eustace well knew the impossibility of his longer stay; he did not seem surprised, but sighed.

"Ah! well I know," said Eloise, violently agitated, "I well know myself to be the occasion of these mis-fortunes. Nempere sought for me; the generous Mountfort would not give me up; and now is he com-pelled to fly—perhaps may not even escape with life. Ah! I fear it is destined that every friend must suffer in the fatality which environs me. Fitzeustace!" she

uttered this with such tenderness, that, almost involuntarily, he clasped her hand, and pressed it to his bosom,
in the silent, yet expressive enthusiasm of love. "Fitzeustace! you will not likewise desert the poor isolated
Eloise ?"

"Say not isolated, dearest love. Can, can you fear
my love, whilst your Fitzeustace exists? Say, adored
Eloise, shall we *now* be united, *never, never* to part
again? Say, will you consent to our immediate union?

"Know you not," exclaimed Eloise, in a low, faltering voice, "know you not that I *have been* another's?"

"Oh! suppose me not," interrupted the impassioned
Fitzeustace, "the slave of such vulgar and narrow-
minded prejudice. Does the frightful vice and ingratitude of Nempere sully the spotless excellence of my
Eloise's soul? No, no,—that must ever continue un-
contaminated by the frailty of the body in which it is
enshrined. It must rise superior to the earth : 'tis that
which I adore, Eloise. Say, say, was *that* Nempere's?"

"Oh! no, never!" cried Eloise, with energy. "Nothing but *fear* was Nempere's."

"Then why say you that ever you were *his?*" said
Fitzeustace, reproachfully. "You never *could* have
been his, destined as you were for mine, from the first
instant the particles composing the soul which I adore,
were assimilated by the God whom I worship."

"Indeed, believe me, dearest Fitzeustace, I love you,
far beyond anything existing—indeed, existence were
valueless, unless enjoyed with you!"

Eloise, though a *something* prevented her from
avowing them, *felt* the enthusiastic and sanguine ideas
of Fitzeustace to be true : her soul, susceptible of the
most exalted virtue and expansion, though cruelly nipped
in its growth, thrilled with delight unexperienced before, when she found a being who could understand
and perceive the truth of her feelings, and indeed *anticipate* them, as did Fitzeustace ; and *he*, while gazing

on the index of that soul, which associated with his, and animated the body of Eloise, but for him, felt delight, which, glowing and enthusiastic as had been his picture of happiness, he never expected to know. His dark and beautiful eye gleamed with tenfold lustre; his every nerve, his every pulse, confessed the awakened consciousness, that *she*, on whom his soul had doted, ever since he acknowledged the existence of his intellectuality, was present before him.

A short space of time passed, and Eloise gave birth to the son of Nempere. Fitzeustace cherished it with the affection of a father; and, when occasionally he necessarily must be absent from the apartment of his beloved Eloise, his whole delight was to gaze on the child, and trace in its innocent countenance the features of the mother who was so beloved by him.

Time no longer dragged heavily to Eloise and Fitzeustace: happy in the society of each other, they wished nor wanted other joys; united by the laws of their God, and assimilated by congeniality of sentiment, they supposed that each succeeding month must be like this, must pass like this, in the full satiety of every innocent union of mental enjoyment. While thus the time sped in rapturous succession of delight, autumn advanced.

The evening was late, when, at the usual hour, Eloise and Fitzeustace took the way to their beloved pavilion. Fitzeustace was unusually desponding, and his ideas for futurity were marked by the melancholy of his mind. Eloise in vain attempted to soothe him; the contention of his mind was but too visible. She led him to the pavilion. They entered it. The autumnal moon had risen; her dimly-gleaming orb, scarcely now visible, was shrouded in the darkness of the atmosphere: like the spirit of the spotless ether, which shrinks from the obtrusive gaze of man, she hung behind a leaden-coloured cloud. The wind in low and melancholy whispering sighed among the branches of the towering trees; the melody of the nightingale, which floated upon its dying cadences, alone broke on the solemnity of the scene. Lives there, whose soul experiences no degree of delight, is susceptible of no gradations of feelings, at change of scenery? Lives there, who can listen to the cadence of the evening zephyr, and not acknowledge, in his mind, the sensations of celestial melancholy which it awakens? for, if he does, his life were valueless, his death were undeplored. Ambition, avarice, ten thousand mean, ignoble passions, had extinguished within him that soft, but indefinable sensorium of unallayed delight, with which his soul, whose susceptibility is not destroyed hy the demands of selfish appetite, thrills exultingly, and wants but the union of another, of whom the feelings are in unison with his own, to constitute almost insupportable delight.

Let Epicureans argue, and say, " There is no pleasure but in the gratification of the senses." Let them enjoy their own opinion; I want not *pleasure*, when I can enjoy *happiness*. Let Stoics say, "Every idea that there are fine feelings, is weak; he who yields to them is even weaker." Let those too, wise in their own conceit, indulge themselves in sordid and degrading hypotheses; let them suppose human nature capable of no influence from any thing but materiality; so long as I enjoy the innocent and *congenial* delight, which it were needless to define to those who are strangers to it, I am satisfied.

"Dear Fitzeustace," said Eloise, "tell me what afflicts you; why are you so melancholy?—Do not we mutually love, and have we not the unrestrained enjoyment of each other's society?"

Fitzeustace sighed deeply; he pressed Eloise's hand. "Why does my dearest Eloise suppose that I am unhappy?" The tone of his voice was tremulous, and a deadly settled paleness dwelt on his cheek.

"Are you not unhappy, then, Fitzeustace?"

"I know I ought not to be so," he replied, with a faint smile;—he paused—"Eloise," continued Fitzeustace, "I know I ought not to grieve, but you will, perhaps, pardon me when I say, that a father's curse, whether from the prejudice of education, or the innate consciousness of its horror, agitates my mind. I cannot leave you, I cannot go to England; and will you then leave your country, Eloise, to accommodate me? No, I do not, I ought not to expect it."

"Oh! with pleasure; what is country? what is everything without you? Come, my love, dismiss these fears, we yet may be happy."

"But before we go to England, before my father will see us, it is necessary that we should be married—nay, do not start, Eloise; I view it in the light that you do: I consider it an human institution, and incapable of furnishing that bond of union by which alone can intellect be conjoined; I regard it as but a chain, which, although it keeps the body bound, still leaves the soul unfettered : it is not so with love. But still, Eloise, to those who think like us, it is at all events harmless; it is but yielding to the prejudices of the world wherein we live, and procuring moral expediency, at a slight sacrifice of what we conceive to be right."

"Well, well, it shall be done, Fitzeustace," resumed Eloise ; "but take the assurance of *my* promise that I cannot love you more."

They soon agreed on a point of, in their eyes, so trifling importance, and arriving in England, tasted that happiness, which love and innocence alone can give. Prejudice may triumph for awhile, but virtue will be eventually the conqueror.

CONCLUSION.

T was night—all was still: not a breeze dared to move, not a sound to break the stillness of horror. Wolfstein has arrived at the village near which St. Irvyne stood ; he has sped him to the château, and has entered the edifice ; the garden door was open, and he entered the vaults.

For a time, the novelty of his situation, and the painful recurrence of past events, which, independently of his own energies, would gleam upon his soul, rendered him too much confused to investigate minutely the recesses of the cavern. Arousing himself, at last, however, from this momentary suspension of faculty, he paced the vaults in eager desire for the arrival of midnight. How inexpressible was his horror when he fell on a body which appeared motionless and without life ! He raised it in his arms, and, taking it to the light, beheld, pallid in death, the features of Megalena. The laugh of anguish which had convulsed her expiring frame, still played around her mouth, as a smile of horror and despair; her hair was loose and wild, seemingly gathered in knots by the convulsive grasp of dissolution. She moved not ; his soul was nerved by almost superhuman powers ; yet the ice of despair chilled his burning brain. Curiosity, resistless curiosity, even in a moment such as this, reigned in his bosom. The body of Megalena was breathless, and yet no visible cause could be assigned for her death. Wolfstein dashed the body convulsively on the earth, and, wildered by the suscitated energies of his soul almost to madness, rushed into the vaults.

Not yet had the bell announced the hour of midnight. Wolfstein sate on a projecting mass of stone ; his frame trembled with a burning anticipation of what was about to occur ; a thirst of knowledge scorched

his soul to madness; yet he stilled his wild energies,—
yet he awaited in silence the coming of Ginotti. At
last the bell struck; Ginotti came; his step was
rapid, and his manner wild; his figure was wasted
almost to a skeleton, yet it retained its loftiness and
grandeur; still from his eye emanated that indefinable expression which ever made Wolfstein shrink
appalled. His cheek was sunken and hollow, yet was
it flushed by the hectic of despairing exertion. "Wolfstein," he said, "Wolfstein, part is past—the hour of
agonizing horror is past; yet the dark and icy gloom
of desperation braces this soul to fortitude;—but come,
let us to business." He spoke, and threw his mantle
on the ground. "I am blasted to endless torment,"
muttered the mysterious. "Wolfstein, dost thou deny
thy Creator?"—"Never, never."—"Wilt thou not?"
—"No, no,—anything but that."

Deeper grew the gloom of the cavern. Darkness
almost visible seemed to press around them; yet did
the scintillations which flashed from Ginotti's burning
gaze dance on its bosom. Suddenly a flash of lightning
hissed through the lengthened vaults; a burst of
frightful thunder seemed to convulse the universal
fabric of nature; and, borne on the pinions of hell's
sulphurous whirlwind, he himself, the frightful prince
of terror, stood before them. "Yes," howled a voice
superior to the bursting thunder-peal; "yes, thou shalt
have eternal life, Ginotti." On a sudden Ginotti's frame
mouldered to a gigantic skeleton, yet two pale and
ghastly flames glared in his eyeless sockets. Blackened
in terrible convulsions, Wolfstein expired; over him
had the power of hell no influence. Yes, endless
existence is thine, Ginotti—a dateless and hopeless ·
eternity of horror.

*   *   *   *   *   *

Ginotti is Nempere. Eloise is the sister of Wolfstein.
Let then the memory of these victims to hell and malice

live in the remembrance of those who can pity the wanderings of error; let remorse and repentance expiate the offences which arise from the delusion of the passions, and let endless life be sought from Him who alone can give an eternity of happiness.

AN ADDRESS,

TO THE

IRISH PEOPLE.

BY PERCY BYSSHE SHELLEY.

ADVERTISEMENT.

The lowest possible price is set on this publication, because it is the intention of the Author to awaken in the minds of the Irish poor, a knowledge of their real state, summarily pointing out the evils of that state, and suggesting rational means of remedy.—Catholic Emancipation, and a Repeal of the Union Act, (the latter, the most successful engine that England ever wielded over the misery of fallen Ireland,) being treated of in the following address, as grievances which unanimity and resolution may remove, and associations conducted with peaceable firmness, being earnestly recommended, as means for embodying that unanimity and firmness, which must finally be successful.

Dublin:

1812.
*Price—*5*d.*

AN ADDRESS TO THE IRISH PEOPLE.

ELLOW MEN,—I am not an Irishman, yet I can feel for you. I hope there are none among you who will read this address with prejudice or levity, because it is made by an Englishman ; indeed, I believe there are not. The Irish are a brave nation. They have a heart of liberty in their breasts, but they are much mistaken if they fancy that a stranger cannot have as warm a one. Those are my brothers and my countrymen who are unfortunate. I should like to know what there is in a man being an Englishman, a Spaniard, or a Frenchman that makes him worse or better than he really is. He was born in one town, you in another, but that is no reason why he should not feel for you, desire your benefit, or be willing to give you some advice, which may make you more capable of knowing your own interest, or acting so as to secure it. There are many Englishmen who cry down the Irish, and think it answers their ends to revile all that belongs to Ireland : but it is not because these men are Englishmen that they maintain such opinions, but because they wish to get money, and titles, and power. They would act in this manner to whatever country they might belong, until mankind is much altered for the better, which reform, I hope, will one day be effected. I address you, then, as my brothers and my fellow-men, for I should wish to see the Irishman who, if England was persecuted as Ireland is, who, if France was persecuted as Ireland is, who, if any set of men that helped to do a public service, were prevented from enjoying its benefits as Irishmen are—I should like to see the man, I say, who would see these misfortunes, and not attempt to succour the sufferers when he could, just that I might tell him that he was no Irishman, but some bastard mongrel bred up in a court, or some coward fool who was a democrat to all above him, and an aristocrat to all below him. I think there are few true Irishmen who would not be ashamed of such a character, still fewer who possess it. I know that there are some, not among you, my friends, but among your enemies, who, seeing the title of this piece, will take it up with a sort of hope that it may recommend violent measures, and thereby disgrace the cause of freedom, that the warmth of an heart desirous that liberty should be possessed equally by all, will vent itself in abuse on the enemies of liberty, bad men who deserve the contempt of the good, and ought not to excite their indignation to the harm of their cause. But these men will be disappointed—I know the warm feelings of an Irishman sometimes carries him beyond the point of prudence. I do not desire to root out, but to moderate this honourable warmth. This will disappoint the pioneers of oppression, and they will be sorry that through this address nothing will occur which can be twisted into any other meaning but what is calculated to fill you with that moderation which they have not, and make you give them that toleration which they refuse to grant to you. You profess the Roman Catholic religion which your fathers professed before you. Whether it is the best religion or not, I will not here inquire : all religions are good which make men good; and the way that a person ought to prove that his method of worshipping God is best, is for himself to be better than all other men. But we will consider what your religion was in old times and what it is now; you may say it is not a fair way for me to proceed as a Protestant, but I am not a Protestant nor am I a Catholic, and therefore not being a follower of either of these religions, I am better able to judge between them. A Protestant is my brother, and a Catholic is my brother. I am happy when I can do either of them a service, and no pleasure is so great to me than that which I should feel if my advice could make men of any professions of faith, wiser, better, and happier.

The Roman Catholics once persecuted the Protestants, the Protestants now persecute the Roman Catholics. Should we think that one is as bad as the other? No, you are not answerable for the faults of your fathers any more than the Protestants are good for the goodness of their fathers. I must judge of people as I see them; the Irish Catholics are badly used. I will not endeavour to hide from them their wretchedness; they would think that I mocked at them if I should make the attempt. The Irish Catholics now demand for themselves and proffer for others unlimited toleration, and the sensible part among them, which I am willing to think constitutes a very large portion of their body, know that the gates of Heaven are open to people of every religion, provided they are good. But the Protestants, although they may think so in their hearts, which certainly, if they think at all, they must seem to act as if they thought that God was better pleased with them than with you; they trust the reins of earthly government only to the hands of their own sect. In spite of this, I never found one of them impudent enough to say that a Roman Catholic, or a Quaker, or a Jew, or a Mahometan, if he was a virtuous man, and did all the good in his power, would go to Heaven a bit the slower for not subscribing to the thirty-nine articles—and if he should say so, how ridiculous in a foppish courtier not six feet high to direct the spirit of universal harmony in what manner to conduct the affairs of the universe !

I.   P

The Protestants say that there was a time when the Roman Catholics burnt and murdered people of different sentiments, and that their religious tenets are now as they were then. This is all very true. You certainly worship God in the same way that you did when these barbarities took place, but is that any reason that you should now be barbarous? There is as much reason to suppose it as to suppose that because a man's great-grandfather, who was a Jew, had been hung for sheep-stealing, that I, by believing the same religion as he did, must certainly commit the same crime. Let us then see what the Roman Catholic religion has been. No one knows much of the early times of the Christian religion until about three hundred years after its beginning ; two great Churches, called the Roman and the Greek Churches, divided the opinions of men. They fought for a very long time—a great many words were wasted, and a great deal of blood shed.

This, as you may suppose, did no good. Each party, however, thought they were doing God a service, and that he would reward them. If they had looked an inch before their noses, they might have found that fighting and killing men, and cursing them and hating them, was the very worst way for getting into favour with a Being who is allowed by all to be best pleased with deeds of love and charity. At last, however, these two religions entirely separated, and the popes reigned like kings and bishops at Rome, in Italy. The Inquisition was set up, and in the course of one year 30,000 people were burnt in Italy and Spain for entertaining different opinions from those of the pope and the priests. There was an instance of shocking barbarity which the Roman Catholic clergy committed in France by order of the pope. The bigoted monks of that country, in cold blood, in one night massacred 80,000 Protestants; this was done under the authority of the Pope, and there was only one Roman Catholic bishop who had virtue enough to refuse to help. The vices of monks and nuns in their convents were in those times shameful. People thought that they might commit any sin, however monstrous, if they had money enough to prevail upon the priests to absolve them. In truth, at that time the priests shamefully imposed upon the people; they got all the power into their own hands; they persuaded them that a man could not be entrusted with the care of his own soul, and by cunningly obtaining possession of their secrets, they became more powerful than kings, princes, dukes, lords, or ministers. This power made them bad men; for although rational people are very good in their natural state, there are now, and ever have been, very few whose good dispositions despotic power does not destroy. I have now given a fair description of what your religion was; and, Irishmen, my brothers, will you make your friend appear a liar, when he takes upon himself to say for you that you are not now what the professors of the same faith were in times of yore? Do I speak false when I say that the Inquisition is the object of your hatred? Am I a liar if I assert that an Irishman prizes liberty dearly, that he will preserve that right, and if it be wrong, does not dream that money can give to a priest, or the talking of another man erring like himself, can in the least influence the judgment of the eternal God? I am not a liar if I affirm in your name, that you believe a Protestant equally with yourself to be worthy of the kingdom of Heaven, if he be equally virtuous, that you will treat men as brethren wherever you may find them, and that difference of opinion in religious matters shall not, does not, in the least on your part obstruct the most perfect harmony on every other subject. Ah! no, Irishmen, I am not a liar. I seek your confidence, not that I may betray it, but that I may teach you to be happy and wise and good. If you will not repose any trust in me I shall lament; but I will do everything in my power that is honourable, fair, and open to gain it. Some teach you that others are heretics, that you alone are right; some teach that rectitude consists in religious opinions, without which no morality is good. Some will tell you that you ought to divulge your secrets to one particular set of men. Beware, my friends, how you trust those who speak in this way. They will, I doubt not, attempt to rescue you from your present miserable state, but they will prepare a worse. It will be out of the frying-pan into the fire. Your present oppressors, it is true, will then oppress you no longer, but you will feel the lash of a master a thousand times more bloodthirsty and cruel. Evil designing men will spring up who will prevent you thinking as you please—will burn you if you do not think as they do. There are always bad men who take advantage of hard times. The monks and priests of old were very bad men; take care no such abuse your confidence again. You are not blind to your present situation; you are villanously treated; you are badly used. That this slavery shall cease, I will venture to prophesy. Your enemies dare not to persecute you longer, the spirit of Ireland is bent, but it is not broken, and that they very well know. But I wish your views to embrace a wider scene—I wish you to think for your children and your children's children; to take great care (for it all rests with you) that whilst one tyranny is destroyed, another more terrible and fierce does not spring up. Take care then of smooth-faced impostors, who talk indeed of freedom, but who will cheat you into slavery. Can there be worse slavery than the depending for the safety of your soul on the will of another man? Is one man more favoured than another by God? No, certainly, they are all favoured according to the good they do, and not according to the rank and profession they hold. God values a poor man as much as a priest, and has given him a soul as much to himself. The worship that a kind

Being must love is that of a simple affectionate heart, that shows its piety in good works, and not in ceremonies, or confessions, or burials, or processions, or wonders. Take care then that you are not led away. Doubt everything that leads you not to charity, and think of the word "heretic" as a word which some selfish knave invented for the ruin and misery of the world, to answer his own paltry and narrow ambition. Do not inquire if a man be a heretic, if he be a Quaker, a Jew, or a Heathen; but if he be a virtuous man, if he loves liberty and truth, if he wish the happiness and peace of human kind. If a man be ever so much a believer and love not these things, he is a heartless hypocrite, a rascal, and a knave. Despise and hate him as ye despise a tyrant and a villain. Oh, Ireland! thou emerald of the ocean, whose sons are generous and brave, whose daughters are honourable and frank and fair, thou art the isle on whose green shores I have desired to see the standard of liberty erected—a flag of fire—a beacon at which the world shall light the torch of Freedom!

We will now examine the Protestant religion. Its origin is called the Reformation. It was undertaken by some bigoted men who showed how little they understood the spirit of reform by burning each other. You will observe that these men burnt each other, indeed they universally betrayed a taste for destroying, and vied with the chiefs of the Roman Catholic religion in not only hating their enemies, but those men who least of all were their enemies, or anybody's enemies. Now do the Protestants or do they not hold the same tenets as they did when Calvin burnt Servetus? They swear that they do. We can have no better proof. Then with what face can the Protestants object to Catholic Emancipation on the plea that Catholics once were barbarous; when their own establishment is liable to the very same objections, on the very same grounds? I think this is a specimen of

barefaced intoleration, which I had hoped would not
have disgraced this age; this age, which is called the age
of reason, of thought diffused, of virtue acknowledged, and
its principles fixed—oh! that it may be so. I have mentioned the Catholic and Protestant religions more to
show that any objection to the toleration of the one forcibly applies to the non-permission of the other, or rather
to show that there is no reason why both might not be
tolerated; why every religion, every form of thinking
might not be tolerated. But why do I speak of *toleration?*
This word seems to mean that there is some merit in the
person who tolerates: he has this merit, if it be one, of
refraining to do an evil act, but he will share the merit with
every other peaceable person who pursues his own business, and does not hinder another of his rights. It is not
a merit to tolerate, but it is a crime to be intolerant: it
is not a merit in me that I sit quietly at home without
murdering any one, but it is a crime if I do so. Besides,
no act of a national representation can make anything
wrong which was not wrong before; it cannot change
virtue and truth, and for a very plain reason: because
they are unchangeable. An Act passed in the British
Parliament to take away the rights of Catholics to act in
that assembly, does not really take them away. It prevents them from doing it by force. This is in such cases
the last and only efficacious way. But force is not the
test of truth; they will never have recourse to violence
who acknowledge no other rule of behaviour but virtue
and justice.

The folly of persecuting men for their religion will
appear if we examine it. Why do we persecute them?
to make them believe as we do. Can anything be more
barbarous or foolish? For, although we may make them
say they believe as we do, they will not in their hearts
do any such thing, indeed they cannot; this devilish
method can only make them false hypocrites. For what is

belief? We cannot believe just what we like, but only what we think to be true; for you cannot alter a man's opinion by beating or burning, but by persuading him that what you think is right, and this can only be done by fair words and reason. It is ridiculous to call a man a heretic because he thinks differently from you; he might as well call you one. In the same sense the word orthodox is used; it signifies "to think rightly," and what can be more vain, presumptuous in any man or any set of men, to put themselves so out of the ordinary course of things as to say—"What we think is right, no other people throughout the world have opinions anything like equal to ours." Anything short of unlimited toleration, and complete charity with all men, on which you will recollect that Jesus Christ principally insisted, is wrong, and for this reason. What makes a man to be a good man? Not his religion, or else there could be no good men in any religion but one, when yet we find that all ages, countries, and opinions have produced them. Virtue and wisdom always so far as they went produced liberty or happiness long before any of the religions now in the world had ever [been] heard of. The only use of a religion that ever I could see, is to make men wiser and better; so far as it does this it is a good one. Now, if people are good, and yet have sentiments differing from you, then all the purposes are answered which any reasonable man could want, and whether he thinks like you or not is of too little consequence to employ means which must be disgusting and hateful to candid minds; nay, they cannot approve of such means. For, as I have before said, you cannot believe or disbelieve what you like— perhaps some of you may doubt this, but just try. I will take a common and familiar instance. Suppose you have a friend of whom you wish to think well; he commits a crime which proves to you that he is a bad man. It is very painful to you to think ill of him, and you would still

think well of him if you could.   But, mark the word, you
cannot think well of him, not even to secure your own
peace of mind can you do so.   You try, but your attempts
are vain.   This shows how little power a man has over
his belief, or rather, that he cannot believe what he does
not think true.   And what shall we think now?   What
fools and tyrants must not those men be who set up a
particular religion, say that this religion alone is right,
and that everyone who disbelieves it ought to be deprived
of certain rights which are really his, and which would
be allowed him if he believed.   Certainly if you cannot
help disbelief, it is not any fault in you.   To take away a
man's rights and privileges, to call him a heretic, or to
think worse of him, when at the same time you cannot
help owning that he has committed no fault, is the
grossest tyranny and intoleration.   From what has been
said I think we may be justified in concluding that people
of all religions ought to have an equal share in the State,
that the words heretic and orthodox were invented by a
vain villain, and have done a great deal of harm in the
world, and that no person is answerable for his belief
whose actions are virtuous and moral, that the religion is
best whose members are the best men, and that no person
can help either his belief or disbelief.   Be in charity with
all men.   It does not therefore signify what your religion
was, or what the Protestant religion *was*, we must consider them as we find them.   What are they *now?*
Yours is not intolerant; indeed, my friends, I have ventured to pledge myself for you that it is not.   You merely
desire to go to Heaven in your own way, nor will you
interrupt fellow travellers, although the road which you
take may not be that which they take.   Believe me that
goodness of heart and purity of life are things of more
value in the eye of the Spirit of Goodness, than idle
earthly ceremonies and things which may have anything
but charity for their object.   And is it for the first or the

last of these things that you or the Protestants contend? It is for the last. Prejudiced people indeed are they who grudge to the happiness and comfort of your souls things which can do harm to no one. They are not compelled to share in these rites. Irishmen! knowledge is more extended than in the early period of your religion, people have learned to think, and the more thought there is in the world, the more happiness and liberty will there be:— men begin now to think less of idle ceremonies and more of realities. From a long night have they risen, and they can perceive its darkness. I know no men of thought and learning who do not consider the Catholic idea of purgatory much nearer the truth than the Protestant one of eternal damnation. Can you think that the Maho-metans and the Indians, who have done good deeds in this life, will not be rewarded in the next? The Protestants believe that they will be eternally damned, at least they swear that they do. I think they appear in a better light as perjurers than believers in a falsehood so hurtful and uncharitable as this. I propose unlimited toleration, or rather the destruction both of toleration and intoleration. The act permits certain people to worship God after such a manner, which, in fact, if not done, would as far as in it lay prevent God from hearing their address. Can we conceive anything more presumptuous, and at the same time more ridiculous, than a set of men granting a licence to God to receive the prayers of certain of his creatures? Oh, Irishmen! I am interested in your cause; and it is not because you are Irishmen or Roman Catholics that I feel with you and feel for you; but because you are men and sufferers. Were Ireland at this moment peopled with Brahmins, this very same Address would have been suggested by the same state of mind. You have suffered not merely for your religion, but some other causes which I am equally desirous of remedying. The Union of England with Ireland has withdrawn the Protestant aristocracy and gentry from their native country, and with these their friends and connexions. Their resources are taken from this country, although they are dissipated in another; the very poor people are most infamously oppressed by the weight of burden which the superior ranks lay upon their shoulders. I am no less desirous of the reform of these evils (with many others) than for the Catholic Emancipation.

Perhaps you all agree with me on both these subjects, We now come to the method of doing these things. I agree with the Quakers so far as they disclaim violence, and trust their cause wholly and solely to its own truth. If you are convinced of the truth of your cause, trust wholly to its truth; if you are not convinced, give it up. In no case employ violence; the way to liberty and happiness is never to transgress the rules of virtue and justice. Liberty and happiness are founded upon virtue and justice; if you destroy the one you destroy the other. However ill others may act, this will be no excuse for you if you follow their example; it ought rather to warn you from pursuing so bad a method. Depend upon it, Irishmen, your cause shall not be neglected. I will fondly hope that the schemes for your happiness and liberty, as well as those for the happiness and liberty of the world, will not be wholly fruitless. One secure method of defeating them is violence on the side of the injured party. If you can descend to use the same weapons as your enemy, you put yourself on a level with him on this score: you must be convinced that he is on these grounds your superior. But appeal to the sacred principles of virtue and justice, then how is he awed into nothing! How does truth show him in his real colours, and place the cause of toleration and reform in the clearest light! I extend my view not only to you as Irishmen, but to all of every persuasion, of every country. Be calm, mild, deliberate, patient; recollect that you can in no measure more effectually forward the cause of reform than by employing your leisure time in reasoning or the cultivation of your minds. Think and talk and discuss : the only subjects you ought to propose are those of happiness and liberty. Be free and be happy, but first be wise and good. For you are not all wise or good. You are a great and a brave nation, but you cannot yet be all wise or good. You may be at some time, and then Ireland will be an earthly paradise. You know what is meant by a mob. It is an assembly of people who, without foresight or thought, collect themselves to disapprove of by force any measure which they dislike. An assembly like this can never do anything but harm ; tumultuous proceedings must retard the period when thought and coolness will produce freedom and happiness, and that to the very people who make the mob. But if a number of human beings, after thinking of their own interests, meet together for any conversation on them, and employ resistance of the mind, not resistance of the body, these people are going the right way to work. But let no fiery passions carry them beyond this point. Let them consider that in some sense the whole welfare of their countrymen depends on their prudence, and that it becomes them to guard the welfare of others as their own. Associations for purposes of violence are entitled to the strongest disapprobation of the real reformist. Always suspect that some knavish rascal is at the bottom of things of this kind, waiting to profit by the confusion. All secret associations are also bad. Are you men of deep designs, whose deeds love darkness better than light? Dare you not say what you think before any man? Can you not meet in the open face of day in conscious innocence? Oh, Irishmen, ye can ! Hidden arms, secret meetings, and designs violently to separate England from Ireland are all very bad. I do not mean to say

the very end of them is bad; the object you have in
view may be just enough, whilst the way you go about
it is wrong—may be calculated to produce an opposite
effect. Never do evil that good may come; always think
of others as well as yourself, and cautiously look how
your conduct may do good or evil, when you yourself
shall be mouldering in the grave. Be fair, open, and
you will be terrible to your enemies. A friend cannot
defend you, much as he may feel for your sufferings, if
you have recourse to methods of which virtue and justice
disapprove. No cause is in itself so dear to liberty as
yours. Much depends on you; far may your efforts
spread either hope or despair:. do not then cover in
darkness wrongs at which the face of day and the tyrants
who bask in its warmth ought to blush. Wherever has
violence succeeded? The French Revolution, although
undertaken with the best intentions, ended ill for the
people, because violence was employed. The cause
which they vindicated was that of truth, but they gave
it the appearance of a lie by using methods which will
suit the purposes of liars as well as their own. Speak
boldly and daringly what you think; an Irishman was
never accused of cowardice, do not let it be thought pos-.
sible that he is a coward. Let him say what he thinks; a
lie is the basest and meanest employment of men : leave
lies and secrets to courtiers and lordlings. Be open,
sincere, and single-hearted. Let it be seen that the
Irish votaries of Freedom dare to speak what they
think; let them resist oppression, not by force of arms,
but by power of mind and reliance on truth and justice.
Will any be arraigned for libel—will imprisonment or
death be the consequences of this mode of proceeding?
Probably not. But if it were so? Is danger frightful
to an Irishman who speaks for his own liberty and the
liberty of his wife and children? No ; he will steadily
persevere, and sooner shall pensioners cease to vote with

their benefactors than an Irishman swerve from the path of duty. But steadily persevere in the system above laid down, its benefits will speedily be manifested. Persecution may destroy some, but cannot destroy all, or nearly all; let it do its will. Ye have appealed to truth and justice, show the goodness of your religion by persisting in a reliance on these things, which must be the rules even of the Almighty's conduct. But before this can be done with any effect, habits of SOBRIETY, REGULARITY, and THOUGHT must be entered into, and firmly resolved upon.

My warm-hearted friends who meet together to talk of the distresses of your countrymen until social chat induces you to drink rather freely, as ye have felt passionately, so reason coolly. Nothing hasty can be lasting; lay up the money with which you usually purchase drunkenness and ill-health to relieve the pains of your fellow sufferers. Let your children lisp of freedom in the cradle—let your deathbed be the school for fresh exertions—let every street of the city and field of the country be connected with thoughts which liberty has made holy. Be warm in your cause, yet rational and charitable and tolerant— never let the oppressor grind you into justifying his conduct by imitating his meanness.

Many circumstances, I will own, may excuse what is called rebellion, but no circumstances can ever make it good for your cause, and however honourable to your feelings, it will reflect no credit on your judgments. It will bind you more closely to the block of the oppressor, and your children's children, whilst they talk of your exploits, will feel that you have done them injury instead of benefit.

A crisis is now arriving which shall decide your fate. The King of Great Britain has arrived at the evening of his days. He has objected to your emancipation; he has been inimical to you; but he will in a certain time be no more. The present Prince of Wales will then be king. It is said that he has promised to restore you to freedom: your real and natural right will, in that case, be no longer kept from you. I hope he has pledged himself to this act of justice, because there will then exist some obligation to bind him to do right. Kings are but too apt to think little as they should do : they think everything in the world is made for them ; when the truth is, that it is only the vices of men that make such people necessary, and they have no other right of being kings but in virtue of the good they do.

The benefit of the governed is the origin and meaning of government. The Prince of Wales has had every opportunity of knowing how he ought to act about Ireland and liberty. That great and good man Charles Fox, who was your friend and the friend of freedom, was the friend of the Prince of Wales. He never flattered nor disguised his sentiments, but spoke them *openly* on every occasion, and the Prince was the better for his instructive conversation. He saw the truth, and he believed it. Now I know not what to say; his staff is gone, and he leans upon a broken reed; his present advisers are not like Charles Fox, they do not plan for liberty and safety, not for the happiness, but for the glory of their country; and what, Irishmen, is the glory of a country divided from their happiness? It is a false light hung out by the enemies of freedom to lure the unthinking into their net. Men like these surround the Prince, and whether or no he has really promised to emancipate you—whether or no he will consider the promise of a Prince of Wales binding to a King of England, is yet a matter of doubt. We cannot at least be quite certain of it: on this you cannot certainly rely. But there are men who, wherever they find a tendency to freedom, go there to increase, support, and regulate that tendency. These men, who join to a rational disdain of danger a practice of speaking the truth, and defending the cause of the oppressed against the oppressor—these men see what is right and will pursue it. On such as these you may safely rely: they love you as they love their brothers; they feel for the unfortunate, and never ask whether a man is an Englishman or an Irishman, a catholic, a heretic, a christian, or a heathen, before their hearts and their purses are opened to feel with their misfortunes and relieve their necessities: such are the men who will stand by you for ever. Depend then not upon the promises of princes, but upon those of virtuous and disinterested men: depend not upon force of arms or violence, but upon the force of the truth of the rights which you have to share equally with others, the benefits and the evils of government.

The crisis to which I allude as the period of your emancipation is not the death of the present King, or any circumstance that has to do with kings, but something that is much more likely to do you good: it is the increase of virtue and wisdom which will lead people to find out that force and oppression are wrong and false; and this opinion, when it once gains ground, will prevent government from severity. It will restore those rights which Government has taken away. Have nothing to do with force or violence, and things will safely and surely make their way to the right point. The Ministers have now in Parliament a very great majority, and the Ministers are against you. They maintain the falsehood that, were you in power, you would prosecute* and burn, on the plea that you once did so. They maintain many other things of the same nature. They command the majority of the House of Commons, or rather the part of that assembly who receive pensions from Government or whose relatives receive them. These men of course are against you, because their employers are. But the sense of the country is not against you; the people of England

* [Persecute ?]

are not against you—they feel warmly for you—in some
respects they feel with you.   The sense of the English
and of their governors is opposite—there must be an end
of this; the goodness of a Government consists in the
happiness of the governed.   If the governed are wretched
and dissatisfied, the government has failed in its end.   It
wants altering and mending.   It will be mended, and a
reform of English government will produce good to the
Irish—good to all human kind, excepting those whose
happiness consists in others' sorrows, and it will be a fit
punishment for these to be deprived of their devilish joy.
This I consider as an event which is approaching, and
which will make the beginning of our hopes for that
period which may spread wisdom and virtue so wide as
to leave no hole in which folly or villany may hide themselves.   I wish you, O Irishmen, to be as careful and
thoughtful of your interests as are your real friends.   Do
not drink, do not play, do not spend any idle time, do not
take everything that other people say for granted—there
are numbers who will tell you lies to make their own
fortunes: you cannot more certainly do good to your
own cause than by defeating the intentions of these men.
Think, read, and talk; let your own condition and that
of your wives and children fill your minds; disclaim all
manner of alliance with violence: meet together if you
will, but do not meet in a mob.   If you think and read
and talk with a real wish of benefiting the cause of truth
and liberty, it will soon be seen how true a service you
are tendering, and how sincere you are in your professions; but mobs and violence must be discarded.   The
certain degree of civil and religious liberty which the
usage of the English Constitution allows, is such as the
worst of men are entitled to, although you have it not; but
that liberty which we may one day hope for, wisdom and
virtue can alone give you a right to enjoy.   This wisdom
and this virtue I recommend on every account that you

should *instantly begin* to practise. Lose not a day, not an hour, not a moment. Temperance, sobriety, charity, and independence will give you virtue; and reading, talking, thinking, and searching will give you wisdom; when you have those things you may defy the tyrant. It is not going often to chapel, crossing yourselves, or confessing that will make you virtuous ; many a rascal has attended regularly at mass, and many a good man has never gone at all. It is not paying priests or believing in what they say that makes a good man, but it is doing good actions or benefiting other people ; this is the true · way to be good, and the prayers and confessions and masses of him who does not these things are good for nothing at all. Do your work regularly and quickly : when you have done, think, read, and talk ; do not spend your money in idleness and drinking, which so far from doing good to your cause, will do it harm. If you have anything to spare from your wife and children, let it do some good to other people, and put them in a way of getting wisdom and virtue, as the pleasure that will come from these good acts will be much better than the headache that comes from a drinking bout. And never quarrel between each other ; be all of one mind as nearly as you can ; do these things, and I will promise you liberty and happiness. But if, on the contrary of these things, you neglect to improve yourselves, continue to use the word heretic, and demand from others the toleration which you are unwilling to give, your friends and the friends of liberty will have reason to lament the death-blow of their hopes. I expect better things from you : it is for yourselves that I fear and hope. Many Englishmen are prejudiced against you ; they sit by their own firesides, and certain rumours artfully spread are ever on the wing against you. But these people who think ill of you and of your nation are often the very men who, if they had better information, would feel for

I.   Q

you most keenly. Wherefore are these reports spread? How do they begin? They originate from the warmth of the Irish character, which the friends of the Irish nation have hitherto encouraged rather than repressed; this leads them in those moments, when their wrongs appear so clearly, to commit acts which justly excite displeasure. They begin therefore from yourselves, although falsehood and tyranny artfully magnify and multiply the cause of offence. Give no offence.

I will for the present dismiss the subject of the Catholic Emancipation; a little reflection will convince you that my remarks are just. Be true to yourselves, and your enemies shall not triumph. I fear nothing, if charity and sobriety mark your proceedings. Everything is to be dreaded—you yourselves will be unworthy of even a restoration to your rights, if you disgrace the cause, which I hope is that of truth and liberty, by violence; if you refuse to others the toleration which you claim for yourselves. But this you will not do. I rely upon it, Irishmen, that the warmth of your character will be shown as much in union with Englishmen and what are called heretics, who feel for you and love you, as in avenging your wrongs, or forwarding their annihilation. It is the heart that glows and not the cheek. The firmness, sobriety, and consistence of your outward behaviour will not at all show any hardness of heart, but will prove that you are determined in your cause, and are going the right way to work. I will repeat that virtue and wisdom are necessary to true happiness and liberty. The Catholic Emancipation, I consider, is certain. I do not see that anything but violence and intolerance among yourselves can leave an excuse to your enemies for continuing your slavery. The other wrongs under which you labour will probably also soon be done away. You will be rendered equal to the people of England in their rights and privileges, and will be in all respects, so far as concerns the State, as happy. And now, Irishmen, another and a more wide prospect opens to my view. I cannot avoid, little as it may appear to have anything to do with your present situation, to talk to you on the subject. It intimately concerns the well-being of your children and your children's children, and will perhaps more than anything prove to you the advantage and necessity of being thoughtful, sober, and regular; of avoiding foolish and idle talk, and thinking of yourselves as of men who are able to be much wiser and happier than you now are; for habits like these will not only conduce to the successful putting aside your present and immediate grievances, but will contain a seed which in future times will spring up into the tree of liberty, and bear the fruit of happiness.

There is no doubt but the world is going wrong, or rather that it is very capable of being much improved. What I mean by this improvement is, the inducement of a more equal and general diffusion of happiness and liberty. Many people are very rich and many are very poor. Which do you think are happiest? I can tell you that neither are happy, so far as their station is concerned. Nature never intended that there should be such a thing as a poor man or a rich one. Being put in an unnatural situation, they can neither of them be happy, so far as their situation is concerned. The poor man is born to obey the rich man, though they both come into the world equally helpless and equally naked. But the poor man does the rich no service by obeying him—the rich man does the poor no good by commanding him. It would be much better if they could be prevailed upon to live equally like brothers—they would ultimately both be happier. But this can be done neither to-day nor to-morrow; much as such a change is to be desired, it is quite impossible. Violence and folly in this, as in the other case, would only put off the period of its event.

Mildness, sobriety, and reason are the effectual methods of forwarding the ends of liberty and happiness.

Although we may see many things put in train during our life-time, we cannot hope to see the work of virtue and reason finished now; we can only lay the foundation for our posterity. Government is an evil; it is only the thoughtlessness and vices of men that make it a necessary evil. When all men are good and wise, government will of itself decay. So long as men continue foolish and vicious, so long will government, even such a government as that of England, continue necessary in order to prevent the crimes of bad men. Society is produced by the wants, government by the wickedness, and a state of just and happy equality by the improvement and reason of man. It is in vain to hope for any liberty and happiness without reason and virtue, for where there is no virtue there will be crime, and where there is crime there must be government. Before the restraints of government are lessened, it is fit that we should lessen the necessity for them. Before government is done away with, we must reform ourselves. It is this work which I would earnestly recommend to you. O Irishmen, RE-FORM YOURSELVES, and I do not recommend it to you particularly because I think that you most need it, but because I think that your hearts are warm and your feelings high, and you will perceive the necessity of doing it more than those of a colder and more distant nature.

I look with an eye of hope and pleasure on the present state of things, gloomy and incapable of improvement as they may appear to others. It delights me to see that men begin to think and to act for the good of others. Extensively as folly and selfishness have predominated in this age, it gives me hope and pleasure at least to see that many know what is right. Ignorance and vice commonly go together: he that would do good must be wise.

A man cannot be truly wise who is not truly virtuous. Prudence and wisdom are very different things. The prudent man is he who carefully consults for his own good : the wise man is he who carefully consults for the good of others.

I look upon Catholic Emancipation and the restoration of the liberties and happiness of Ireland, so far as they are compatible with the English Constitution, as great and important events. I hope to see them soon. But if all ended here, it would give me little pleasure. I should still see thousands miserable and wicked ; things would still be wrong. I regard then the accomplishment of these things as the road to a greater reform, that reform after which virtue and wisdom shall have con-quered pain and vice—when no government will be wanted but that of your neighbour's opinion. I look to these things with hope and pleasure, because I consider that they will certainly happen, and because men will not then be wicked and miserable. But I do not consider that they will or can immediately happen ; their arrival will be gradual, and it all depends upon yourselves how soon or how late these great changes will happen. If all of you to-morrow were virtuous and wise, govern-ment which to-day is a safeguard, would then become a tyranny. But I cannot expect a rapid change. Many are obstinate and determined in their vice, whose selfish-ness makes them think only of their own good, when in fact the best way even to bring that about is to make others happy. I do not wish to see things changed now, because it cannot be done without violence, and we may assure ourselves that none of us are fit for any change, however good, if we condescend to employ force in a cause which we think right. Force makes the side that employs it directly wrong, and as much as we may pity we cannot approve the headstrong and intolerant zeal of its adherents.

Can you conceive, O Irishmen! a happy state of
society—conceive men of every way of thinking living
together like brothers? The descendant of the greatest
prince would then be entitled to no more respect than
the son of a peasant. There would be no pomp and no
parade; but that which the rich now keep to themselves
would then be distributed among the people. None
would be in magnificence, but the superfluities then taken
from the rich would be sufficient when spread abroad to
make every one comfortable. No lover would then be
false to his mistress, no mistress could desert her lover.
No friend would play false; no rents, no debts, no
taxes, no frauds of any kind would disturb the general
happiness: good as they would be, wise as they would
be, they would be daily getting better and wiser. No
beggars would exist, nor any of those wretched women
who are now reduced to a state of the most horrible
misery and vice by men whose wealth makes them
villainous and hardened; no thieves or murderers,
because poverty would never drive men to take away
comforts from another when he had enough for himself.
Vice and misery, pomp and poverty, power and obedience,
would then be banished altogether. It is for such a state
as this, Irishmen, that I exhort you to prepare. "A camel
shall as soon pass through the eye of a needle, as a rich
man enter the kingdom of heaven." This is not to be
understood literally. Jesus Christ appears to me only to
have meant that riches have generally the effect of
hardening and vitiating the heart; so has poverty. I
think those people then are very silly, and cannot see
one inch beyond their noses, who say that human nature
is depraved; when at the same time wealth and poverty,
those two great sources of crime, fall to the lot of a great
majority of people; and when they see that people in
moderate circumstances are always most wise and good.
People say that poverty is no evil; they have never felt

it, or they would not think so ; that wealth is necessary to encourage the arts—but are not the arts very inferior things to virtue and happiness?—the man would be very dead to all generous feelings who would rather see pretty pictures and statues than a million free and happy men.

It will be said that my design is to make you dissatisfied with your present condition, and that I wish to raise a Rebellion. But how stupid and sottish must those men be who think that violence and uneasiness of mind have anything to do with forwarding the views of peace, harmony, and happiness. They should know that nothing was so well fitted to produce slavery, tyranny, and vice as the violence which is attributed to the friends of liberty, and which the real friends of liberty are the only persons who disdain. As to your being dissatisfied with your present condition, anything that I may say is certainly not likely to increase that dissatisfaction. I have advanced nothing concerning your situation but its real case ; but what may be proved to be true. I defy any one to point out a falsehood that I have uttered in the course of this Address. It is impossible but the blindest among you must see that everything is not right. This sight has often pressed some of the poorest among you to take something from the rich man's store by violence, to relieve his own necessities. I cannot justify, but I can pity him. I cannot pity the fruits of the rich man's intemperance. I suppose some are to be found who will justify him. This sight has often brought home to a day-labourer the truth which I wish to impress upon you that all is not right. But I do not merely wish to convince you that our present state is bad, but that its alteration for the better depends on your own exertions and resolutions.

But he has never found out the method of mending it who does not first mend his own conduct, and then prevail upon others to refrain from any vicious habits which they may have contracted, much less does the poor man suppose that wisdom as well as virtue is necessary, and that the employing his little time in reading and thinking, is really doing all that he has in his power to do towards the state, when pain and vice shall perish altogether.

I wish to impress upon your minds that without virtue or wisdom there can be no liberty or happiness; and that temperance, sobriety, charity, and independence of soul will give you virtue, as thinking, inquiring, reading, and talking will give you wisdom. Without the first the last is of little use, and without the last the first is a dreadful curse to yourselves and others.

I have told you what I think upon this subject, because I wish to produce in your minds an awe and caution necessary, before the happy state of which I have spoken can be introduced. This cautious awe is very different from the prudential fear which leads you to consider yourself as the first object, as, on the contrary, it is full of that warm and ardent love for others that burns in your hearts, O Irishmen! and from which I have fondly hoped to light a flame that may illumine and invigorate the world.

I have said that the rich command and the poor obey, and that money is only a kind of sign which shows that according to government the rich man has a right to command the poor man, or rather that the poor man, being urged by having no money to get bread, is forced to work for the rich man, which amounts to the same thing. I have said that I think all this very wrong, and that I wish the whole business was altered. I have also said that we can expect little amendment in our own time, and that we must be contented to lay the foundation of liberty and happiness by virtue and wisdom. This, then, shall be my work; let this be yours, Irishmen. Never shall that glory fail, which I am anxious that you shall deserve—

the glory of teaching to a world the first lessons of virtue
and wisdom.

Let poor men still continue to work. I do not wish to
hide from them a knowledge of their relative condition
in society, I esteem it next [to] impossible to do so. Let
the work of the labourer, of the artificer—let the work of
every one, however employed, still be exerted in its
accustomed way. The public communication of this
truth ought in no manner to impede the established
usages of society, however it is fitted in the end to do
them away. For this reason it ought not to impede
them, because if it did, a violent and unaccustómed and
sudden sensation * would take place in all ranks
of men, which would bring on violence and destroy
the possibility of the event of that which in its own
nature must be gradual, however rapid, and rational however warm. It is founded on the reform of private men,
and without individual amendment it is vain and foolish
to expect the amendment of a state or government. I
would advise them, therefore, whose feelings this Address
may have succeeded in affecting (and surely those feelings which charitable and temperate remarks excite can
never be violent and intolerant), if they be, as I hope,
those whom poverty has compelled to class themselves in
the lower orders of society, that they will as usual attend
to their business and the discharge of those public or
private duties which custom has ordained. Nothing can
be more rash and thoughtless than to show in ourselves
singular instances of any particular doctrine before the
general mass of the people are so convinced by the reasons of the doctrine, that it will be no longer singular.
That reasons as well as feelings may help the establishment of happiness and liberty, on the basis of wisdom
and virtue, be our aim and intention. Let us not be led
into any means which are unworthy of this end, nor, as

* [Cessation ?]

so much depends upon yourselves, let us cease carefully to watch over our conduct, that when we talk of reform it be not objected to us, that reform ought to begin at home.   In the interval that public or private duties and necessary labours allow, husband your time so that you may do to others and yourselves the most real good.   To improve your own minds is to join these two views ; conversation and reading are the principal and chief methods of awaking the mind to knowledge and goodness.   Reading or thought will principally bestow the former of these —the benevolent exercise of the powers of the mind in communicating useful knowledge will bestow an habit of the latter ; both united will contribute so far as lies in your individual power to that great reform which will be perfect and finished the moment every one is virtuous and wise.   Every folly refuted, every bad habit conquered, every good one confirmed, are so much gained in this great and excellent cause.

To begin to reform the government is immediately necessary, however good or bad individuals may be ; it is the more necessary, if they are eminently the latter, in some degree to palliate or do away the cause, as political institution has even* the greatest influence on the human character, and is that alone which differences the Turk from the Irishman.

I write now not only with a view for Catholic Emancipation, but for universal emancipation ; and this emancipation complete and unconditional, that shall comprehend every individual of whatever nation or principles, that shall fold in its embrace all that think and all that feel : the Catholic cause is subordinate, and its success preparatory to this great cause, which adheres to no sect but society, to no cause but that of universal happiness, to no party but the people.   I desire Catholic Emancipation, but I desire not to stop here ; and I hope

* [Ever ?]

there are few, who having perused the preceding arguments, will not concur with me in desiring a complete,
a lasting, and a happy amendment. That all steps, however good and salutary, which may be taken, all reforms
consistent with the English constitution that may be
effectuated, can only be subordinate and preparatory to
the great and lasting one which shall bring about the
peace, the harmony, and the happiness of Ireland,
England, Europe, the World. I offer merely an outline
of that picture which your own hopes may gift with the
colours of reality.

Government will not allow a peaceable and reasonable
discussion of its principles by any association of men
who assemble for that express purpose. But have not
· human beings a right to assemble to talk upon what subject they please? Can anything be more evident than
that as government is only of use as it conduces to the
happiness of the governed, those who are governed have
a right to talk on the efficacy of the safeguard employed
for their benefit? Can any topic be more interesting or
useful than one discussing how far the means of government is or could be made in a higher degree effectual to producing the end? Although I deprecate violence, and the cause which depends for its influence on
force, yet I can by no means think that assembling together merely to talk of how things go on—I can by no
means think that societies formed for talking on any
subject, however Government may dislike them, come
in any way under the head of force or violence—I think
that associations conducted in the spirit of sobriety, regularity, and thought, are one of the best and most
efficient of those means which I would recommend for
the production of happiness, liberty, and virtue.

Are you slaves or are you men? If slaves, then crouch
to the rod and lick the feet of your oppressors ; glory
[in] your shame ; it will become you, if brutes, to act

according to your nature. But you are men : a real man
is free, so far as circumstances will permit him. Then
firmly yet quietly resist. When one cheek is struck, turn
the other to the insulting coward. You will be truly
brave : you will resist and conquer. The discussion of
any subject is a right that you have brought into the
world with your heart and tongue. Resign your heart's
blood before you part with this inestimable privilege of
man. For it is fit that the governed should inquire into
the proceedings of government, which is of no use the
moment it is conducted on any other principle but that
of safety. You have much to think of. Is war necessary to your happiness and safety? The interests of the
poor gain nothing from the wealth or extension of a
nation's boundaries, they gain nothing from glory, a word
that has often served as a cloak to the ambition or avarice
of statesmen. The barren victories of Spain, gained in
behalf of a bigoted and tyrannical government, are nothing to them. The conquests in India, by which England
has gained glory indeed, but a glory which is not more
honourable than that of Buonaparte, are nothing to them.
The poor purchase this glory and this wealth at the ex-
pense of their blood and labour and happiness and
virtue. They die in battle for this infernal cause. Their
labour supplies money and food for carrying it into
effect; their happiness is destroyed by the oppression
they undergo ; their virtue is rooted out by the depravity
and vice that prevail throughout the army, and which
under the present system are perfectly unavoidable. Who
does not know that the quartering of a regiment on any
town will soon destroy the innocence and happiness of
its inhabitants? The advocates for the happiness and
liberty of the great mass of the people, who pay for war
with their lives and labour, ought never to cease writing
and speaking until nations see, as they must feel, the
folly of fighting and killing each other in uniform for

nothing at all. Ye have much to think of. The state of your representation in the House, which is called the collective representation of the country, demands your attention.

It is horrible that the lower classes must waste their lives and liberty to furnish means for their oppressors to oppress them yet more terribly. It is horrible that the poor must give in taxes what would save them and their families from hunger and cold ;—it is still more horrible that they should do this to furnish further means of their own abjectedness and misery. But what words can express the enormity of the abuse that prevents them from choosing representatives with authority to inquire into the manner in which their lives and labour, their happiness and innocence, are expended, and what advantages result from their expenditure which may counterbalance so horrible and monstrous an evil ? There is an outcry raised against amendment ; it is called innovation and condemned by many unthinking people who have a good fire and plenty to eat and drink. Hard-hearted or thoughtless beings, how many are famishing whilst you deliberate, how many perish to contribute to your pleasures ? I hope that there are none such as these native Irishmen, indeed I scarcely believe that there are.

Let the object of your associations (for I conceal not my approval of assemblies conducted with regularity, *peaceableness*, and thought for any purpose) be the amendment of these abuses, it will have for its object universal emancipation, liberty, happiness, and virtue. There is yet another subject, "the Liberty of the Press." The liberty of the Press consists in a right to publish any opinion on any subject which the writer may entertain. The Attorney-General in 1793, on the trial of Mr. Percy, said, "I never will dispute the right of any man fully to discuss topics respecting Government, and honestly to point out what he may consider a proper remedy of grievances." The liberty of the Press is placed as a sentinel to alarm us when any attempt is made on our liberties. It is this sentinel, oh, Irishmen, whom I now awaken! I create to myself a freedom which exists not. There is no liberty of the Press for the subjects of British government.

It is really ridiculous to hear people yet boasting of this inestimable blessing, when they daily see it successfully muzzled and outraged by the lawyers of the Crown, and by virtue of what are called *ex officio* informations. Blackstone says, that "if a person publishes what is improper, mischievous, or illegal, he must take the consequences of his own temerity." And Lord Chief Baron Comyns defines libel as "a contumely, or reproach, published to the defamation of the Government, of a magistrate, or of a private person." Now I beseech you to consider the words mischievous, improper, illegal, contumely, reproach, or defamation. May they not make that mischievous or improper which they please? Is not law with them as clay in the potter's hand? Do not the words contumely, reproach, or defamation express all degrees and forces of disapprobation? It is impossible to express yourself displeased at certain proceedings of Government, or the individuals who conduct it, without uttering a reproach. We cannot honestly point out a proper remedy of grievances with safety, because the very mention of these grievances will be reproachful to the personages who countenance them; and therefore will come under a definition of libel. For the persons who thus directly or indirectly undergo reproach, will say for their own sakes that the exposure of their corruption is mischievous and improper; therefore the utterer of the reproach is a fit subject for three years' imprisonment. Is there anything like the liberty of the Press in restrictions so positive yet pliant as these? The little freedom which we enjoy in this most important point comes from the clemency of our rulers, or their fear lest public opinion, alarmed at the discovery of its enslaved state, should violently assert a right to extension and diffusion. Yet public opinion may not always be so formidable ; rulers may not always be so merciful or so timid; at any rate, evils, and great evils, do result from the present system of intellectual slavery, and you have enough to think of if this grievance alone remained in the constitution of society. I will give but one instance of the present state of our Press.

A countryman of yours is now confined in an English gaol. His health, his fortune, his spirits suffer from close confinement. The air which comes through the bars ot a prison-grate does not invigorate the frame nor cheer the spirits. But Mr. Finnerty, much as he has lost, yet retains the fair name of truth and honour. He was imprisoned for persisting in the truth. His judge told him on his trial that truth and falsehood were indifferent to the law, and that if he owned the publication, any consideration whether the facts that it related were well or ill-founded, was totally irrelevant. Such is the libel law; such the liberty of the Press—there is enough to think of. The right of withholding your individual assent to war, the right of choosing delegates to represent you in the assembly of the nation, and that of freely opposing intellectual power to any measure of Government of which you may disapprove, are, in addition to the indifference with which the Legislative and the Executive power ought to rule their conduct towards professors of every religion, enough to think of.

I earnestly desire peace and harmony :—peace, that whatever wrongs you may have suffered, benevolence and a spirit of forgiveness should mark your conduct towards those who have persecuted you :—harmony, that among yourselves may be no divisions, that Protestants and Catholics unite in a common interest, and that whatever be the belief and principles of your countryman and fellow sufferer, you desire to benefit his cause at the same time that you vindicate your own. Be strong and unbiassed by selfishness or prejudice— for, Catholics, your religion has not been spotless, crimes in past ages have sullied it with a stain, which let it be your glory to remove. Nor, Protestants, hath your religion always been characterized by the mildness of benevolence which Jesus Christ recommended. Had it anything to do with the present subject I could account for the spirit of intolerance which marked both religions; I will, however, only adduce the fact, and earnestly exhort you to root out from your own minds everything which may lead to uncharitableness, and to reflect that yourselves as well as your brethren may be deceived. Nothing on earth is infallible. The priests that pretend to it are wicked and mischievous impostors ; but it is an imposture which every one more or less assumes who encourages prejudice in his breast against those who differ from him in opinion, or who sets up his own religion as the only right and true one, when no one is so blind as not to see that every religion is right and true which makes men beneficent and sincere. I therefore earnestly exhort both Protestants and Catholics to act in brotherhood and harmony, never forgetting because the Catholics alone are heinously deprived of religious rights, that the Protestants and a certain rank of people of every persuasion, share with them all else that is terrible, galling, and intolerable in the mass of political grievance.

In no case employ violence or falsehood. I cannot too often or too vividly endeavour to impress upon your minds that these methods will produce nothing but wretchedness and slavery—that they will at the same time rivet the fetters with which ignorance and oppression bind you to abjectness, and deliver you over to a tyranny which shall render you incapable of renewed efforts.

Violence will immediately render your cause a bad one. If you believe in a providential God, you must also believe that he is a good one. And it is not likely a merciful God would befriend a bad cause. Insincerity is no less hurtful than violence; those who are in the habit of either, would do well to reform themselves. A lying bravo will never promote the good of his country— he cannot be a good man. The courageous and sincere may, at the same time, successfully oppose corruption, by uniting their voice with that of others, or individually raise up intellectual opposition to counteract the abuses of Government and society. In order to benefit your- selves and your country to any extent, habits of sobriety, regularity, and thought are previously so necessary that, without these preliminaries, all that you have done falls to the ground. You have built on sand; secure a good foundation, and you may erect a fabric to stand for ever —the glory and the envy of the world.

I have purposely avoided any lengthened discussion on those grievances to which your hearts are, from cus· tom and the immediate interest of the circumstances, probably most alive at present. I have not, however, wholly neglected them. Most of all have I insisted on their instant palliation and ultimate removal; nor have I omitted a consideration of the means which I deem most effectual for the accomplishment of this great end. How far you will consider the former worthy of your adoption, so far shall I deem the latter probable and interesting to the lovers of human kind. And I have opened to your view a new scene—does not your heart bound at the bare possibility of your posterity possessing that liberty and happiness of which, during our lives, powerful exertions and habitual abstinence may give us a foretaste? Oh! if your hearts do not vibrate at such as this, then ye are dead and cold—ye are not men.

I now come to the application of my principles, the

I.   R conclusion of my Address; and, O Irishmen, whatever conduct ye may feel yourselves bound to pursue, the path which duty points to lies before me clear and un-obscured. Dangers may lurk around it, but they are not the dangers which lie beneath the footsteps of the hypo-crite or temporizer.

For I have not presented to you the picture of happi-ness on which my fancy doats as an uncertain meteor to mislead honourable enthusiasm, or blindfold the judg-ment which makes virtue useful. I have not proposed crude schemes, which I should be incompetent to mature, or desired to excite in you any virulence against the abuses of political institution; where I have had occa-sion to point them out, I have recommended moderation whilst yet I have earnestly insisted upon energy and perseverance; I have spoken of peace, yet declared that resistance is laudable; but the intellectual resistance which I recommend, I deem essential to the introduction of the millennium of virtue, whose period every one can, so far as he is concerned, forward by his own proper power. I have not attempted to show that the Catholic claims, or the claims of the people to a full representation in Parliament, or any of these claims to real rights, which I have insisted upon as introductory to the ultimate claim of *all*, to universal happiness, freedom and equality; I have not attempted, I say, to show that these can be granted consistently with the spirit of the English Con-stitution;* this is a point which I do not feel myself inclined to discuss, and which I consider foreign to my subject. But I have shown that these claims have for their basis truth and justice, which are immutable, and

* The excellence of the Constitution of Great Britain appears to me to be its indefiniteness and versatility, whereby it may be unre-sistingly accommodated to the progression of wisdom and virtue. Such accommodation I desire; but I wish for the cause before the effect.

which in the ruin of governments shall rise like a phœnix from their ashes.

Is any one inclined to dispute the possibility of a happy change in society? Do they say that the nature of man is corrupt, and that he was made for misery and wickedness? Be it so. Certain as are opposite conclusions, I will concede the truth of this for a moment. What are the means which I take for melioration? Violence, corruption, rapine, crime? Do I do evil that good may come? I have recommended peace, philanthropy, wisdom. So far as my arguments influence, they will influence to these; and if there is any one *now* inclined to say that "private vices are public benefits," and that peace, philanthropy, and wisdom will, if once they gain ground, ruin the human race, he may revel in his happy dreams; though were *I* this man I should envy Satan's hell. The wisdom and charity of which I speak are the *only* means which I will countenance for the redress of your grievances and the grievances of the world. So far as they operate, I am willing to stand responsible for their evil effects. I expect to be accused of a desire for renewing in Ireland the scenes of revolutionary horror which marked the struggles of France twenty years ago. But it is the renewal of that unfortunate era which I strongly deprecate, and which the tendency of this Address is calculated to obviate. For can burthens be borne for ever, and the slave crouch and cringe the while? Is misery and vice so consonant to man's nature that he will hug it to his heart? But when the wretched one in bondage beholds the emancipation near, will he not endure his misery awhile with hope and patience, then spring to his preserver's arms, and start into a man?

It is my intention to observe the effect on your minds, O Irishmen, which this Address, dictated by the fervency of my love and hope, will produce. I have come to this country to spare no pains where expenditure may purchase you real benefit. The present is a crisis which of all others is the most valuable for fixing the fluctuation of public feeling; as far as my poor efforts may have succeeded in fixing it to virtue, Irishmen, so far shall I esteem myself happy. I intend this Address as introductory to another. The organization of a society whose institution shall serve as a bond to its members for the purposes of virtue, happiness, liberty, and wisdom, by the means of intellectual opposition to grievances, would probably be useful. For the formation of such society I avow myself anxious.

Adieu, my friends! May every sun that shines on your green island see the annihilation of an abuse, and the birth of an embryon of melioration! Your own hearts—may they become the shrines of purity and freedom, and never may smoke to the Mammon of unrighteousness ascend from the unpolluted altar of their devotion!

No. 7, Lower Sackville Street, Feb. 22nd.

POSTSCRIPT.

I have now been a week in Dublin, during which time I have endeavoured to make myself more accurately acquainted with the state of the public mind on those great topics of grievances which induced me to select Ireland as a theatre, the widest and fairest, for the operations of the determined friend of religious and political freedom.

The result of my observations has determined me to propose an association for the purposes of restoring Ireland to the prosperity which she possessed before the Union Act; and the religious freedom which the involuntariness of faith ought to have taught all monopolists of Heaven long, long ago, that every one had a right to possess.

For the purpose of obtaining the emancipation of the Catholics from the penal laws that aggrieve them, and a repeal of the Legislative Union Act, and grounding upon the remission of the church-craft and oppression, which caused these grievances ; *a plan of amendment and regeneration in the moral and political state of society, on a comprehensive and systematic philanthropy which shall be sure though slow in its projects: and as it is without the rapidity and danger of revolution, so will it be devoid of the time-servingness of temporizing reform* —which in its deliberate capacity, having investigated the state of the Government of England, shall oppose those parts of it, by intellectual force, which will not bear the touchstone of reason.

For information respecting the principles which I possess, and the nature and spirit of the association which I propose, I refer the reader to a small pamphlet, which I shall publish on the subject in the course of a few days.

I have published the above Address (written in England) in the cheapest possible form, and have taken pains that the remarks which it contains should be intelligible to the most uneducated minds. Men are not slaves and brutes because they are poor ; it has been the policy of the thoughtless.or wicked of the higher ranks (as a proof of the decay of which policy I am happy to see the rapid success of a comparatively enlightened system of education) to conceal from the poor the truths which I have endeavoured to teach them. In doing so I have but translated my thoughts into another language ; and, as language is only useful as it communicates ideas, I shall think my style so far good as it is successful as a means to bring about the end which I desire on any occasion to accomplish.

A Limerick paper, which I suppose professes to support certain *loyal* and *John Bullish* principles of freedom, has, in an essay for advocating the liberty of the Press, the following clause : " For lawless licence of discussion never did we advocate, nor do we now." What is lawless licence of discussion ? Is it not as indefinite as the words *contumely, reproach, defamation*, that allow at present such latitude to the outrages that are committed on the free expression of individual sentiment ? Can they not see that what is rational will stand by its reason, and what is true stand by its truth, as all that is foolish will fall by its folly, and all that is false be controverted by its own falsehood ? Liberty gains nothing by the reform of politicians of this stamp, any more than it gains from a change of Ministers in London. What at present is contumely and defamation, would at the period of this Limerick amendment be "lawless licence of discussion," and such would be the mighty advantage which this doughty champion of liberty proposes to effect.

I conclude with the words of Lafayette, a name endeared by its peerless bearer to every lover of the human race, " For a nation to love liberty it is sufficient that she knows it, to be free it is sufficient that she wills it."

PROPOSALS

FOR AN

ASSOCIATION

OF THOSE

PHILANTHROPISTS,

WHO CONVINCED OF THE INADEQUACY OF THE MORAL AND
POLITICAL STATE OF IRELAND TO PRODUCE BENEFITS
WHICH ARE NEVERTHELESS ATTAINABLE, ARE WILLING
TO UNITE TO ACCOMPLISH ITS REGENERATION.

BY

PERCY BYSSHE SHELLEY.

Dublin:

PRINTED BY I. ETON, WINETAVERN STREET.

[1812.]

PROPOSALS FOR AN ASSOCIATION,

ETC,

I PROPOSE an Association which shall have for its immediate objects Catholic Emancipation and the Repeal of the Act of Union between Great Britain and Ireland; and grounding on the removal of these grievances, an annihilation or palliation of whatever moral or political evil it may be within the compass of human power to assuage or eradicate.

MAN cannot make occasions, but he may seize those that offer. None are more interesting to philanthropy than those which excite the benevolent passions, that generalize and expand private into public feelings, and make the hearts of individuals vibrate not merely for themselves, their families, and their friends, but for posterity, *for a people*; till their country becomes the world, and their family the sensitive creation.

A recollection of the absent, and a taking into consideration the interests of those unconnected with ourselves, is a principal source of that feeling which generates occasions wherein a love for human kind may become eminently useful and active. Public topics of fear and hope, such as sympathize with general grievance, or hold out hopes of general amendment, are those on which the philanthropist would dilate with the warmest feeling; because these are accustomed to place individuals at a distance from self; for in proportion as he is absorbed in public feeling, so will a consideration of his proper benefit be generalized. In proportion as he feels with or for a nation or a world, so will man consider himself less as that centre to which we are but too prone to believe that every line of human concern does or ought to converge.

I should not here make the trite remark that selfish motive biasses, brutalizes, and degrades the human mind, did it not thence follow, that to seize those occasions wherein the opposite spirit predominates, is a duty which Philanthropy imperiously exacts of her votaries; that occasions like these are the proper ones for leading mankind to their own interest by awakening in their minds a love for the interest of their fellows. A plant that grows in every soil, though too often it is choked by tares before its lovely blossoms are expanded. Virtue produces pleasure, it is as the cause to the effect; I feel pleasure in doing good to my friend, because I love him. I do not love him for the sake of that pleasure.

I regard the present state of the public mind in Ireland to be one of those occasions which the ardent votary of the religion of Philanthropy dare not leave unseized. I perceive that the public interest is excited, I perceive that individual interest has, in a certain degree, quitted individual concern to generalize itself with universal feeling. Be the Catholic Emancipation a thing of great or of small misfortune,* be it a means of adding happiness to four millions of people, or a reform which will only give honour to a few of the higher ranks, yet a benevolent and disinterested feeling has gone abroad, and I am willing that it should never subside. I desire that means should be taken with energy and expedition in this important yet fleeting crisis, to feed the unpolluted flame at which nations and ages may light the torch of Liberty and Virtue!

It is my opinion that the claims of the Catholic inhabitants of Ireland, if gained to-morrow, would in a very small degree aggrandize their liberty and happiness. The disqualifications principally affect the higher orders of the Catholic persuasion, these would principally be benefited by their removal. Power and wealth do not

* Query, a misprint for *importance* ?

benefit, but injure, the cause of virtue and freedom. I am happy, however, at the near approach of this emancipation, because I am inimical to all disqualifications for opinion. It gives me pleasure to see the approach of this enfranchisement, not for the good which it will bring with it, but because it is a sign of benefits approaching, a prophet of good about to come; and therefore do I sympathize with the inhabitants of Ireland in this great cause; a cause which though in its own accomplishment will add not one comfort to the cottager, will snatch not one from the dark dungeon, will root not out one vice, alleviate not one pang, yet it is the foreground of a picture, in the dimness of whose distance I behold the lion lay down with the lamb, and the infant play with the basilisk. For it supposes the extermination of the eyeless monster Bigotry, whose throne has tottered for two hundred years. I hear the teeth of the palsied beldame Superstition chatter, and I see her descending to the grave! Reason points to the open gates of the Temple of Religious Freedom, Philanthropy kneels at the altar of the common God! There, wealth and poverty, rank and abjectness, are names known but as memorials of past time: meteors which play over the loathsome pool of vice and misery, to warn the wanderer where dangers lie. Does a God rule this illimitable universe? Are you thankful for his beneficence—do you adore his wisdom—do you hang upon his altar the garland of your devotion? Curse not your brother, though he hath enwreathed with his flowers of a different hue; the purest religion is that of Charity, its loveliness begins to proselyte the hearts of men. The tree is to be judged of by its fruit. I regard the admission of the Catholic claims and the Repeal of the Union Act as blossoms of that fruit which the summer sun of improved intellect and progressive virtue is destined to mature.

I will not pass unreflected on the Legislative Union of Great Britain and Ireland, nor will I speak of it as a grievance so tolerable or unimportant in its own nature as that of Catholic disqualification. The latter affects few, the former affects thousands. The one disqualifies the rich from power, the other impoverishes the peasant, adds beggary to the city, famine to the country, multiplies abjectedness, whilst misery and crime play into each other's hands under its withering auspices. I esteem, then, the annihilation of this second grievance to be something more than a mere sign of coming good. I esteem it to be in itself a substantial benefit. The aristocracy of Ireland—(for much as I may disapprove other distinctions than those of virtue and talent, I consider it useless, hasty, and violent, not for the present to acquiesce in their continuance)—the aristocracy of Ireland suck the veins of its inhabitants and consume the blood in England. I mean not to deny the unhappy truth that there is much misery and vice in the world. I mean to say that Ireland shares largely of both.—England has made her poor ; and the poverty of a rich nation will make its people very desperate and wicked.

I look forward, then, to the redress of both these grievances ; or rather, I perceive the state of the public mind, that precedes them as the crisis of beneficial innovation. The latter I consider to be the cause of the former, as I hope it will be the cause of more comprehensively beneficial amendments. It forms that occasion which should energetically and quickly be occupied. The voice of the whole human race; their crimes, their miseries, and their ignorance, invoke us to the task. For the miseries of the Irish poor, exacerbated by the union of their country with England, are not peculiar to themselves. England, the whole civilized world, with few exceptions, is either sunk in disproportioned abjectness, or raised to unnatural elevation. The repeal of the Union

Act will place Ireland on a level, so far as concerns the well-being of its poor, with her sister nation. Benevolent feeling has gone out in this country in favour of the happiness of its inhabitants ; may this feeling be corroborated, methodized, and continued ! May it never fail ! But it will not be kept alive by each citizen sitting quietly by his own fireside, and saying that things are going on well, because the rain does not beat on *him*, because *he* has books and leisure to read them, because *he* has money and is at liberty to accumulate luxuries to *himself.* Generous feeling dictates no such sayings. When the heart recurs to the thousands who have no liberty and no leisure, it must be rendered callous by long contemplation of wretchedness, if after such recurrence it can beat with contented evenness. Why do I talk thus? Is there anyone who doubts that the present state of politics and morals is wrong? They say, Show us a safe method of improvement. There is no safer than the corroboration and propagation of generous and philanthropic feeling, than the keeping continually alive a love for the human race, than the putting in train causes which shall have for their consequences virtue and freedom ; and, because I think that individuals acting singly, with whatever energy, can never effect so much as a society, I propose that all those whose views coincide with those that I have avowed, who perceive the state of the public mind in Ireland, who think the present a fit opportunity for attempting to fix its fluctuations at Philanthropy, who love all mankind, and are willing actively to engage in its cause, or passively to endure the persecutions of those who are inimical to its success; I propose to these to form an association for the purposes, first, of debating on the propriety of whatever measures may be agitated; and secondly, for carrying, by united or individual exertion, such measures into effect when determined on. That it should be an association for discussing * knowledge and virtue throughout the poorer classes of society in Ireland, for co-operating with any enlightened system of education ; for discussing topics calculated to throw light on any methods of alleviation of moral and political evil, and, as far as lays in its power, actively interesting itself, in whatever occasions may arise for benefiting mankind.

When I mention Ireland, I do not mean to confine the influence of the association to this or to any other country, but for the time being.   Moreover, I would recommend that this association should attempt to form others, and to actuate them with a similar spirit ; and I am thus indeterminate in my description of the association which I propose, because I conceive that an assembly of men meeting to do all the good that opportunity will permit them to do, must be in its nature as indefinite and varying as the instances of human vice and misery that precede, occasion, and call for its institution.

As political institution and its attendant evils constitute the majority of those grievances which philanthropists desire to remedy, it is probable that existing Governments will frequently become the topic of their discussions, the results of which may little coincide with the opinions which those who profit by the supineness of human belief desire to impress upon the world. It is probable that this freedom may excite the odium of certain well-meaning people, who pin their faith upon their grandmother's apron-string. The minority in number are the majority in intellect and power. The former govern the latter, though it is by the sufferance of the latter that this originally delegated power is exercised. This power is become hereditary, and hath ceased to be necessarily united with intellect.

It is certain, therefore, that any questioning of established principles would excite the abhorrence and opposi-

* Query, *diffusing* ?

tion of those who derived power and honour (such as it is) from their continuance.

As the association which I recommend would question those principles (however they may be hedged in with antiquity and precedent) which appeared ill adapted for the benefit of human kind, it would probably excite the odium of those in power. It would be obnoxious to the Government, though nothing would be farther from the views of associated philanthropists than attempting to subvert establishments forcibly, or even hastily. Aristocracy would oppose it, whether oppositionists or ministerialists (for philanthropy is of no party), because its ultimate views look to a subversion of all factitious distinctions, although from its immediate intentions I fear that aristocracy can have nothing to dread. The priesthood would oppose it, because a union of Church and State—contrary to the principles and practice of Jesus, contrary to that equality which he fruitlessly endeavoured to teach mankind—is, of all institutions that from the rust of antiquity are called venerable, the least qualified to stand free and cool reasoning, because it least conduces to the happiness of human kind; yet, did either the minister, the peer, or the bishop know their true interest, nstead of that virulent opposition which some among them have made to freedom and philanthropy, they would rejoice and co-operate with the diffusion and corroboration of those principles that would remove a load of paltry equivocation, paltrier grandeur, and of wigs that crush into emptiness the brains below them, from their shoulders; and, by permitting them to reassume the degraded and vilified title of man, would preclude the necessity of mystery and deception, would bestow on them a title more ennobling, and a dignity which, though it would be without the gravity of an ape, would possess the ease and consistency of a man.

For the reasons above alleged, falsely, prejudicedly, and

narrowly, will those very persons whose ultimate benefit is included in the general good, whose promotion is the essence of a philanthropic association, will they persecute those who have the best intentions towards them, malevolence towards none.

I do not, therefore, conceal that those who make the favour of Government the sunshine of their moral day, confide in the political creed-makers of the hour, are willing to think things that are rusty and decayed venerable, and are uninquiringly satisfied with evils as these are, because they find them established and unquestioned as they do sunlight and air when they come into existence ; that they had better not even think of philanthropy. I conceal not from them that the discountenance which Government will show to such an association as I am desirous to establish will come under their comprehensive definition of danger : that virtue, and any assembly instituted under its auspices, demands a voluntariness on the part of its devoted individuals, to sacrifice personal to public benefit ; and that it is possible that a party of beings associated for the purposes of disseminating virtuous principles, may, considering the ascendency which long custom has conferred on opposite motives to action, meet with inconveniences that may amount to personal danger. These considerations are, however, to the mind of the philanthropist, as is a drop to an ocean ; they serve by their possible existence as tests whereby to discover the really virtuous man from him who calls himself a patriot for dishonourable and selfish purposes. I propose then, to such as think with me, a Philanthropic Association, in spite of the danger that may attend the attempt. I do not this beneath the shroud of mystery and darkness. I propose not an Association of Secrecy. Let it [be?] open as the beam of day. Let it rival the sunbeam in its stainless purity, as in the extensiveness o its effulgence.

I disclaim all connexion with insincerity and concealment. The latter implies the former, as much as the former stands in need of the latter. It is a very latitudinarian system of morality that permits its professor to employ bad means for any end whatever. Weapons which vice *can* use are unfit for the hands of virtue. Concealment implies falsehood ; it is bad, and can therefore never be serviceable to the cause of philanthropy.

I propose therefore that the association shall be established and conducted in the open face of day, with the utmost possible publicity. It is only vice that hides itself in holes and corners, whose effrontery shrinks from scrutiny, whose cowardice

> lets "I *dare not*" wait upon "I would,"
> Like the poor cat i' th' adage.*

But the eye of virtue, eagle-like, darts through the undazzling beam of eternal truth, and from the undiminished fountain of its purity gathers wherewith to vivify and illuminate a universe.

I have hitherto abstained from inquiring whether the association which I recommend be or be not consistent with the English Constitution. And here it is fit briefly to consider what a constitution is.

Government can have no rights, it is a delegation for the purpose of securing them to others. Man becomes a subject of government, not that he may be in a worse, but that he may be in a better state than that of unorganized society. The strength of government is the happiness of the governed. All government existing for the happiness of others is just only so far as it exists by their consent, and useful only so far as it operates to their well-being. Constitution is to government what government is to law. Constitution may, in this view of the subject, be defined to be not merely something con-

* Macbeth, act i. sc. 7.

I.   S

stituted for the benefit of any nation or class of people, but something constituted by themselves for their own benefit. The nations of England and Ireland have no constitution, because at no one time did the individuals that compose them constitute a system for the general benefit. If a system determined on by a very few, at a great length of time; if Magna Charta, the Bill of Rights, and other usages for whose influence the improved state of human knowledge is rather to be looked to than any system which courtiers pretend to exist, and perhaps believe to exist—a system whose spring of agency they represent as something secret, undiscoverable, and awful as the law of nature; if these make a constitution, then England has one. But if (as I have endeavoured to show they do not) a constitution is something else, then the speeches of kings or commissioners, the writings of courtiers, and the journals of Parliament, which teem with its glory, are full of political cant, exhibit the skeleton of national freedom, and are fruitless attempts to hide evils in whose favour they cannot prove an alibi. As, therefore, in the true sense of the expression, the spot of earth on which we live is destitute of constituted government, it is impossible to offend against its principles, or to be with justice accused of wishing to subvert what has no real existence. If a man was accused of setting fire to a house, which house never existed, and from the nature of things could not have existed, it is impossible that a jury in their senses would find him guilty of arson. The English Constitution then could not be offended by the principles of virtue and freedom. In fact, the manner in which the Government of England has varied since its earliest establishment, proves that its present form is the result of a progressive accommodation to existing principles. It has been a continual struggle for liberty on the part of the people, and an uninterrupted attempt at tightening the reins of oppression, and encouraging ignorance and imposture, by the oligarchy to whom the first William parcelled out the property of the aborigines at the conquest of England by the Normans. I hear much of its being a tree so long growing which to cut down is as bad as cutting down an oak where there are no more. But the best way, on topics similar to these, is to tell the plain truth, without the confusion and ornament of metaphor. I call expressions similar to these, political cant, which, like the songs of "Rule Britannia" and "God save the King," are but abstracts of the caterpillar creed of courtiers, cut down to the taste and comprehension of a mob ; the one to disguise to an alehouse politician the evils of that devilish practice of war, and the other to inspire among clubs of all descriptions a certain feeling which some call loyalty and others servility. A Philanthropic Association has nothing to fear from the English Constitution, but it may expect danger from its government. So far, however, from thinking this an argument against its institution, establishment, and augmentation, I am inclined to rest much of the weight of the cause which my duties call upon me to support, on the very fact that government forcibly interferes when the opposition that is made to its proceedings is profoundly and undeniably nothing but intellectual. A good cause may be shown to be good, violence instantly renders bad what might before have been good. "Weapons that falsehood can use are unfit for the hands of truth "—truth can reason, and falsehood cannot.

A political or religious system may burn and imprison those who investigate its principles ; but it is an invariable proof of their falsehood and hollowness. Here there is another reason for the necessity of a Philanthropic Association, and I call upon any fair and rational opponent to controvert the argument which it contains ; for there is no one who even calls himself a philanthropist that thinks personal danger or dishonour terrible in any other light than as it affects his usefulness.

Man has a heart to feel, a brain to think, and a tongue to utter. The laws of his moral as of his physical nature are immutable, as is everything of nature; nor can the ephemeral institutions of human society take away those rights, annihilate or strengthen the duties that have for their basis the imperishable relations of his constitution.

Though the Parliament of England were to pass a thousand bills, to inflict upon those who determined to utter their thoughts a thousand penalties, it could not render that criminal which was in its nature innocent before the passing of such bills.

Man has a right to feel, to think, and to speak, nor can any acts of legislature destroy that right. He will feel, he must think, and he *ought* to give utterance to those thoughts and feelings with the readiest sincerity and the strictest candour. A man must have a right to do a thing before he can have a duty; this right must permit before his duty can enjoin him to any act. Any law is bad which attempts to make it criminal to do what the plain dictates within the breast of every man tell him that he ought to do.

The English Government permits a fanatic to assemble any number of persons to teach them the most extravagant and immoral systems of faith; but a few men meeting to consider its own principles are marked with its hatred and pursued by its jealousy.

The religionist who agonizes the death-bed of the cottager, and, by picturing the hell which hearts black and narrow as his own alone could have invented, and which exists but in their cores, spreads the uncharitable doctrines which devote *heretics* to eternal torments, and represents heaven to be what earth is, a monopoly in the hands of certain favoured ones whose merit consists in slavishness, whose success is the reward of sycophancy.

Thus much is permitted, but a public inquiry that involves any doubt of their rectitude into the principles of government is not permitted. When Jupiter and a countryman were one day walking out, conversing familiarly on the affairs of earth, the countryman listened to Jupiter's assertions on the subject for some time in acquiescence, at length, happening to hint a doubt, Jupiter threatened him with his thunder. "Ah, ah," says the countryman, "now, Jupiter, I know that you are wrong ; you are always wrong when you appeal to your thunder." The essence of virtue is disinterestedness. Disinterestedness is the quality which preserves the character of virtue distinct from that of either innocence or vice. This, it will be said, is mere assertion. It is so: but it is an assertion whose truth, I believe, the hearts of philanthropists are disinclined to deny. Those who have been convinced by their grandam of the doctrine of an original hereditary sin, or by the apostles of a degrading philosophy of the necessary and universal selfishness of man, cannot be philanthropists. Now, as an action, or a motive to action, is only virtuous so far as it is disinterested, or partakes (I adopt this mode of expression to suit the taste of some) of the nature of generalized self-love, then reward or punishment, attached even by omnipotence to any action, can in no wise make it either good or bad.

It is no crime to act in contradiction to an English judge or an English legislator, but it is a crime to transgress the dictates of a monitor which feels the spring of every motive, whose throne is the human sensorium, whose empire the human conduct. Conscience is a government before which all others sink into nothingness ; it surpasses, and, where it can act, supersedes all other, as nature surpasses art, as God surpasses man.

In the preceding pages, during the course of an investigation of the possible objections which might be urged

278 PROPOSALS FOR AN ASSOCIATION.

by philanthropy to an association such as I recommend,
as I have rather sought to bring forward than conceal
my principles, it will appear that they have their origin
from the discoveries in the sciences of politics and morals
which preceded and occasioned the revolutions of America
and France. It is with openness that I confess, nay,
with pride I assert, that they are so. The names of
Paine and Lafayette will outlive the p[o]etic aristocracy
of an expatriated Jesuit,* as the executive of a bigoted
policy will die before the disgust at the sycophancy of
their eulogists can subside.

It will be said, perhaps, that much as principles such
as these may appear marked on the outside with peace,
liberty, and virtue, that their ultimate tendency is to a
Revolution, which, like that of France, will end in bloodshed, vice, and slavery. I must offer, therefore, my
thoughts on that event, which so suddenly and so lament-
ably extinguished the overstrained hopes of liberty which
it excited. I do not deny that the Revolution of France
was occasioned by the literary labours of the encyclo-
pædists. When we see two events together, in certain
cases, we speak of one as the cause, the other the effect.
We have no other idea of cause and effect but that which
arises from necessary connexion ; it is, therefore, still
doubtful whether D'Alembert, Boulanger, Condorcet, and
other celebrated characters, were the causes of the over-
throw of the ancient monarchy of France. Thus much
is certain, that they contributed greatly to the extension
and diffusion of knowledge, and that knowledge is incompatible with slavery. The French nation was bowed to
the dust by ages of uninterrupted despotism. They were
plundered and insulted by a succession of oligarchies,
each more bloodthirsty and unrelenting than the foregoing. In a state like this her soldiers learned to fight
for Freedom on the plains of America, whilst at this very

* See *Mémoires de Jacobinisme*, par l'Abbé Baruel.

conjuncture a ray of science burst through the clouds of bigotry that obscured the moral day of Europe. The French were in the lowest state of human degradation, and when the truth, unaccustomed to their ears, that they were men and equals, was promulgated, they were the first to vent their indignation on the monopolizers of earth, because they were most glaringly defrauded of the immunities of nature.

Since the French were furthest removed by the sophistications of political institution from the genuine condition of human beings, they must have been most unfit for that happy state of equal law which proceeds from consummated civilization, and which demands habits of the strictest virtue before its introduction.

The murders during the period of the French Revolution, and the despotism which has since been established, prove that the doctrines of philanthropy and freedom were but shallowly understood. Nor was it until after that period that their principles became clearly to be explained, and unanswerably to be established.

Voltaire was the flatterer of kings, though in his heart he despised them—so far has he been instrumental in the present slavery of his country. Rousseau gave licence by his writings to passions that only incapacitate and contract the human heart—so far hath he prepared the necks of his fellow-beings for that yoke of galling and dishonourable servitude which at this moment it bears. Helvetius and Condorcet established principles ; but if they drew conclusions, their conclusions were unsystematical, and devoid of the luminousness and energy of method. They were little understood in the Revolution. But this age of ours is not stationary. Philosophers have not developed the great principles of the human mind that conclusions from them should be unprofitable and impracticable. We are in a state of continually progressive improvement. One truth that has been dis-

covered can never die, but will prevent the revivification
of its apportioned opposite falsehood. By promoting
truth and discouraging its opposite—the means of philanthropy are principally to be forwarded. Godwin wrote
during the Revolution of France, and certainly his writings
were totally devoid of influence with regard to its purposes. Oh! that they had not! In the Revolution of France
were engaged men whose names are inerasable from the
records of Liberty. Their genius penetrated with a
glance the gloom and glare which Church-craft and
State-craft had spread before the imposture and villany
of their establishments. They saw the world. Were they
men? Yes! They felt for it! They risked their lives
and happiness for its benefit! Had there been more of
those men, France would not now be a beacon to warn
us of the hazard and horror of Revolutions, but a pattern
of society rapidly advancing to a state of perfection, and
holding out an example for the gradual and peaceful
regeneration of the world. I consider it to be one of the
effects of a Philanthropic Association to assist in the
production of such men as these, in an extensive
development of those germs of excellence whose favourite
soil is the cultured garden of the human mind.

Many well-meaning persons may think that the attainment of the good which I propose as the ultimatum of
philanthropic exertion is visionary and inconsistent with
human nature; they would tell me not to make people
happy for fear of overstocking the world, and to permit
those who found dishes placed before them on the table
of partial nature to enjoy their superfluities in quietness,
though millions of wretches crowded around but to pick
a morsel,* which morsel was still refused to the prayers
of agonizing famine.

I cannot help thinking this an evil, nor help endeavouring, by the safest means that I can devise, to palliate

* See Malthus on *Population.*

at present, and in fine to eradicate, this evil. War, vice, and misery are undeniably bad, they embrace all that we can conceive of temporal and eternal evil. Are we to be told that these are remediless, because the earth would, in case of their remedy, be overstocked? That the rich are still to glut, that the ambitious are still to plan, that the fools whom these knaves mould, are still to murder their brethren and call it glory, and that the poor are to pay with their blood, their labour, their happiness, and their innocence for the crimes and mistakes which the hereditary monopolists of earth commit? Rare sophism! How will the heartless rich hug thee to their bosoms, and lull their conscience into slumber with the opiate of thy reconciling dogmas!

But when the philosopher and philanthropist contemplates the universe, when he perceives existing evils that admit of amendment, and hears tell of other evils, which, in the course of sixty centuries, may again derange the system of happiness which the amendment is calculated to produce, does he submit to prolong a positive evil, because, if that were eradicated, after a millennium of 6000 years (for such space of time would it take to people the earth) another evil would take place?

To how contemptible a degradation of grossest credulity will not prejudice lower the human mind! We see in winter that the foliage of the trees is gone, that they present to the view nothing but leafless branches—we see that the loveliness of the flower decays, though the root continues in the earth. What opinion should we form of that man who, when he walked in the freshness of the spring, beheld the fields enamelled with flowers, and the foliage bursting from the buds, should find fault with this beautiful order, and murmur his contemptible discontents because winter must come, and the landscape be robbed of its beauty for a while again? Yet this man is Mr. Malthus. Do we not see that the laws of nature perpetually act by disorganization and reproduction, each alternately becoming cause and effect. The analogies that we can draw from physical to moral topics are of all others the most striking.

Does anyone yet question the possibility of inducing radical reform of moral and political evil? Does he object, from that impossibility, to the association which I propose, which I frankly confess to be one of the means whose instrumentality I would employ to attain this reform. Let them look to the methods which I use. Let me put my object out of their view and propose their own, how would they accomplish it? By diffusing virtue and knowledge, by promoting human happiness. Palsied be the hand, for ever dumb be the tongue that would by one expression convey sentiments differing from these: I will use no bad means for any end whatever. Know then, ye philanthropists—to whatever profession of faith, or whatever determination of principles, chance, reason, or education may have conducted you— that the endeavours of the truly virtuous necessarily converge to one point, though it be hidden from them what point that is; they all labour for one end, and that controversies concerning the nature of that end serve only to weaken the strength which for the interest of virtue should be consolidated.

The diffusion of true and virtuous principles (for in the first principles of morality *none* disagree) will produce the best of possible terminations.

I invite to an Association of Philanthropy those, of whatever ultimate expectations, who will employ the same means that I employ; let their designs differ as much as they may from mine, I shall rejoice at their co-operation: because, if the ultimatum of my hopes be founded on the unity of truth, I shall then have auxiliaries in its cause, and if it be false I shall rejoice that means are not neglected for forwarding that which is true.

The accumulation of evil which Ireland has for the last twenty years sustained, and considering the unremittingness of its pressure I may say patiently sustained; the melancholy prospect which the unforeseen conduct of the Regent of England holds out of its continuance, demands of every Irishman whose pulses have not ceased to throb with the life-blood of his heart, that he should individually consult, and unitedly determine on some measures for the liberty of his countrymen. That those measures should be pacific though resolute, that their movers should be calmly brave and temperately unbending, though the whole heart and soul should go with the attempt, is the opinion which my principles command me to give.

And I am induced to call an association such as this occasion demands, an Association of Philanthropy, because good men ought never to circumscribe their usefulness by any name which denotes their exclusive devotion to the accomplishment of its signification.

When I began the preceding remarks, I conceived that on the removal of the restrictions from the Regent a ministry less inimical than the present to the interests of liberty would have been appointed. I am deceived, and the disappointment of the hopes of freedom on this subject affords an additional argument towards the necessity of an Association.

I conclude these remarks, which I have indited principally with a view of unveiling my principles, with a proposal for an Association for the purposes of Catholic Emancipation, a repeal of the Union Act, and grounding upon the attainment of these objects a reform of whatever moral or political evil may be within its compass of human power to remedy.

Such as are favourably inclined towards the institution would highly gratify the Proposer if they would personally communicate with him on this important subject;

by which means the plan might be matured, errors in the Proposer's original system be detected, and a meeting for the purpose convened with that resolute expedition which the nature of the present crisis demands.

No. 7, Lower Sackville Street.

DECLARATION OF RIGHTS.

I.

GOVERNMENT has no rights; it is a delegation from several individuals for the purpose of securing their own. It is therefore just, only so far as it exists by their consent, useful only so far as it operates to their well-being.

II.

If these individuals think that the form of government which they or their forefathers constituted is ill adapted to produce their happiness, they have a right to change it.

III.

Government is devised for the security of Rights. The rights of man are liberty, and an equal participation of the commonage of Nature.

IV.

As the benefit of the governed is, or ought to be, the origin of government, no men can have any authority that does not expressly emanate from *their* will.

V.

Though all governments are not so bad as that of Turkey, yet none are so good as they might be. The majority of every country have a right to perfect their government. The minority should not disturb them;

they ought to secede, and form their own system in their own way.

VI.

All have a right to an equal share in the benefits and burdens of Government. Any disabilities for opinion imply, by their existence, bare-faced tyranny on the side of Government, ignorant slavishness on the side of the governed.

VII.

The rights of man, in the present state of society, are only to be secured by some degree of coercion to be exercised on their violator. The sufferer has a right that the degree of coercion employed be as slight as possible.

VIII.

It may be considered as a plain proof of the hollowness of any proposition if power be used to enforce instead of reason to persuade its admission. Government is never supported by fraud until it cannot be supported by reason.

IX.

No man has a right to disturb the public peace by personally resisting the execution of a law, however bad. He ought to acquiesce, using at the same time the utmost powers of his reason to promote its repeal.

X.

A man must have a right to act in a certain manner, before it can be his duty. He may, before he ought.

XI.

A man has a right to think as his reason directs; it is a duty he owes to himself to think with freedom, that he may act from conviction.

XII.

A man has a right to unrestricted liberty of discussion. Falsehood is a scorpion that will sting itself to death.

XIII.

A man has not only a right to express his thoughts, but it is his duty to do so.

XIV.

No law has a right to discourage the practice of truth. A man ought to speak the truth on every occasion. A duty can never be criminal ; what is not criminal cannot be injurious.

XV.

Law cannot make what is in its nature virtuous or innocent to be criminal, any more than it can make what is criminal to be innocent. Government cannot make a law; it can only pronounce that which was the law before its organization ; viz., the moral result of the imperishable relations of things.

XVI.

The present generation cannot bind their posterity: the few cannot promise for the many.

XVII.

No man has a right to do an evil thing that good may come.

XVIII.

Expediency is inadmissible in morals. Politics are only sound when conducted on principles of morality : they are, in fact, the morals of nations.

XIX.

Man has no right to kill his brother. It is no excuse that he does so in uniform : he only adds the infamy of servitude to the crime of murder.

XX.

Man, whatever be his country, has the same rights in one place as another—the rights of universal citizenship.

XXI.

The government of a country ought to be perfectly indifferent to every opinion. Religious differences, the bloodiest and most rancorous of all, spring from partiality.

XXII.

A delegation of individuals, for the purpose of securing their rights, can have no undelegated power of restraining the expression of their opinion.

XXIII.

Belief is involuntary; nothing involuntary is meritorious or reprehensible. A man ought not to be considered worse or better for his belief.

XXIV.

A Christian, a Deist, a Turk, and a Jew, have equal rights : they are men and brethren.

XXV.

If a person's religious ideas correspond not with your own, love him nevertheless. How different would yours have been had the chance of birth placed you in Tartary or India !

XXVI.

Those who believe that Heaven is, what earth has been, a monopoly in the hands of a favoured few, would do well to reconsider their opinion ; if they find that it came from their priest or their grandmother, they could not do better than reject it.

XXVII.

No man has a right to be respected for any other possessions but those of virtue and talents. Titles are tinsel, power a corruptor, glory a bubble, and excessive wealth a libel on its possessor.

XXVIII.

No man has a right to monopolise more than he can enjoy; what the rich give to the poor, whilst millions are starving, is not a perfect favour, but an imperfect right.

XXIX.

Every man has a right to a certain degree of leisure and liberty, because it is his duty to attain a certain degree of knowledge. He may, before he ought.

XXX.

Sobriety of body and mind is necessary to those who would be free; because, without sobriety, a high sense of philanthropy cannot actuate the heart, nor cool and determined courage execute its dictates.

XXXI.

The only use of government is to repress the vices of man. If man were to-day sinless, to-morrow he would have a right to demand that government and all its evils should cease.

_____

Man! thou whose rights are here declared, be no longer forgetful of the loftiness of thy destination. Think of thy rights, of those possessions which will give thee virtue and wisdom, by which thou mayest arrive at happiness and freedom. They are declared to thee by one who knows thy dignity, for every hour does his heart swell with honourable pride in the contemplation of what thou mayest attain—by one who is not forgetful of thy degeneracy, for every moment brings home to him the bitter conviction of what thou art.

Awake!—arise!—or be for ever fallen.

A

REFUTATION

OF

DEISM:

IN

A DIALOGUE.

———

ΣΥΝΕΤΟΙΣΙΝ.

———————————————————

London:

PRINTED BY SCHULZE AND DEAN,

13, POLAND STREET.

——
1814.

PREFACE.

The object of the following Dialogue is to prove that the system of Deism is untenable. It is attempted to shew that there is no alternative between Atheism and Christianity; that the evidences of the Being of a God are to be deduced from no other principles than those of Divine Revelation.

The Author endeavours to shew how much the cause of natural and revealed Religion has suffered from the mode of defence adopted by Theosophistical Christians. How far he will accomplish what he proposed to himself, in the composition of this Dialogue, the world will finally determine.

The mode of printing this little work may appear too expensive, either for its merits or its length. However inimical this practice confessedly is, to the general diffusion of knowledge, yet it was adopted in this instance with a view of excluding the multitude from the abuse of a mode of reasoning, liable to misconstruction on account of its novelty.

EUSEBES AND THEOSOPHUS.

EUSEBES.

THEOSOPHUS, I have long regretted and observed the strange infatuation which has blinded your understanding. It is not without acute uneasiness that I have beheld the progress of your audacious scepticism trample on the most venerable institutions of our forefathers, until it has rejected the salvation which the only begotten Son of God deigned to proffer in person to a guilty and unbelieving world. To this excess, then, has the pride of the human understanding at length arrived? To measure itself with Omniscience! To scan the intentions of Inscrutability!

You can have reflected but superficially on this awful and important subject. The love of paradox, an affectation of singularity, or the pride of reason has seduced you to the barren and gloomy paths of infidelity. Surely you have hardened yourself against the truth with a spirit of coldness and cavil.

Have you been wholly inattentive to the accumulated evidence which the Deity has been pleased to attach to the revelation of his will? The antient books in which the advent of the Messiah was predicted, the miracles by which its truth has been so conspicuously confirmed, the martyrs who have undergone every variety of torment in attestation of its veracity? You seem to require mathematical demonstration in a case which admits of no more than strong moral probability. Surely the merit of that faith which we are required to repose in our Redeemer would be thus entirely done away. Where is the difficulty of according credit to that which is perfectly plain and evident ? How is he entitled to a recompense who believes what he cannot disbelieve ?

When there is satisfactory evidence that the witnesses of the Christian miracles passed their lives in labours, dangers, and sufferings, and consented severally to be racked, burned, and strangled, in testimony of the truth of their account, will it be asserted that they were actuated by a disinterested desire of deceiving others ? That they were hypocrites for no end but to teach the purest doctrine that ever enlightened the world, and martyrs without any prospect of emolument or fame ? The sophist, who gravely advances an opinion thus absurd, certainly sins with gratuitous and indefensible pertinacity.

The history of Christianity is itself the most indisputable proof of those miracles by which its origin was sanctioned to the world. It is itself one great miracle. A few humble men established it in the face of an opposing universe. In less than fifty years an astonishing multitude was converted, as Suetonius,* Pliny,† Tacitus,‡ and Lucian attest ; and shortly afterwards thousands who had boldly overturned the altars, slain the priests and burned the temples of Paganism, were loud in demanding the recompense of martyrdom from the hands of the infuriated heathens. Not until three centuries after the

---

* *Judæi, impulsore Chresto, turbantes, facile comprimuntur.—Suet. in Tib.*

Affecti suppliciis Christiani, genus hominum superstitionis novæ et maleficæ.—Id. in Nerone.

† *Multi omnis ætatis utriusque sexus etiam; neque enim civitates tantum, sed vicos etiam et agros superstitionis istius contagio pervagata est.—Plin. Epist.*

‡ Tacit. Annal L. xv., Sect. xlv.

coming of the Messiah did his holy religion incorporate itself with the institutions of the Roman Empire, and derive support from the visible arm of fleshly strength. Thus long without any assistance but that of its Omnipotent author, Christianity prevailed in defiance of incredible persecutions, and drew fresh vigour from circumstances the most desperate and unpromising. By what process of sophistry can a rational being persuade himself to reject a religion, the original propagation of which is an event wholly unparalleled in the sphere of human experience?

The morality of the Christian religion is as original and sublime, as its miracles and mysteries are unlike all other portents. A patient acquiescence in injuries and violence ; a passive submission to the will of sovereigns; a disregard of those ties by which the feelings of humanity have ever been bound to this unimportant world ; humility and faith, are doctrines neither similar nor comparable to those of any other system.* Friendship, patriotism, and magnanimity ; the heart that is quick in sensibility, the hand that is inflexible in execution ; genius, learning and courage, are qualities which have engaged the admiration of mankind, but which we are taught by Christianity to consider as splendid and delusive vices.

I know not why a Theist should feel himself more inclined to distrust the historians of Jesus Christ than those of Alexander the Great. What do the tidings of redemption contain which render them peculiarly obnoxious to discredit? It will not be disputed that a revelation of the Divine will is a benefit to mankind.† It will not be asserted that even under the Christian revelation, we have too clear a solution of the vast enigma of the Universe, too satisfactory a justification of the attributes

* See the *Internal Evidence of Christianity;* see also Paley's Evidences, Vol. II., p 27.

† Paley's Evidences, Vol. I., p. 3.

of God. When we call to mind the profound ignorance in which, with the exception of the Jews, the philosophers of antiquity were plunged ; when we recollect that men, eminent for dazzling talents and fallacious virtues, Epicurus, Democritus, Pliny, Lucretius,* Euripides, and innumerable others, dared publicly to avow their faith in Atheism with impunity, and that the Theists, Anaxagoras, Pythagoras and Plato, vainly endeavoured by that human reason, which is truly incommensurate to so vast a purpose, to establish among philosophers the belief in one Almighty God, the creator and preserver of the world; when we recollect that the multitude were grossly and ridiculously idolatrous, and that the magistrates, if not Atheists, regarded the being of a God in the light of an abstruse and uninteresting speculation ;† when we add to these considerations a remembrance of the wars and the oppressions, which about the time of the advent of the Messiah, desolated the human race, is it not more credible that the Deity actually interposed to check the rapid progress of human deterioration, than that he permitted a specious and pestilent imposture to seduce mankind into the labyrinth of a deadlier superstition? Surely the Deity has not created man immortal, and left him for ever in ignorance of his glorious destination. If the Christian Religion is false, I see not upon what foundation our belief in a moral governor of the universe, or our hopes of immortality can rest.

Thus then the plain reason of the case, and the suffrage ·of the civilized world, conspire with the more indisputable

* Plin. Nat. His. Cap. de Deo., Euripides, Bellerophon, Frag. xxv.

Hunc igitur terrorem animi, tenebrasque necesse est
Non radii solis, neque lucida tela diei
Discutient, sed naturæ species ratioque :
Principium hinc cujus nobis exordia sumet,
NULLAM REM NIHILO GIGNI DIVINITUS UNQUAM.

Luc. de Rer. Nat. Lib. 1 [*v*. 147-151].

† See Cicero de Natura Deorum.

suggestions of faith, to render impregnable that system which has been so vainly and so wantonly assailed. Suppose, however, it were admitted that the conclusions of human reason and the lessons of worldly virtue should be found, in the detail, incongruous with Divine Revelation; by the dictates of which would it become us to abide? Not by that which errs whenever it is employed, but by that which is incapable of error : not by the ephemeral systems of vain philosophy, but by the word of God, which shall endure for ever.

Reflect, O Theosophus, that if the religion you reject be true, you are justly excluded from the benefits which result from a belief in its efficiency to salvation. Be not regardless, therefore, I entreat you, of the curses so emphatically heaped upon infidels by the inspired organs of the will of God: the fire which is never quenched, the worm that never dies. I dare not think that the God in whom I trust for salvation, would terrify his creatures with menaces of punishment which he does not intend to inflict. The ingratitude of incredulity is, perhaps, the only sin to which the Almighty cannot extend his mercy without compromising his justice. How can the human heart endure, without despair, the mere conception of so tremendous an alternative? Return, I entreat you, to that tower of strength which securely overlooks the chaos of the conflicting opinions of men. Return to that God who is your creator and preserver, by whom alone you are defended from the ceaseless wiles of your eternal enemy. Are human institutions so faultless that the principle upon which they are founded may strive with the voice of God? Know that faith is superior to reason, in as much as the creature is surpassed by the Creator; and that whensoever they are incompatible, the suggestions of the latter, not those of the former, are to be questioned.

Permit me to exhibit in their genuine deformity the

errors which are seducing you to destruction. State to me
with candour the train of sophisms by which the evil
spirit has deluded your understanding. Confess the
secret motives of your disbelief; suffer me to administer
a remedy to your intellectual disease. I fear not the con-
tagion of such revolting sentiments: I fear only lest
patience should desert me before you have finished the
detail of your presumptuous credulity.

THEOSOPHUS.

I AM not only prepared to confess, but to vindicate my
sentiments. I cannot refrain, however, from premising,
that in this controversy I labour under a disadvantage
from which you are exempt. You believe that incredulity
is immoral, and regard him as an object of suspicion and
distrust whose creed is incongruous with your own. But
truth is the perception of the agreement or disagreement
of ideas. I can no more conceive that a man who perceives
the disagreement of any ideas should be persuaded of
their agreement, than that he should overcome a physical
impossibility. The reasonableness or the folly of the
articles of our creed is therefore no legitimate object of
merit or demerit; our opinions depend not on the will,
but on the understanding.

If I am in error (and the wisest of us may not presume
to deem himself secure from all illusion) that error is the
consequence of the prejudices by which I am prevented,
of the ignorance by which I am incapacitated from form-
ing a correct estimation of the subject. Remove those
prejudices, dispel that ignorance, make truth apparent,
and fear not the obstacles that remain to be encountered
But do not repeat to me those terrible and frequent curses,
by whose intolerance and cruelty I have so often been
disgusted in the perusal of your sacred books. Do
not tell me that the All-Merciful will punish me for the
conclusions of that reason by which he has thought fit to

distinguish me from the beasts that perish. Above all, refrain from urging considerations drawn from reason, to degrade that which you are thereby compelled to acknowledge as the ultimate arbiter of the dispute. Answer my objections as I engage to answer your assertions, point by point, word by word.

You believe that the only and ever-present God begot a Son whom he sent to reform the world, and to propitiate its sins ; you believe that a book, called the Bible, contains a true account of this event, together with an infinity of miracles and prophecies which preceded it from the creation of the world. Your opinion that these circumstances really happened appears to me, from some considerations which I will proceed to state, destitute of rational foundation.

To expose all the inconsistency, immorality and false pretensions which I perceive in the Bible, demands a minuteness of criticism at least as voluminous as itself. I shall confine myself, therefore, to the confronting of your tenets with those primitive and general principles which are the basis of all moral reasoning.

In creating the Universe, God certainly proposed to himself the happiness of his creatures. It is just, therefore, to conclude that he left no means unemployed, which did not involve an impossibility, to accomplish this design. In fixing a residence for this image of his own Majesty, he was doubtless careful that every occasion of detriment, every opportunity of evil, should be removed. He was aware of the extent of his powers, he foresaw the consequences of his conduct, and doubtless modelled his being consentaneously with the world of which he was to be the inhabitant, and the circumstances which were destined to surround him.

The account given by the Bible has but a faint concordance with the surmises of reason concerning this event.

According to this book, God created Satan, who, instigated by the impulses of his nature, contended with the
Omnipotent for the throne of Heaven. After a contest
for the empire, in which God was victorious, Satan was
thrust into a pit of burning sulphur. On man's creation,
God placed within his reach a tree whose fruit he forbade
him to taste, on pain of death ; permitting Satan, at the
same time, to employ all his artifice to persuade this
innocent and wondering creature to transgress the fatal
prohibition.

The first man yielded to this temptation ; and to satisfy
Divine Justice the whole of his posterity must have been
eternally burned in hell, if God had not sent his only Son
on earth, to save those few whose salvation had been foreseen and determined before the creation of the world.

God is here represented as creating man with certain
passions and powers, surrounding him with certain circumstances, and then condemning him to everlasting torments because he acted as omniscience had foreseen, and
was such as omnipotence had made him. For to assert
that the Creator is the author of all good, and the creature
the author of all evil, is to assert that one man makes a
straight line and a crooked one, and that another makes
the incongruity.*

Barbarous and uncivilized nations have uniformly
adored, under various names, a God of which themselves
were the model : revengeful, blood-thirsty, grovelling
and capricious. The idol of a savage is a demon that
delights in carnage. The steam of slaughter, the disson-
ance of groans, the flames of a desolated land, are the
offerings which he deems acceptable, and his innumerable
votaries throughout the world have made it a point of
duty to worship him to his taste.† The Phenicians, the
Druids and the Mexicans have immolated hundreds at
the shrines of their divinity, and the high and holy name

* Hobbes.   † See Preface to Le Bon Sens.

of God has been in all ages the watchword of the most unsparing massacres, the sanction of the most atrocious perfidies.

But I appeal to your candour, O Eusebes, if there exist a record of such grovelling absurdities and enormities so atrocious, a picture of the Deity so characteristic of a dcmon as that which the sacred writings of the Jews contain. I demand of you, whether as a conscientious Theist you can reconcile the conduct which is attributed to the God of the Jews with your conceptions of the purity and benevolence of the divine nature.

The loathsome and minute obscenities to which the inspired writers perpetually descend, the filthy observances which God is described as personally instituting,* the total disregard of truth and contempt of the first principles of morality, manifested on the most public occasions by the chosen favourites of Heaven, might corrupt, were they not so flagitious as to disgust.

When the chief of this obscure and brutal horde of assassins asserts that the God of the Universe was enclosed in a box of shittim wood,† "two feet long and three feet wide,"‡ and brought home in a new cart, I smile at the impertinence of so shallow an imposture. But it is blasphemy of a more hideous and unexampled nature to maintain that the Almighty God expressly commanded Moses to invade an unoffending nation ; and, on account of the difference of their worship, utterly to destroy every human being it contained, to murder every infant and unarmed man in cold blood, to massacre the captives, to rip up the matrons, and to retain the maidens

* See Hosea, chap. i., chap. ix. Ezekiel, chap. iv., chap. xvi., chap. xxiii. Heyne, speaking of the opinions entertained of the Jews by ancient poets and philosophers, says :—*Meminit quidem superstitionis Judaicæ Horatius, verum ut eam risu exploderet.*— *Heyn. ad Virg. Poll. in Arg.*

† I. Sam. chap. v., 8.   ‡ Wordsworth's Lyrical Ballads.

alone for concubinage and violation.* At the very time
that philosophers of the most enterprising benevolence

* Then Moses stood in the gate of the camp, and said, Who is on
the Lord's side? let him come unto me. And all the sons of Levi
gathered themselves together unto him. And he said unto them,
Thus saith the Lord God of Israel, Put every man his sword by his
side, and go in and out from gate to gate throughout the camp, *and
slay every man his brother, and every man his companion, and every
man his neighbour.* And the children of Levi did according to the
word of Moses : and there fell of the people on that day twenty-three
thousand men.—*Exodus* xxxii., 26.

And they warred against the Midianites, as the Lord commanded Moses ; and they slew all the males. And the children of
Israel took all the women of Midian captives, and their little ones,
and took the spoil of all their cattle, and all their flocks, and all
their goods. And they burned all their huts wherein they dwelt, and
all their goodly castles, with fire. And Moses, and Eleazar the
priest, and all the princes of the congregation, went forth to meet
them without the camp. And Moses was [wroth] with the officers
of the host, with the captains over thousands, and captains over hundreds, which came from the battle. And Moses said unto them,
Have ye saved all the women alive? behold, these caused the children of Israel, through the counsel of Balaam, to commit trespass
against the Lord in the matter of Peor, and there was a plague
among the congregation of the Lord. *Now therefore kill every
male among the little ones, and kill every woman that hath known
man by lying with him. But all the women-children, that have not
known a man by lying with him,* KEEP ALIVE FOR YOURSELVES.
—*Numbers* xxxi., 7-18.

And we utterly destroyed them, as we did unto Sihon, king of
Heshbon, utterly destroying the men, women, and children of every
city.—*Deut.* iii., 6.

And they utterly destroyed all that was in the city, both man and
woman, young and old, and ox and sheep and ass, with the edge of
the sword.—*Joshua.*

So Joshua fought against Debir, and utterly destroyed all the
souls that were therein : he left none remaining, but utterly destroyed all that breathed, as the Lord God of Israel commanded.—
Joshua, chap. x.

And David gathered all the people together, and went to Rabbah,
and took it. And he brought forth the people therein, and *put them*

were founding in Greece those institutions which have rendered it the wonder and luminary of the world, am I required to believe that the weak and wicked king of an obscure and barbarous nation, a murderer, a traitor and a tyrant, was the man after God's own heart? A wretch, at the thought of whose unparalleled enormities the sternest soul must sicken in dismay! An unnatural monster, who sawed his fellow beings in sunder, harrowed them to fragments under harrows of iron, chopped them to pieces with axes, and burned them in brick-kilns, because they bowed before a different, and less bloody idol than his own. It is surely no perverse conclusion of an infatuated understanding that the God of the Jews is not the benevolent author of this beautiful world.

The conduct of the Deity in the promulgation of the Gospel, appears not to the eye of reason more compatible with his immutability and omnipotence than the history of his actions under the law accords with his benevolence.

You assert that the human race merited eternal reprobation because their common father had transgressed the divine command, and that the crucifixion of the Son of God was the only sacrifice of sufficient efficacy to satisfy eternal justice. But it is no less inconsistent with justice and subversive of morality that millions should be responsible for a crime which they had no share in committing, than that, if they had really committed it, the crucifixion of an innocent being could absolve them from moral turpitude. *Ferretne ulla civitas latorem istiusmodi legis, ut condemnaretur filius, aut nepos, si pater aut avus deliquisset?* Certainly this is a mode of legislation peculiar to a state of savageness and anarchy; this is the irrefragable logic of tyranny and imposture.

under saws, and under harrows of iron, and made them pass through the brick kiln; this did he also unto all the children of Ammon.—II. Sam. xii., 29.

The supposition that God has ever supernaturally revealed his will to man at any other period than the original creation of the human race, necessarily involves a compromise of his benevolence. It assumes that he withheld from mankind a benefit which it was in his power to confer. That he suffered his creatures to remain in ignorance of truths essential to their happiness and salvation. That during the lapse of innumerable ages, every individual of the human race had perished without redemption, from an universal stain which the Deity at length descended in person to erase. That the good and wise of all ages, involved in one common fate with the ignorant and wicked, have been tainted by involuntary and inevitable error which torments infinite in duration may not avail to expiate.

In vain will you assure me with amiable inconsistency that the mercy of God will be extended to the virtuous, and that the vicious will alone be punished. The foundation of the Christian Religion is manifestly compromised by a concession of this nature. A subterfuge thus palpable plainly annihilates the necessity of the incarnation of God for the redemption of the human race, and represents the descent of the Messiah as a gratuitous display of Deity, solely adapted to perplex, to terrify and to embroil mankind.

It is sufficiently evident that an omniscient being never conceived the design of reforming the world by Christianity. Omniscience would surely have foreseen the inefficacy of that system, which experience demonstrates not only to have been utterly impotent in restraining, but to have been most active in exhaling the malevolent propensities of men. During the period which elapsed between the removal of the seat of empire to Constantinople in 328, and its capture by the Turks in 1453, what salutary influence did Christianity exercise upon that world which it was intended to enlighten? Never before was

Europe the theatre of such ceaseless and sanguinary wars; never were the people so brutalized by ignorance and debased by slavery.

I will admit that one prediction of Jesus Christ has been indisputably fulfilled. *I come not to bring peace upon earth, but a sword.* Christianity indeed has equalled Judaism in the atrocities, and exceeded it in the extent of its desolation. Eleven millions of men, women, and children, have been killed in battle, butchered in their sleep, burned to death at public festivals of sacrifice, poisoned, tortured, assassinated, and pillaged in the spirit of the Religion of Peace, and for the glory of the most merciful God.

In vain will you tell me that these terrible effects flow not from Christianity, but from the abuse of it. No such excuse will avail to palliate the enormities of a religion pretended to be divine. A limited intelligence is only so far responsible for the effects of its agency as it foresaw, or might have foreseen them; but Omniscience is manifestly chargeable with all the consequences of its conduct. Christianity itself declares that the worth of the tree is to be determined by the quality of its fruit. The extermination of infidels; the mutual persecutions of hostile sects; the midnight massacres and slow burning of thousands, because their creed contained either more or less than the orthodox standard, of which Christianity has been the immediate occasion; and the invariable opposition which philosophy has ever encountered from the spirit of revealed religion, plainly show that a very slight portion of sagacity was sufficient to have estimated at its true value the advantages of that belief to which some Theists are unaccountably attached.

You lay great stress upon the originality of the Christian system of morals. If this claim be just, either your religion must be false, or the Deity has willed that opposite modes of conduct should be pursued by mankind at

1. · U

different times, under the same circumstances ; which is absurd.

The doctrine of acquiescing in the most insolent despotism ; of praying for and loving our enemies ; of faith and humility, appears to fix the perfection of the human character in that abjectness and credulity which priests and tyrants of all ages have found sufficiently convenient for their purposes. It is evident that a whole nation of Christians (could such an anomaly maintain itself a day) would become, like cattle, the property of the first occupier. It is evident that ten highwaymen would suffice to subjugate the world if it were composed of slaves who dared not to resist oppression.

The apathy to love and friendship, recommended by your creed, would, if attainable, not be less pernicious. This enthusiasm of ánti-social misanthropy, if it were an actual rule of conduct, and not the speculation of a few interested persons, would speedily annihilate the human race. A total abstinence from sexual intercourse is not perhaps enjoined, but is strenuously recommended,* and was actually practised to a frightful extent by the primitive Christians.†

The penalties inflicted by that monster· Constantine, the first Christian Emperor, on the pleasures of unlicensed love, are so iniquitously severe, that no modern legislator could have affixed them to the most atrocious crimes.‡ This cold-blooded and hypocritical ruffian cut his son's throat, strangled his wife, murdered his father-in-law and his brother-in-law, and maintained at his court a set of

---

* Now concerning the things whereof ye wrote to me ; it is good for a man not to touch a woman.

I say, therefore, to the unmarried and widows, it is good for them if they abide even as I. But if they cannot contain, let them marry ; it is better to marry than burn.—*I. Cor.* chap. vii.

† *See* Gibbon's "Decline and Fall," vol. ii., p. 210.

‡ Ibid. Vol. ii., p. 269.

blood-thirsty and bigoted Christian Priests, one of whom was sufficient to excite the one half of the world to massacre the other.

I am willing to admit that some few axioms of morality, which Christianity has borrowed from the philosophers of Greece and India, dictate, in an unconnected state, rules of conduct worthy of regard; but the purest and most elevated lessons of morality must remain nugatory, the most probable inducements to virtue must fail of their effect, so long as the slightest weight is attached to that dogma which is the vital essence of revealed religion.

Belief is set up as the criterion of merit or demerit; a man is to be judged not by the purity of his intentions but by the orthodoxy of his creed; an assent to certain propositions, is to outweigh in the balance of Christianity the most generous and elevated virtue.

But the intensity of belief, like that of every other passion, is precisely proportioned to the degrees of excitement. A graduated scale, on which should be marked the capabilities of propositions to approach to the test of the senses, would be a just measure of the belief which ought to be attached to them: and but for the influence of prejudice or ignorance this invariably *is* the measure of belief. That is believed which is apprehended to be true, nor can the mind by any exertion avoid attaching credit to an opinion attended with overwhelming evidence. Belief is not an act of volition, nor can it be regulated by the mind: it is manifestly incapable therefore of either merit or criminality. The system which assumes a false criterion of moral virtue, must be as pernicious as it is absurd. Above all, it cannot be divine, as it is impossible that the Creator of the human mind should be ignorant of its primary powers.

The degree of evidence afforded by miracles and prophecies in favour of the Christian Religion is lastly to be considered.

Evidence of a more imposing and irresistible nature
is required in proportion to the remoteness of any event
from the sphere of our experience. Every case of
miracles is a contest of opposite improbabilities, whether
it is more contrary to experience that a miracle should
be true, or that the story on which it is supported
should be false : whether the immutable laws of this
harmonious world should have undergone violation, or
that some obscure Greeks and Jews should have conspired to fabricate a tale of wonder.

The actual appearance of a departed spirit would be
a circumstance truly unusual and portentous ; but the
accumulated testimony of twelve old women that a spirit
had appeared is neither unprecedented nor miraculous.

It seems less credible that the God whose immensity
is uncircumscribed by space, should have committed
adultery with a carpenter's wife, than that some bold
knaves or insane dupes had deceived the credulous
multitude.*   We have perpetual and mournful experience
of the latter : the former is yet under dispute.   History
affords us innumerable examples of the possibility of the
one : Philosophy has in all ages protested against the
probability of the other.

Every superstition can produce its dupes, its miracles,
and its mysteries ; each is prepared to justify its peculiar
tenets by an equal assemblage of portents, prophecies
and martyrdoms.

Prophecies, however circumstantial, are liable to the
same objection as direct miracles: it is more agreeable
to experience that the historical evidence of the prediction really having preceded the event pretended to be
foretold should be false, or that a lucky conjuncture of
events should have justified the conjecture of the prophet,
than that God should communicate to a man the discern-

* See Paley's Evidences.   Vol. i. chap. 1.

ment of future events.* I defy you to produce more than one instance of prophecy in the Bible, wherein the inspired writer speaks so as to be understood, wherein his prediction has not been so unintelligible and obscure as to have been itself the subject of controversy among Christians.

That one prediction which I except is certainly most explicit and circumstantial. It is the only one of this nature which the Bible contains. Jesus himself here predicts his own arrival in the clouds to consummate a period of supernatural desolation, before the generation which he addressed should pass away.† Eighteen hundred years have past, and no such event is pretended to have happened. This single plain prophecy, thus conspicuously false, may serve as a criterion of those which are more vague and indirect, and which apply in an hundred senses to an hundred things.

Either the pretended predictions in the Bible were meant to be understood, or they were not. If they were, why is there any dispute concerning them : if they were not, wherefore were they written at all? But the God of Christianity spoke to mankind in parables, that seeing they might not see, and hearing they might not under-. stand.

---

* See the Controversy of Bishop Watson and Thomas Paine.— Paine's Criticism on the xixth chapter of Isaiah.

† Immediately after the tribulation of these days shall the sun be darkened, and the moon shall not give her light, and the stars shall fall from heaven, and the powers of the heavens shall be shaken : and then shall appear the sign of the Son of man in heaven : and then shall all the tribes of the earth mourn, and they shall see the Son of man coming in the clouds of heaven with power and great glory. And he shall send his angel with a great sound of a trumpet, and they shall gather together his elect from the four winds, from one end of heaven to the other. *Verily I say unto you, this genera-tion shall not pass, until all these things be fulfilled.—Matt.* chap. xxiv.

The Gospels contain internal evidence that they were not written by eye-witnesses of the event which they pretend to record. The Gospel of St. Matthew was plainly not written until some time after the taking of Jerusalem, that is, at least forty years after the execution of Jesus Christ : for he makes Jesus say that *upon you may come all the righteous blood shed upon the earth, from the blood of righteous Abel unto the blood of Zacharias son of Barachias whom ye slew between the altar and the temple.** Now Zacharias, son of Barachias, was assassinated between the altar and the temple by a faction of zealots, during the siege of Jerusalem.†

You assert that the design of the instances of supernatural interposition which the Gospel records was to convince mankind that Jesus Christ was truly the expected Redeemer. But it is as impossible that any human sophistry should frustrate the manifestation of Omnipotence, as that Omniscience should fail to select the most efficient means of accomplishing its design. Eighteen centuries have passed and the tenth part of the human race have a blind and mechanical belief in that Redeemer, without a complete reliance on the merits of whom, their lot is fixed in everlasting misery : surely if the Christian system be thus dreadfully important its Omnipotent author would have rendered it incapable of those abuses from which it has never been exempt, and to which it is subject in common with all human institutions, he would not have left it a matter of ceaseless cavil or complete indifference to the immense majority of mankind. Surely some more conspicuous evidences of its authenticity would have been afforded than driving out devils, drowning pigs, curing blind men, animating a dead body, and turning water into wine. Some theatre worthier of the transcendent event, than Judea, would have been chosen, some historians more adapted by

* See Matthew, chap. xxiii. v. 35.   † Josephus.

their accomplishments and their genius to record the
incarnation of the immutable God. The humane
society restores drowned persons ; every empiric can
cure every disease ; drowning pigs is no very difficult
matter, and driving out devils was far from being an
original or an unusual occupation in Judea. Do not
recite these stale absurdities as proofs of the Divine
origin of Christianity.

If the Almighty has spoken, would not the Universe
have been convinced ? If he had judged the knowledge
of his will to have been more important than any other
science to mankind, would he not have rendered it more
evident and more clear ?

Now, O Eusebes, have I enumerated the general
grounds of my disbelief of the Christian Religion.—I
could have collated its Sacred Writings with the Brah-
minical record of the early ages of the world, and
identified its institutions with the antient worship of the
Sun. I might have entered into an elaborate comparison of the innumerable discordances which exist
between the inspired historians of the same event.
Enough however has been said to vindicate me from the
charge of groundless and infatuated scepticism. I trust
therefore to your candour for the consideration, and to
your logic for the refutation, of my arguments.

EUSEBES.

I WILL not dissemble, O Theosophus, the difficulty of
solving your general objections to Christianity, on the
grounds of human reason. I did not assist at the councils
of the Almighty when he determined to extend his mercy
to mankind, nor can I venture to affirm that it exceeded
the limits of his power to have afforded a more conspicuous or universal manifestation of his will.

But this is a difficulty which attends Christianity in
common with the belief in the being and attributes of

God. This whole scheme of things might have been, according to our partial conceptions, infinitely more admirable and perfect. Poisons, earthquakes, disease, war, famine and venomous serpents ; slavery and persecution are the consequences of certain causes, which according to human judgment might well have been dispensed with an arranging the economy of the globe.

Is this the reasoning which the Theist will choose to employ ? Will he impose limitations on that Deity whom he professes to regard with so profound a veneration ? Will he place his God between the horns of a logical dilemma which shall restrict the fulness either of his power or his bounty ?

Certainly he will prefer to resign his objections to Christianity, than pursue the reasoning upon which they are found, to the dreadful conclusions of cold and dreary Atheism.

I confess that Christianity appears not unattended with difficulty to the understanding which approaches it with a determination to judge its mysteries by reason. I will ever* confess that the discourse, which you have just delivered, ought to unsettle any candid mind engaged in a similar attempt. The children of this world are wiser in their generation than the children of light.

But if I succeed in convincing you that reason conducts to conclusions destructive of morality, happiness, and the hope of futurity, and inconsistent with the very existence of human society, I trust that you will no longer confide in a director so dangerous and faithless.

I require you to declare, O Theosophus, whether you would embrace Christianity or Atheism, if no other systems of belief shall be found to stand the touchstone of enquiry.

[* Qy. ? *even.*]

THEOSOPHUS.

I DO not hesitate to prefer the Christian system, or indeed any system of religion, however rude and gross, to Atheism. Here we truly sympathize; nor do I blame, however I may feel inclined to pity, the man who in his zeal to escape this gloomy faith, should plunge into the most abject superstition.

The Atheist is a monster among men. Inducements, which are omnipotent over the conduct of others, are impotent for him. His private judgment is his criterion of right and wrong. He dreads no judge but his own conscience, he fears no hell but the loss of his self-esteem. He is not to be restrained by punishments, for death is divested of its terror, and whatever enters into his heart to conceive, that will he not scruple to execute. *Iste non timet omnia providentem et cogitantem, et anim-advertentem, et omnia ad se pertinere putantem, curiosum et plenum negotii Deum.*

This dark and terrible doctrine was surely the abortion of some blind speculator's brain; some strange and hideous perversion of intellect, some portentous distortion of reason. There can surely be no metaphysician sufficiently bigoted to his own system to look upon this harmonious world, and dispute the necessity of intelligence; to contemplate the design and deny the designer; to enjoy the spectacle of this beautiful Universe and not feel himself instinctively persuaded to gratitude and adoration. What arguments of the slightest plausibility can be adduced to support a doctrine rejected alike by the instinct of the savage and the reason of the sage?

I readily engage, with you, to reject reason as a faithless guide, if you can demonstrate that it conducts to Atheism. So little, however, do I mistrust the dictates of reason, concerning a supreme Being, that I promise, in the event of your success, to subscribe the wildest and most monstrous creed which you can devise. I will call credulity, faith ; reason, impiety ; the dictates of the understanding shall be the temptations of the Devil, and the wildest dreams of the imagination, the infallible inspirations of Grace.

EUSEBES.

LET me request you then to state, concisely, the grounds of your belief in the being of a God. In my reply I shall endeavour to controvert your reasoning, and shall hold myself acquitted by my zeal for the Christian religion, of the blasphemies which I must utter in the progress of my discourse.

THEOSOPHUS.

I WILL readily state the grounds of my belief in the being of a God. You can only have remained ignorant of the obvious proofs of this important truth, from a superstitious reliance upon the evidence afforded by a revealed religion. The reasoning lies within an extremely narrow compass ; *quicquid enim nos vel meliores vel beatiores facturum est, aut in aperto, aut in proximo posuit natura.*

From every design we justly infer a designer. If we examine the structure of a watch, we shall readily confess the existence of a watch-maker. No work of man could possibly have existed from all eternity. From the contemplation of any product of human art, we conclude that there was an artificer who arranged its several parts. In like manner, from the marks of design and contrivance exhibited in the Universe, we are necessitated to infer a designer, a contriver. If the parts of the Universe have been designed, contrived, and adapted, the existence of a God is manifest.

But design is sufficiently apparent. The wonderful adaptation of substances which act to those which are acted upon ; of the eye to light, and of light to the eye ; of the ear to sound, and of sound to the ear ; of every object of sensation to the sense which it impresses prove that neither blind chance, nor undistinguishing necessity has brought them into being. The adaptation of certain animals to certain climates, the relation borne to each other by animals and vegetables, and by different tribes of animals; the relation, lastly, between man and the circumstances of his external situation are so many demonstrations of Deity.

All is order, design, and harmony, so far as we can descry the tendency of things, and every new enlargement of our views, every new display of the material world, affords a new illustration of the power, the wisdom and the benevolence of God.

The existence of God has never been the topic of popular dispute. There is a tendency to devotion, a thirst for reliance on supernatural aid inherent in the human mind. Scarcely any people, however barbarous, have been discovered, who do not acknowledge with reverence and awe the supernatural causes of the natural effects which they experience. They worship, it is true, the vilest and most inanimate substances, but they firmly confide in the holiness and power of these symbols, and thus own their connexion with what they can neither see nor perceive.

If there is motion in the Universe, there is a God.* The power of beginning motion is no less an attribute of mind than sensation or thought. Wherever motion exists it is evident that mind has operated. The phenomena of the Universe indicate the agency of powers which cannot belong to inert matter.

Every thing which begins to exist must have a cause: every combination, conspiring to an end, implies intelligence.

EUSEBES.

DESIGN must be proved before a designer can be inferred. The matter in controversy is the existence of design in the Universe, and it is not permitted to assume the con-

---

* See Dugald Stewart's Outlines of Moral Philosophy, and Paley's Natural Theology.

tested premises and thence infer the matter in dispute. Insidiously to employ the words contrivance, design, and adaptation before these circumstances are made apparent in the Universe, thence justly inferring a contriver, is a popular sophism against which it behoves us to be watchful.

To assert that motion is an attribute of mind, that matter is inert, that every combination is the result of intelligence is also an assumption of the matter in dispute.

Why do we admit design in any machine of human contrivance? Simply because innumerable instances of machines having been contrived by human art are present to our mind, because we are acquainted with persons who could construct such machines; but if, having no previous knowledge of any artificial contrivance, we had accidentally found a watch upon the ground, we should have been justified in concluding that it was a thing of Nature, that it was a combination of matter with whose cause we were unacquainted, and that any attempt to account for the origin of its existence would be equally presumptuous and unsatisfactory.

The analogy which you attempt to establish between the contrivances of human art, and the various existences of the Universe, is inadmissible. We attribute these effects to human intelligence, because we know beforehand that human intelligence is capable of producing them. Take away this knowledge, and the grounds of our reasoning will be destroyed. Our entire ignorance, therefore, of the Divine Nature leaves this analogy defective in its most essential point of comparison.

What consideration remains to be urged in support of the creation of the Universe by a supreme Being? Its admirable fitness for the production of certain effects, that wonderful consent of all its parts, that universal harmony by whose changeless laws innumerable systems of worlds perform their stated revolutions, and the blood is driven through the veins of the minutest animalcule that sports in the corruption of an insect's lymph : on this account did the Universe require an intelligent Creator, because it exists producing invariable effects, and inasmuch as it is admirably organised for the production of these effects, so the more did it require a creative intelligence.

Thus have we arrived at the substance of your assertion, " That whatever exists, producing certain effects, stands in need of a Creator, and the more conspicuous is its fitness for the production of these effects, the more certain will be our conclusion that it would not have existed from eternity, but must have derived its origin from an intelligent creator."

In what respect then do these arguments apply to the Universe, and not apply to God? From the fitness of the Universe to its end you infer the necessity of an intelligent Creator. But if the fitness of the Universe, to produce certain effects, be thus conspicuous and evident, how much more exquisite fitness to his end must exist in the Author of this Universe? If we find great difficulty from its admirable arrangement in conceiving that the Universe has existed from all eternity, and to resolve this difficulty suppose a Creator, how much more clearly must we perceive the necessity of this very Creator's creation whose perfections comprehend an arrangement far more accurate and just.

The belief of an infinity of creative and created Gods, each more eminently requiring an intelligent author of his being than the foregoing, is a direct consequence of the premises which you have stated. The assumption that the Universe is a design, leads to a conclusion that there are [an] infinity of creative and created Gods, which is absurd. It is impossible indeed to prescribe limits to learned error, when Philosophy relinquishes experience and feeling for speculation.

Until it is clearly proved that the Universe was created, we may reasonably suppose that it has endured from all eternity. In a case where two propositions are diametrically opposite, the mind believes that which is less incomprehensible : it is easier to suppose that the Universe has existed from all eternity, than to conceive an eternal being capable of creating it. If the mind sinks beneath the weight of one, is it an alleviation to increase the intolerability of the burthen?

A man knows, not only that he now is, but that there was a time when he did not exist ; consequently there must have been a cause. But we can only infer, from effects, causes exactly adequate to those effects. There certainly is a generative power which is effected by particular instruments; we cannot prove that it is inherent in these instruments, nor is the contrary hypothesis capable of demonstration. We admit that the generative power is incomprehensible, but to suppose that the same effects are produced by an eternal Omnipotent and Omniscient Being, leaves the cause in the same obscurity, but renders it more incomprehensible.

We can only infer from effects causes exactly adequate to those effects. An infinite number of effects demand an infinite number of causes, nor is the philosopher justified in supposing a greater connexion or unity in the latter, than is perceptible in the former. The same energy cannot be at once the cause of the serpent and the sheep ; of the blight by which the harvest is destroyed, and the sunshine by which it is matured ; of the ferocious propensities by which man becomes a victim to himself, and of the accurate judgment by which his institutions are improved. The spirit of our accurate and exact philosophy is outraged by conclusions which contradict each other so glaringly.

The greatest, equally with the smallest motions of the Universe, are subjected to the rigid necessity of inevitable laws. These laws are the unknown causes of the known effects perceivable in the Universe. Their effects are the boundaries of our knowledge, their names the expressions of our ignorance. To suppose some existence beyond, or above them, is to invent a second and superfluous hypothesis to account for what has already been accounted for by the laws of motion and the properties of matter. I admit that the nature of these laws is incomprehensible, but the hypothesis of a Deity adds a gratuitous difficulty, which so far from alleviating those which it is adduced to explain, requires new hypotheses for the elucidation of its own inherent contradictions.

The laws of attraction and repulsion, desire and aversion, suffice to account for every phenomenon of the moral and physical world. A precise knowledge of the properties of any object, is alone requisite to determine its manner of action. Let the mathematician be acquainted with the weight and volume of a cannon ball, together with the degree of velocity and inclination with which it is impelled, and he will accurately delineate the course it must describe, and determine the force with which it will strike an object at a given distance. Let the influencing motive, present to the mind of any person be given, and the knowledge of his consequent conduct will result. Let the bulk and velocity of a comet be discovered, and the astronomer, by the accurate estimation of the equal and contrary actions of the centripetal and centrifugal forces, will justly predict the period of its return.

The anomalous motions of the heavenly bodies, their unequal velocities and frequent aberrations, are corrected by that gravitation by which they are caused. The illustrious Laplace has shewn that the approach of the Moon to the Earth, and the Earth to the Sun, is only a secular equation of a very long period, which has its maximum and minimum. The system of the Universe then is upheld solely by physical powers. The necessity of matter is the ruler of the world. It is vain philosophy which supposes more causes than are exactly adequate to explain the phenomena of things. *Hypotheses non fingo: quicquid enim ex phænomenis non deducitur, hypothesis vocanda est; et hypotheses vel metaphysicæ, vel physicæ, vel qualitatum occultarum, seu mechanicæ, in philosophiâ locum non habent.*

You assert that the construction of the animal machine, the fitness of certain animals to certain situations, the connexion between the organs of perception and that which is perceived ; the relation between everything which exists, and that which tends to preserve it in its existence, imply design. It is manifest that if the eye could not see, nor the stomach digest, the human frame could not preserve its present mode of existence. It is equally certain, however, that the elements of its composition, if they did not exist in one form, must exist in another ; and that the combinations which they would form, must so long as they endured, derive support for their peculiar mode of being from their fitness to the circumstances of their situation.

It by no means follows, that because a being exists, performing certain functions, he was fitted by another being to the performance of these functions. So rash a conclusion would conduct, as I have before shewn, to an absurdity ; and it becomes infinitely more unwarrantable from the consideration that the known laws of matter and motion, suffice to unravel, even in the present imperfect state of moral and physical science, the majority of those difficulties which the hypothesis of a Deity was invented to explain.

Doubtless no disposition of inert matter, or matter deprived of qualities, could ever have composed an animal, a tree, or even a stone. But matter deprived of qualities, is an abstraction, concerning which it is impossible to form an idea. Matter, such as we behold it, is not inert. It is infinitely active and subtile. Light, electricity, and magnetism are fluids not surpassed by thought itself in tenuity and activity : like thought they are sometimes the cause and sometimes the effect of motion ; and, distinct as they are from every other class of substances with which we are acquainted, seem to possess equal claims with thought to the unmeaning distinction of immateriality.

The laws of motion and the properties of matter suffice to account for every phenomenon, or combination of phenomena exhibited in the Universe. That certain animals exist in certain climates, results from the consentaneity of their frames to the circumstances of their situation : let these circumstances be altered to a sufficient degree, and the elements of their composition must exist in some new combination no less resulting than the former from those inevitable laws by which the Universe is governed.

It is the necessary consequence of the organization of man, that his stomach should digest his food : it inevitably results also from his gluttonous and unnatural appetite for the flesh of animals that his frame be diseased and his vigour impaired ; but in neither of these cases is adaptation of means to end to be perceived. Unnatural diet, and the habits consequent upon its use are the means, and every complication of frightful disease is the end, but to assert that these means were adapted to this end by the Creator of the world, or that human caprice can avail to traverse the precautions of Omnipotence, is absurd. These are the consequences of the properties of organized matter ; and it is a strange perversion of the understanding to argue that a certain sheep was created to be butchered and devoured by a certain individual of the human species, when the conformation of the latter, as is manifest to the most superficial student of comparative anatomy,

I.   X classes him with those animals who feed on fruits and vegetables.*

The means by which the existence of an animal is sustained, requires a designer in no greater degree than the existence itself of the animal. If it exists, there must be means to support its existence. In a world where *omne mutatur nihil interit*, no organized being can exist without a continual separation of that substance which is incessantly exhausted, nor can this separation take place otherwise than by the invariable laws which result from the relations of matter. We are incapacitated only by our ignorance from referring every phenomenon, however unusual, minute or complex, to the laws of motion and the properties of matter ; and it is an egregious

* See Cuvier Leçons d'Anat. Comp. tom. iii. p. 169, 373, 448, 465, 480. Rees' Cyclopædia, Art. Man.

Οὐκ αἰδεῖσθε τους ἡμέρους καρπους αἵματι και φόνῳ μιγνύοντες ; ἀλλὰ δράκοντας ἀγρίους καλεῖτε καὶ παρδάλεις καὶ λέοντας, αὐτοὶ δὲ μιαιφονεῖτε εἰς ὠμότητα καταλιπόντες ἐκείνοις οὐδέν. Ἐκείνοις μὲν γὰρ ὁ φόνος τροφὴ, ὑμῖν δε ὄψον ἐστίν. ῞Οτι γὰρ οὐκ ἔστιν ἀνθρώπῳ κατὰ φύσιν τὸ σαρκοφαγεῖν, πρῶτον μὲν ἀπὸ τῶν σωμάτων δηλοῦται τῆς κατασκευῆς. Οὐδενὶ γὰρ ἔοικε τὸ ἀνθρώπου σῶμα τῶν ἐπὶ σαρκοφαγίᾳ γεγονότων, οὐ γρυπότης χείλους, οὐκ ὀξύτης ὄνυχος, οὐ τραχύτης ὀδόντων πρόσεστιν, οὐ κοιλίας εὐτονία καὶ πνεύματος θερμότης, τρέψαι καὶ κατεργάσασθαι δυνατὴ τό βαρὺ καὶ κρεῶδες. Ἀλλ' αὐτόθεν ἡ φύσις τῇ λειότητι τῶν ὀδόντων, καὶ τῇ σμικρότητι τοῦ στόματος, καὶ τῇ μαλακότητι τῆς γλώσσης, καὶ τῇ πρὸς πέψιν ἀμβλύτητι τοῦ πνεύματος, ἐξόμνυται τὴν σαρκοφαγίαν. Εἰ δὲ λέγεις, πεφυκέναι σεαυτὸν ἐπὶ τοιαύτην ἐδωδὴν, ὃ βούλει φαγεῖν, πρῶτος αὐτὸς ἀπόκτεινον· ἀλλ' αὐτός, διὰ σεαυτοῦ, μὴ χρησάμενος κοπίδι, μηδὲ τυμπάνῳ τινὶ μηδὲ πελέκει· ἀλλὰ, ὡς λύκοι καὶ ἄρκτοι, καὶ λέοντες αὐτόι ὡς ἐσθίουσι φονευούσιν, ἄνελε δήγματι βοῦν, ἢ σώματι σῦν, ἢ ἄρνα ἢ λαγὼον διάῤῥηξον, καὶ φάγε προσπεσὼν ἔτι ζῶντος ὡς ἐκεῖνα.

Πλουτ. περὶ Σαρκοφαγ. Λογ. β.

[The same passage is quoted in the Notes to Queen Mab (Vol. iii. p. 359—360).]

offence against the first principles of reason to suppose an immaterial creator of the world, *in quo omnia moventur sed sine mutuâ passione :* which is equally a superfluous hypothesis in the mechanical philosophy of Newton, and a useless excrescence on the inductive logic of Bacon.

What then is this harmony, this order which you maintain to have required for its establishment, what it needs not for its maintenance, the agency of a supernatural intelligence? Inasmuch as the order visible in the Universe requires one cause, so does the disorder whose operation is not less clearly apparent, demand another. Order and disorder are no more than modifications of our own perceptions of the relations which subsist between ourselves and external objects, and if we are justified in inferring the operation of a benevolent power from the advantages attendant on the former, the evils of the latter bear equal testimony to the activity of a malignant principle, no less pertinacious in inducing evil out of good, than the other is unremitting in procuring good from evil.

If we permit our imagination to traverse the obscure regions of possibility, we may doubtless imagine, according to the complexion of our minds, that disorder may have a relative tendency to unmingled good, or order be relatively replete with exquisite and subtile evil. To neither of these conclusions, which are equally presumptuous and unfounded, will it become the philosopher to assent. Order and disorder are expressions denoting our perceptions of what is injurious or beneficial to ourselves, or to the beings in whose welfare we are compelled to sympathize by the similarity of their conformation to our own.*

A beautiful antelope panting under the fangs of a tiger, a defenceless ox, groaning beneath the butcher's axe, is a spectacle which instantly awakens compassion in a vir-

* See Godwin's Political Justice, Vol. i. p. 449.

tuous and unvitiated breast.   Many there are, however, sufficiently hardened to the rebukes of justice and the precepts of humanity, as to regard the deliberate butchery of thousands of their species, as a theme of exultation and a source of honour, and to consider any failure in these remorseless enterprises as a defect in the system of things. The criteria of order and disorder are as various as those beings from whose opinions and feelings they result.

Populous cities are destroyed by earthquakes, and desolated by pestilence.   Ambition is everywhere devoting its millions to incalculable calamity.   Superstition, in a thousand shapes, is employed in brutalizing and degrading the human species, and fitting it to endure without a murmur the oppression of its innumerable tyrants.   All this is abstractedly neither good nor evil, because good and evil are words employed to designate that peculiar state of our own perceptions, resulting from the encounter of any object calculated to produce pleasure or pain. Exclude the idea of relation, and the words good and evil are deprived of import.

Earthquakes are injurious to the cities which they destroy, beneficial to those whose commerce was injured by their prosperity, and indifferent to others which are too remote to be affected by their influence.   Famine is good to the corn-merchant, evil to the poor, and indifferent to those whose fortunes can at all times command a superfluity.   Ambition is evil to the restless bosom it inhabits, to the innumerable victims who are dragged by its ruthless thirst for infamy, to expire in every variety of anguish, to the inhabitants of the country it depopulates, and to the human race whose improvement it retards ; it is indifferent with regard to the system of the Universe, and is good only to the vultures and the jackalls that track the conqueror's career, and to the worms who feast in security on the desolation of his progress.   It is manifest that we cannot reason with respect to the universal system from that which only exists in relation to our own perceptions.

You allege some considerations in favour of a Deity from the universality of a belief in his existence.

The superstitions of the savage, and the religion of civilized Europe appear to you to conspire to prove a first cause. I maintain that it is from the evidence of revelation alone that this belief derives the slightest countenance.

That credulity should be gross in proportion to the ignorance of the mind which it enslaves, is in strict consistency with the principles of human nature. The idiot, the child, and the savage, agree in attributing their own passions and propensities * to the inanimate substances by which they are either benefited or injured. The former become Gods and the latter Demons; hence prayers and sacrifices, by the means of which the rude Theologian imagines that he may confirm the benevolence of the one, or mitigate the malignity of the other. He has averted the wrath of a powerful enemy by supplications and submission ; he has secured the assistance of his neighbour by offerings; he has felt his own anger subside before the entreaties of a vanquished foe, and has cherished gratitude for the kindness of another. Therefore does he believe that the elements will listen to his vows. He is capable of love and hatred towards his fellow beings, and is variously impelled by those principles to benefit or injure them. The source of his error is sufficiently obvious. When the winds, the waves and the atmosphere, act in such a manner as to thwart or forward his designs, he attributes to them the same propensities of whose existence within himself he is conscious when he is instigated by benefits to kindness, or by injuries to revenge. The bigot of the woods can form no conception of beings possessed of properties differing from his own : it requires,

* See Southey's History of Brazil, p. 255.

indeed, a mind considerably tinctured with science, and enlarged by cultivation to contemplate itself, not as the centre and model of the Universe, but as one of the infinitely various multitude of beings of which it is actually composed.

There is no attribute of God which is not either borrowed from the passions and powers of the human mind, or which is not a negation. Omniscience, Omnipotence, Omnipresence, Infinity, Immutability, Incomprehensibility, and Immateriality, are all words which designate properties and powers peculiar to organised beings, with the addition of negations, by which the idea of limitation is excluded.*

That the frequency of a belief in God (for it is not universal) should be any argument in its favour, none to whom the innumerable mistakes of men are familiar, will assert. It is among men of genius and science that Atheism alone is found, but among these alone is cherished an hostility to those errors, with which the illiterate and vulgar are infected.

How small is the proportion of those who really believe in God, to the thousands who are prevented by their occupations from ever bestowing a serious thought upon the subject, and the millions who worship butterflies, bones, feathers, monkeys, calabashes and serpents. The word God, like other abstractions, signifies the agreement of certain propositions, rather than the presence of any idea. If we found our belief in the existence of God on the universal consent of mankind, we are duped by the most palpable of sophisms. The word God cannot mean at the same time an ape, a snake, a bone, a calabash, a Trinity, and a Unity. Nor can that belief be accounted universal against which men of powerful intellect and spotless virtue have in every age protested.

* See Le Systeme de la Nature: this book is one of the most eloquent vindications of Atheism.

*Non pudet igitur physicum, id est speculatorem vena-
toremque naturæ, ex animis consuetudine imbutis petere
testimonium veritatis ?*

Hume has shewn, to the satisfaction of all philosophers,
that the only idea which we can form of causation is
derivable* from the constant conjunction of objects, and
the consequent inference of one from the other. We
denominate that phenomenon the cause of another which
we observe with the fewest exceptions to precede its occurrence. Hence it would be inadmissible to deduce the
being of a God from the existence of the Universe; even if
this mode of reasoning did not conduct to the monstrous
conclusion of an infinity of creative and created Gods,
each more eminently requiring a Creator than its pre-
decessor.

If Power† be an attribute of existing substance, substance could not have derived its origin from power. One
thing cannot be at the same time the cause and the effect
of another.—The word power expresses the capability of
any thing to be or act. The human mind never hesitates
to annex the idea of power to any object of its experience.
To deny that power is the attribute of being, is to deny
that being can be. If power be an attribute of substance,
the hypothesis of a God is a superfluous and unwarrantable assumption.

Intelligence is that attribute of the Deity, which you
hold to be most apparent in the Universe. Intelligence
is only known to us as a mode of animal being. We
cannot conceive intelligence distinct from sensation and
perception, which are attributes to organized bodies. To
assert that God is intelligent, is to assert that he has
ideas ; and Locke has proved .that ideas result from
sensation. Sensation can exist only in an organized body,

[* Printed *deniable.*]

† For a very profound disquisition on this subject, see Sir William
Drummond's Academical Questions, chap. i. p. 1.

an organised body is necessarily limited both in extent and operation. The God of the rational Theosophis is a vast and wise animal.

You have laid it down as a maxim that the power of beginning motion is an attribute of mind as much as thought and sensation.

Mind cannot create, it can only perceive. Mind is the recipient of impressions made on the organs of sense, and without the action of external objects we should not only be deprived of all knowledge of the existence of mind, but totally incapable of the knowledge of any thing. It is evident, therefore, that mind deserves to be considered as the effect, rather than the cause of motion. The ideas which suggest themselves too are prompted by the circumstances of our situation, these are the elements of thought, and from the various combinations of these our feelings, opinions, and volitions inevitably result.

That which is infinite necessarily includes that which is finite. The distinction therefore between the Universe, and that by which the Universe is upheld, is manifestly erroneous. To devise the word God, that you may express a certain portion of the universal system, can answer no good purpose in philosophy: In the language of reason, the words God and Universe are synonymous. *Omnia enim per Dei potentiam facta sunt, imo, quia naturæ potentia nulla est nisi ipsa Dei potentia, artem est nos catemus Dei potentiam non intelligere quatenus causas naturales ignoramus: adeoque stultè ad eandam Dei potentiam recurritur, quando rei alicujus, causam naturalem, sive est, ipsam Dei potentiam ignoramus.* *

Thus from the principles of that reason to which you so rashly appealed as the ultimate arbiter of our dispute, have I shewn that the popular arguments in favour of the

* Spinosa. Tract. Theologico.-Pol., chap. i. p. 14. [Quoted also in the Notes to Queen Mab (Vol. iii. p. 328).]

being of a God are totally destitute of colour. I have shewn the absurdity of attributing intelligence to the cause of those effects which we perceive in the Universe, and the fallacy which lurks in the argument from design. I have shewn that order is no more than a peculiar manner of contemplating the operation of necessary agents, that mind is the effect, not the cause of motion, that power is the attribute, not the origin of Being. I have proved that we can have no evidence of the existence of a God from the principles of reason.

You will have observed, from the zeal with which I have urged arguments so revolting to my genuine sentiments, and conducted to a conclusion in direct contradiction to that faith which every good man must eternally preserve, how little I am inclined to sympathise with those of my religion who have pretended to prove the existence of God by the unassisted light of reason. I confess that the necessity of a revelation has been compromised by treacherous friends to Christianity, who have maintained that the sublime mysteries of the being of a God and the immortality of the soul are discoverable from other sources than itself.

I have proved that on the principles of that philosophy to which Epicurus, Lord Bacon, Newton, Locke and Hume were addicted, the existence of God is a chimera.

The Christian Religion then, alone, affords indisputable assurance that the world was created by the power, and is preserved by the Providence of an Almighty God, who, in justice has appointed a future life for the punishment of the vicious and the remuneration of the virtuous.

Now, O Theosophus, I call upon you to decide between Atheism and Christianity ; to declare whether you will pursue your principles to the destruction of the bonds of civilized society, or wear the easy yoke of that religion which proclaims "peace upon earth, good-will to all men."

THEOSOPHUS.

I AM not prepared at present, I confess, to reply clearly to your unexpected arguments. I assure you that no considerations, however specious, should seduce me to deny the existence of my Creator.

I am willing to promise that if, after mature deliberation, the arguments which you have advanced in favour of Atheism should appear incontrovertible, I will endeavour to adopt so much of the Christian scheme as is consistent with my persuasion of the goodness, unity, and majesty of God.

HISTORY

OF

A SIX WEEKS' TOUR

THROUGH

A PART OF FRANCE,
SWITZERLAND, GERMANY, AND HOLLAND:

WITH LETTERS

DESCRIPTIVE OF

A SAIL ROUND THE LAKE OF GENEVA, AND OF
THE GLACIERS OF CHAMOUNI.

LONDON:

PUBLISHED BY T. HOOKHAM, JUN.
OLD BOND STREET;
AND C. AND J. OLLIER,
WELBECK STREET.

1817.

[The two following Letters were addressed by SHELLEY *to* THOMAS LOVE PEACOCK. *The remainder of the little volume was written by* MRS. SHELLEY.]

To T. P. Esq.

Montalegre, near Coligni. Geneva,
July 12th, 1816.

T is nearly a fortnight since I have returned from Vevai. This journey has been on every account delightful, but most especially, because then I first knew the divine beauty of Rousseau's imagination, as it exhibits itself in *Julie*. It is inconceivable what an enchantment the scene itself lends to those delineations, from which its own most touching charm arises. But I will give you an abstract of our voyage, which lasted eight days, and if you have a map of Switzerland, you can follow me.

We left Montalegre at half-past two on the 23rd of June. The lake was calm, and after three hours of rowing we arrived at Hermance, a beautiful little village, containing a ruined tower, built, the villagers say, by Julius Cæsar. There were three other towers similar to it, which the Genevese destroyed for their own fortifications in 1560. We got into the tower by a kind of window. The walls are immensely solid, and the stone of which it is built so hard, that it yet retained the mark of chisels. The boatmen said, that this tower was once three times higher than it is now. There are two staircases in the thickness of the walls, one of which is entirely demolished, and the other half ruined, and only accessible by a ladder. The town itself, now an inconsiderable village inhabited by a few fishermen, was built by a Queen of Burgundy, and reduced to its present state by the inhabitants of Berne, who burnt and ravaged everything they could find.

Leaving Hermance, we arrived at sunset at the village of Nerni. After looking at our lodgings, which were gloomy and dirty, we walked out by the side of the lake. It was beautiful to see the vast expanse of these purple and misty waters broken by the craggy islets near to its slant and "beached margin." There were many fish sporting in the lake, and multitudes were collected close to the rocks to catch the flies which inhabited them.

On returning to the village, we sat on a wall beside the lake, looking at some children who were playing at a game like nine-pins. The children here appeared in an extraordinary way deformed and diseased. Most of them were crooked, and with enlarged throats; but one little boy had such exquisite grace in his mien and motions, as I never before saw equalled in a child. His countenance was beautiful for the expression with which it overflowed. There was a mixture of pride and gentleness in his eyes and lips, the indications of sensibility, which his education will probably pervert to misery or seduce to crime; but there was more of gentleness than of pride, and it seemed that the pride was tamed from its original wildness by the habitual exercise of milder feelings. My companion gave him a piece of money, which he took without speaking, with a sweet smile of easy thankfulness, and then, with an unembarrassed air, turned to his play. All this might scarcely be; but the imagination surely could not forbear to breathe into the most inanimate forms some likeness of its own visions, on such a serene and glowing evening, in this remote and romantic village, beside the calm lake that bore us hither.

On returning to our inn, we found that the servant had arranged our rooms, and deprived them of the greater portion of their former disconsolate appearance. They reminded my companion of Greece : it was five years, he said, since he had slept in such beds. The influence of the recollections excited by this circumstance on our conversation gradually faded, and I retired to rest with no unpleasant sensations, thinking of our journey to-morrow, and of the pleasure of recounting the little adventures of it when we return.

The next morning we passed Yvoire, a scattered village with an ancient castle, whose houses are interspersed with trees, and which stands at a little distance from Nerni, on the promontory which bounds a deep bay, some miles in extent. So soon as we arrived at this promontory, the lake began to assume an aspect of wilder magnificence. The mountains of Savoy, whose summits were bright with snow, descended in broken slopes to the lake: on high, the rocks were dark with pine-forests, which become deeper and more immense, until the ice and snow mingle with the points of naked rock that pierce the blue air; but below, groves of walnut, chesnut, and oak, with openings of lawny fields, attested the milder climate.

As soon as we had passed the opposite promontory, we saw the river Drance, which descends from between a chasm in the mountains, and makes a plain near the lake, intersected by its divided streams. Thousands of *besolets*, beautiful water-birds, like sea-gulls, but smaller, with purple on their backs, take their station on the shallows, where its waters mingle with the lake. As we approached Evian, the mountains descended more precipitously to the lake, and masses of intermingled wood and rock overhung its shining spire.

We arrived at this town about seven o'clock, after a day which involved more rapid changes of atmosphere than I ever recollect to have observed before. The morning was cold and wet; then an easterly wind, and the clouds hard and high; then thunder showers, and wind shifting to 'every quarter; then a warm blast from the south, and summer clouds hanging over the peaks, with bright blue sky between. About half an hour after we had arrived at Evian, a few flashes of lightning came from a dark cloud, directly overhead, and continued after the cloud had dispersed. "Diespiter, per pura tonantes egit equos :" a phenomenon which certainly had no influence on me, corresponding with that which it produced on Horace.

The appearance of the inhabitants of Evian is more wretched, diseased, and poor, than I ever recollect to have seen. The contrast indeed between the subjects of the King of Sardinia and the citizens of the independent republics of Switzerland, affords a powerful illustration of the blighting mischiefs of despotism, within the space of a few miles. They have mineral waters here, *eaux savon-neuses*, they call them. In the evening we had some difficulty about our passports, but so soon as the syndic heard my companion's rank and name, he apologized for the circumstance. The inn was good. During our voyage, on the distant height of a hill, covered with pine-forests, we saw a ruined castle, which reminded me of those on the Rhine.

We left Evian on the following morning, with a wind of such violence as to permit but one sail to be carried. The waves also were exceedingly high, and our boat so heavily laden, that there appeared to be some danger. We arrived, however, safe at Mellerie, after passing with great speed mighty forests which overhung the lake, and lawns of exquisite verdure, and mountains with bare and icy points, which rose immediately from the summit of the rocks, whose bases were echoing to the waves.

We here heard that the Empress Maria Louisa had slept at Mellerie, before the present inn was built, and when the accommodations were those of the most wretched village, in remembrance of St. Preux. How beautiful it is to find that the common sentiments of human nature can attach themselves to those who are the most removed from its duties and its enjoyments, when Genius pleads for their admission at the gate of Power. To own them was becoming in the Empress, and con-firms the affectionate praise contained in the regret of a great and enlightened nation. A Bourbon dared not even to have remembered Rousseau. She owed this power to that democracy which her husband's dynasty outraged, and of which it was, however, in some sort the representative among the nations of the earth. This little incident shows at once how unfit and how impossible it is for the ancient system of opinions, or for any power built upon a conspiracy to revive them, permanently to subsist among mankind. We dined there, and had some honey, the best I have ever tasted, the very essence of the mountain flowers, and as fragrant. Probably the village derives its name from this production. Mellerie is the well-known scene of St. Preux's visionary exile; but Mellerie is indeed enchanted ground, were Rousseau no magician. Groves of pine, chesnut, and walnut over-shadow it; magnificent and unbounded forests to which England affords no parallel. In the midst of these woods are dells of lawny expanse, inconceivably verdant, adorned with a thousand of the rarest flowers and odorous with thyme.

The lake appeared somewhat calmer as we left Mellerie, sailing close to the banks, whose magnificence augmented with the turn of every promontory. But we congratulated ourselves too soon : the wind gradually increased in violence, until it blew tremendously ; and as it came from the remotest extremity of the lake, pro-duced waves of a frightful height, and covered the whole surface with a chaos of foam. One of our boatmen, who was a dreadfully stupid fellow, persisted in holding the

I.   Y

sail at a time when the boat was on the point of being
driven under water by the hurricane. On discovering
his error, he let it entirely go, and the boat for a moment
refused to obey the helm ; in addition, the rudder was so
broken as to render the management of it very difficult ;
one wave fell in, and then another. My companion, an
excellent swimmer, took off his coat; I did the same, and
we sat with our arms crossed, every instant expecting to
be swamped. The sail was however again held, the
boat obeyed the helm, and, still in imminent peril from
the immensity of the waves, we arrived in a few minutes
at a sheltered port, in the village of St. Gingoux.

I felt in this near prospect of death a mixture of sensations, among which terror entered, though but subordi-
nately. My feelings would have been less painful had I
been alone; but I know that my companion would have
attempted to save me, and I was overcome with humilia-
tion, when I thought that his life might have been risked
to preserve mine. When we arrived at St. Gingoux, the
inhabitants, who stood on the shore, unaccustomed to
see a vessel as frail as ours and fearing to venture at all
on such a sea, exchanged looks of wonder and congratu-
lation with our boatmen, who, as well as ourselves, were
well pleased to set foot on shore.

St. Gingoux is even more beautiful than Mellerie ; the
mountains are higher, and their loftiest points of elevation
descend more abruptly to the lake. On high, the aerial
summits still cherish great depths of snow in their
ravines, and in the paths of their unseen torrents. One
of the highest of these is called Roche de St. Julien,
beneath whose pinnacles the forests become deeper and
more extensive; the chesnut gives a peculiarity to the
scene, which is most beautiful, and will make a picture
in my memory, distinct from all other mountain scenes
which I have ever before visited.

As we arrived here early, we took a *voiture* to visit

the mouth of the Rhone. We went between the mountains and the lake, under groves of mighty chesnut trees, beside perpetual streams, which are nourished by the snows above, and form stalactites on the rocks, over which they fall. We saw an immense chesnut tree, which had been overthrown by the hurricane of the morning. The place where the Rhone joins the lake was marked by a line of tremendous breakers ; the river is as rapid as when it leaves the lake, but is muddy and dark. We went about a league farther on the road to La Valais, and stopped at a castle called La Tour de Bouverie, which seems to be the frontier of Switzerland and Savoy, as we were asked for our passports, on the supposition of our proceeding to Italy.

On one side of the road was the immense Roche de St. Julien, which overhung it ; through the gateway of the castle we saw the snowy mountains of La Valais, clothed in clouds, and on the other side was the willowy plain of the Rhone, in a character of striking contrast with the rest of the scene, bounded by the dark mountains that overhang Clarens, Vevai, and the lake that rolls between. In the midst of the plain rises a little isolated hill, on which the white spire of a church peeps from among the tufted chesnut-woods. We returned to St. Gingoux before sunset, and I passed the evening in reading *Julie.*

As my companion rises late, I had time before breakfast, on the ensuing morning, to hunt the waterfalls of the river that fall into the lake at St. Gingoux. The stream is indeed, from the declivity over which it falls, only a succession of waterfalls, which roar over the rocks with a perpetual sound, and suspend their unceasing spray on the leaves and flowers that overhang and adorn its savage banks. The path that conducted along this river sometimes avoided the precipices of its shores, by leading through meadows ; sometimes threaded the base of the perpendicular and caverned rocks. I gathered in these meadows a nosegay of such flowers as I never saw in England, and which I thought more beautiful for that rarity.

On my return, after breakfast, we sailed for Clarens, determining first to see the three mouths of the Rhone, and then the castle of Chillon; the day was fine, and the water calm. We passed from the blue waters of the lake over the stream of the Rhone, which is rapid even at a great distance from its confluence with the lake; the turbid waters mixed with those of the lake, but mixed with them unwillingly. (*See Nouvelle Héloise, Lettre* 17, *Part* 4.) I read *Julie* all day; an overflowing, as it now seems, surrounded by the scenes which it has so wonderfully peopled, of sublimest genius, and more than human sensibility. Mellerie, the Castle of Chillon, Clarens, the mountains of La Valais and Savoy, present themselves to the imagination as monuments of things that were once familiar, and of beings that were once dear to it. They were created indeed by one mind, but a mind so powerfully bright as to cast a shade of falsehood on the records that are called reality.

We passed on to the Castle of Chillon, and visited its dungeons and towers. These prisons are excavated below the lake; the principal dungeon is supported by seven columns, whose branching capitals support the roof. Close to the very walls, the lake is 800 feet deep; iron rings are fastened to these columns, and on them were engraven a multitude of names, partly those of visitors, and partly doubtless of the prisoners, of whom now no memory remains, and who thus beguiled a solitude which they have long ceased to feel. One date was as ancient as 1670. At the commencement of the Reformation, and indeed long after that period, this dungeon was the receptacle of those who shook, or who denied the system of idolatry from the effects of which man-kind is even now slowly emerging.

Close to this long and lofty dungeon was a narrow cell, and beyond it one larger and far more lofty and dark, supported upon two unornamented arches. Across one of these arches was a beam, now black and rotten, on which prisoners were hung in secret. I never saw a monument more terrible of that cold and inhuman tyranny which it has been the delight of man to exercise over man. It was indeed one of those many tremendous fulfilments which render the "pernicies humani generis" of the great Tacitus, so solemn and irrefragable a pro-phecy. The gendarme, who conducted us over this castle, told us that there was an opening to the lake, by means of a secret spring, connected with which the whole dungeon might be filled with water before the prisoners could possibly escape !

We proceeded with a contrary wind to Clarens, against a heavy swell. I never felt more strongly than on landing at Clarens, that the spirit of old times had deserted its once cherished habitation. A thousand times, thought I, have Julia and St. Preux walked on this terrassed road, looking towards these mountains which I now behold; nay, treading on the ground where I now tread. From the window of our lodging our landlady pointed out "le bosquet de Julie." At least the inha-bitants of this village are impressed with an idea, that the persons of that romance had actual existence. In the evening we walked thither. It is indeed Julia's wood. The hay was making under the trees; the trees them-selves were aged, but vigorous, and interspersed with younger ones, which are destined to be their successors, and in future years, when we are dead, to afford a shade to future worshippers of nature, who love the memory of that tenderness and peace of which this was the imaginary abode. We walked forward among the vineyards, whose

narrow terraces overlook this affecting scene. Why did
the cold maxims of the world compel me at this moment
to repress the tears of melancholy transport which it
would have been so sweet to indulge, immeasurably, even
until the darkness of night had swallowed up the objects
which excited them?

I forgot to remark, what indeed my companion re-
marked to me, that our danger from the storm took place
precisely in the spot where Julie and her lover were
nearly overset, and where St. Preux was tempted to
plunge with her into the lake.

On the following day we went to see the castle of
Clarens, a square strong house, with very few windows,
surrounded by a double terrace that overlooks the valley,
or rather the plain of Clarens. The road which conducted to it wound up the steep ascent through woods of
walnut and chesnut. We gathered roses on the terrace,
in the feeling that they might be the posterity of some
planted by Julia's hand. We sent their dead and withered
leaves to the absent.

We went again to the " bosquet de Julie," and found
that the precise spot was now utterly obliterated, and a
heap of stones marked the place where the little chapel
had once stood. Whilst we were execrating the author
of this brutal folly, our guide informed us that the land
belonged to the convent of St. Bernard, and that this
outrage had been committed by their orders. I knew
before, that if avarice could harden the hearts of men, a
system of prescriptive religion has an influence far more
inimical to natural sensibility. I know that an isolated
man is sometimes restrained by shame from outraging
the venerable feelings arising out of the memory of
genius, which once made nature even lovelier than itself;
but associated man holds it as the very sacrament of his
union to forswear all delicacy, all benevolence, all remorse, all that is true, or tender, or sublime.

We sailed from Clarens to Vevai. Vevai is a town more beautiful in its simplicity than any I have ever seen. Its market-place, a spacious square interspersed with trees, looks directly upon the mountains of Savoy and La Valais, the lake, and the valley of the Rhone. It was at Vevai that Rousseau conceived the design of *Julie.*

From Vevai we came to Ouchy, a village near Lausanne. The coasts of the Pays de Vaud, though full of villages and vineyards, present an aspect of tranquillity and peculiar beauty which well compensates for the solitude which I am accustomed to admire. The hills are very high and rocky, crowned and interspersed with woods. Waterfalls echo from the cliffs, and shine afar. In one place we saw the traces of two rocks of immense size, which had fallen from the mountain behind. One of these lodged in a room where a young woman was sleeping, without injuring her. The vineyards were utterly destroyed in its path, and the earth torn up.

The rain detained us two days at Ouchy. We, however, visited Lausanne, and saw Gibbon's house. We were shown the decayed summer-house where he finished his History, and the old acacias on the terrace from which he saw Mont Blanc after having written the last sentence. There is something grand and even touching in the regret which he expresses at the completion of his task. It was conceived amid the ruins of the Capitol. The sudden departure of his cherished and accustomed toil must have left him, like the death of a dear friend, sad and solitary.

My companion gathered some acacia leaves to preserve in remembrance of him. I refrained from doing so, fearing to outrage the greater and more sacred name of Rousseau; the contemplation of whose imperishable creations had left no vacancy in my heart for mortal things. Gibbon had a cold and unimpassioned spirit. I never felt more inclination to rail at the prejudices which cling to such a thing, than now that Julie and Clarens, Lausanne and the Roman empire, compelled me to a contrast between Rousseau and Gibbon.

When we returned, in the only interval of sunshine during the day, I walked on the pier which the lake was lashing with its waves. A rainbow spanned the lake, or rather rested one extremity of its arch upon the water, and the other at the foot of the mountains of Savoy. Some white houses, I know not if they were those of Mellerie, shone through the yellow fire.

On Saturday the 30th of June we quitted Ouchy, and after two days of pleasant sailing arrived on Sunday evening at Montalegre.   S.

TO T. P. ESQ.

ST. MARTIN—SERVOZ—CHAMOUNI—MONTANVERT— MONT BLANC.

Hôtel de Londres, Chamouni,
July 22nd, 1816.

Whilst you, my friend, are engaged in securing a home for us, we are wandering in search of recollections to embellish it. I do not err in conceiving that you are interested in details of all that is majestic or beautiful in nature; but how shall I describe to you the scenes by which I am now surrounded? To exhaust the epithets which express the astonishment and the admiration—the very excess of satisfied astonishment, where expectation scarcely acknowledged any boundary, is this to impress upon your mind the images which fill mine now even till it overflow? I too have read the raptures of travellers; I will be warned by their example; I will simply detail to you all that I can relate, or all that, if related, would enable you to conceive of what we have done or seen since the morning of the 20th, when we left Geneva.

We commenced our intended journey to Chamouni at half-past eight in the morning. , We passed through the champain country, which extends from Mont Salêve to the base of the higher Alps. The country is sufficiently fertile, covered with corn-fields and orchards, and intersected by sudden acclivities with flat summits. The day was cloudless and excessively hot, the Alps were perpetually in sight, and as we advanced, the mountains, which form their outskirts, closed in around us. We passed a bridge over a stream, which discharges itself into the Arve. The Arve itself, much swoln by the rains, flows constantly to the right of the road.

As we approached Bonneville through an avenue composed of a beautiful species of drooping poplar, we observed that the corn-fields on each side were covered with inundation. Bonneville is a neat little town, with no conspicuous peculiarity, except the white towers of the prison, an extensive building overlooking the town. At Bonneville the Alps commence, one of which, clothed by forests, rises almost immediately from the opposite bank of the Arve.

From Bonneville to Cluses the road conducts through a spacious and fertile plain, surrounded on all sides by mountains, covered like those of Mellerie with forests of intermingled pine and chesnut. At Cluses the road turns suddenly to the right, following the Arve along the chasm, which it seems to have hollowed for itself among the perpendicular mountains. The scene assumes here a more savage and colossal character: the valley becomes narrow, affording no more space than is sufficient for the river and the road. The pines descend to the banks, imitating with their irregular spires, the pyramidal crags which lift them-

selves far above the regions of forest into the deep azure
of the sky, and among the white dazzling clouds. The
scene, at the distance of half a mile from Cluses, differs
from that of Matlock in little else than in the immensity of its proportions, and in its untameable, inaccessible solitude, inhabited only by the goats which we saw
browsing on the rocks.

Near Maglans, within a league of each other, we saw
two waterfalls. They were no more than mountain rivu-
lets, but the height from which they fell, at least of
twelve hundred feet, made them assume a character
inconsistent with the smallness of their stream. The
first fell from the overhanging brow of a black precipice
on an enormous rock, precisely resembling some colossal
Egyptian statue of a female deity. It struck the head
of the visionary image, and, gracefully dividing there,
fell from it in folds of foam more like to cloud than
water, imitating a veil of the most exquisite woof. It
then united, concealing the lower part of the statue, and
hiding itself in a winding of its channel, burst into a
deeper fall, and crossed our route in its path towards
the Arve.

The other waterfall was more continuous and larger.
The violence with which it fell made it look more like
some shape which an exhalation had assumed than like
water, for it streamed beyond the mountain, which appeared dark behind it, as it might have appeared behind
an evanescent cloud.

The character of the scenery continued the same until
we arrived at St. Martin (called in the maps Sallanches),
the mountains perpetually becoming more elevated, exhibiting at every turn of the road more craggy summits,
loftier and wider extent of forests, darker and more deep
recesses.

The following morning we proceeded from St. Martin
on mules to Chamouni, accompanied by two guides.

We proceeded, as we had done the preceding day, along the valley of the Arve, a valley surrounded on all sides by immense mountains, whose rugged precipices are intermixed on high with dazzling snow. Their bases were still covered with the eternal forests, which perpetually grew darker and more profound as we approached the inner regions of the mountains.

On arriving at a small village, at the distance of a league from St. Martin, we dismounted from our mules, and were conducted by our guides to view a cascade. We beheld an immense body of water fall two hundred and fifty feet, dashing from rock to rock, and casting a spray which formed a mist around it, in the midst of which hung a multitude of sunbows, which faded or became unspeakably vivid, as the inconstant sun shone through the clouds. When we approached near to it, the rain of the spray reached us, and our clothes were wetted by the quick-falling but minute particles of water. The cataract fell from above into a deep craggy chasm at our feet, where, changing its character to that of a mountain stream, it pursued its course towards the Arve, roaring over the rocks that impeded its progress.

As we proceeded, our route still lay through the valley, or rather, as it had now become, the vast ravine, which is at once the couch and the creation of the terrible Arve. We ascended, winding between mountains whose immensity staggers the imagination. We crossed the path of a torrent, which three days since had descended from the thawing snow, and torn the road away.

We dined at Servoz, a little village, where there are lead and copper mines, and where we saw a cabinet of natural curiosities, like those of Keswick and Bethgelert. We saw in this cabinet some chamois' horns, and the horns of an exceedingly rare animal called the bouquetin, which inhabits the deserts of snow to the south of Mont Blanc : it is an animal of the stag kind ; its horns weigh

at least twenty-seven English pounds. It is inconceivable how so small an animal could support so inordinate a weight. The horns are of a very peculiar conformation, being broad, massy, and pointed at the ends,
and surrounded with a number of rings, which are
supposed to afford an indication of its age: there were
seventeen rings on the largest of these horns.

From Servoz three leagues remain to Chamouni.—
Mont Blanc was before us—the Alps, with their innumerable glaciers on high all around, closing in the complicated windings of the single vale—forests inexpressibly
beautiful, but majestic in their beauty—intermingled
beech and pine, and oak, overshadowed our road, or
receded, whilst lawns of such verdure as I have never
seen before occupied these openings, and gradually
became darker in their recesses. Mont Blanc was before us, but it was covered with cloud; its base, furrowed
with dreadful gaps, was seen above. Pinnacles of snow
intolerably bright, part of the chain connected with Mont
Blanc, shone through the clouds at intervals on high. I
never knew—I never imagined what mountains were
before. The immensity of these aerial summits excited,
when they suddenly burst upon the sight, a sentiment of
ecstatic wonder, not unallied to madness. And remember
this was all one scene, it all pressed home to our regard
and our imagination. Though it embraced a vast extent
of space, the snowy pyramids which shot into the bright
blue sky seemed to overhang our path; the ravine,
clothed with gigantic pines, and black with its depth
below, so deep that the very roaring of the untameable
Arve, which rolled through it, could not be heard above
—all was as much our own, as if we had been the creators
of such impressions in the minds of others as now occupied our own. Nature was the poet, whose harmony
held our spirits more breathless than that of the divinest.

As we entered the valley of Chamouni (which in fact

may be considered as a continuation of those which we
have followed from Bonneville and Cluses) clouds hung
upon the mountains at the distance perhaps of 6000 feet
from the earth, but so as effectually to conceal not only
Mont Blanc, but the other *aiguilles*, as they call them
here, attached and subordinate to it. We were travelling along the valley, when suddenly we heard a sound
as of the burst of smothered thunder rolling above;
yet there was something earthly in the sound, that told
us it could not be thunder. Our guide hastily pointed
out to us a part of the mountain opposite, from whence
the sound came. It was an avalanche. We saw the
smoke of its path among the rocks, and continued to
hear at intervals the bursting of its fall. It fell on the
bed of a torrent, which it displaced, and presently we
saw its tawny-coloured waters also spread themselves
over the ravine, which was their couch.

We did not, as we intended, visit the *Glacier de Boisson* to-day, although it descends within a few minutes'
walk of the road, wishing to survey it at least when un-
fatigued. We saw this glacier which comes close to the
fertile plain, as we passed ; its surface was broken into a
thousand unaccountable figures: conical and pyramidical
crystallizations, more than fifty feet in height, rise from
its surface, and precipices of ice, of dazzling splendour,
overhang the woods and meadows of the vale. This
glacier winds upwards from the valley, until it joins the
masses of frost from which it was produced above, winding through its own ravine like a bright belt flung over
the black region of pines. There is more in all these
scenes than mere magnitude of proportion: there is a
majesty of outline; there is an awful grace in the very
colours which invest these wonderful shapes—a charm
which is peculiar to them, quite distinct even from the
reality of their unutterable greatness.

July 2 {.

Yesterday morning we went to the source of the Arveiron. It is about a league from this village; the river
rolls forth impetuously from an arch of ice, and spreads
itself in many streams over a vast space of the valley,
ravaged and laid bare by its inundations. The glacier by
which its waters are nourished, overhangs this cavern
and the plain, and the forests of pine which surround it,
with terrible precipices of solid ice. On the other side
rises the immense glacier of Montanvert, fifty miles in
extent, occupying a chasm among mountains of inconceivable height, and of forms so pointed and abrupt, that
they seem to pierce the sky. From this glacier we saw,
as we sat on a rock close to one of the streams of the
Arveiron, masses of ice detach themselves from on high,
and rush with a loud dull noise into the vale. The violence of their fall turned them into powder, which flowed
over the rocks in imitation of waterfalls, whose ravines
they usurped and filled.

In the evening I went with Ducrée, my guide, the only
tolerable person I have seen in this country, to visit the
glacier of Boisson. This glacier, like that of Montanvert,
comes close to the vale, overhanging the green meadows
and the dark woods with the dazzling whiteness of its precipices and pinnacles, which are like spires of radiant
crystal, covered with a net-work of frosted silver. These
glaciers flow perpetually into the valley, ravaging in their
slow but irresistible progress the pastures and the forests
which surround them, performing a work of desolation in
ages which a river of lava might accomplish in an hour,
but far more irretrievably; for where the ice has once
descended the hardiest plant refuses to grow; if even, as
in some extraordinary instances, it should recede after its
progress has once commenced. The glaciers perpetually
move onward, at the rate of a foot each day, with a

motion that commences at the spot where, on the boundaries of perpetual congelation, they are produced by the
freezing of the waters which arise from the partial melting of the eternal snows. They drag with them from the
regions whence they derive their origin all the ruins of
the mountain, enormous rocks, and immense accumula-
tions of sand and stones. These are driven onwards by
the irresistible stream of solid ice ; and when they arrive
at a declivity of the mountain, sufficiently rapid, roll
down, scattering ruin. I saw one of these rocks which
had descended in the spring (winter here is the season of
silence and safety) which measured forty feet in every
direction.

The verge of a glacier, like that of Boisson, presents
the most vivid image of desolation that it is possible to
conceive. No one dares to approach it ; for the enormous pinnacles of ice which perpetually fall, are perpetually reproduced. The pines of the forest, which
bound it at one extremity, are overthrown and shattered
to a wide extent at its base. There is something inexpressibly dreadful in the aspect of the few branchless
trunks, which, nearest to the ice rifts, still stand in the
uprooted soil. The meadows perish, overwhelmed with
sand and stones. Within this last year, these glaciers
have advanced three hundred feet into the valley. Saus-
sure, the naturalist, says, that they have their periods of
increase and decay : the people of the country hold an
opinion entirely different ; but as I judge, more probable.
It is agreed by all, that the snow on the summit of Mont
Blanc and the neighbouring mountains perpetually aug-
ments, and that ice, in the form of glaciers, subsists without melting in the valley of Chamouni during its transient
and variable summer. If the snow which produces this
glacier must augment, and the heat of the valley is no
obstacle to the perpetual existence of such masses of ice
as have already descended into it. the consequence is

obvious; the glaciers must augment and will subsist, at
least until they have overflowed this vale.

I will not pursue Buffon's sublime but gloomy theory—
that this globe which we inhabit will at some future
period be changed into a mass of frost by the encroach-
ments of the polar ice, and of that produced on the most
elevated points of the earth. Do you, who assert the
supremacy of Ahriman, imagine him throned among
these desolating snows, among these palaces of death
and frost, so sculptured in this their terrible magnificence
by the adamantine hand of necessity, and that he casts
around him, as the first essays of his final usurpation,
avalanches, torrents, rocks, and thunders, and above all
these deadly glaciers, at once the proof and symbols of
his reign;—add to this, the degradation of the human
species—who in these regions are half deformed or
idiotic, and most of whom are deprived of anything that
can excite interest or admiration. This is a part of the
subject more mournful and less sublime; but such as
neither the poet nor the philosopher should disdain to
regard.

This morning we departed, on the promise of a fine
day, to visit the glacier of Montanvert. In that part
where it fills a slanting valley, it is called the Sea of Ice.
This valley is 950 toises, or 7600 feet above the level of
the sea. We had not proceeded far before the rain began
to fall, but we persisted until we had accomplished more
than half our journey, when we returned, wet through.

Chamouni, July 25th.

We have returned from visiting the glacier of Montanvert, or, as it is called, the Sea of Ice, a scene in truth of
dizzying wonder. The path that winds to it along the
side of a mountain, now clothed with pines, now intersected with snowy hollows, is wide and steep. The cabin
of Montanvert is three leagues from Chamouni. half of

which distance is performed on mules, not so sure footed, but that on the first day the one which I rode fell in what the guides call a *mauvais pas,* so that I narrowly escaped being precipitated down the mountain. We passed over a hollow covered with snow, down which vast stones are accustomed to roll. One had fallen the preceding day, a little time after we had returned: our guides desired us to pass quickly, for it is said that sometimes the least sound will accelerate their descent. We arrived at Montanvert, however, safe.

On all sides precipitous mountains, the abodes of unrelenting frost, surround this vale: their sides are banked up with ice and snow, broken, heaped high, and exhibiting terrific chasms. The summits are sharp and naked pinnacles, whose overhanging steepness will not even permit snow to rest upon them. Lines of dazzling ice occupy here and there their perpendicular rifts, and shine through the driving vapours with inexpressible brilliance: they pierce the clouds like things not belonging to this earth. The vale itself is filled with a mass of undulating ice, and has an ascent sufficiently gradual even to the remotest abysses of these horrible deserts. It is only half a league (about two miles) in breadth, and seems much less. It exhibits an appearance as if frost had suddenly bound up the waves and whirlpools of a mighty torrent. We walked some distance upon its surface. The waves are elevated about 12 or 15 feet from the surface of the mass, which is intersected by long gaps of unfathomable depth, the ice of whose sides is more beautifully azure than the sky. In these regions everything changes, and is in motion. This vast mass of ice has one general progress, which ceases neither day nor night; it breaks and bursts for ever: some undulations sink while others rise; it is never the same. The echo of rocks, or of the ice and snow which fall from their overhanging precipices, or roll from their aerial summits, scarcely ceases for one moment. One would think that Mont Blanc, like the god of the Stoics, was a vast animal, and that the frozen blood for ever circulated through his stony veins.

We dined (M***, C***, and I) on the grass, in the open air, surrounded by this scene. The air is piercing and clear. We returned down the mountain, sometimes encompassed by the driving vapours, sometimes cheered by the sunbeams, and arrived at our inn by seven o'clock.

Montalegre, July 28th.

The next morning we returned through the rain to St. Martin. The scenery had lost something of its immensity, thick clouds hanging over the highest mountains ; but visitings of sunset intervened between the showers, and the blue sky shone between the accumulated clouds of snowy whiteness which brought them ; the dazzling mountains sometimes glittered through a chasm of the clouds above our heads, and all the charm of its grandeur remained. We repassed *Pont Pellisier*, a wooden bridge over the Arve, and the ravine of the Arve. We repassed the pine-forests which overhang the defile, the château of St. Michel, a haunted ruin, built on the edge of a precipice, and shadowed over by the eternal forest. We repassed the vale of Servoz, a vale more beautiful, because more luxuriant, than that of Chamouni. Mont Blanc forms one of the sides of this vale also, and the other is inclosed by an irregular amphitheatre of enormous mountains, one of which is in ruins, and fell fifty years ago into the higher part of the valley; the smoke of its fall was seen in Piedmont, and people went from Turin to investigate whether a volcano had not burst forth among the Alps. It continued falling many days, spreading, with the shock and thunder of its ruin, consternation into the neighbouring vales. In the evening we arrived at St. Martin. The next day we wound through the valley, which I have described before, and arrived in the evening at our home.

We have bought some specimens of minerals and plants, and two or three crystal seals, at Mont Blanc, to preserve the remembrance of having approached it. There is a cabinet of *Histoire Naturelle* at Chamouni, just as at Keswick, Matlock, and Clifton, the proprietor of which is the very vilest specimen of that vile species of quack that, together with the whole army of aubergistes and guides, and indeed the entire mass of the population, subsist on the weakness and credulity of travellers as leeches subsist on the sick. The most interesting of my purchases is a large collection of all the seeds of rare alpine plants, with their names written upon the outside of the papers that contain them. These I mean to colonize in my garden in England, and to permit you to make what choice you please from them They are companions which the Celandine—the classic Celandine, need not despise ; they are as wild and more daring than he, and will tell him tales of things even as touching and sublime as the gaze of a vernal poet.

Did I tell you that there are troops of wolves among these mountains? In the winter they descend into the valleys, which the snow occupies six months of the year, and devour everything that they can find out of doors. A wolf is more powerful than the fiercest and strongest dog. There are no bears in these regions. We heard, when we were at Lucerne, that they were occasionally found in the forests which surround that lake. Adieu.

S.

A Proposal

FOR PUTTING

REFORM TO THE VOTE

THROUGHOUT THE KINGDOM.

BY THE HERMIT OF MARLOW.

LONDON:

PRINTED FOR C. AND J. OLLIER,

3, WELBECK STREET, CAVENDISH SQUARE;

By C. H. Reynell, 21, Piccadilly.

——

1817.

A PROPOSAL, &c.

A GREAT question is now agitating in this nation, which no man or party of men is competent to decide; indeed there are no materials of evidence which can afford a foresight of the result. Yet on its issue depends whether we are to be slaves or free men.

It is needless to recapitulate all that has been said about Reform. Every one is agreed that the House of Commons is not a representation of the people. The only theoretical question that remains is, whether the people ought to legislate for themselves, or be governed by laws and impoverished by taxes originating in the edicts of an assembly which represents somewhat less than a thousandth part of the entire community. I think they ought not to be so taxed and governed. An hospital for lunatics is the only theatre where we can conceive so mournful a comedy to be exhibited as this mighty nation now exhibits: a single person bullying and swindling a thousand of his comrades out of all they possessed in the world, and then trampling and spitting upon them, though he were the most contemptible and degraded of mankind, and they had strength in their arms and courage in their hearts. Such a parable realized in political society is a spectacle worthy of the utmost indignation and abhorrence.

The prerogatives of Parliament constitute a sovereignty which is exercised in contempt of the People, and it is in strict consistency with the laws of human nature that it should have been exercised for the People's misery and ruin. Those whom they despise, men instinctively seek to render slavish and wretched, that their scorn may be secure. It is the object of the Reformers to restore the People to a sovereignty thus held in their contempt. It is my object, or I would be silent now.

Servitude is sometimes voluntary. Perhaps the People choose to be enslaved ; perhaps it is their will to be degraded and ignorant and famished ; perhaps custom is their only God, and they its fanatic worshippers will shiver in frost and waste in famine rather · than deny that idol, perhaps the majority of this nation decree that they will not be represented in Parliament, that they will not deprive of power those who have reduced them to the miserable condition in which they now exist. It is *their* will—it is their own concern. If such be their decision, the champions of the rights and the mourners over the errors and calamities of man, must retire to their homes in silence, until accumulated sufferings shall have produced the effect of reason.

The question now at issue is, whether the majority of the adult individuals of the United Kingdom of Great Britain and Ireland desire or no a complete representation in the Legislative Assembly.

I have no doubt that such is their will, and I believe this is the opinion of most persons conversant with the state of the public feeling. But the fact ought to be formally ascertained before we proceed. If the majority of the adult population should solemnly state their desire to be, that the representatives whom they might appoint should constitute the Commons House of Parliament, there is an end to the dispute. Parliament would then be required, not petitioned, to prepare some effectual plan for carrying the general will into effect ; and if Parliament should then refuse, the consequences

of the contest that might ensue would rest on its presumption and temerity. Parliament would have rebelled against the People then.

If the majority of the adult population shall, when seriously called upon for their opinion, determine on grounds, however erroneous, that the experiment of innovation by Reform in Parliament is an evil of greater magnitude than the consequences of misgovernment to which Parliament has afforded a constitutional sanction, then it becomes us to be silent ; and we should be guilty of the great crime which I have conditionally imputed to the House of Commons, if after unequivocal evidence that it was the national will to acquiesce in the existing system we should, by partial assemblies of the multitude, or by any party acts, excite the minority to disturb this decision.

The first step towards Reform is to ascertain this point. For which purpose I think the following plan would be effectual :—

That a Meeting should be appointed to be held at the *Crown and Anchor* Tavern on .the —— of ——, to take into consideration the most effectual measures for ascertaining whether or no, a Reform in Parliament is the will of the majority of the individuals of the British Nation.

That the most eloquent and the most virtuous and the most venerable among the Friends of Liberty, should employ their authority and intellect to persuade men to lay aside all animosity and even discussion respecting the topics on which they are disunited, and by the love which they bear to their suffering country conjure them to contribute all their energies to set this great question at rest—whether the Nation desires a Reform in Parliament or no ?

That the friends of Reform, residing in any part of the country, be earnestly entreated to lend perhaps their last and the decisive effort to set their hopes and fears at rest ; that those who can should go to London, and those who cannot, but who yet feel that the aid of their talents might be beneficial, should address a letter to the Chairman of the Meeting, explaining their sentiments : let these letters be read aloud, let all things be transacted in the face of day.   Let Resolutions, of an import similar to those that follow be proposed.

1. That those who think that it is the duty of the People of this nation to exact such a Reform in the Commons House of Parliament, as should make that House a complete representation of their will, and that the People have a right to perform this duty, assemble here for the purpose of collecting evidence as to how far it is the will of the majority of the People to acquit themselves of this duty, and to exercise this right.

2. That the population of Great Britain and Ireland be divided into three hundred distinct portions, each to contain an equal number of inhabitants, and three hundred persons be commissioned, each personally to visit every individual within the district named in his commission, and to inquire whether or no that individual is willing to sign the declaration contained in the third Resolution, requesting him to annex to his signature any explanation or exposure of his sentiments which he might choose to place on record.   That the following Declaration be proposed for signature :—

3. That the House of Commons does not represent the will of the People of the British Nation ; we the undersigned therefore declare, and publish, and our signatures annexed shall be evidence of our firm and solemn conviction that the liberty, the happiness, and the majesty of the great nation to which it is our boast to belong, have been brought into danger and suffered to decay through the corrupt and inadequate manner in which Members are chosen to sit in the Commons

House of Parliament ; we hereby express, before God and our country, a deliberate and unbiassed persuasion, that it is our duty, if we shall be found in the minority in this great question, incessantly to petition ; if among the majority, to require and exact that that House should originate such measures of Reform as would render its Members the actual Representatives of the Nation.

4. That this Meeting shall be held day after day, until it determines on the whole detail of the plan for collecting evidence as to the will of the nation on the subject of a Reform in Parliament.

5. That this Meeting disclaims any design, however remote, of lending their sanction to the revolutionary and disorganizing schemes which have been most falsely imputed to the Friends of Reform, and declares that its object is purely constitutional.

6. That a subscription be set on foot to defray the expenses of this Plan.

In the foregoing proposal of Resolutions, to be submitted to a National Meeting of the Friends of Reform, I have purposely avoided detail. If it shall prove that I have in any degree afforded a hint to men who have earned and established their popularity by personal sacrifices and intellectual eminence such as I have not the presumption to rival, let it belong to them to pursue and develop all suggestions relating to the great cause of liberty which has been nurtured (I am scarcely conscious of a metaphor) with their very sweat, and blood, and tears : some have tended it in dungeons, others have cherished it in famine, all have been constant to it amidst persecution and calumny, and in the face of the sanctions of power :—so accomplish what ye have begun.

I shall mention therefore only one point relating to the practical part of my Proposal. Considerable expenses, according to my present conception, would be

necessarily incurred : funds should be created by subscription to meet these demands.   I have an income of
a thousand a year, on which I support my wife and
children in decent comfort, and from which I satisfy
certain large claims of general justice.   Should any
plan resembling that which I have proposed be determined on by you, I will give £100, being a tenth part
of one year's income, towards its object ; and I will not
deem so proudly of myself, as to believe that I shall
stand alone in this respect, when any rational and consistent scheme for the public benefit shall have received
the sanction of those great and good men who have
devoted themselves for its preservation.

A certain degree of coalition among the sincere
Friends of Reform, in whatever shape, is indispensable
to the success of this proposal.   The friends of Universal or of Limited Suffrage, of Annual or Triennial
Parliaments, ought to settle these subjects on which
they disagree, when it is known whether the Nation
desires that measure on which they are all agreed.   It
is trivial to discuss what species of Reform shall have
place, when it yet remains a question whether there
will be any Reform or no.

Meanwhile, nothing remains for me but to state
explicitly my sentiments on this subject of Reform.
The statement is indeed quite foreign to the merits of
the Proposal in itself, and I should have suppressed it
until called upon to subscribe such a requisition as I
have suggested, if the question which it is natural to
ask, as to what are the sentiments of the person who
originates the scheme, could have received in any other
manner a more simple and direct reply.   It appears to
me that Annual Parliaments ought to be adopted as an
immediate measure, as one which strongly tends to
preserve the liberty and happiness of the Nation ; it
would enable men to cultivate those energies on which
the performance of the political duties belonging to the

citizen of a free state as the rightful guardian of its prosperity essentially depends; it would familiarize men with liberty by disciplining them to an habitual acquaintance with its forms. Political institution is undoubtedly susceptible of such improvements as no rational person can consider possible, so long as the present degraded condition to which the vital imperfections in the existing system of government has reduced the vast multitude of men, shall subsist. The securest method of arriving at such beneficial innovations, is to proceed gradually and with caution ; or in the place of that order and freedom which the Friends of Reform assert to be violated now, anarchy and despotism will follow. Annual Parliaments have my entire assent. I will not state those general reasonings in their favour which Mr. Cobbett and other writers have already made familiar to the public mind.

With respect to Universal Suffrage, I confess I consider its adoption, in the present unprepared state of public knowledge and feeling, a measure fraught with peril. I think that none but those who register their names as paying a certain small sum in *direct taxes* ought at present to send Members to Parliament. The consequences of the immediate extension of the elective franchise to every male adult, would be to place power in the hands of men who have been rendered brutal and torpid and ferocious by ages of slavery. It is to suppose that the qualities belonging to a demagogue are such as are sufficient to endow a legislator. I allow Major Cartwright's arguments to be unanswerable ; abstractedly it is the right of every human being to have a share in the government. But Mr. Paine's arguments are also unanswerable ; a pure republic may be shown, by inferences the most obvious and irresistible, to be that system of social order the fittest to produce the happiness and promote the genuine eminence of man. Yet nothing can less con-

sist with reason, or afford smaller hopes of any
beneficial issue, than the plan which should abolish the
regal and the aristocratical branches of our constitution,
before the public mind, through many gradations of
improvement, shall have arrived at the maturity which
can disregard these symbols of its childhood.

"WE PITY THE PLUMAGE, BUT FORGET
THE DYING BIRD."

AN

ADDRESS to the PEOPLE

ON

The Death of the Princess Charlotte.

BY

𝕿𝖍𝖊 𝕳𝖊𝖗𝖒𝖎𝖙 𝖔𝖋 𝕸𝖆𝖗𝖑𝖔𝖜.

AN ADDRESS, &c.

I. THE Princess Charlotte is dead. She no longer moves, nor thinks, nor feels. She is as inanimate as the clay with which she is about to mingle. It is a dreadful thing to know that she is a putrid corpse, who but a few days since was full of life and hope ; a woman young, innocent, and beautiful, snatched from the bosom of domestic peace, and leaving that single vacancy which none can die and leave not.

II. Thus much the death of the Princess Charlotte has in common with the death of thousands. How many women die in childbed and leave their families of motherless children and their husbands to live on, blighted by the remembrance of that heavy loss ? How many women of active and energetic virtues ; mild, affectionate, and wise, whose life is as a chain of happiness and union, which once being broken, leaves those whom it bound to perish, have died, and have been deplored with bitterness, which is too deep for words ? Some have perished in penury or shame, and their orphan baby has survived, a prey to the scorn and neglect of strangers. Men have watched by the bedside of their expiring wives, and have gone mad when the hideous death-rattle was heard within the throat, regardless of the rosy child sleeping in the lap of the unobservant nurse. The countenance of the physician had been read by the stare of this distracted husband, till the legible despair sunk into his heart. All this has been and is. You walk with a merry heart through

the streets of this great city, and think not that such
are the scenes acting all around you. You do not
number in your thought the mothers who die in childbed. It is the most horrible of ruins :—In sickness, in
old age, in battle, death comes as to his own home ;
but in the season of joy and hope, when life should
succeed to life, and the assembled family expects one
more, the youngest and the best beloved, that the wife,
the mother—she for whom each member of the family
was so dear to one another, should die !—Yet thousands
of the poorest poor, whose misery is aggravated by
what cannot be spoken now, suffer this. And have they
no affections? Do not their hearts beat in their bosoms,
and the tears gush from their eyes ? Are they not
human flesh and blood ? Yet none weep for them—
none mourn for them—none when their coffins are
carried to the grave (if indeed the parish furnishes a
coffin for all) turn aside and moralize upon the sadness
they have left behind.

III. The Athenians did well to celebrate, with public
mourning, the death of those who had guided the
republic with their valour and their understanding, or
illustrated it with their genius. Men do well to mourn
for the dead ; it proves that we love something beside
ourselves ; and he must have a hard heart who can see
his friend depart to rottenness and dust, and speed him
without emotion on his voyage to "that bourne whence
no traveller returns." To lament for those who have
benefited the State, is a habit of piety yet more favour-
able to the cultivation of our best affections. When
Milton died it had been well that the universal English
nation had been clothed in solemn black, and that the
muffled bells had tolled from town to town. The French
nation should have enjoined a public mourning at the
deaths of Rousseau and Voltaire. We cannot truly
grieve for every one who dies beyond the circle of those

especially dear to us ; yet in the extinction of the objects of public love and admiration, and gratitude, there is something, if we enjoy a liberal mind, which has departed from within that circle. It were well done also, that men should mourn for any public calamity which has befallen their country or the world, though it be not death. This helps to maintain that connexion between one man and another, and all men considered as a whole, which is the bond of social life. There should be public mourning when those events take place which make all good men mourn in their hearts,—the rule of foreign or domestic tyrants, the abuse of public faith, the wresting of old and venerable laws to the murder of the innocent, the established insecurity of all those, the flower of the nation, who cherish an unconquerable enthusiasm for public good. Thus, if Horne Tooke and Hardy had been convicted of high treason, it had been good that there had been not only the sorrow and the indignation which would have filled all hearts, but the external symbols of grief. When the French Republic was extinguished, the world ought to have mourned.

IV. But this appeal to the feelings of men should not be made lightly, or in any manner that tends to waste, on inadequate objects, those fertilizing streams of sympathy, which a public mourning should be the occasion of pouring forth. This solemnity should be used only to express a wide and intelligible calamity, and one which is felt to be such by those who feel for their country and for mankind; its character ought to be universal, not particular.

V. The news of the death of the Princess Charlotte, and of the execution of Brandreth, Ludlam, and Turner, arrived nearly at the same time. If beauty, youth, innocence, amiable manners, and the exercise of the domestic virtues could alone justify public sorrow when they are extinguished for ever, this interesting Lady would well deserve that exhibition. She was the last and the best of her race. But there were thousands of others equally distinguished as she, for private excellences, who have been cut off in youth and hope. The accident of her birth neither made her life more virtuous nor her death more worthy of grief. For the public she had done nothing either good or evil; her education had rendered her incapable of either in a large and comprehensive sense. She was born a Princess; and those who are destined to rule mankind are dispensed with acquiring that wisdom and that experience which is necessary even to rule themselves. She was not like Lady Jane Grey, or Queen Elizabeth, a woman of profound and various learning. She had accomplished nothing, and aspired to nothing, and could understand nothing respecting those great political questions which involve the happiness of those over whom she was destined to rule. Yet this should not be said in blame, but in compassion: let us speak no evil of the dead. Such is the misery, such the impotence of royalty—Princes are prevented from the cradle from becoming anything which may deserve that greatest of all rewards next to a good conscience, public admiration and regret.

VI. The execution of Brandreth, Ludlam, and Turner is an event of quite a different character from the death of the Princess Charlotte. These men were shut up in a horrible dungeon for many months, with the fear of a hideous death and of everlasting hell thrust before their eyes; and at last were brought to the scaffold and hung. They too had domestic affections, and were remarkable for the exercise of private virtues. Perhaps their low station permitted the growth of those affections in a degree not consistent with a more exalted rank. They had sons, and brothers, and sisters, and fathers, who loved them, it should seem, more than the Princess Charlotte could be loved by those whom the regulations of her rank had held in perpetual estrangement from her. Her husband was to her as father, mother, and brethren. Ludlam and Turner were men of mature years, and the affections were ripened and strengthened within them. What these sufferers felt shall not be said. But what must have been the long and various agony of their kindred may be inferred from Edward Turner, who, when he saw his brother dragged along upon the hurdle, shrieked horribly and fell in a fit, and was carried away like a corpse by two men. How fearful must have been their agony, sitting in solitude on that day when the tempestuous voice of horror from the crowd, told them that the head so dear to them was severed from the body! Yes—they listened to the maddening shriek which burst from the multitude : they heard the rush of ten thousand terror-stricken feet, the groans and the hootings which told them that the mangled and distorted head was then lifted into the air. The sufferers were dead. What is death? Who dares to say that which will come after the grave?* Brandreth was calm, and evidently believed that the consequences of our errors were limited by that tremendous barrier. Ludlam and Turner were full of fears, lest God should plunge them in everlasting fire. Mr. Pickering, the clergyman, was evidently anxious that Brandreth should not by a false confidence lose the single opportunity of reconciling himself with the Ruler of the future world. None knew what death was, or could know. Yet these men were presumptuously thrust into that unfathomable gulf, by other men, who knew as little and who reckoned not the present or the future sufferings

---

* " Your death has eyes in his head—mine is not painted so."

Cymbeline.

of their victims. Nothing is more horrible than that man should for any cause shed the life of man. For all other calamities there is a remedy or a consolation. When that Power through which we live ceases to maintain the life which it has conferred, then is grief and agony, and the burthen which must be borne: such sorrow improves the heart. But when man sheds the blood of man, revenge, and hatred, and a long train of executions, and assassinations, and proscriptions is perpetuated to remotest time. ·

VII. Such are the particular, and some of the general considerations depending on the death of these men. But, however deplorable, if it were a mere private or customary grief, the public as the public should not mourn. But it is more than this. The events which led to the death of those unfortunate men are a public calamity. I will not impute blame to the jury who pronounced them guilty of high treason, perhaps the law requires that such should be the denomination of their offence. Some restraint ought indeed to be imposed on those thoughtless men who imagine they can find in violence a remedy for violence, even if their oppressors had tempted them to this occasion of their ruin. They are instruments of evil, not so guilty as the hands that wielded them, but fit to inspire caution. But their death, by hanging and beheading, and the circumstances of which it is the characteristic and the consequence, constitute a calamity such as the English nation ought to mourn with an unassuageable grief.

VIII. Kings and their ministers have in every age been distinguished from other men by a thirst for expenditure and bloodshed. There existed in this country, until the American war, a check, sufficiently feeble and pliant indeed, to this desolating propensity. Until America proclaimed itself a Republic, England was perhaps the freest and most glorious nation subsisting on the surface of the earth. It was not what is to the full desirable that a nation should be, but all that it can be, when it does not govern itself. The consequences, however, of that fundamental defect soon became evident. The government which the imperfect constitution of our representative assembly threw into the hands of a few aristocrats, improved the method of anticipating the taxes by loans, invented by the ministers of William III., until an enormous debt had been created. In the war against the Republic of France, this policy was followed up, until now, the *mere interest* of the public debt amounts to more than twice as much as the lavish expenditure of the public treasure, for maintaining the standing army, and the royal family, and the pensioners, and the placemen. The effect of this debt is to produce such an unequal distribution of the means of living, as saps the foundation of social union and civilized life. It creates a double aristocracy, instead of one which was sufficiently burthensome before, and gives twice as many people the liberty of living in luxury and idleness on the produce of the industrious and the poor. And it does not give them this because they are more wise and meritorious than the rest, or because their leisure is spent in schemes of public good, or in those exercises of the intellect and the imagination, whose creations ennoble or adorn a country. They are not like the old aristocracy, men of pride and honour, *sans peur et sans tache*, but petty peddling slaves, who have gained a right to the title of public creditors, either by gambling in the funds, or by subserviency to government, or some other villainous trade. They are not the "Corinthian capital of polished society," but the petty and creeping weeds which deface the rich tracery of its sculpture. The effect of this system is, that the day labourer gains no more now by working sixteen hours a day than he gained before by

working eight. I put the thing in its simplest and
most intelligible shape. The labourer, he that tills the
ground and manufactures cloth, is the man who has to
provide, out of what he would bring home to his wife
and children, for the luxuries and comforts of those
whose claims are represented by an annuity of forty-
four millions a year levied upon the English nation.
Before, he supported the army and the pensioners, and
the royal family, and the landholders ; and this is a
hard necessity to which it was well that he should
submit. Many and various are the mischiefs flowing
from oppression, but this is the representative of them
all—namely, that one man is forced to labour for
another in a degree not only not necessary to the support of the subsisting distinctions among mankind, but
so as by the excess of the injustice to endanger the
very foundations of all that is valuable in social
order, and to provoke that anarchy which is at once the
enemy of freedom, and the child and the chastiser of
misrule. The nation, tottering on the brink of two
chasms, began to be weary of a continuance of such
dangers and degradations, and the miseries which are
the consequence of them ; the public voice loudly demanded a free representation of the people. It began
to be felt that no other constituted body of men could
meet the difficulties which impend. Nothing but the
nation itself dares to touch the question as to whether
there is any remedy or no to the annual payment of
forty-four millions a year, beyond the necessary expenses
of State, for ever and for ever. A nobler spirit also
went abroad, and the love of liberty, and patriotism,
and the self-respect attendant on those glorious emotions, revived in the bosoms of men. The government
had a desperate game to play.

IX. In the manufacturing districts of England discontent and disaffection had prevailed for many years ;

this was the consequence of that system of double aristocracy produced by the causes before mentioned. The
manufacturers, the helots of luxury, are left by this
system famished, without affections, without health,
without leisure or opportunity for such instruction as
might counteract those habits of turbulence and dissi-
pation, produced by the precariousness and insecurity
of poverty. Here was a ready field for any adven-
turer who should wish, for whatever purpose, to incite
a few ignorant men to acts of illegal outrage. So soon
as it was plainly seen that the demands of the people
for a free representation must be conceded if some
intimidation and prejudice were not conjured up, a conspiracy of the most horrible atrocity was laid in train.
It is impossible to know how far the higher members
of the government are involved in the guilt of their
infernal agents. It is impossible to know how numerous or how active they have been, or by what false
hopes they are yet inflaming the untutored multitude
to put their necks under the axe and into the halter.
But thus much is known, that so soon as the whole
nation lifted up its voice for parliamentary reform, spies
were sent forth. These were selected from the most
worthless and infamous of mankind, and dispersed
among the multitude of famished and illiterate labourers.
It was their business if they found no discontent to
create it. It was their business to find victims, no
matter whether right or wrong. It was their business
to produce upon the public an impression, that if any
attempt to attain national freedom, or to diminish the
burthens of debt and taxation under which we groan,
were successful, the starving multitude would rush in,
and confound all orders and distinctions, and institutions and laws, in common ruin. The inference with
which they were required to arm the ministers was,
that despotic power ought to be eternal. To produce
this salutary impression, they betrayed some innocent

and unsuspecting rustics into a crime whose penalty is
a hideous death.   A few hungry and ignorant manufacturers, seduced by the splendid promises of these
remorseless blood-conspirators, collected together in
what is called rebellion against the State.   All was
prepared, and the eighteen dragoons assembled in
readiness, no doubt, conducted their astonished victims
to that dungeon which they left only to be mangled by
the executioner's hand.   The cruel instigators of their
ruin retired to enjoy the great revenues which they had
earned by a life of villainy.   The public voice was overpowered by the timid and the selfish, who threw the
weight of fear into the scale of public opinion, and
Parliament confided anew to the executive government
those extraordinary powers which may never be laid
down, or which may be laid down in blood, or which
the regularly constituted assembly of the nation must
wrest out of their hands.   Our alternatives are a
despotism, a revolution, or reform.

X. On the 7th of November, Brandreth, Turner, and
Ludlam ascended the scaffold.   We feel for Brandreth
the less, because it seems he killed a man.   But recollect who instigated him to the proceedings which led
to murder.   On the word of a dying man, Brandreth
tells us, that "OLIVER *brought him to this*"—that,
"*but for* OLIVER *he would not have been there.*"   See,
too, Ludlam and Turner, with their sons, and brothers,
and sisters, how they kneel together in a dreadful
agony of prayer.   Hell is before their eyes, and they
shudder and feel sick with fear, lest some unrepented
or some wilful sin should seal their doom in everlasting
fire.   With that dreadful penalty before their eyes—
with that tremendous sanction for the truth of all he
spoke, Turner exclaimed loudly and distinctly, *while
the executioner was putting the rope round his neck,*
"THIS IS ALL OLIVER AND THE GOVERNMENT."   What
more he might have said we know not, because the

chaplain prevented any further observations. Troops of
horse, with keen and glittering swords, hemmed in the
multitudes collected to witness this abominable exhibition. "When the stroke of the axe was heard, there
was a burst of horror from the crowd.* The instant
the head was exhibited, there was a tremendous shriek
set up, and the multitude ran violently in all directions,
as if under the impulse of sudden frenzy. Those who
resumed their stations, groaned and hooted." It is a
national calamity, that we endure men to rule over us,
who sanction for whatever ends a conspiracy which is
to arrive at its purpose through such a frightful pouring
forth of human blood and agony. But when that purpose is to trample upon our rights and liberties for
ever, to present to us the alternatives of anarchy and
oppression, and triumph when the astonished nation
accepts the latter at their hands, to maintain a vast
standing army, and add year by year to a public debt,
which already, they know, cannot be discharged ; and
which, when the delusion that supports it fails, will
produce as much misery and confusion through all
classes of society as it has continued to produce of
famine and degradation to the undefended poor ; to
imprison and calumniate those who may offend them at
will ; when this, if not the purpose, is the effect of that
conspiracy, how ought we not to mourn ?

XI. Mourn then people of England. Clothe yourselves in solemn black. Let the bells be tolled. Think
of mortality and change. Shroud yourselves in solitude and the gloom of sacred sorrow. Spare no symbol
of universal grief. Weep—mourn—lament. Fill the
great city—fill the boundless fields with lamentation
and the echo of groans. A beautiful Princess is dead :
—she who should have been the Queen of her beloved
nation, and whose posterity should have ruled it for

* These expressions are taken from *The Examiner*, Sunday.
Nov. 9th.—*Author's Note.*

ever. She loved the domestic affections, and cherished arts which adorn, and valour which defends. She was amiable and would have become wise, but she was young, and in the flower of youth the destroyer came. LIBERTY is dead. Slave! I charge thee disturb not the depth and solemnity of our grief by any meaner sorrow. If One has died who was like her that should have ruled over this land, like Liberty, young, innocent, and lovely, know that the power through which that one perished was God, and that it was a private grief. But *man* has murdered Liberty, and whilst the life was ebbing from its wound, there descended on the heads and on the hearts of every human thing, the sympathy of an universal blast and curse. Fetters heavier than iron weigh upon us, because they bind our souls. We move about in a dungeon more pestilential than damp and narrow walls, because the earth is its floor and the heavens are its roof. Let us follow the corpse of British Liberty slowly and reverentially to its tomb: and if some glorious Phantom should appear, and make its throne of broken swords and sceptres and royal crowns trampled in the dust, let us say that the Spirit of Liberty has arisen from its grave and left all that was gross and mortal there, and kneel down and worship it as our Queen.

LETTERS TO LEIGH HUNT.*

LETTER I.

LYONS, *March 22,* 1818.

MY DEAR FRIEND,—Why did you not wake me that night before we left England, you and Marianne ? I take this as rather an unkind piece of kindness in you ; but which, in consideration of the six hundred miles between us, I forgive.

We have journeyed towards the spring that has been hastening to meet us from the south ; and though our weather was at first abominable, we have now warm sunny days, and soft winds, and a sky of deep azure, the most serene I ever saw. The heat in this city to-day, is like that of London in the midst of summer. My spirits and health sympathize in the change. Indeed, before I left London, my spirits were as feeble as my health, and I had demands upon them which I found difficult to supply. I have read *Foliage :*—with most of the poems I was already familiar. What a delightful poem the " Nymphs" is ! especially the second part. It is truly *poetical* in the intense and emphatic sense of the word. If six hundred miles were not between us, I should say what pity that *glib* was not omitted, and that the poem is not as faultless as it is beautiful. But for fear I should *spoil* your next poem, I will not let slip a word on the subject. Give my love to Marianne and her sister, and

* Originally printed by Leigh Hunt in his work on *Lord Byron and some of his Contemporaries,* 1828 ; afterwards included by Mrs. Shelley in her collection of Shelley's *Letters from Abroad.*—ED.

tell Marianne she defrauded me of a kiss by not waking
me when she went away, and that as I have no better mode
of conveying it, I must take the best, and ask you to pay
the debt. When shall I see you all again? Oh that it
might be in Italy! I confess that the thought of how
long we may be divided, makes me very melancholy.
Adieu, my dear friend. Write soon. ·

Ever most affectionately yours,

P. B. S.

LIVORNO, *August* 15, 1819.

MY DEAR FRIEND,—How good of you to write to us
so often, and such kind letters ! But it is like lending to
a beggar. What can I offer in return?

Though surrounded by suffering and disquietude, and
latterly almost overcome by our strange misfortune, I
have not been idle. My Prometheus is finished, and I
am also on the eve of completing another work, totally
different from anything you might conjecture that I should
write, of a more popular kind ; and, if anything of mine
could deserve attention, of higher claims. " Be innocent of
the knowledge, dearest chuck, till thou approve the performance."

I send you a little poem* to give to Ollier for publication, but *without my name :* Peacock will correct the
proofs. I wrote it with the idea of offering it to the
Examiner, but I find it is too long. It was composed last
year at Este ; two of the characters you will recognize ;
the third is also in some degree a painting from nature,
but, with regard to time and place, ideal. You will find
the little piece, I think, in some degree consistent with
your own ideas of the manner in which poetry ought to

* Julian and Maddalo.

be written. I have employed a certain familiar style of language to express the actual way in which people talk with each other, whom education and a certain refinement of sentiment have placed above the use of vulgar idioms. I use the word *vulgar* in its most extensive sense; the vulgarity of rank and fashion is as gross in its way, as that of poverty, and its cant terms equally expressive of base conceptions, and therefore equally unfit for poetry. Not that the familiar style is to be admitted in the treatment of a subject wholly ideal, or in that part of any subject which relates to common life, where the passion, exceeding a certain limit, touches the boundaries of that which is ideal. Strong passion expresses itself in metaphor, borrowed from all objects alike remote or near, *and casts over all the shadow of its own greatness.* But what am I about? if my grandmother sucks eggs, was it I who taught her?

If *you* would really correct the proof, I need not trouble Peacock, who, I suppose has enough. Can you take it as a compliment that I prefer to trouble you?

I do not particularly wish this poem to be known as mine, but, at all events, I would not put my name to it. I leave you to judge whether it is best to throw it into the fire, or to publish it. So much for self—*self,* that burr will stick to one. Your kind expressions about my Eclogue* gave me great pleasure : indeed, my great stimulus in writing is to have the approbation of those who feel kindly towards me. The rest is mere duty. I am also delighted to hear that you think of us, and form fancies about us. We cannot yet come home.

*   *   *   *   *   *

Most affectionately yours,

P. B. SHELLEY.

* Rosalind and Helen.

LIVORNO, *September 3rd*, 1819.

MY DEAR FRIEND,—At length has arrived Ollier's parcel, and with it the portrait. What a delightful present ! It is almost yourself, and we sate talking with it, and of it, all the evening. . . . . It is a great pleasure to us to possess it, a pleasure in a time of need ; coming to us when there are few others. How we wish it were you, and not your picture ! How I wish we were with you !

This parcel, you know, and all its letters, are now a year old ; some older. There are all kinds of dates, from March to August, 1818, and " your date," to use Shakespeare's expression, " is better in a pie or a pudding, than in your letter." " Virginity," Parolles says,—but letters are the same thing in another shape.

With it came, too, Lamb's Works. I have looked at none of the other books yet. What a lovely thing is his " Rosamond Gray!" how much knowledge of the sweetest and deepest part of our nature in it ! When I think of such a mind as Lamb's,—when I see how unnoticed remain things of such exquisite and complete perfection, what should I hope for myself, if I had not higher objects in view than fame ?

I have seen too little of Italy and of pictures. Perhaps Peacock has shown you some of my letters to him. But at Rome I was very ill, seldom able to go out without a carriage ; and though I kept horses for two months there, yet there is so much to see ! Perhaps I attended more to sculpture than painting,—its forms being more easily intelligible than those of the latter. Yet I saw the famous works of Raphael, whom I agree with the whole world in thinking the finest painter. Why, I can tell you another time. With respect to Michael Angelo, I dissent, and think with astonishment and indignation on the common notion that he equals, and in some respects exceeds

Raphael. He seems to me to have no sense of moral dignity and loveliness ; and the energy for which he has been so much praised, appears to me to be a certain rude, external, mechanical quality, in comparison with anything possessed by Raphael ; or even much inferior artists. His famous painting in the Sistine Chapel, seems to me deficient in beauty and majesty, both in the conception and the execution. He has been called the Dante of painting ; but if we find some of the gross and strong outlines, which are employed in the few most distasteful passages of the Inferno, where shall we find your Francesca,—where, the spirit coming over the sea in a boat, like Mars rising from the vapours of the horizon,—where, Matilda gathering flowers, and all the exquisite tenderness, and sensibility, and ideal beauty, in which Dante excelled all poets except Shakespeare ?

As to Michael Angelo's *Moses*—but you have seen a cast of that in England.—I write these things, Heaven knows why !

I have written something and finished it,* different from any thing else, and a new attempt for me ; and I mean to dedicate it to you. I should not have done so without your approbation, but I asked your picture last night, and it smiled assent. If I did not think it in some degree worthy of you, I would not make you a public offering of it. I expect to have to write to you soon about it. If Ollier is not turned Christian, Jew, or become infected with *the Murrain*, he will publish it. Don't let him be frightened, for it is nothing which by any courtesy of language can be termed either moral or immoral.

Mary has written to Marianne for a parcel, in which I beg you will make Ollier enclose what you know would most interest me,—your " Calendar " (a sweet extract from which I saw in the Examiner), and the other poems belonging to you ; and for some friends of mine, my Eclogue.

* The Cenci.

I. 2 B

This parcel, which must be sent instantly, will reach me
by October ; but don't trust letters to it, except just a line
or so.   When you write, write by the post.

Ever your affectionate,

P. B. S.

My love to Marianne and Bessy, and Thornton too,
and Percy, &c., and if you could imagine any way in
which I could be useful to them here, tell me.   I will inquire about the Italian chalk.   You have no idea of the
pleasure this portrait gives us.

FIRENZE, *Nov.* 13, 1819.

'MY DEAR FRIEND, — Yesterday morning Mary
brought me a little boy.   She suffered but two hours'
pain, and is now so well that it seems a wonder that she
stays in bed.   The babe is also quite well, and has begun
to suck.   You may imagine this is a great relief and a
great comfort to me, amongst all my misfortunes, past,
present, and to come.

Since I last wrote to you, some circumstances have
occurred, not necessary to explain by letter, which make
my pecuniary condition a very difficult one.   The physicians absolutely forbid my travelling to England in the
winter, but I shall probably pay you a visit in the spring.
With what pleasure, among all the other sources of
regret and discomfort with which England abounds for
me, do I *think* of looking on the original of that kind
and earnest face which is now opposite Mary's bed.   It
will be the only thing which Mary will envy me, or will
need to envy me, in that journey : for I shall come alone.
Shaking hands with you is worth all the trouble ; the
rest is clear loss.

I will tell you more about myself and my pursuits in
my next letter.

Kind love to Marianne, Bessie, and all the children.
Poor Mary begins (for the first time) to look a little con-

soled. For we have spent, as you may imagine, a miserable five months.

Good-bye, my dear Hunt,

Your affectionate friend,

P. B. S.

I have had no letter from you for a *month*.

FLORENCE, *Nov. 23rd*, 1819.

MY DEAR HUNT,—*Why* don't you write to us? I was preparing to send you something for your "Indicator," but I have been a drone instead of a bee in this business, thinking that perhaps, as you did not acknowledge any of my late enclosures, it would not be welcome to you, whatever I might send.

What a state England is in! But you will never write politics. I don't wonder;—but I wish, then, that you would write a paper in " The Examiner," on the actual state of the country, and what, under all the circumstances of the conflicting passions and interests of men, we are to expect. Not what we ought to expect, or what, if so and so were to happen, we might expect,—but what, as things are, there is reason to believe will come ;—and send it me for my information. Every word a man has to say is valuable to the public now; and thus you will at once gratify your friend, nay, instruct, and either exhilarate him or force him to be resigned,—and awaken the minds of the people.

I have no spirits to write what I do not know whether you will care much about ; I know well, that if I were in great misery, poverty, &c., you would think of nothing else but how to amuse and relieve me. You omit me if I am prosperous.

I could laugh if I found a joke, in order to put you in good humour with me after my scolding ;—in good humour enough to write to us. * * * * * Affectionate love to and from all. This ought not only to be the *vale* of a letter, but a superscription over the gate of life.

Your sincere friend,
P. B. SHELLEY.

I send you a *sonnet*. I don't expect you to publish it; but you may show it to whom you please.

FLORENCE, *November* 1819.

MY DEAR FRIEND,—Two letters, both bearing date Oct. 20, arrive on the same day :—one is always glad of twins.

We hear of a box arrived at Genoa with books and clothes : it must be yours. Meanwhile the babe is wrapped in flannel petticoats, and we get on with him as we can. He is small, healthy, and pretty. Mary is recovering rapidly. Marianne, I hope, is quite recovered.

You do not tell me whether you have received my lines on the Manchester affair. They are of the exoteric species, and are meant, not for "The Indicator," but "The Examiner." I would send for the former, if you like, some letters on such subjects of art as suggest themselves in Italy. Perhaps I will, at a venture, send you a specimen of what I mean next post. I enclose you in this a piece for "The Examiner ;" or let it share the fate, whatever that fate may be, of the "Mask of Anarchy."

I am sorry to hear that you have employed yourself in translating "Aminta," though I doubt not it will be a just and beautiful translation. You ought to write Amintas. You ought to exercise your fancy in the perpetual creation of new forms of gentleness and beauty.

*   *   *   *   *   *

With respect to translation, even *I* will not be seduced by it ; although the Greek plays, and some of the ideal dramas of Calderon (with which I have lately, and with inexpressible wonder and delight, become acquainted), are perpetually tempting me to throw over their perfect and glowing forms the grey veil of my own words. And you know me too well to suspect, that I refrain from the belief that what I would substitute for them would deserve the regret which yours would, if suppressed. I have confidence in my moral sense alone; but that is a kind of originality. I have only translated the Cyclops of Euripides when I could absolutely do nothing else, and the Symposium of Plato, which is the delight and astonishment of all who read it :—I mean the original, or so much of the original as is seen in my translation, not the translation itself. * * * * *

I think I have an accession of strength since my residence in Italy, though the disease itself in the side, whatever it may be, is not subdued. Some day we shall return from Italy. I fear that in England things will be carried violently by the rulers, and that they will not have learned to yield in time to the spirit of the age. The great thing to do is to hold the balance between popular impatience and tyrannical obstinacy: to inculcate with fervour both the right of resistance and the duty of forbearance. You know, my principles incite me to take all I can get in politics, for ever aspiring to something more. I am one of those whom nothing will fully satisfy, but who am ready to be partially satisfied, by all that is practicable. We shall see.

Give Bessy a thousand thanks from me for writing out in that pretty neat hand your kind and powerful defence. Ask what she would like best from Italian land. We mean to bring you all something ; and Mary and I have been wondering what it shall be. Do you, each of you, choose. * * * * * *

Adieu, my dear friend,
Yours affectionately ever,
P. B. S.

PISA, *August* 26*th*, 1821.

MY DEAREST FRIEND,—Since I last wrote to you, I have been on a visit to Lord Byron, at Ravenna. The result of this visit was a determination on his part to come and live at Pisa, and I have taken the finest palace on the Lung' Arno for him. But the material part of my visit consists in a message which he desires me to give you, and which I think ought to add to your determination—for such a one I hope you have formed—of restoring your shattered health and spirits by a migration to these "regions mild of calm and serene air."

He proposes that you should come and go shares with him and me, in a periodical work, to be conducted here ; in which each of the contracting parties should publish all their original compositions, and share the profits. He proposed it to Moore, but for some reason it was never brought to bear. There can be no doubt that the *profits* of any scheme in which you and Lord Byron engage must, from various yet co-operating reasons, be very great. As to myself, I am, for the present, only a sort of link between you and him, until you can know each other and effectuate the arrangement ; since (to entrust you with a secret which, for your sake, I withhold from Lord Byron) nothing would induce me to share in the profits, and still less in the borrowed splendour, of such a partnership. You and he, in different manners, would be equal, and would bring, in a different manner, but in the same proportion, equal stocks of reputation and success ; do not let my frankness with you, nor my belief that you deserve it more than Lord Byron, have the effect of deterring you from assuming a station in modern literature, which the universal voice of my contemporaries forbids me either to stoop or aspire to. I am, and I desire to be, nothing.

I did not ask Lord Byron to assist me in sending a remittance for your journey ; because there are men, however excellent, from whom we would never receive an obligation, in the worldly sense of the word; and I am as jealous for my friend as for myself. I, as you know, have it not; but I suppose that at last I shall make up an impudent face, and ask Horace Smith to add to the many obligations he has conferred on me. I know I need only ask.

I think I have never told you how very much I like your "Amyntas;" it almost reconciles me to translations. In another sense I still demur. You might have written another poem such as the "Nymphs," with no great access of effort. I am full of thoughts and plans, and should do something if the feeble and irritable frame which incloses it was willing to obey the spirit. I fancy then that I should do great things. Before this you will have seen "Adonais." Lord Byron, I suppose from modesty on account of his being mentioned in it, did not say a word of "Adonais," though he was loud in his praise of "Prometheus," and what you will not agree with him in, censure of the "Cenci." Certainly if "Marino Faliero" is a dream, the "Cenci" is not : but that between ourselves. Lord Byron is reformed, as far as gallantry goes, and lives with a beautiful and sentimental Italian lady, who is as much attached to him as may be. I trust greatly to his intercourse with you, for his creed to become as pure as he thinks his conduct is. He has many generous and exalted qualties, but the canker o. aristocracy wants to be cut out.

*　　*　　*　　*　　*　　*

THE COLISEUM.

A FRAGMENT.*

T the hour of noon, on the feast of the Passover,
an old man, accompanied by a girl, apparently
his daughter, entered the Coliseum at Rome.
They immediately passed through the Arena, and seek-
ing a solitary chasm among the arches of the southern
part of the ruin, selected a fallen column for their seat,
and clasping each other's hands, sate as in silent contemplation of the scene. But the eyes of the girl were
fixed upon her father's lips, and his countenance, sublime and sweet, but motionless as some Praxitelean
image of the greatest of poets, filled the silent air with
smiles, not reflected from external forms.

It was the great feast of the Resurrection, and the
whole native population of Rome, together with all the
foreigners who flock from all parts of the earth to contemplate its celebration, were assembled round the
Vatican. The most awful religion of the world went
forth surrounded by emblazonry of mortal greatness,
and mankind had assembled to wonder at and worship

---

* Imperfectly printed in *The Shelley Papers*, 1833 : first printed
correctly and completely in the two-volume edition of Shelley's
Essays and Letters, edited by Mrs. Shelley.

the creations of their own power. No straggler was to be met with in the streets and grassy lanes which led to the Coliseum. The father and daughter had sought this spot immediately on their arrival.

A figure, only visible at Rome in night or solitude, and then only to be seen amid the desolated temples of the Forum, or gliding among the weed-grown galleries of the Coliseum, crossed their path. His form, which, though emaciated, displayed the elementary outlines of exquisite grace, was enveloped in an ancient chlamys, which half concealed his face; his snow-white feet were fitted with ivory sandals, delicately sculptured in the likeness of two female figures, whose wings met upon the heel, and whose eager and half-divided lips seemed quivering to meet. It was a face, once seen, never to be forgotten. The mouth and the moulding of the chin resembled the eager and impassioned tenderness of the statues of Antinous; but instead of the effeminate sullenness of the eye, and the narrow smoothness of the forehead, shone an expression of profound and piercing thought; the brow was clear and open, and his eyes deep, like two wells of crystalline water which reflect the all-beholding heavens. Over all was spread a timid expression of womanish tenderness and hesitation, which contrasted, yet intermingled strangely, with the abstracted and fearless character that predominated in his form and gestures.

He avoided, in an extraordinary degree, all communication with the Italians, whose language he seemed scarcely to understand, but was occasionally seen to converse with some accomplished foreigner, whose gestures and appearance might attract him amid his solemn haunts. He spoke Latin, and especially Greek, with fluency, and with a peculiar but sweet accent; he had apparently acquired a knowledge of the northern languages of Europe. There was no circumstance connected with him that gave the least intimation of his country, his origin, or his occupation. His dress was strange, but splendid and solemn. He was forever alone. The literati of Rome thought him a curiosity, but there was something in his manner unintelligible but impressive, which awed their obtrusions into distance and silence. The countrymen, whose path he rarely crossed, returning by starlight from their market at Campo Vaccino, called him, with that strange mixture of religious and historical ideas so common in Italy, *Il Diavolo di Bruto.*

Such was the figure which interrupted the contemplations, if they were so engaged, of the strangers, by addressing them in the clear, and exact, but unidiomatic phrases of their native language :—" Strangers, you are two ; behold the third in this great city, to whom alone the spectacle of these mighty ruins is more delightful than the mockeries of a superstition which destroyed them."

" I see nothing," said the old man.

" What do you here, then ? "

" I listen to the sweet singing of the birds, and the sound of my daughter's breathing composes me like the soft murmur of water—and I feel the sun-warm wind— and this is pleasant to me."

" Wretched old man, know you not that these are the ruins of the Coliseum ? "—

" Alas ! stranger," said the girl, in a voice like mournful music, " speak not so—he is blind."—

The stranger's eyes were suddenly filled with tears, and the lines of his countenance became relaxed. " Blind ! " he exclaimed, in a tone of suffering, which was more than an apology ; and seated himself apart on a flight of shattered and mossy stairs which wound up among the labyrinths of the ruin.

" My sweet Helen," said the old man, " you did not tell me that this was the Coliseum."

" How should I tell you, dearest father, what I knew

not ?   I was on the point of inquiring the way to that building, when we entered this circle of ruins, and, until the stranger accosted us, I remained silent, subdued by the greatness of what I see."

"It is your custom, sweetest child, to describe to me the objects that gave you delight.   You array them in the soft radiance of your words, and whilst you speak I only feel the infirmity which holds me in such dear dependence, as a blessing.   Why have you been silent now ? "

"I know not—first the wonder and pleasure of the sight, then the words of the stranger, and then thinking on what he had said, and how he had looked—and now, beloved father, your own words."

"Well, tell me now, what do you see ?"

"I see a great circle of arches built upon arches, and shattered stones lie around, that once made a part of the solid wall.   In the crevices, and on the vaulted roofs, grow a multitude of shrubs, the wild olive and the myrtle —and intricate brambles, and entangled weeds and plants I never saw before.   The stones are immensely massive, and they jut out one from the other.   There are terrible rifts in the wall, and broad windows through which you see the blue heaven.   There seems to be more than a thousand arches, some ruined, some entire, and they are all immensely high and wide.   Some are shattered, and stand forth in great heaps, and the under-wood is tufted on their crumbling summits.   Around us lie enormous columns, shattered and shapeless—and fragments of capitals and cornice, fretted with delicate sculptures."—

"It is opened to the blue sky ?" said the old man.

"Yes.   We see the liquid depth of heaven above through the rifts and the windows; and the flowers, and the weeds, and the grass and creeping moss, are nourished by its unforbidden rain.   The blue sky is above—the wide, bright, blue sky—it flows through the great rents on high, and through the bare boughs of the marble rooted fig-tree, and through the leaves and flowers of the weeds, even to the dark arcades beneath. I see—I feel its clear and piercing beams fill the universe, and impregnate the joy-inspiring wind with life and light, and casting the veil of its splendour over all things—even me. Yes, and through the highest rift the noonday waning moon is hanging, as it were, out of the solid sky, and this shows that the atmosphere has all the clearness which it rejoices me that you feel."

"What else see you?"

"Nothing."

"Nothing?"

"Only the bright-green mossy ground, speckled by tufts of dewy clover-grass that run into the interstices of the shattered arches, and round the isolated pinnacles of the ruin."

"Like the lawny dells of soft short grass which wind among the pine forests and precipices in the Alps of Savoy?"

"Indeed, father, your eye has a vision more serene than mine."

"And the great wrecked arches, the shattered masses of precipitous ruin, overgrown with the younglings of the forest, and more like chasms rent by an earthquake among the mountains, than like the vestige of what was human workmanship—what are they?"

"Things awe-inspiring and wonderful."

"Are they not caverns such as the untamed elephant might choose, amid the Indian wilderness, wherein to hide her cubs; such as, were the sea to overflow the earth, the mightiest monsters of the deep would change into their spacious chambers?"

"Father, your words image forth what I would have expressed, but, alas! could not."

"I hear the rustling of leaves, and the sound of

waters—but it does not rain,—like the fast drops of a fountain among woods."

"It falls from among the heaps of ruin over our heads—it is, I¹ suppose, the water collected in the rifts by the showers."

"A nursling of man's art, abandoned by his care, and transformed by the enchantment of Nature into a likeness of her own creations, and destined to partake their immortality! Changed into a mountain cloven with woody dells, which overhang its labyrinthine glades, and shattered into toppling precipices. Even the clouds, intercepted by its craggy summit, feed its eternal fountains with their rain. By the column on which I sit, I should judge that it had once been crowned by a temple or a theatre, and that on sacred days the multitude wound up its craggy path to spectacle or the sacrifice——It was such itself!* Helen, what sound of wings is that?"

* Nor does a recollection of the use to which it may have been destined interfere with these emotions. Time has thrown its purple shadow athwart this scene, and no more is visible than the broad and everlasting character of human strength and genius, that pledge of all that is to be admirable and lovely in ages yet to come. Solemn temples, where the senate of the world assembled, palaces, triumphal arches, and cloud-surrounded columns, loaded with the sculptured annals of conquest and domination—what actions and deliberations have they been destined to enclose and commemorate? Superstitious rites, which in their mildest form, outrage reason, and obscure the moral sense of mankind; schemes for wide-extended murder, and devastation, and misrule, and servitude; and, lastly, these schemes brought to their tremendous consummations, and a human being returning in the midst of festival and solemn joy, with thousands and thousands of his enslaved and desolated species chained behind his chariot, exhibiting, as titles to renown, the labour of ages, and the admired creations of genius, overthrown by the brutal force, which was placed as a sword within his hand, and,—contemplation fearful and abhorred!—he himself a being capable of the gentlest and best emotions, inspired with the persuasion that he has done a virtuous deed! We do not forget these things. • • •

"It is the wild pigeons returning to their young. Do you not hear the murmur of those that are brooding in their nests?"

"Ay, it is the language of their happiness. They are as happy as we are, child, but in a different manner. They know not the sensations which this ruin excites within us. Yet it is pleasure to them to inhabit it; and the succession of its forms as they pass, is connected with associations in their minds, sacred to them, as these to us. The internal nature of each being is surrounded by a circle, not to be surmounted by his fellows; and it is this repulsion which constitutes the misfortune of the condition of life. But there is a circle which comprehends, as well as one which mutually excludes all things which feel. And, with respect to man, his public and his private happiness consists in diminishing the circumference which includes those resembling himself, until they become one with him, and he with them. It is because we enter into the meditations, designs and destinies of something beyond ourselves, that the contemplation of the ruins of human power excites an elevating sense of awfulness and beauty. It is therefore, that the ocean, the glacier, the cataract, the tempest, the volcano, have each a spirit which animates the extremities of our frame with tingling joy. It is therefore, that the singing of birds, and the motion of leaves, the sensation of the odorous earth beneath, and the freshness of the living wind around, is sweet. And this is Love. This is the religion of eternity, whose votaries have been exiled from among the multitude of mankind. O, Power!" cried the old man, lifting his sightless eyes towards the undazzling sun, "thou which interpenetratest all things, and without which this glorious world were a blind and formless chaos, Love, Author of Good, God, King, Father! Friend of these thy worshippers! Two solitary hearts invoke thee, may they be divided never! If the

contentions of mankind have been their misery; if to give
and seek that happiness which thou art, has been their
choice and destiny; if, in the contemplation of these
majestic records of the power of their kind, they see
the shadow and the prophecy of that which thou mayst
have decreed that he should become; if the justice, the
liberty, the loveliness, the truth, which are thy footsteps,
have been sought by them, divide them not! It is
thine to unite, to eternize; to make outlive the limits of
the grave those who have left among the living, memorials of thee. When this frame shall be senseless
dust, may the hopes, and the desires, and the delights
which animate it now, never be extinguished in my
child; even as, if she were borne into the tomb, my
memory would be the written monument of all her
nameless excellencies!"

The old man's countenance and gestures, radiant
with the inspiration of his words, sunk, as he ceased,
into more than its accustomed calmness, for he heard
his daughter's sobs, and remembered that he had spoken
of death,—"My father, how can I outlive you?" said
Helen.

"Do not let us talk of death," said the old man,
suddenly changing his tone. "Heraclitus, indeed, died
at my age, and if I had so sour a disposition, there
might be some danger. But Democritus reached a
hundred and twenty, by the mere dint of a joyous and
unconquerable mind. He only died at last, because he
had no gentle and beloved ministering spirit, like my
Helen, for whom it would have been his delight to live.
You remember his gay old sister requested him to put
off starving himself to death until she had returned from
the festival of Ceres; alleging, that it would spoil her
holiday if he refused to comply, as it was not permitted
to appear in the procession immediately after the death
of a relation; and how good-temperedly the sage acceded
to her request."

The old man could not see his daughter's grateful smile, but he felt the pressure of her hand by which it was expressed.—"In truth," he continued, "that mystery, death, is a change which neither for ourselves nor for others is the just object of hope or fear. We know not if it be good or evil, we only know, it is. The old, the young, may alike die; no time, no place, no age, no foresight exempts us from death, and the chance of death. We have no knowledge, if death be a state of sensation, of any precaution that can make those sensations fortunate, if the existing series of events shall not produce that effect. Think not of death, or think of it as something common to us all. It has happened," said he, with a deep and suffering voice, "that men have buried their children."

"Alas! then, dearest father, how I pity you. Let us speak no more."

They rose to depart from the Coliseum, but the figure which had first accosted them interposed itself:— "Lady," he said, "if grief be an expiation of error, I have grieved deeply for the words which I spoke to your companion. The men who anciently inhabited this spot, and those from whom they learned their wisdom, respected infirmity and age. If I have rashly violated that venerable form, at once majestic and defenceless, may I be forgiven?"

"It gives me pain to see how much your mistake afflicts you," she said; "if you can forget, doubt not that we forgive."

"You thought me one of those who are blind in spirit," said the old man, "and who deserve, if any human being can deserve, contempt and blame. Assuredly, contemplating this monument as I do, though in the mirror of my daughter's mind, I am filled with astonishment and delight; the spirit of departed generations seems to animate my limbs, and circulate through all the fibres of my frame. Stranger, if I have

I.

expressed what you have ever felt, let us know each other more."

" The sound of your voice, and the harmony of your thoughts, are delightful to me," said the youth, "and it is a pleasure to see any form which expresses so much beauty and goodness as your daughter's; if you reward me for my rudeness, by allowing me to know you, my error is already expiated, and you remember my ill words no more. I live a solitary life, and it is rare that I encounter any stranger with whom it is pleasant to talk ; besides, their meditations, even though they be learned, do not always agree with mine ; and, though I can pardon this difference, they cannot. Nor have I ever explained the cause of the dress I wear, and the difference which I perceive between my language and manners, and those with whom I have intercourse. Not but that it is painful to me to live without communion with intelligent and affectionate beings. You are such, I feel."

CRITICAL NOTICES OF THE SCULPTURE
IN THE FLORENCE GALLERY.*

ON THE NIOBE.

OF all that remains to us of Greek antiquity, this figure is perhaps the most consummate personification of loveliness, with regard to its countenance, as that of the Venus of the Tribune is with regard to its entire form of woman. It is colossal ; the size adds to its value ; because it allows to the spec-

* From *The Shelley Papers*, 1833. A facsimile of the title-page of this little volume, edited by Captain Medwin, has already been given in the third volume of Shelley's Poetical Works—ED.

tator the choice of a greater number of points of view, and affords him a more analytical one, in which to catch a greater number of the infinite modes of expression, of which any form approaching ideal beauty is necessarily composed. It is the figure of a mother in the act of sheltering, from some divine and inevitable peril, the last, we may imagine, of her surviving children.

The little creature, terrified, as we may conceive, at the strange destruction of all its kindred, has fled to its mother and is hiding its head in the folds of her robe, and casting back one arm, as in a passionate appeal for defence, where it never before could have been sought in vain. She is clothed in a thin tunic of delicate woof; and her hair is fastened on her head into a knot, probably by that mother whose care will never fasten it again. Niobe is enveloped in profuse drapery, a portion of which the left hand has gathered up, and is in the act of extending it over the child in the instinct of shielding her from what reason knows to be inevitable. The right (as the restorer has properly imagined,) is drawing up her daughter to her : and with that instinctive gesture, and by its gentle pressure, is encouraging the child to believe that it can give security. The countenance of Niobe is the consummation of feminine majesty and loveliness, beyond which the imagination scarcely doubts that it can conceive anything.

That masterpiece of the poetic harmony of marble expresses other feelings. There is embodied a sense of the inevitable and rapid destiny which is consummating around her, as if it were already over. It seems as if despair and beauty had combined, and produced nothing but the sublimity of grief. As the motions of the form expressed the instinctive sense of the possibility of protecting the child, and the accustomed and affectionate assurance that she would find an asylum within her arms, so reason and imagination speak in the countenance the certainty that no mortal defence is of avail.

There is no terror in the countenance, only grief—deep, remediless grief. There is no anger:—of what avail is indignation against what is known to be omnipotent? There is no selfish shrinking from personal pain—there is no panic at supernatural agency—there is no adverting to herself as herself: the calamity is mightier than to leave scope for such emotions.

Everything is swallowed up in sorrow: she is all tears; her countenance, in assured expectation of the arrow piercing its last victim in her embrace, is fixed on her omnipotent enemy. The pathetic beauty of the expression of her tender, and inexhaustible, and unquenchable despair, is beyond the effect of sculpture. As soon as the arrow shall pierce her last tie upon earth, the fable that she was turned into stone, or dissolved into a fountain of tears, will be but a feeble emblem of the sadness of hopelessness, in which the few and evil years of her remaining life, we feel, must flow away.

It is difficult to speak of the beauty of the countenance, or to make intelligible in words, from what such astonishing loveliness results.

The head, resting somewhat backward upon the full and flowing contour of the neck, is as in the act of watching an event momently to arrive. The hair is delicately divided on the forehead, and a gentle beauty gleams from the broad and clear forehead, over which its strings are drawn. The face is of an oval fulness, and the features conceived with the daring of a sense of power. In this respect it resembles the careless majesty which Nature stamps upon the rare masterpieces of her creation, harmonising them as it were from the harmony of the spirit within. Yet all this not only consists with, but is the cause of the subtlest delicacy of clear and tender beauty—the expression at once of innocence and sublimity of soul—of purity and strength —of all that which touches the most removed and

divine of the chords that make music in our thoughts
—of that which shakes with astonishment even the most
superficial.

THE MINERVA.

THE head is of the highest beauty. It has a close
helmet, from which the hair delicately parted on the
forehead, half escapes. The attitude gives entire effect
to the perfect form of the neck, and to that full and
beautiful moulding of the lower part of the face and
mouth, which is in living beings the seat of the expression of a simplicity and integrity of nature. Her
face, upraised to heaven, is animated with a profound,
sweet, and impassioned melancholy, with an earnest,
and fervid, and disinterested pleading against some
vast and inevitable wrong. It is the joy and poetry
of sorrow making grief beautiful, and giving it that
nameless feeling which, from the imperfection of language, we call pain, but which is not all pain, though
a feeling which makes not only its possessor, but the
spectator of it, prefer it to what is called pleasure, in
which all is not pleasure. It is difficult to think
that this head, though of the highest ideal beauty,
is the head of Minerva, although the attributes and
attitude of the lower part of the statue certainly suggest
that idea. The Greeks rarely, in their representations
of the characters of their gods,—unless we call the poetic
enthusiasm of Apollo a mortal passion,—expressed the
disturbance of human feeling ; and here is deep and
impassioned grief animating a divine countenance. It
is, indeed, divine. Wisdom (which Minerva may be
supposed to emblem,) is pleading earnestly with Power,
—and invested with the expression of that grief, because it must ever plead so vainly. The drapery of the
statue, the gentle beauty of the feet, and the grace of
the attitude, are what may be seen in many other statues.

belonging to that astonishing era which produced it; such a countenance is seen in few.

This statue happens to be placed on a pedestal, the subject of whose relief is in a spirit wholly the reverse. It was probably an altar to Bacchus—possibly a funeral urn. Under the festoons of fruits and flowers that grace the pedestal, the corners of which are ornamented with the skulls of goats, are sculptured some figures of Mænads under the inspiration of the god. Nothing can be conceived more wild and terrible than their gestures, touching, as they do, the verge of distortion, into which their fine limbs and lovely forms are thrown. There is nothing, however, that exceeds the possibility of nature, though it borders on its utmost line.

The tremendous spirit of superstition, aided by drunkenness, producing something beyond insanity, seems to have caught them in its whirlwinds, and to bear them over the earth, as the rapid volutions of a tempest have the ever-changing trunk of a waterspout, or as the torrent of a mountain river whirls the autumnal leaves resistlessly along in its full eddies. The hair, loose and floating, seems caught in the tempest of their own tumultuous motion; their heads are thrown back, leaning with a strange delirium upon their necks, and looking up to heaven whilst they totter and stumble even in the energy of their tempestuous dance.

One represents Agave with the head of Pentheus in one hand, and in the other a great knife; a second has a spear with its pine cone, which was the Thyrsus; another dances with mad voluptuousness; the fourth is beating a kind of tambourine.

This was indeed a monstrous superstition, even in Greece, where it was alone capable of combining ideal beauty and poetical and abstract enthusiasm with the wild errors from which it sprung. In Rome it had a more familiar, wicked, and dry appearance; it was not suited to the severe and exact apprehensions of the

Romans, and their strict morals were violated by it, and sustained a deep injury, little analogous to its effects upon the Greeks, who turned all things—superstition, prejudice, murder, madness—to beauty.

ON THE VENUS CALLED ANADYOMINE.

SHE has just issued from the bath, and yet is animated with the enjoyment of it.

She seems all soft and mild enjoyment, and the curved lines of her fine limbs flow into each other with a never-ending sinuosity of sweetness. Her face expresses a breathless, yet passive and innocent voluptuousness, free from affectation. Her lips, without the sublimity of lofty and impetuous passion, the grandeur of enthusiastic imagination of the Apollo of the Capitol, or the union of both, like the Apollo Belvidere, have the tenderness of arch, yet pure and affectionate desire, and the mode of which the ends of the mouth are drawn in, yet lifted or half-opened, with the smile that for ever circles round them, and the tremulous curve into which they are wrought by inextinguishable desire, and the tongue lying against the lower lip, as in the listlessness of passive joy, express love, still love.

Her eyes seem heavy and swimming with pleasure, and her small forehead fades on both sides into that sweet swelling and thin declension of the bone over the eye, in the mode which expresses simple and tender feelings.

The neck is full, and panting as with the aspiration of delight, and flows with gentle curves into her perfect form.

Her form is indeed perfect. She is half-sitting and half-rising from a shell, and the fulness of her limbs, and their complete roundness and perfection, do not diminish the vital energy with which they seem to be

animated.   The position of the arms, which are lovely
beyond imagination, is natural, unaffected, and easy.
This, perhaps, is the finest personification of Venus,
the deity of superficial desire, in all antique statuary.
Her pointed and pear-like person, ever virgin, and her
attitude modesty itself.

A BAS-RELIEF.

Probably the sides of a Sarcophagus.

THE lady is lying on a couch, supported by a young
woman, and looking extremely exhausted; her dishevelled hair is floating about her shoulder, and she is
half-covered with drapery that falls on the couch.

Her tunic is exactly like a chemise, only the sleeves
are longer, coming half way down the upper part of the
arm.   An old wrinkled woman, with a cloak over her
head, and an enormously sagacious look, has a most
professional appearance, and is taking hold of her arm
gently with one hand, and with the other is supporting
it.   I think she is feeling her pulse.   At the side of the
couch sits a woman as in grief, holding her head in her
hands.   At the bottom of the bed is another matron
tearing her hair, and in the act of screaming out most
violently, which she seems, however, by the rest of her
gestures, to do with the utmost deliberation, as having
come to the resolution, that it was a correct thing to do
so.   Behind her is a gossip of the most ludicrous
ugliness, crying, I suppose, or praying, for her arms are
crossed upon her neck.   There is also a fifth setting up
a wail.   To the left of the couch a nurse is sitting on
the ground dangling the child in her arms, and wholly
occupied in so doing.   The infant is swaddled.   Behind
her is a female who appears to be in the act of rushing
in with dishevelled hair and violent gesture, and in one
hand brandishing a whip or a thunder-bolt.   This is

probably some emblematic person, the messenger of death, or a fury, whose personification would be a key to the whole. What they are all wailing at, I know not; whether the lady is dying, or the father has directed the child to be exposed; but if the mother be not dead, such a tumult would kill a woman in the straw in these days.

The other compartment, in the second scene of the drama, tells the story of the presentation of the child to its father. An old man has it in his arms, and with professional and mysterious officiousness is holding it out to the father. The father, a middle-aged and very respectable-looking man, perhaps not long married, is looking with the admiration of a bachelor on his first child, and perhaps thinking, that he was once such a strange little creature himself. His hands are clasped, and he is gathering up between his arms the folds of his cloak, an emblem of his gathering up all his faculties to understand the tale the gossip is bringing.

An old man is standing beside him, probably his father, with some curiosity, and much tenderness in his looks. Around are collected a host of his relations, of whom the youngest, a handsome girl, seems the least concerned. It is altogether an admirable piece, quite in the spirit of the comedies of Terence.*

MICHAEL ANGELO'S BACCHUS.

THE countenance of this figure is a most revolting mistake of the spirit and meaning of Bacchus. It looks drunken, brutal, narrow-minded, and has an expression of dissoluteness the most revolting. The lower part of the figure is stiff, and the manner in which the shoulders are united to the breast, and the neck to the head, abundantly inharmonious. It is altogether with-

---

* This bas-relief is not antique. It is of the Cinquecento.

out unity, as was the idea of the deity of Bacchus in the conception of a Catholic. On the other hand, considered only as a piece of workmanship, it has many merits. The arms are executed in a style of the most perfect and manly beauty. The body is conceived with great energy, and the manner in which the lines mingle into each other, of the highest boldness and truth. It wants unity as a work of art—as a representation of Bacchus it wants everything.

A JUNO.

A STATUE of great merit. The countenance expresses a stern and unquestioned severity of dominion, with a certain sadness. The lips are beautiful—susceptible of expressing scorn—but not without sweetness. With fine lips a person is never wholly bad, and they never belong to the expression of emotions wholly selfish—lips being the seat of imagination. The drapery is finely conceived, and the manner in which the act of throwing back one leg is expressed, in the diverging folds of the drapery of the left breast fading in bold yet graduated lines into a skirt, as it descends from the left shoulder, is admirably imagined.

AN APOLLO,

with serpents twining round a wreath of laurel on which the quiver is suspended. It probably was, when complete, magnificently beautiful. The restorer of the head and arms, following the indication of the muscles of the right side, has lifted the arm, as in triumph, at the success of an arrow, imagining to imitate the Lycian Apollo in that, so finely described by Apollonius Rhodius, when the dazzling radiance of his beautiful limbs shone over the dark Euxine. The action, energy, and godlike animation of these limbs speak a spirit which seems as if it could not be consumed.

ARCH OF TITUS.*

N the inner compartment of the Arch of Titus, is sculptured in deep relief, the desolation of a city. On one side, the walls of the Temple, split by the fury of conflagration, hang tottering in the act of ruin. The accompaniments of a town taken by assault, matrons and virgins and children and old men gathered into groups, and the rapine and licence of a barbarous and enraged soldiery, are imaged in the distance. The foreground is occupied by a procession of the victors, bearing in their profane hands the holy candlesticks and the tables of shewbread, and the sacred instruments of the eternal worship of the Jews. On the opposite side, the reverse of this sad picture, Titus is represented standing in a chariot drawn by four horses, crowned with laurel, and surrounded by the tumultuous numbers of his triumphant army, and the magistrates, and priests, and generals, and philosophers, dragged in chains beside his wheels. Behind him stands a Victory eagle-winged.

The arch is now mouldering into ruins, and the imagery almost erased by the lapse of fifty generations. Beyond this obscure monument of Hebrew desolation, is seen the tomb of the Destroyer's family, now a mountain of ruins.

The Flavian amphitheatre has become a habitation for owls and dragons. The power, of whose possession it was once the type, and of whose departure it is now the emblem, is become a dream and a memory. Rome is no more than Jerusalem.

* From *The Shelley Papers*, 1833.

REMARKS ON "MANDEVILLE" AND MR. GODWIN.*

HE author of "Mandeville" is one of the most illustrious examples of intellectual power of the present age. He has exhibited that variety and universality of talent which distinguishes him who is destined to inherit lasting renown, from the possessors of temporary celebrity. If his claims were to be measured solely by the accuracy of his researches into ethical and political science, still it would be difficult to name a contemporary competitor. Let us make a deduction of all those parts of his moral system which are liable to any possible controversy, and consider simply those which only to allege is to establish, and which belong to that most important class of truths which he that announces to mankind seems less to teach than to recall.

"Political Justice" is the first moral system explicitly founded upon the doctrine of the negativeness of rights and the positiveness of duties,—an obscure feeling of which has been the basis of all the political liberty and private virtue in the world. But he is also the author of "Caleb Williams"; and if we had no record of a mind, but simply some fragment containing the conception of the character of Falkland, doubtless we should say, "This is an extraordinary mind, and undoubtedly was capable of the very sublimest enterprises of thought."

St. Leon and Fleetwood are moulded with somewhat inferior distinctness, in the same character of a union of delicacy and power. The Essay on Sepulchres has all the solemnity and depth of passion which belong to a mind that sympathises, as one man with his friend in the interest of future ages, in the concerns of the vanished generations of mankind.

It may be said with truth, that Godwin has been

* From *The Shelley Papers*, 1833.

treated unjustly by those of his countrymen, upon whose favour temporary distinction depends. If he had devoted his high accomplishments to flatter the selfishness of the rich, or enforced those doctrines on which the powerful depend for power, they would, no doubt, have rewarded him with their countenance, and he might have been more fortunate in that sunshine than Mr. Malthus or Dr. Paley. But the difference would have been as wide as that which must for ever divide notoriety from fame. Godwin has been to the present age in moral philosophy what Wordsworth is in poetry. The personal interest of the latter would probably have suffered from his pursuit of the true principles of taste in poetry, as much as all that is temporary in the fame of Godwin has suffered from his daring to announce the true foundations of minds, if servility, and dependence, and superstition, had not been too easily reconcileable with his species of dissent from the opinions of the great and the prevailing. It is singular that the other nations of Europe should have anticipated, in this respect, the judgment of posterity ; and that the name of Godwin and that of his late illustrious and admirable wife, should be pronounced, even by those who know but little of English literature, with reverence and admiration ; and that the writings of Mary Wollstonecraft should have been translated, and universally read, in France and Germany, long after the bigotry of faction has stifled them in our own country.

"Mandeville" is Godwin's last production. In interest it is perhaps inferior to "Caleb Williams." There is no character like Falkland, whom the author, with that sublime casuistry which is the parent of toleration and forbearance, persuades us personally to love, whilst his actions must for ever remain the theme of our astonishment and abhorrence. Mandeville challenges our compassion, and no more. His errors arise from an immutable necessity of internal nature, and from much constitutional antipathy and suspicion, which soon spring up into hatred and contempt, and barren misanthropy, which, as it has no root in genius or virtue, produces no fruit uncongenial with the soil wherein it grew. Those of Falkland sprang from a high, though perverted conception of human nature, from a powerful sympathy with his species, and from a temper which led him to believe that the very reputation of excellence should walk among mankind unquestioned and unassailed. So far as it was a defect to link the interest of the tale with anything inferior to Falkland, so is Mandeville defective. But the varieties of human character, the depth and complexity of human motive,— those sources of the union of strength and weakness— those powerful sources of pleading for universal kindness and toleration,—are just subjects for illustration and development in a work of fiction ; as such, "Mandeville" yields in interest and importance to none of the productions of the author. The events of the tale flow like the stream of fate, regular and irresistible, growing at once darker and swifter in their progress : there is no surprise, no shock : we are prepared for the worst from the very opening of the scene, though we wonder whence the author drew the shadows which render the moral darkness, every instant more fearful, at last so appalling and so complete. The interest is awfully deep and rapid. To struggle with it, would be the gossamer attempting to bear up against the tempest. In this respect it is more powerful than "Caleb Williams"; the interest of "Caleb Williams" being as rapid, but not so profound, as that of "Mandeville." It is a wind that tears up the deepest waters of the ocean of mind.

The language is more rich and various, and the expressions more eloquently sweet, without losing that energy and distinctness which characterize "Political

Justice" and "Caleb Williams." The moral speculations
have a strength, and consistency, and boldness, which
has been less clearly aimed at in his other works of
fiction. The pleadings of Henrietta to Mandeville,
after his recovery from madness, in favour of virtue
and of benevolent energy, compose, in every respect,
the most perfect and beautiful piece of writing of
modern times. It is the genuine doctrine of "Political
Justice," presented in one perspicacious and impressive
river, and clothed in such enchanting melody of language, as seems, not less than the writings of Plato, to
realize those lines of Milton :

> How charming is divine philosophy—
> Not harsh and crabbed—
> But musical as is Apollo's lute !

Clifford's talk, too, about wealth, has a beautiful, and
readily to be disentangled intermixture of truth and
error. Clifford is a person, who, without those charac-
teristics which usually constitute the sublime, is sublime
from the mere excess of loveliness and innocence.
Henrietta's first appearance to Mandeville, at Mandeville
House, is an occurrence resplendent with the sunrise of
life ; it recalls to the memory many a vision—or
perhaps but one—which the delusive exhalations of
unbaffled hope have invested with a rose-like lustre as
of morning, yet unlike morning—a light which, once
extinguished, never can return. Henrietta seems at
first to be all that a susceptible heart imagines in the
object of its earliest passion. We scarcely can see her,
she is so beautiful. There is a mist of dazzling loveliness which encircles her, and shuts out from the sight
all that is mortal in her transcendent charms. But the
veil is gradually undrawn, and she "fades into the
light of common day." Her actions, and even her
sentiments, do not correspond to the elevation of her
speculative opinions, and the fearless sincerity which
should be the accompaniment of truth and virtue. But

she has a divided affection, and she is faithful there
only where infidelity would have been self-sacrifice.
Could the spotless Henrietta have subjected her love to
Clifford, to the vain and insulting accident of wealth
and reputation, and the babbling of a miserable old
woman, and yet have proceeded unshrinking to her
nuptial feast from the expostulations of Mandeville's
impassioned and pathetic madness ?   It might be well
in the author to show the foundations of human hope
thus overthrown, for his picture might otherwise have
been illumined with one gleam of light.   It was his
skill to enforce the moral, "that all things are vanity,"
and "that the house of mourning is better than the
house of feasting"; and we are indebted to those who
make us feel the instability of our nature, that we may
lay the knowledge (which is its foundation) deep, and
make the affections (which are its cement) strong.   But
one regrets that Henrietta,—who soared far beyond her
contemporaries in her opinions, who was so beautiful
that she seemed a spirit among mankind,—should act
and feel no otherwise than the least exalted of her sex ;
and still more, that the author, capable of conceiving
something so admirable and lovely, should have been
withheld, by the tenour of the fiction which he chose,
from executing it in its full extent.   It almost seems
in the original conception of the character of Henrietta,
that something was imagined too vast and too uncommon
to be realized ; and the feeling weighs like disappointment on the mind.   But these objections, considered
with reference to the close of the story, are extrinsical.

The reader's mind is hurried on as he approaches
the end with breathless and accelerated impulse.   The
noun *smorfia* comes at last, and touches some nerve
which jars the inmost soul, and grates, as it were,
along the blood ; and we can scarcely believe that that
grin which must accompany Mandeville to his grave, is
not stamped upon our own visage.

ON "FRANKENSTEIN."*

HE novel of "Frankenstein; or, The Modern Prometheus," is undoubtedly, as a mere story, one of the most original and complete productions of the day. We debate with ourselves in wonder, as we read it, what could have been the series of thoughts—what could have been the peculiar experiences that awakened them—which conduced, in the author's mind, to the astonishing combinations of motives and incidents, and the startling catastrophe, which compose this tale. There are, perhaps, some points of subordinate importance, which prove that it is the author's first attempt. But in this judgment, which requires a very nice discrimination, we may be mistaken; for it is conducted throughout with a firm and steady hand. The interest gradually accumulates and advances towards the conclusion with the accelerated rapidity of a rock rolled down a mountain. We are led breathless with suspense and sympathy, and the heaping up of incident on incident, and the working of passion out of passion. We cry "hold, hold! enough!" —but there is yet something to come; and, like the victim whose history it relates, we think we can bear no more, and yet more is to be borne. Pelion is heaped on Ossa, and Ossa on Olympus. We climb Alp after Alp, until the horizon is seen blank, vacant, and limitless; and the head turns giddy, and the ground seems to fail under our feet.

This novel rests its claim on being a source of powerful and profound emotion. The elementary feelings of the human mind are exposed to view; and those who are accustomed to reason deeply on their origin and tendency will, perhaps, be the only persons who can sympathize, to the full extent, in the interest of the actions which are their result. But, founded on nature as they are, there is perhaps no reader, who can endure

* From *The Shelley Papers*, 1833.

I.   2 D anything beside a new love-story, who will not feel a responsive string touched in his inmost soul. The sentiments are so affectionate and so innocent—the characters of the subordinate agents in this strange drama are clothed in the light of such a mild and gentle mind—the pictures of domestic manners are of the most simple and attaching character : the father's is irresistible and deep. Nor are the crimes and malevolence of the single Being, though indeed withering and tremendous, the offspring of any unaccountable propensity to evil, but flow irresistibly from certain causes fully adequate to their production. They are the children, as it were, of Necessity and Human Nature. In this the direct moral of the book consists ; and it is perhaps the most important, and of the most universal application, of any moral that can be enforced by example. Treat a person ill, and he will become wicked. Requite affection with scorn ;—let one being be selected, for whatever cause, as the refuse of his kind—divide him, a social being, from society, and you impose upon him the irresistible obligations—malevolence and selfishness. It is thus that, too often in society, those who are best qualified to be its benefactors and its ornaments, are branded by some accident with scorn, and changed, by neglect and solitude of heart, into a scourge and a curse.

The Being in "Frankenstein" is, no doubt, a tremendous creature. It was impossible that he should not have received among men that treatment which led to the consequences of his being a social nature. He was an abortion and an anomaly ; and though his mind was such as its first impressions framed it, affectionate and full of moral sensibility, yet the circumstances of his existence are so monstrous and uncommon, that, when the consequences of them became developed in action, his original goodness was gradually turned into inextinguishable misanthropy and revenge. The scene between the Being and the blind De Lacey in the cottage, is one of the most profound and extraordinary instances of pathos that we ever recollect. It is impossible to read this dialogue,—and indeed many others of a somewhat similar character,—without feeling the heart suspend its pulsations with wonder, and the "tears stream down the cheeks." The encounter and argument between Frankenstein and the Being on the sea of ice, almost approaches, in effect, to the expostulation of Caleb Williams with Falkland. It reminds us, indeed, somewhat of the style and character of that admirable writer, to whom the author has dedicated his work, and whose productions he seems to have studied.

There is only one instance, however, in which we detect the least approach to imitation ; and that is the conduct of the incident of Frankenstein's landing in Ireland. The general character of the tale, indeed, resembles nothing that ever preceded it. After the death of Elizabeth, the story, like a stream which grows at once more rapid and profound as it proceeds, assumes an irresistible solemnity, and the magnificent energy and swiftness of a tempest.

The churchyard scene, in which Frankenstein visits the tombs of his family, his quitting Geneva, and his journey through Tartary to the shores of the Frozen Ocean, resemble at once the terrible reanimation of a corpse and the supernatural career of a spirit. The scene in the cabin of Walton's ship—the more than mortal enthusiasm and grandeur of the Being's speech over the dead body of his victim—is an exhibition of intellectual and imaginative power, which we think the reader will acknowledge has seldom been surpassed.

ON THE REVIVAL OF LITERATURE.*

N the fifteenth century of the Christian era, a new and extraordinary event roused Europe from her lethargic state, and paved the way to her present greatness. The writings of Dante in the thirteenth, and of Petrarch in the fourteenth, were the bright luminaries which had afforded glimmerings of literary knowledge to the almost benighted traveller toiling up the hill of Fame. But on the taking of Constantinople, a new and sudden light appeared: the dark clouds of ignorance rolled into distance, and Europe was inundated by learned monks, and still more by the quantity of learned manuscripts which they brought with them from the scene of devastation. The Turks settled themselves in Constantinople, where they adopted nothing but the vicious habits of the Greeks: they neglected even the small remains of its ancient learning, which, filtered and degenerated as it was by the absurd mixture of Pagan and Christian philosophy, proved, on its retirement to Europe, the spark which spread gradually and successfully the light of knowledge over the world.

Italy, France, and England,—for Germany still remained many centuries less civilized than the surrounding countries,—swarmed with monks and cloisters. Superstition, of whatever kind, whether earthly or divine, has hitherto been the weight which clogged man to earth, and prevented his genius from soaring aloft amid its native skies. The enterprises, and the effects of the human mind, are something more than stupendous: the works of nature are material and tangible: we have a half insight into their kind, and in many instances we predict their effects with certainty. But mind seems to govern the world without visible or substantial means. Its birth is unknown; its action and influence unperceived; and its being seems eternal.

* From *The Shelley Papers*, 1833.

To the mind both humane and philosophical, there cannot exist a greater subject of grief, than the reflection of how much superstition has retarded the progress of intellect, and consequently the happiness of man.

The monks in their cloisters were engaged in trifling and ridiculous disputes: they contented themselves with teaching the dogmas of their religion, and rushed impatiently forth to the colleges and halls, where they disputed with an acrimony and meanness little befitting the resemblance of their pretended holiness. But the situation of a monk is a situation the most unnatural that bigotry, proud in the invention of cruelty, could conceive ; and their vices may be pardoned as resulting from the wills and devices of a few proud and selfish bishops, who enslaved the world that they might live at ease.

The disputes of the schools were mostly scholastical ; it was the discussion of words, and had no relation to morality. Morality,—the great means and end of man,—was contained, as they affirmed, in the extent of a few hundred pages of a certain book, which others have since contended were but scraps of martyrs' last dying words, collected together and imposed on the world. In the refinements of the scholastic philosophy, the world seemed in danger of losing the little real wisdom that still remained as her portion; and the only valuable part of their disputes was such as tended to develop the system of the Peripatetic Philosophers. Plato, the wisest, the profoundest, and Epicurus, the most humane and gentle among the ancients, were entirely neglected by them. Plato interfered with their peculiar mode of thinking concerning heavenly matters ; and Epicurus, maintaining the rights of man to pleasure and happiness, would have afforded a seducing contrast to their dark and miserable code of morals. It has been asserted, that these holy men solaced their lighter moments in a contraband worship of Epicurus and profaned the philosophy which maintained the rights of all by a selfish indulgence of the rights of a few.   Thus it is: the laws of nature are invariable, and man sets them aside that he may have the pleasure of travelling through a labyrinth in search of them again.

Pleasure, in an open and innocent garb, by some strange process of reasoning, is called vice ; yet man (so closely is he linked to the chains of necessity—so irresistibly is he impelled to fulfil the end of his being,) must seek her at whatever price : he becomes a hypocrite, and braves damnation with all its pains.

Grecian literature,—the finest the world has ever produced,—was at length restored : its form and mode we obtained from the manuscripts which the ravages of time, of the Goths, and of the still more savage Turks, had spared.   The burning of the library at Alexandria was an evil of importance.   This library is said to have contained volumes of the choicest Greek authors.

A SYSTEM OF GOVERNMENT BY JURIES.

A FRAGMENT.*

GOVERNMENT, as it now subsists, is perhaps an engine at once the most expensive and inartificial that could have been devised as a remedy for the imperfections of society.   Immense masses of the product of labour are committed to the discretion of certain individuals for the purpose of executing its intentions, or interpreting its meaning.   These have not been consumed, but wasted, in the principal part of the past history of political society.

Government may be distributed into two parts :— First, the fundamental—that is, the permanent forms, which regulate the deliberation or the action of the whole ; from which it results that a state is democrat-

* From *The Shelley Papers*, 1833.

ical, or aristocratical, or despotic, or a combination of all these principles.

And Secondly—the necessary or accidental—that is, those that determine, *not* the forms according to which the deliberation or the action of the mass of the community is to be regulated, but the opinions or moral principles which are to govern the particular instances of such action or deliberation. These may be called, with little violence to the popular acceptation of those terms, Constitution, and Law : understanding by the former, the collection of those written institutions or traditions which determine the individuals who are to exercise, in a nation, the discretionary right of peace and war, of death or imprisonment, fines and penalties, and the imposition and collection of taxes, and their application, thus vested in a king, or an hereditary senate, or in a representative assembly, or in a combination of all ; and by the latter, the mode of determining those opinions, according to which the constituted authorities are to decide on any action; for law is either a collection of opinions expressed by individuals without constitutional authority, or the decision of a constitutional body of men, the opinion of some or all of whom it expresses—and no more.

To the former, or constitutional topics, this treatise has no direct reference. Law may be considered, simply—an opinion regulating political power. It may be divided into two parts—General Law, or that which relates to the external and integral concerns of a nation, and decides on the competency of a particular person or collection of persons to discretion in matters of war and peace—the assembling of the representative body —the time, place, manner, form, of holding judicial courts, and other concerns enumerated before, and in reference to which this community is considered as a whole ;—and Particular Law, or that which decides upon contested claims of property, which punishes or restrains violence and fraud, which enforces compacts, and preserves to every man that degree of liberty and security, the enjoyment of which is judged not to be inconsistent with the liberty and security of another.

To the former, or what is here called general law, this treatise has no direct reference.   How far law, in its general form or constitution, as it at present exists in the greater part of the nations of Europe, may be affected by inferences from the ensuing reasonings, it is foreign to the present purpose to inquire—let us confine our attention to particular law, or law strictly so termed.

The only defensible intention of law, like that of every other human institution, is very simple and clear —the good of the whole.   If law is found to accomplish this object very imperfectly, that imperfection makes no part of the design with which men submit to its institution.   Any reasonings which tend to throw light on a subject hitherto so dark and intricate, cannot fail, if distinctly stated, to impress mankind very deeply, because it is a question in which the life and property and liberty and reputation of every man are vitally involved.

For the sake of intelligible method, let us assume the ordinary distinctions of law, those of civil and criminal law, and of the objects of it, private and public wrongs.   The author of these pages ought not to suppress his conviction, that the principles on which punishment is usually inflicted are essentially erroneous; and that, in general, ten times more is apportioned to the victims of law, than is demanded by the welfare of society, under the shape of reformation or example. He believes that, although universally disowned, the execrable passion of vengeance, exasperated by fear, exists as a chief source among the secret causes of this exercise of criminal justice.   He believes also, that in questions of property, there is a vague but most effective favouritism in courts of law and among lawyers, against the poor to the advantage of the rich—against the tenant in favour of the landlord—against the creditor in favour of the debtor ; thus enforcing and illustrating that celebrated maxim, against which moral science is a perpetual effort : *To whom much is given, of him shall much be required; and to whom men have committed much, of him they will ask the more.*

But the present purpose is, not the exposure of such mistakes as actually exist in public opinion, but an attempt to give to public opinion its legitimate dominion, and an uniform and unimpeded influence to each particular case which is its object.

When law is once understood to be no more than the recorded opinion of men, no more than the apprehensions of individuals on the reasoning of a particular case, we may expect that the sanguinary or stupid mistakes which disgrace the civil and criminal jurisprudence of civilized nations will speedily disappear. How long, under its present sanctions, do not the most exploded violations of humanity maintain their ground in courts of law, after public opinion has branded them with reprobation ; sometimes even until by constantly maintaining their post under the shelter of venerable names, they out-weary the very scorn and abhorrence of mankind, or subsist unrepealed and silent, until some check, in the progress of human improvement, awakens them, and that public opinion, from which they should have received their reversal, is infected by their influence. Public opinion would never long stagnate in error, were it not fenced about and frozen over by forms and superstitions. If men were accustomed to reason, and to hear the arguments of others, upon each particular case that concerned the life, or liberty, or property, or reputation of their peers, those mistakes, which at present render these possessions so insecure to all but those who enjoy enormous wealth, never could subsist. If the administration of law ceased to appeal from the common sense, or the enlightened minds of twelve contemporary *good and true men*, who should be the peers of the accused, or, in cases of property, of the claimant, to the obscure records of dark and barbarous epochs, or the precedents of what venal and enslaved judges might have decreed to please their tyrants, or the opinion of any man or set of men who lived when bigotry was virtue, and passive obedience that discretion which is the better part of valour,—all those mistakes now fastened in the public opinion, would be brought at each new case to the   *   *   *   *   *

*   *   *   *   *   *   *

ON LOVE.*

HAT is Love?   Ask him who lives what is life ; ask him who adores what is God.

I know not the internal constitution of other men, nor even of thine whom I now address.   I see that in some external attributes they resemble me, but when, misled by that appearance, I have thought to appeal to something in common and unburthen my inmost soul to them, I have found my language misunderstood, like one in a distant and savage land.   The more opportunities they have afforded me for experience, the wider has appeared the interval between us, and to a greater distance have the points of sympathy been withdrawn.   With a spirit ill-fitted to sustain such proof, trembling and feeble through its tenderness, I have everywhere sought, and have found only repulse and disappointment.

Thou demandest what is Love.   It is that powerful attraction towards all we conceive, or fear, or hope

* Printed in The Keepsake, Lond. 1829.

beyond ourselves, when we find within our own
thoughts the chasm of an insufficient void, and seek to
awaken in all things that are, a community with what
we experience within ourselves. If we reason we would
be understood ; if we imagine we would that the airy
children of our brain were born anew within another's ;
if we feel we would that another's nerves should vibrate
to our own, that the beams of their eyes should kindle
at once and mix and melt into our own ; that lips of
motionless ice should not reply to lips quivering and
burning with the heart's best blood :—this is Love.
This is the bond and the sanction which connects not
only man with man, but with every thing which exists.
We are born into the world, and there is something
within us, which from the instant that we live, more
and more thirsts after its likeness. It is probably in
correspondence with this law that the infant drains
milk from the bosom of its mother ; this propensity
develops itself with the development of our nature.
We dimly see within our intellectual nature, a miniature
as it were of our entire self, yet deprived of all that we
condemn or despise, the ideal prototype of every thing
excellent and lovely that we are capable of conceiving
as belonging to the nature of man. Not only the portrait of our external being, but an assemblage of the
minutest particles of which our nature is composed * :
a mirror whose surface reflects only the forms of purity
and brightness : a soul within our own soul that de-
scribes a circle around its proper Paradise, which pain
and sorrow and evil dare not overleap. To this we
eagerly refer all sensations, thirsting that they should
resemble and correspond with it. The discovery of its
antitype ; the meeting with an understanding capable
of clearly estimating our own ; an imagination which

* These words are ineffectual and metaphorical. Most words
are so,—no help !

should enter into and seize upon the subtle and delicate peculiarities which we have delighted to cherish and unfold in secret, with a frame, whose nerves, like the chords of two exquisite lyres, strung to the accompaniment of one delightful voice, vibrate with the vibrations of our own ; and a combination of all these in such proportion as the type within demands : this is the invisible and unattainable point to which Love tends ; and to attain which, it urges forth the powers of man to arrest the faintest shadow of that, without the possession of which, there is no rest nor respite to the heart over which it rules. Hence in solitude, or that deserted state when we are surrounded by human beings and yet they sympathize not with us, we love the flowers, the grass, the waters, and the sky. In the motion of the very leaves of spring, in the blue air, there is then found a secret correspondence with our heart. There is eloquence in the tongueless wind, and a melody in the flowing brooks and the rustling of the reeds beside them, which by their inconceivable relation to something within the soul awaken the spirits to dance of breathless rapture, and bring tears of mysterious tenderness to the eyes, like the enthusiasm of patriotic success, or the voice of one beloved singing to you alone. Sterne says that if he were in a desert he would love some cypress. So soon as this want or power is dead, man becomes a living sepulchre of himself, and what yet survives is the mere husk of what once he was.

END OF VOL. I.

PRINTED BY BALLANTYNE, HANSON AND CO.
EDINBURGH AND LONDON

www.ingramcontent.com/pod-product-compliance
Lightning Source LLC
Chambersburg PA
CBHW030954110726
47900CB00004B/1264